PRAISE FOR

THE LAST ADAM

Ron Echols's *The Last Adam* is a bold and genre-blending supernatural thriller that successfully balances cinematic storytelling with intimate, character-driven drama. Readers are treated to a high-stakes narrative that moves between the spiritual battlegrounds of Heaven and Earth, anchored by memorable and familiar characters like Mary Levitt, a struggling singer whose journey from rejection to divine purpose is both grounded and gripping. Echols weaves together elements of suspense, faith, and speculative fiction with remarkable confidence, making this a title that's equally at home on a church book club shelf or among fans of *The Screwtape Letters* and *The Matrix*. With a brisk pace and skillful worldbuilding, *The Last Adam* keeps readers invested through moments of wonder, fear, tenderness, and hope. It's rare to see a debut that balances accessibility with ambition this well.
—**Josh**, CEO of *Skookum Hill Publishing*

***

The Last Adam is a daring, emotionally charged thriller that reimagines the Nativity through a contemporary, high-stakes lens. Ron Echols masterfully blends biblical prophecy with cinematic action, weaving angels, adversaries, and human frailty into a gripping narrative that spans from Los Angeles to Jerusalem. At the heart of the story is Mary, a young, talented singer whose life spirals into divine chaos, and Joseph, a man caught between legacy, love, and a growing war he doesn't yet understand. The characters are richly drawn, the pacing relentless, and the spiritual themes handled with both reverence and bold imagination. Think The Da Vinci Code meets This Present Darkness, but with fresher emotional stakes and a thoroughly modern pulse. Echols isn't just telling a story, he's constructing a world where ancient powers still pull the strings of everyday lives. A truly compelling debut.
—**Hammad Khalid**, MDPublishing.com

***

The Last Adam is a bold, genre-defying novel that reimagines the birth of Jesus in a modern, suspense-filled setting. With vivid prose and haunting imagery, it plunges readers into a contemporary America gripped by unseen spiritual warfare, where angels and demons battle over the destiny of mankind. The author masterfully blends biblical allegory with supernatural suspense, crafting a narrative that is both thought-provoking and pulse-pounding. This is not just a retelling, it's a reimaging that invites readers to wrestle with faith, doubt, and the unseen forces that shape our world.

This novel stands out for its emotional depth, cinematic pacing, and characters who feel vividly real, especially the conflicted modern-day Joseph and Mary, whose struggles mirror the timeless tension between destiny and free will. *The Last Adam* is as much a spiritual thriller as it is a deeply human story, and it lingers in the mind long after the final page.

—**Rachel S. Kim**, author of *Prophets and Shadows* and contributing editor at *Faith & Fiction Quarterly*

***

Ron Echols has done something I rarely see—he's taken the most important story in human history and made it visceral, immediate, and impossible to put down. *The Last Adam* doesn't just retell the Incarnation; it drops you into the middle of a spiritual war where every choice matters and every soul hangs in the balance.

This isn't your grandmother's Christian fiction. It's raw, it's real, and it wrestles with the messy intersection of divine purpose and human frailty. Echols writes with the urgency of someone who knows the stakes are eternal. The result? A book that will grip your heart, challenge your assumptions, and leave you changed.

If you're tired of safe, predictable Christian novels, *The Last Adam* is the wake-up call you've been waiting for.

—**Jeff B. Miller**, author of *From Heart to Page* and *"The Newsletter for Christian Writers on Substack"*, founder, *ChristianGhostwriting.com LLC*, *IndieChristianBook.com*, *ChristianWritingCoach.net*, Pastor of *Godspeed-Church.com*

***

The Last Adam asks what I think is one of the most important questions of faith: Are ancient lessons truly timeless? Or, in Echols creative experiment, if we lay the framework of the past in our modern times, will we get the same result? By setting this exciting stage, Echols allows the reader to decide for themselves. Through a blend of speculative fiction and contemporary drama, he reimagines the quiet moments of spiritual reflections and the battlegrounds of spiritual warfare. With cinematic prose, mythic characters who feel grounded, and an emotionally driven narrative full of surprises, Echols lets the reader wrestle with questions of purpose, identity, and redemption without the need for any definitive answers. Readers who enjoy faith-driven stories with a touch of the supernatural will be excited to explore familiar characters forced to find their way in our strange new world.

—David Ridd

THE LAST ADAM

RON ECHOLS

Published by KHARIS PUBLISHING,
an imprint of KHARIS MEDIA LLC.

ISBN-13: 978-1-63746-655-1

ISBN-10: 1-63746-655-2

Library of Congress Control Number: 2025950413

All KHARIS PUBLISHING products are available at special quantity discounts for bulk purchases for sales promotions, premiums, fund-raising, and educational needs. For details, contact:

Kharis Media LLC
Tel: +1 (331) 312-2376
support@kharispublishing.com
www.kharispublishing.com

To God, for Your perfect love and mercy. Every word on these pages exists because of You. Thank You for giving me the Story

To my wife Cheryl, who gave me the strength to write it down. You believed in it long before I did. Thank you for your love, faith, and patience through every late night and long draft. This book is as much yours as it is mine.

CONTENTS

PROLOGUE xi

CHAPTER 1: THE SHOW 17

CHAPTER 2: FAMILY BUSINESS 44

CHAPTER 3: JOY AND PAIN 56

CHAPTER 4: CHANGE OF PLANS 72

CHAPTER 5: MOVING PIECES 88

CHAPTER 6: TRUST 103

CHAPTER 7: BLAME 114

CHAPTER 8: TAPESTRY 131

CHAPTER 9: THE GATHERING 145

CHAPTER 10: THE WEDDING 153

CHAPTER 11: PULLING OUT THE RUG 168

CHAPTER 12: THE TRIAL 176

CHAPTER 13: DESPERATE DECISIONS 181

CHAPTER 14: FLIGHT 200

CHAPTER 15: STRIKE 221

CHAPTER 16: BATTLE 236

CHAPTER 17: RESPITE AND RESCUE 251

CHAPTER 18: THE APPROACHING STORM 286

CHAPTER 19: THE SIEGE 292

CHAPTER 20: FINAL CONFRONTATION 303

EPILOGUE: VISITORS FROM THE EAST 323

ABOUT KHARIS PUBLISHING: 329

PROLOGUE

Location: The Lunar Surface, Tranquility Base, southwestern corner of the Sea of Tranquility.

The moon hung motionless, like a dead thing in the void of space. Its pockmarked exterior reflecting the sun's merciless glare and millennia of asteroids pummeling its surface. In that airless waste where humans had once taken a small step, the lunar dust lay since undisturbed, marked only by boot prints and machinery left behind.

Piercing through the silence of the void, a voice called out.

"Raphael!"

A brilliant white light erupted into existence, hovering above the moon's surface like a tear in the fabric of space itself. The light intensified until it seemed to bend space around it, taking form. A figure of a man emerged. Behind him, the first suggestion of wings. Translucent, but appearing stronger than steel, they folded against his armor etched with ancient angelic symbols that seemed to move when viewed directly. Dark hair, wild and untamed accentuated his sapphire eyes and caressed his polished, glass-like skin.

The being that called itself Gabriel stood motionless on the lunar surface, its feet leaving no prints in the ancient dust. The face that poets had tried and failed to capture for millennia turned slowly, searching.

"Raphael?"

The name rippled out without sound, more like a thought given form in the vacuum. Gabriel's wings stirred restlessly, creating eddies in the dust that danced like spirits in the harsh light.

"Here, Gabriel," reverberated a voice, bright but commanding, from the shadowed surface. Another angel sat casually reclined within the lunar rover, abandoned by the humans who briefly touched the face of Heaven before retreating to their warm blue marble decades ago. His eyes were fixated upon the Earth, suspended in the cosmic darkness. Raphael mirrored Gabriel, but adorned in silver armor with fiery ginger hair framing his serene face.

"I've been searching for you," Gabriel said, moving closer. In the moon's one-sixth gravity, each step seemed to take too long, as if time itself was stretching.

"Observing," Raphael replied simply, still watching Earth.

"Observing…anyone in particular?" Gabriel asked, also redirecting his gaze toward Earth. From this distance, cities glowed like constellations, tiny lights poking through the darkness that surrounded them.

Maintaining his stare, Raphael revealed what he had been witnessing, his voice heavy from countless years of disappointment. "There in Houston, a man, after a night of heavy drinking, returned home to engage in an argument with his wife, he killed her in a drunken fit of jealousy. Across the sea in Madrid, Spain, a young prostitute on the cusp of adulthood prepares to inject herself with an HIV-contaminated needle provided by a friend. There, in Manila, a corrupt politician embezzles funds meant for the poor, channeling them to fuel his business ventures. Wherever I look, human virtue becomes more scarce."

Raphael shifted his gaze to Gabriel, his glowing eyes piercing the darkness. "Who is worthy down there? Even among ourselves, evil found a way to take root. We cast him down to Earth, and he has only brought misery and death upon everyone there. Since the dawn of humanity, the stain of evil has tainted them all. They have no hope."

Gabriel hung his head in solemn contemplation of Raphael's declaration. They both knew who "he" was. Neither needed to speak the name that had once been brightest among them.

"You have manifested yourself on the human plane of reality. What if you're spotted?" Gabriel snapped, briefly changing the subject.

A small chuckle escaped Raphael's lips. "I am on the MOON, Gabriel, not Times Square New York. Besides, you're doing it too. Did you even hear anything I said?"

"We do not materialize on this plane without purpose," Gabriel scolded. "And yes, I heard you. I came to you because I have news."

"What news?" Raphael asked.

"Your complaining is timely for once," Gabriel chided.

He stepped closer to the rover, standing beside Raphael. "You are correct; there is no one on Earth capable of saving them. However, he has devised a plan."

Raphael peered up at Gabriel, rising from his reclined posture. "What plan?"

Gabriel leaned in, his voice whispering the secret. "He will go directly to them. He will send a part of himself to help them."

"So, the time for final battle has come? He will lead us against the adversary?" Raphael asked, energy crackling around his form at the thought.

"No, this is not Armageddon," Gabriel corrected. "This is the beginning. He will walk the Earth himself, using his own words, his truth, will be carried directly to them."

Gabriel's eyes widened. "That's too much. They will panic at the sight," he warned.

"As usual, you are not understanding. He will be born there." Gabriel explained.

"What? Why?" Raphael's bewilderment unusual for someone who existed since the earth was formed. "Become a human child? What could that possibly accomplish?"

Amused by the confusion etched on Raphael's face, Gabriel continued, "He will birth himself into their world, experience their joys and their sorrows, breathe their air, and shed human tears. He will BE human. He says only then can he deliver what is necessary for their redemption. It is a necessary madness."

"Incredible," Raphael murmured, the word carrying both wonder and doubt. His gaze returned to Earth, that fragile sphere that held such consequence in the cosmic order. Resting his foot upon the rover's steering wheel, he reclined once more, assuming his former pose, his mind wrestling with what he had just heard.

"Childlike vulnerability," Gabriel finally said. His voice holding the hint of wonder that even angels could feel. "Yet with a power never before seen on earth," Gabriel approached the rover. "Two have already been chosen to protect him," Gabriel revealed.

"Who?" Raphael inquired, his form tense with anticipation.

Gabriel stood. Hesitating to respond.

Raphael continued to probe, his curiosity burning. "Are they dignitaries? Kings or Presidents?"

"A carpenter and his young girlfriend," Gabriel responded.

"Stop joking," Raphael demanded. His voice bore a tinge of annoyance.

"I'm not joking. It is just as I said," Gabriel clearly stated.

Raphael fell silent, as the two of them resumed gazing into the cosmic expanse at the earth. The moon's darkness began to recede, yielding to the creeping sun. Elongated shadows cast by the angels began to dance upon the lunar terrain. Their ethereal wings shimmered, glistening beneath the radiant golden rays that reflected off their celestial armor.

"Lucifer," Raphael whispered. He then turned to face Gabriel. "He is aware?"

"He is aware of the prophecy. But ignorant of the specifics. Like you, he probably anticipates the prophesy is speaking about the arrival of a conqueror or ruler. But once he is born on Earth, Lucifer will sense his presence and seek to eliminate the child," Gabriel explained. "And likely the mother as well for good measure."

"And we shall be there, as we always have," Raphael declared, his voice unwavering.

"He has instructed us not to directly intervene. Likewise, our fallen friends cannot directly harm him," Gabriel contradicted. "The young humans must either prevail or fail on their own. They must make their own choices, raise and teach him as one of their own. That is the sole path. It is his will. And his will be done on Earth, as it is in Heaven."

"Lucifer won't follow rules," Raphael whispered, his voice touched with an old sorrow. "And if it is chaos he wants, I'll make sure he encounters it."

Gabriel rested his gloved hand upon Raphael's shoulder; a touch steeped in camaraderie and old history. "No interference," he stated firmly.

A portal of light materialized a gateway between worlds. "The elders summon us," Gabriel affirmed. "Your presence is required. Are you finished here?"

"I am ready," Raphael replied. But in that instant, he abruptly turned toward Earth and briskly advanced several steps. "We have been spotted," he declared. "An astronomer with a telescope."

"So much for your moon theory," Gabriel quipped. "This is why we refrain from manifesting in the physical realm without purpose. She must have caught sight of us as the sun crossed our location."

The astronomer fumbled for her phone as she jerked back from the viewer of the telescope, hands shaking so badly she almost dropped it. This was it. Proof of… something. Aliens? No, not aliens. The word 'alien' felt too quaint, too inadequate When she looked back through the telescope, she somehow knew they knew she had seen them. Just before she passed out, she heard a voice in her head. It wasn't a sound, exactly. More like a memory. Telling her to sleep. When they found her the next morning, slumped over her telescope, she remembered nothing. Just a vague feeling of unease, like the kind of dream that leaves you checking the locks twice and leaving the lights on, even though you can't explain why.

Raphael raised his index finger, sketching a symbol in the air, akin to those adorning their armor. A luminous trail of blue energy lingered before him as he drew, an inverted triangle with a half-circle at its base. The image hovered momentarily before dissipating like a wisp of smoke.

"What did you do?" Gabriel asked.

"I put her to sleep," Raphael responded. "When she wakes up, she will think it was just a dream."

"Shall we go now?" Gabriel's tone bore irritation. "There is much to discuss, much to plan." The radiant light that had transported him reappeared behind Gabriel. And as they stepped into the radiant embrace of the portal, it closed behind them, allowing the lunar surface to reclaim its silence. With the fate of humanity and the Heavens in the balance, the countdown had begun.

Chapter 1

THE SHOW

The cell phone alarm in Mary Levitt's small LA apartment blared into the stillness of the morning. Her eyes shot open, and she groaned, frantically reaching out to silence the incessant noise. As her fingers fumbled with the buttons, the accusing digits glared back at her: 7:30 AM. She had exactly 90 minutes to make it to the audition.

Startled from the alarm, her heart pounded as she lay there in her dimly lit room, her mind racing with a million thoughts. The tiny apartment was a clutter of clothes strewn about the floor and music posters plastered on the walls. Among the posters were her favorite singers and bands, all representing the dream that consumed her days and nights. The artists' faces seemed to be smiling down at her, urging her to keep pushing forward, their success a beacon of hope.

With a jolt, she remembered that time was slipping away. She shot up from the bed, fighting her way free of sheets that seemed determined to keep her trapped. Her dark, wavy hair was a wild mess around her. She stumbled to her feet and rushed to the bathroom, the sound of running shower water echoed in the small space.

As she welcomed the warm splash of water on her face, hoping to shake off the sleepy fog that clung to her, she caught a glimpse of herself in the mirror. Her reflection looked like it had its own opinions about her chances today. Dark circles under her eyes that had seen too many late-night gigs, but held a flicker of determination, hair that belonged in a "before" picture for a shampoo commercial.

Trembling with excitement and nerves, she whispered to her reflection, hoping to bolster her spirits. "Today's the big day. You can do this."

The thought of the audition made her heart race. Years of singing into the late hours of the night, rehearsing songs until even she grew tired of hearing them. From the dark smoke-filled bars, to the trendy coffee houses filled with pretentious hipsters, she had poured her soul into honing her musical talents. Today, that talent would be heard by those who held the power to make or break her dreams.

Mary hurriedly dressed in her favorite outfit, a flowy dress that swayed with her every movement, a symbol of the free spirit within her. It still fit, thank God. The sneakers were worn but comfortable. Lucky sneakers, she called them, though they hadn't brought much luck so far. Just endless auditions and rejections, each one carving away another piece of her dream. Her trusty companions that had seen her through countless performances.

With a hurried glance at the clock, she grabbed her guitar and dashed toward the door. As she bounded over the piles of clothes, she misjudged her step and tripped. Landing face first, smacking her cheekbone on the wood with a loud thud.

"Owww!" she groaned, as she rolled onto her back, holding her face. As it grew numb from the pain, she could feel it was already beginning to swell. Using the wall as a brace, she slowly brought herself to her feet, carefully navigating the rest of the distance out the door.

The city was just beginning to wake up, the sun on the horizon casting a warm, golden glow over the streets and the mountains in the distance. Flurries of cars hurried past her building, the driver's faces buried in their phones or lost in their own thoughts.

The bus stop was two blocks away. She had to run. Time seemed to stretch and compress with each tap of her footsteps on the sidewalk. Seeming to echo in sync with her increasing pulse and labored breathing. Her guitar case bounced against her back like a reminder of everything at stake.

She could hear the hiss of the bus's air brakes as it pulled up to the stop. The door opening with the familiar squeak and the line of usual suspects began to file inside. She bounced onto the first step as the driver's hand was reaching for the button to close the door.

The driver, same one she'd had a hundred times before, gave her a knowing look as she climbed aboard. "Today?" he asked. Eyebrows raised in anticipation.

Mary briskly nodded yes, mustering up a wide grin, not able to trust her voice after her morning workout.

"Then I'll say a prayer for you," he told her. Proudly confident in the difference he believed it would make.

She fumbled her guitar case across her front as she made her way through the narrow lane between the seats, her breath coming in ragged gasps. Thankfully, there was a seat nearby. She plopped down, beads of sweat running down and stinging her eyes.

Lost in thought for what seemed like hours, she nearly missed her stop. The bus' breaks squealed as it slowed to a stop in front of the theatre. Mary looked up at the marquee as she emerged through the doors and stepped off the bus. The building loomed over her like a grand cathedral with spires and elaborate stonework that seemed out of place in modern LA. Mary had passed it a thousand times before, but today it looked different. The shadows seemed deeper, the stone darker.

Her hand trembled slightly as she pushed open the heavy doors with a firm shove. The receptionist carefully maintained smile faltered for just a moment as she took in Mary's disheveled appearance, that brief crack in professional courtesy revealing something that might have been pity. But there was understanding there too, the kind that comes from watching countless dreams die in fluorescent-lit hallways. She gave Mary a sympathetic smile as she signed in, her signature looking strange and foreign on the page.

Inside the studio waiting room the air was charged with nervous energy. Bodies packed the space, other dreamers all pretending not to look at each other while stealing desperate glances. The air felt thick, charged with competitive tension and anxious perspiration sweat. This wasn't just another audition, this was for a modern movie musical, a retelling of a Broadway classic. One role. Hundreds of hopefuls. The odds felt like a physical weight pressing down on them all.

Mary found a spot on the floor, carefully setting down her guitar case. The case had seen better days, just like its owner. She'd decorated it with stickers from every bar and coffee shop she'd played in, creating a map of her disappointments across its surface. Each venue's logo reminding her of nights spent singing to crowds more interested in their phones than her music. The side door burst open with a bang that made everyone jump. A young intern appeared: her clipboard held like a shield. All heads snapped toward her in synchronization.

"Leslie?" she called out.

"I'm here," said a confident voice from among the throng. Leslie's head popped into view as she stood up from her spot on the floor. As she pushed through the group, her eyes met Mary's just before she disappeared through the door. Mary had seen her around the scene, good voice, decent stage presence. The kind of safe choice casting directors loved.

Mary claimed Leslie's abandoned spot, the floor still warm where she'd been sitting. Through the walls, other auditioners' voices filtered through. Beautiful voices, professional voices. They were good. Very good. Too good. Mary could hear Leslie hitting all the right pitches, every note exactly where it should be. The doubt that had been circling like a vulture finally sank its claws in deep. Mary tried to push it away, but it was too late. The doubt was already whispering in her ear, reminding her of every rejection, every failed attempt, every dream that had withered under harsh fluorescent lights just like these.

"Mary?" The intern's voice cut through her doubt-spiral like a knife. "You're up.

"Here!" she replied, struggling to stand. Her legs had fallen asleep, sending needles of pain shooting up her calves as she stood. The pretty intern's face blurred slightly as she passed, or maybe that was just blood rushing back to her legs making her vision swim.

The audition room stretched out before her in the dim light. Three judges sat at a table that seemed miles away, their faces lost in shadow. Only their eyes sometimes caught the light, reflecting it back like cats' eyes in headlights. The spotlight waited center stage, a perfect circle of harsh white that promised either salvation or execution.

"Hello," she said nervously as she stepped into the light. Her voice small in the vast space. "I'm Mary."

"We know," came the retort, flat and final. "What happened to your face?"

Mary's hand flew to her cheek, confusion giving way to remembrance of her morning collision with the floor. The bruise throbbed at her touch, as if acknowledging its role in this farce. "Oh that," she managed. "I... fell down." Perfect timing, as always.

The shadowed figures offered no response to her excuse.

“You may begin.”

Mary squatted down and placed her guitar on the floor, flipped open the clasps and lifted the lid.

“No music,” one of the judges said sharply.

“Oh,” said Mary. The word slipped out before she could stop it. This was unexpected. But no time to worry about that. Rising slowly, she approached the microphone, her trembling fingers reached out to touch the mic. The metal felt warm under her touch. The room held its breath as she began to sing. This was her own composition, a tactical choice she'd made believing it would give her an edge, keeping the judges from comparing her to the original artist. The melody poured out of her, filling the space between her and those shadowed figures with something that felt almost like magic. Her voice didn't shake, didn't falter. For those brief minutes, she was perfect. As the final note faded, floating away like a bird into darkness, she stood still. Waiting. Smiling. Ready for the validation that had eluded her for so long. The fluorescent lights hummed overhead, seeming to grow louder in the silence that followed.

The judges exchanged glances, their faces maintaining that careful neutrality she'd seen too many times before. But their eyes, held that slight softening she'd learned to recognize. It was the look that always preceded rejection, that gentle preparation for the axe about to fall. The demon of self-doubt didn't need to claw its way in this time. It had never left.

A judge cleared her throat, breaking the stillness. “Thank you. You sound great, but not what we were looking for. Thank you for coming.” The words were polite, almost gentle, wrapped in professional courtesy like a blade wrapped in silk. But they cut just as deep. Another rejection. Another small death under these merciless lights.

Mary nodded mechanically, her cheeks burning with familiar humiliation. She heard herself thank them, her voice small and far away, as if someone else was speaking through her mouth. Her hands moved on autopilot, gathering her guitar case, that faithful companion to so many failures. She made her exit quickly, before the tears could start.

Outside the studio, she leaned against the wall, letting its cold surface ground her in reality. But the tears came anyway, stinging her eyes. The sting of failure once again settled onto her shoulders, a burden she knew too well.

The vultures of doubts and insecurities now descended, picking at the carcass of her dreams.

As she trudged back to the waiting area, she avoided the glances of the other hopefuls. Their once-familiar faces now seemed like blurred silhouettes, all absorbed in their own private anxieties. She could feel their eyes on her, judging her failure. Her eyes burned with tears, and she swallowed hard, desperate to maintain composure. Even the room itself appeared to have dimmed, the fluorescent lights casting an oppressive glow. The walls seemed to close in, suffocating her spirit and mocking her dreams. She wanted to scream, to vent her frustration at the unfairness of it all, but the words caught in her throat, trapped by her fear of appearing weak in front of the others.

Mary slipped out of the audition venue and into the rain-soaked streets. The rain poured down in torrents, as if the Heavens themselves were weeping in disappointment. The droplets cascaded down her face, mingling with her own tears. As she walked away, each step felt like a burden, her soaked clothes clinging to her body, mirroring the heaviness of the guitar case in her hand. The evening sun began peeking through, painting the city in hues of amber and gold as Mary stepped into her favorite coffee shop. She ordered her usual, a creamy latte with a sprinkle of cinnamon. She hoped this cozy piece of Heaven would offer solace.

As Mary settled into a corner seat near the window, she gazed out at the city, the familiar sights and sounds creating a sense of home amidst the turmoil. Coffee grinders and casual conversation, phones chiming and chairs scraping the floor. Her thoughts continued drifting to the audition earlier. Her once-confident inner voice had now faltered, and she pulled her hoodie over her head to hide her bruised face from side-glancing patrons. She took the first sip of her latte, the warmth spreading through her body like a comforting hug.

In another corner of the coffee shop, Joseph walked in, his eyes scanning the room with a hint of trepidation. He moved like a man who was both exactly where he was supposed to be and completely lost at the same time. As if guided by some unseen force, Joseph's gaze fell upon Mary, and something within him stirred. The feeling was like a key turning in a lock he hadn't known existed. He hesitated for a moment, not wanting to intrude, but there was a pull that drew him toward her.

"Mind if I join you?" he asked, his voice gentler than she'd expected. Deeper too.

Mary looked up, her eyes meeting his inquisitively. She noticed his hands first. Builder's hands, strong and calloused, with the kind of permanent dirt under the nails that doesn't wash away. The kind of hands that create things. They wrapped around his coffee cup like they were trying to draw warmth from it, though the LA afternoon was anything but cold.

She felt oddly at ease, as if they were old friends reuniting after a lifetime apart. She gestured to the empty chair across from her that had stayed empty. "Sure, go ahead."

"I'm Joseph," he introduced himself, extending a hand across the table.

"Mary," she replied, taking it. The handshake lasted a fraction too long, and she could have sworn she felt something pass between them. Static electricity, probably. Had to be.

Joseph settled into the chair. They exchanged small talk at first, a hesitant dance of words as they tiptoed around the initial pleasantries. The coffee shop's usual sounds seemed to fade into the background, as if the world was giving them space for something important.

"So, what brings you here?" Joseph asked, his eyes soft with genuine interest.

She debated lying, making up a story more interesting than failed auditions and dying dreams. But something made her tell the truth.

"I had an audition today," she said, her voice catching slightly. "It didn't go well."

"Is that why they hit you?" he asked with a slight smile, nodding towards her bruised face.

"Oh no, that happened earlier. Just clumsy," she said, self-consciously brushing her hair forward to cover the bruise.

His expression softened with empathy. "I'm sorry about the audition. But hey, their loss, right?"

"Yeah," she managed a weak smile. "Their loss."

Mary began feeling a strong sense of comfort in Joseph's presence. There was something about him that felt strangely familiar, as if they had crossed paths in another lifetime. Perhaps it was the way he looked at her, with a mixture of understanding and curiosity, that made her feel seen in a way she hadn't felt in a long time.

"So, Joseph," Mary began, trying to steer the conversation away from her. "What brings you here tonight?"

He hesitated for a moment before replying, as if unsure how much to reveal. "I needed a break from work, I suppose. I work in the family business and that world can be a bit suffocating sometimes."

Mary nodded sympathetically, her eyes locking with his. "I can imagine. It must be tough feeling like you have to live up to certain expectations."

"You have no idea," he admitted, a hint of weariness in his voice. "My father's expectations know no bounds."

Mary leaned in closer as they got to know one another, their conversation now growing into an exchange of confessions and secrets. "You don't have to be what others expect you to be," she said softly. "You have the power to choose your own path, to follow your heart." She took another sip of her brew. "At least, that's the way I am thinking about it with my currently non-existent singing career," she joked.

"Yea, but the difference is you have only yourself to deal with. But I have a family legacy being placed like a target on my back. What if I disappoint everyone? What if I fail to live up to their expectations?"

Mary placed a reassuring hand on his. "First of all, I also have a family that is not thrilled I am pointing my life in another direction. And second, failure is a part of life," she said gently. "You're more than what others expect you to be. You have dreams and desires of your own, and they're worth pursuing."

"Do you hear yourself? What a total hypocrite you are," Mary thought. Mere moments ago, she was ready to give it all up, and now here she was providing words of wisdom like an overly cheerful motivational post on a Facebook feed.

Joseph's eyes softened, and a faint smile graced his lips. "Thank you," he said sincerely. "I needed to hear that."

Their conversation flowed on like a river, carrying with it their shared dreams and aspirations. They spoke of their passions, the things that made their souls come alive, and the obstacles that stood in their way. There was an inexplicable comfort in each other's presence, as if they were soulmates brought together by the hands of fate.

As the evening sun dipped below the horizon, casting a warm glow over the coffee shop, their conversation gradually began to drift to a close. Just then, a mesmerizing melody began to fill the coffee shop. Mary turned in the direction of the sound, her curiosity piqued. The music seemed to dance through the air, captivating her. But to her surprise, Joseph was unmoved and appeared puzzled.

"You don't hear that?" Mary asked, her eyes widening with wonder.

Joseph shook his head, a touch of bewilderment in his expression. "Hear what?"

"The music," she said, her voice tinged with awe. "It's like nothing I've ever heard before. Is there a performer here somewhere? A band?"

Joseph leaned back, as if trying to tune into a frequency only she could perceive. "I'm sorry, Mary. I don't hear anything." But he saw the expression on her face and knew there was something happening with her.

Then just as suddenly as it began, it stopped. "It's gone now," said Mary. "That was so weird."

"Probably just a car playing music as it went by," Joseph reasoned. "With one of those loud sound systems."

"Maybe," Mary said, unconvinced.

"I should probably get going," Joseph said reluctantly, not wanting the night to end. The coffee shop had grown quieter, as if to give them these last few moments.

"Same here," Mary replied, though neither of them moved to leave.

He smiled, a genuine warmth in his gaze. Digging deeper into his courage he asked, "Do you think I can call you sometime? Maybe have dinner?"

"Sure," replied Mary. Her hand trembled slightly as she typed her number into his phone, but that was just nerves. Had to be. "I could eat."

"I'll call you. Really looking forward to seeing you again Mary," Joseph said as he grabbed his coat, replaced his chair under the table, and made his exit.

Mary couldn't help but feel that their encounter was more than just chance. Exchanging phone numbers was such a small act, but always felt like a profound declaration of some kind. But there was definitely a pull she felt between them.

And that melody. What was that melody? And where were the two people who had been sitting at the table across from me? Mary was facing them the entire time, but didn't actually see them leave. Her eyes darted around the coffee shop, searching for any sign of their presence, but there was none. As if they had vanished into thin air. Of course, she knew better than that.

I guess I was just preoccupied and missed them. Gathering her things and chugging the last gulp of coffee from her cup, she tossed it into the bin and once more stepped out into the city.

The journey home was a quiet one. The moon hung low in the night sky, its silvery glow casting haunting shadows on the streets. Each step felt like a march toward uncertainty as she continuously replayed the events of the day in her mind, trying to make sense of everything that had happened, the failed audition, the strange music, then meeting Joseph. Everything felt both ordinary and strange all at once.

Maybe I really should consider going back to law school.

She pushed open the door to her small apartment, the loud creaking sound breaking the silence of the night. The room welcomed her with its familiar smells like an embrace, the soft glow of fairy lights creating an ambiance of warmth and comfort.

"That you, girl?" Martha's voice carried from the kitchen, along with the smell of something almost burning. Her roommate's cooking adventures usually ended in either triumph or disaster, with little middle ground.

She found Martha in the kitchen, waving a dish towel at the smoke detector while something that might have once been pasta sat cremated in a pot.

"So," Martha said, giving up on dinner and reaching for the takeout menus they kept in a drawer specifically for nights like this. "How bad was it?"

Mary slumped into a kitchen chair. "Got anything stronger?"

"That bad, huh?" Martha asked concerningly, her voice tight with worry.

"Oh well, you know. Same thing," she confessed, her eyes welling once again with tears. "They said I'm not what they were looking for."

Martha settled beside her, offering a comforting hug. "Oh, Mary, I'm so sorry," she whispered, her heart aching for her friend.

"I just don't know if I'm meant to do this," Mary confessed. "Maybe I'm just not good enough. Maybe I'll never be good enough."

Martha pulled back slightly, her eyes locking with Mary's. "Don't you dare say that," she said firmly, her voice unwavering. "You are an incredible singer, Mary. You have a gift. You just had an off day, that's all. It happens to the best of us."

"But what if it's not just an off day?" she questioned. "What if I'm not cut out for this? What if I'm chasing a hopeless dream that will never come true?"

Martha's grip tightened, determination gleaming in her eyes. "You can't give up, Mary," she said fiercely. "You can't let one setback define your entire journey. You owe it to yourself to keep trying."

Mary felt torn, her heart warring with her mind. A part of her wanted to believe Martha's words, to cling onto the hope that she could rise above these repeated moments of failure. But another part of her was drowning in a sea of insecurities.

"I don't know if I have the strength to keep going," she admitted, her voice barely a whisper. Her dreams felt like distant stars, just out of reach. But as she looked into Martha's unwavering eyes, she found a glimmer of hope, a spark of determination that she had nearly lost.

Martha cupped Mary's face in her hands, forcing her to meet her gaze once again. "You are stronger than you think, Mary," she said fiercely. "I believe in you, and I know you can do this."

"I'll try," Mary said softly, a sense of determination returning to her voice. "I'll keep trying."

Martha smiled, a mix of relief and pride in her eyes. "That's all I ask," she said, pulling Mary into another hug.

"But," Mary continued, and something in her voice made Martha look up sharply, "I met someone."

"Girl, what? Spill!"

Mary told her about Joseph, the normal parts, anyway. The coffee shop meeting, the easy conversation, the way his eyes seemed to change color in different lights. She left out the strange music and the vanishing coffee shop patrons.

"Wow," Martha said when she finished. "Sounds like somebody up there is looking out for you. One door closes, a handsome guy in a suit opens the other."

Mary's hand tightened on her drink glass. That phrase; looking out for you, suddenly felt strange to hear. The lights flickered, just once, just briefly. Probably someone running the microwave in 4B again. Their building's wiring was older than both of them combined.

They sat there; their hearts entwined in a moment of shared vulnerability. Martha knew that this was a pivotal moment, one that could either break Mary's spirit or ignite the fire within her.

"Mary," Martha said gently. "I want you to do something for me."

Mary looked up, her eyes searching Martha's face for guidance.

"I want you to close your eyes," Martha instructed. "Take a deep breath. Forget about the audition, forget about what anyone else thinks. Just listen to your own voice, your own soul."

Mary hesitated for a moment, but then she closed her eyes and followed Martha's instructions. She took a deep breath, trying to calm the storm within her. And then she listened.

In the depths of her being, Mary could hear the faint strains of the melody she heard in the coffee shop. She imagined it was a melody of hope and passion, of dreams and desires. She imagined it was a melody that had been with her since the day she was born, a melody that had called to her today. It was a feeling of belonging, of knowing that she was meant for something greater than the doubts that plagued her. The melody was her anchor, her guiding star in the vast sea of uncertainty. She felt warm.

"I hear it," Mary whispered, her eyes still closed.

Martha smiled, her heart swelling with pride. "That's all that matters, Mary," she said softly. "As long as you can hear the music, as long as you can feel it in your soul, then you know you're on the right path."

Mary opened her eyes, "Thank you, Martha," she said, her voice filled with gratitude. "Thank you for always believing in me."

Martha hugged her tightly, her heart overflowing with love for her friend. "I'll always believe in you, Mary," she said. "No matter what happens, no matter how tough things get, I'll be right here, cheering you on."

"Thanks," Mary said. She stood up, suddenly restless. "I'm going to turn in."

"You sure? We could order pizza, watch bad movies, properly mourn your failed audition..."

"Rain check? I just... I think I just need to get some quiet time."

Martha's eyes narrowed slightly. In the fluorescent kitchen light, her face took on an odd cast, like she was seeing something in Mary that hadn't been there before. "Okay, but if you need anything..."

"I know where to find you," Mary finished with a smile that felt only slightly strained.

Mary sat on the bed in her room. Outside her window, a church bell tolled nine times, though the nearest church was miles away. Her phone buzzed-a text from Joseph.

"Really looking forward to seeing you again," it read. Simple. Normal. She started to reply, but movement caught her eye. In the mirror above her desk, just for a moment, she thought she saw someone standing behind her.

When she spun around, her room was empty. Of course it was empty. Just shadows and fairy lights and her own imagination running wild after a long, tiring day. But some nights, maybe it was better to order pizza and watch silly movies with your best friend than to think too hard about shadows and songs and strange meetings in coffee shops.

She found Martha still in the kitchen, now on the phone with their favorite pizza place. Their eyes met, and something passed between them, an understanding.

"Extra cheese?" Martha asked, covering the phone's mouthpiece.

"Extra cheese," Mary agreed, and for a moment everything felt normal again.

Sunday morning spilled through the Temple's stained-glass windows, painting the floor in fragments of colored light. In the broadcast booth, the producer's voice cut through the pre-show chaos with practiced authority: "Ok let's hold this up for three, two, one, fade to black. Cue opener on five, four, three, two, one and opener is rolling."

The Temple logo flashed across the monitors, theme music swelling through the speakers. The voiceover boomed its familiar welcome: "Live, From Los Angeles, Welcome, to The Temple Hour."

"Luke, let's get a sweeping shot over the audience." The producer's commands came rapid-fire, each one precise. "Good, good. Camera two give me a tight shot on Gwen. Be ready on my mark."

"Rex, camera three wide shot of the choir. Nicely done Rex. Roll montage footage. Luke gives me a view of the audience enjoying the music. Rex keeps panning the stage. Good, that good. Two, stay on Gwen during the solo. Luke, I want you on Mary for her solo. We want to be sure everyone hears that beautiful voice of hers. Kim checks the audio. Seems a bit off. Ok Luke, Gwen is almost on. And to Gwen in three, two, one, cue."

Gwen stood at the center of it all, lost in her own thoughts as she counted performances in her head, one hundred and thirty-four now. The number felt important, though she couldn't have said why. Maybe someday an interviewer would ask, when the record companies finally recognized what she knew in her bones: that she was meant for bigger things than this weekly broadcast, bigger than this building full of people who didn't understand real talent.

She imagined the future that surely waited just around the corner, paparazzi flashbulbs, adoring fans screaming her name, red carpets and award shows where she'd finally be recognized for what she was. The fantasy was so vivid she could almost taste it, metallic and sharp on her tongue.

The music cue snapped her back to reality. This was her moment, even if it wasn't the one she daydreamed of. She hit her mark perfectly, that first note ringing pure and clear through the Temple's vast space. The song was an old standard, slower than her usual fare, one that everyone in the building knew by heart. She poured everything into it, almost forgetting that it was a duet.

Almost.

But there was Mary, right on cue, her voice blending in with an effortlessness that made Gwen's jaw tighten. Two years ago, Mary had been nobody, just another hopeful at an audition. Now she was impossible to ignore. The congregation certainly noticed, their response swelling as Mary's voice soared above the melody. Gwen watched the monitors, saw how the cameras lingered on Mary's face, how the light seemed to find her no matter where she stood.

Something twisted in Gwen's chest. She'd worked too hard, waited too long, to be upstaged by this girl who'd appeared from nowhere with her gift wrapped in phony modesty. But anger built behind her professional smile, boiling beneath the surface.

But Gwen was nothing if not practiced at hiding her true feelings. When her part came again, she threw herself into the performance with everything she had. She worked the stage like she owned it, making sure every eye that wasn't already on Mary had to be on her.

Every eye was…except one.

Joseph sat in his usual spot. He rarely missed a service. He thought he recognized Mary at the coffee shop, but hadn't connected it was her until later. They had furiously exchanged increasingly flirtatious texts every day since they met, but had not yet been able to align their schedules to get together for their date. He just couldn't get her out of his mind. She was a very attractive girl. Thin and a tiny bit awkward, but mostly, it was her kindness that drew him in. But for now, it was his turn to take her in. Proud to now know her in a new way, and excited to get closer to her.

Mary and Gwen finished their duet to the sound of thunderous applause. The song had ended, but Gwen stood on stage, basking in the spotlight she felt should have been hers alone. Too busy to see Mary walk offstage or to notice everyone had settled back into their seats and the Temple ministers waiting for her exit so they could begin delivering the day's message. Slightly embarrassed and gathering herself, she quickly trotted off.

In the center of it all stood Zachariah, the founder. "Zee" as his friends called him, was a captivating speaker with a magnetic personality. Beloved by the congregation and the viewers at home. However, something had changed in him over the past few months. He had become strangely silent, no longer speaking both on and off the stage. Joseph recalled hearing that it had been over five months since he had uttered a word, refusing any medical help despite the concerns of his loved ones. Speculations arose, ranging from Alzheimer's, to a stroke, to even being under a curse from God . Some felt he was under a self-imposed penance of some sort. Whatever the case was, he was the main draw to the Temple and his silence did not bode well for the show. TV ratings and Temple attendance were always highest when he was scheduled to speak.

A few years ago, his wife Elizabeth, who was the Temple's business manager, came up with the idea of having associate ministers sometimes stand in for him on occasion. But her idea was radical in a unique way. Elizabeth switched to being non-denominational and having clergy from various cultures and belief systems on staff. This approach gave the Temple a reputation for progressiveness and modernity, attracting more followers. Regardless of one's beliefs or background, everyone was welcome, free of judgment. Attendance boomed, and Elizabeth struck a deal with a local TV station to broadcast the services weekly. The show became a hit, leading to the network allocating additional time slots. Now, *The Temple Hour* could be seen four times a week and was one of the fastest-growing churches in the country. Today's speaker was the new Evangelical minister, known for his entertaining delivery and enlightening messages. It was always an enjoyable time at the Temple.

After the service, Joseph waited for Mary in the outside hallway, eagerly hoping to surprise her. But it had been 20 minutes. He began to think he had missed her when he heard a voice call out from the crowd.

"Girl, you were amazing tonight!" Martha's enthusiastic voice rang through the hallway.

Joseph spun around to see Martha trotting his way, arms open wide for a hug from her friend Mary, who had just emerged from the changing room.

"That was so good! I wish I could sing like you." Martha exclaimed, twirling Mary around in her excitement.

"You have a fantastic voice," Mary replied. "Way better than mine."

"Are you crazy? I wish I could sing like that. That's why they put me in the back," Martha said, her Filipino accent adding a unique charm to her words. Martha proudly flaunted her uniqueness. Mary cherished their friendship and the honesty that always came with it.

As they chatted, Mary's eyes scanned the crowd, searching for Joseph. "Did he come?" she asked Martha, straining to see over the heads of people.

"I didn't see him, but I know he did. Because he is totally into you," Martha teased, pinching Mary's cheek playfully.

Mary chuckled, giving Martha a playful shove. "Stop it," she kidded. "We practically just met."

"Hey, I only say what I see. And I know when a man is interested in a woman. And he is definitely interested in you," Martha insisted, her smile widening.

"Hey Mary!" Joseph's voice called out from a short distance away. Mary spotted him and waved her arm in the air to make sure he saw her.

"Oh, here's your little puppy now. No more time for little old Martha. I'll call you later, okay?" Martha teased, giving Mary a nudge with her shoulder before walking away.

"You better!" Mary responded, watching Martha disappear into the crowd. Turning her attention back to Joseph, her eyes shining with affection.

Joseph spotted her hand waving above the heads of the crowd and began moving toward her. He had only taken a few steps when…

"Well, hello there! Long time no see," Gwen said with a coy smile, seizing Joseph's arm and spinning him around mid-stride.

Joseph forced a polite smile, dreading Gwen's presence. They had once been caught in a whirlwind romance, but Joseph had learned the hard way that Gwen's passion could quickly turn possessive and suffocating. Her relentless pressure to take their relationship to the next level and marry became an insurmountable obstacle that ultimately drove them apart. Unfortunately for Joseph, Gwen's tenaciousness was legendary.

She wore a low cut, tight fitting blue cashmere blouse with a short black skirt revealing the tempting curves of her body. Way too risqué for church. He remembered to control his eyes but it was too late. Gwen caught him looking and intended to take advantage of it.

"Uh, hi Gwen. How are you?" Joseph replied, trying to maintain a polite distance.

"I'm great! How did you like the number?" Gwen asked, seeming unfazed by Joseph's lack of enthusiasm.

"Of course, I enjoyed it as usual. You guys keep getting better and better each time I see you," Joseph replied, hoping to keep the conversation casual.

"I know, right? So, what's up with you today? Any plans? I was thinking we could catch the new Denzel movie. I heard the special effects are mind-blowing," Gwen suggested.

"You know better than that," Joseph said, trying to hint that he was not interested.

"What do you mean? Can't two friends go to a movie together?" Gwen pressed. Her eyes were gleaming and her body language spoke of mischief and intention.

Gwen followed Joseph's gaze and spotted Mary approaching them. Gwen had seen that look in his eyes before, he'd once watched her that way, before she'd pushed too hard, wanted too much too fast. Now he looked at Mary like she was the answer to questions he hadn't known he was asking.

She couldn't resist teasing him, "New girl, huh? Does she have you on such a tight leash that you don't have a life of your own anymore?"

"You know what I mean, Gwen. We're not together anymore," Joseph said firmly, not wanting to give her false hope.

"I've got to go," he said, hoping Mary would rescue him.

Gwen locked eyes with Mary making her way towards them. "Uh-oh, guess we are in trouble now." she said as she giggled and poked Joseph in the ribs with her finger.

"Knock it off Gwen." He said through clenched teeth.

"Hey, guys! What's up?" Mary greeted them, not yet sensing the tension.

"Nothing," Joseph replied, moving closer to Mary, and leaning in to give her a welcome hug, pressing his face against her warm cheeks.

"Aw, no kiss?" Gwen said, pouting her lips.

"Just a church kiss," Mary responded, glancing at Gwen out of the corner of her eye.

“Let’s keep it rated G. I’m right here you know,” Gwen said, with animosity in her stare.

Joseph couldn’t hold back his irritation any longer. “You don’t have to be,” he snapped back.

"Joseph! That was rude," Mary scolded him.

Gwen couldn't resist adding, "Yeah, that was rude. We just left church, for goodness' sake. Anyway, I really do have to go. Bye, Joseph. See you later," she said as she left, pointedly ignoring Mary.

“Do you know Gwen?” Mary asked.

"When will she quit? I'm tempted to set her straight once and for all," Joseph grumbled as they began walking outside. “Yes, I know her. Ex-girlfriend, in fact,” Joseph said reluctantly, wondering what would happen next.

“Wow small world!” exclaimed Mary, unsure how he felt about the new news.

"Hey, don't worry about her. She just needs time. After all, she's a woman," Mary finally said, trying to defuse the situation. "We women feel deeply, so it takes a while. Are you still interested in her?"

Mary’s tone stopped Joseph from walking, a tinge of panic in his voice. “Who, me? No way!” He was embarrassed by the scene and the last thing he wanted was for Gwen to drive a wedge of doubt between them.

"Touchy, huh?" Mary teased, quickly hiding her smile as she spun around and walked away from him. Joseph quickly strode to catch up with her. He knew he had to reassure her.

“Mary, you don’t believe that do you?”

"Sure, if you say so," she said as she turned and smiled into his eyes. Her smile captivated him. Suppressing the urge to laugh out loud, he couldn't find the words to respond, just like earlier.

"Can I see you tomorrow night?" he asked, suddenly serious. “Finally get that date you promised me?”

"Wild horses couldn't keep me away," she assured him, the playful tone returning to her voice.

"Awesome. I’ll pick you up after my meeting with my dad."

"I would love to meet him one day," Mary said thoughtfully, looking out over the now-thinning parking lot.

"One day. My dad is kind of an acquired taste,” Joseph chuckled, grabbing Mary's hand. "He doesn't like me being distracted from things.”

Mary smiled, lacing her fingers through his. "And what do you think? Am I a distraction?" she asked playfully, her eyes locking with his.

"Yes, you are." Joseph pulled her closer, unable to resist. "The best kind."

"How do I distract you?" Mary asked, holding his hands tighter, moving closer herself.

"You're doing it right now," Joseph murmured. Slowly, he moved his face closer to hers, feeling a warmth spread through his chest. "But there's nothing else I'd rather be than distracted by you."

They shared a tender kiss, their bodies pressed close together, lost in the moment of their connection. Suddenly, Mary inhaled sharply, abruptly pulling away.

"My mother's waiting for me. I need to bring some things home for dinner."

"Of course. Sorry if I've made you late," Joseph said, still caressing her face.

"I'll call you later tonight, okay?" He leaned in carefully for a goodnight kiss.

She closed her eyes and once again kissed him gently but meaningfully. Mary had promised herself she wouldn't rush into physical intimacy before marriage, but there was an unearthly strong urge at play here. If they were alone... she wasn't entirely sure she could keep that promise. But for now, it was just a kiss.

"Goodnight," she said quickly, pushing herself away and stepping back toward her car.

"Goodnight," he echoed, watching her walk into the night under the parking lot light. She opened the door to her Uber and flipped him one last smile as she got in. He watched until the taillights disappeared into the darkness.

Mary's Uber pulled up to her parents' house, the drive passing more quickly than usual. Through the kitchen window, she could see her mother Anne preparing dinner, no doubt waiting for the lemons she'd asked Mary to pick up. As she made her way down the driveway to the back door, her mother Anne was there to greet her with a warm embrace, one arm wrapped around her, while the other accepted the bag of lemons.

"Hello, honey," Anne said, her eyes twinkling with motherly affection. "You're just in time. How was the performance tonight? You must tell me all about it. And don't you dare leave anything out."

"Well, I think I did okay." Mary's voice was quiet, understated.

"That's all? You are way too modest. You have a beautiful voice. That's why they picked you. I am so glad you auditioned for the solo. It is nice to have someone else singing up there for a change."

Mary removed her coat and hung it on the hallway hook. After washing her hands, she moved over to the stove and lifted the lid. The stew smelled delicious. Unable to resist, she snuck a tasty spoonful.

"It smells great, Mom," Mary said, stirring the pot gently.

As Anne sliced vegetables, Mary added, "Gwen actually was outstanding tonight. You should have seen her work the stage. She is a natural-born performer."

"And a natural-born pain in the you know what." Anne responded. She noticed Mary sneaking another sip of the stew and playfully took the spoon out of Mary's hand, nudging her aside. "Lord forgive me for saying so, but it is true. I mean the nerve of that girl."

Mary set about arranging the table, finding comfort in the familiar ritual. Each plate, each utensil had its place, a small order she could control in a world that felt increasingly chaotic.

"She is harmless, Mom. Just immature." Mary said.

"She is older than you by almost nine years." Anne reminded her, hand on her hip, wooden spoon pointed like an accusatory finger. "Just keep an eye on her is all I am saying."

She turned her head towards the living room and shouted for her husband, "Joachim! Dinner's ready! Mary is here. Come on down!"

"Okay!" The muffled response came back.

"Hello sweetie." Joachim said as he came thumping down the stairs and into the kitchen. He kissed Anne on the forehead. He removed his favorite white satin yarmulke as he sat down at the table.

"Hey dad, how have you been? How was work today?" Mary asked sweetly.

"You know, the same as usual," he said looking eagerly at the steaming bowl of stew Anne had set before him. "They threw a retirement party for me today."

"Really? That's terrific!" said Mary as she reached out to hold the hand of her now seated mother and father for the prayer.

Joachim shrugged, "It was all right, I guess. I don't like being the center of attention." He went on to begin the family ritual of the dinner prayer in Hebrew.

"*Ba-ruch a-tah A-do-nai E-lo-hei-nu Me-lech Ha-o-lam, she-ha-kol ni-h"yeh bid-va-ro. Ba-ruch a-tah A-do-nai E-lo-hei-nu Me-lech Ha-o-lam, bo-rei p"ri ha-a-da-mah.* Blessed are You, our God, King of the Universe, who creates the fruit of the earth. Blessed are You, our God, King of the Universe, who creates the fruit of the tree."

He continued, "For health and strength and daily food, we praise thy name, O Lord. We are truly grateful for the blessings of this day. This food, which you have already blessed in the giving, so further bless in our partaking. May the peace and blessing of God descend upon us as we receive of His bounty, and may our hearts be filled with love for one another. Amen."

"Amen" echoed Mary and Anne.

Mary raised her spoon to her mouth and blew. "Ah, I am starving. Mom, this smells so good" Turning to her father, "So tell me more about the party. What did they do for you?"

"It was really festive" Joshim said as he began to eat. "Balloons, streamers, cake, music, the whole nine yards. Everyone wrote their well wishes on a big poster and people gave speeches about how green I was when I first started at the firm. It was just all so awkward."

"You deserved every minute of it," Anne said, her voice warm with pride as she ladled more stew into Joachim's bowl. "That firm wouldn't be standing without your thirty-five years of dedication and hard work."

"That's right, Dad. Time to take your bow," Mary added, though she could see the tension building in his shoulders.

"I've never needed applause," Joachim muttered, stirring his stew without eating it. He looked older suddenly, more tired than Mary remembered. "Unlike some of us at this table." The words carried a sharp edge that made Anne's hands still on her napkin.

"Mary," he continued, setting his spoon down with careful precision. "We need to discuss law school."

Mary sighed inwardly. She had been down this road with her father before. She watched her mother's fingers worry at the napkin's edge, creasing and un-creasing the white fabric.

"Dad, I don't understand why you're always against my singing. It's my passion, and I love sharing my voice with others."

Anne interjected, "Mary, I don't think now is the time to discuss..."

"I pulled lots of strings to get you that internship last summer. Donald himself promised to bring you on after you pass the bar. If you pass the bar," his voice hardened. "Which won't happen if you keep wasting time with this hobby."

"It's not just a hobby," Mary said quietly, clutching her hands under the table. "Dad, singing is my dream. And my internship was an eye-opener for me. Law isn't my path, Dad. It never was. I love singing at The Temple"

"The Temple," Joachim scoffed. "Ever since Zachariah went silent, Elizabeth's turned it into a circus. Television cameras, pop music, my own daughter prancing around on some stage. What happened to reverence? To tradition?"

Mary fidgeted with her fork. She had been waiting for the right moment to share her recent romantic encounter with her parents, and up until now, tonight seemed like the perfect opportunity. As the meal progressed, the conversation flowed, and Mary's courage and anticipation grew. She admired her father, Joachim Levitt, for his intelligence and dedication as the chief accountant of a prestigious construction company. Her mother, Anne, was an esteemed architect, and the dinner table often buzzed with discussions about their respective careers. But when the topic moved to Mary, his only child, it always put him in a mood.

Finally finding a moment, Mary cleared her throat during a break in the conversation and spoke up, "There's something I want to tell you both. I met someone recently."

Joachim and Anne exchanged curious glances, their curiosity piqued as she continued.

"His name is Joseph," she began, "and he's incredible. We have this amazing connection, and I can't stop thinking about him." Outside, a car passed, its headlights sweeping across the dining room windows like searchlights.

Anne smiled warmly, "That's wonderful, dear. Tell us more about him."

"He's funny, kind, and just so easy to talk to," Mary gushed, her eyes alight with excitement. "We met at a coffee shop. He works in construction. We have so much in common, and I can't wait to see where this goes."

Joachim raised an eyebrow, intrigued by his daughter's enthusiasm. "Well, it sounds like you had quite the eventful past few weeks. You said he works in the same field as me?"

Mary hesitated for a moment, not wanting to give away too much too soon. "Yes, he is a builder, but it's a family business."

"Oh, how interesting," Elizabeth chimed in. "And what does he do in the company?"

"He didn't mention his exact job, but his family owns it. He's involved in the business side of things," Mary replied, avoiding the specifics.

Mary noticed her father's demeanor change subtly. His eyes narrowed slightly, and she sensed a flicker of recognition in his expression.

"We're going out tomorrow night," Mary said, excitement in her voice.

"Did he mention his last name?" Joachim asked, his voice measured.

"Yes, his last name is Reisman," she admitted.

"You've got to be kidding me." Joachim's voice dropped to a low murmur. "Mary, are you aware that Joseph Reisman is the son of my boss?"

Mary's eyes widened in surprise, her mind racing to make sense of the revelation.

"I... I had no idea," Mary stammered, feeling the ground shift beneath her perfect moment. Her mother reached across the table to touch her hand, but Mary pulled back. "Why should that matter?"

"Why does it matter?" Joachim pushed back from the table, his chair scraping against the floor. "Our professional lives are intertwined with the Reisman's, and getting involved with Joseph will complicate things for us." He added as he continued to spoon the stew into his mouth, "That Joseph. I have heard about him over the years from his father. He has a bit of a reputation. Probably just looking for his next thrill."

"Joachim, that's enough." Anne interjected firmly. She looked over at Mary apologetically. She could see that a change had come over Mary now and her usually bright expression was quieter, less animated. Anne added, "You seem to forget that my father was not sold on you at first either."

"He accepted me because I did it the right way. I came and talked to him like a man. I showed respect for the traditions of our faith. Joseph has never set foot in this house to talk to me." Joachim said.

Anne said, "Joachim, you have been with Reisman Construction for 30 years. You know him and his father already. It is not like he is a stranger to you. He is a nice boy from a respectable family. I am sure he will be very respectful of Mary."

Mary agreed. "That's true dad. Anyway, I thought you would like that I may have a boyfriend who comes from a Jewish background."

Joachim felt control slipping through his fingers like sand, each word from his wife and daughter clipping away at his authority. A vein pulsed at his temple as he watched them dismiss his concerns with casual waves of their hands. *Where was the respect for his position as head of the house?* The thought burned like acid.

"Anne, he is too old for her," he protested. "They are nearly 10 years apart for crying out loud." Joachim spooned another helping of stew into his mouth, using the mundane action to accentuate his irritation. "His father told me that Joseph has not been the same since his last girlfriend. What was her name again? Gwen, I think. He has had so many that his father told me he lost count. Who knows what baggage he is carrying? You can't know him that well yet."

He spooned another spoonful of stew into his mouth. "One used to be able to tell who the bad seeds were, but nowadays people are sleeping around with whomever...."

"Joachim, that's enough I said!" Anne's voice cracked like a whip. "You are taking this too far."

"Is that what you want Mary, to take someone else's leftovers?" Joachim's voice rose as he glared across the table. His harsh words hung in the air, forcing a brief stunned silence. Mary felt the tears welling up, hot and traitorous. Her father's words planted doubts that began to take root. The possibility of something special with Joseph seemed to be withering right before her eyes.

"Look at what you have done!" Anne reached across the table, her hand once again finding Mary's like a lifeline. "Don't mind your father honey. You know he always just lets old things tumble out of his mouth. He doesn't mean to hurt you." Mary turned toward the window, but found only her own reflection staring back, ghostlike and uncertain against the darkness beyond. The familiar urge to flee upstairs to her childhood room pulled at her legs, a siren song of escape. But something else stirred within her, something stronger than fear.

No, she thought, steel entering her spine. *I have a right to express my feelings. My feelings are not wrong and I will not run away from them.*

"Dad, I don't know what secrets Joseph might have had in his life before. And I don't know what happened between him and other women. I haven't asked because frankly, I don't think it's any of my business. What I do know is how he is with me. He seems kind, and respectful of me in every way. If I felt that he meant any harm or had anything other than the best intentions, you can believe I would not waste my time with him."

Mary got up from the table and walked around behind her father. She wrapped her arms around his shoulders, laid her head on his and gave him a squeeze. "You raised me well dad. Can't you trust my decisions? Don't you believe I will do the right thing?"

Joachim's heart melted from the thoughtful words of his daughter. If there was ever a daddy's little girl, Mary was it. Visions of her childhood fondly flashed through his mind. She was his life. But still, his approval would not come easily.

"Yes, well I guess you are right." He finally said as he patted her arm with his hand. "I have tried to be a good father."

Mary giggled and playfully swatted her father in the shoulder. "Stubborn as stone, but I love you anyway." She pressed a kiss to his cheek, tasting the faint salt of worry that had gathered there during their argument. Rising from the table, she gathered herself, eager for the sanctuary of her old room.

"Thanks mom, goodnight dad. I think I will go to my old room for the night." said Mary.

"Goodnight sweetie," said Anne. She then turned to Joachim with raised eyebrows and said, "Now let's talk about your parenting skills."

The sound of her mother's words followed Mary down the hallway, drawing a knowing smile to her lips. Some conversations never changed, no matter how many years passed beneath this roof.

The house spoke to her in familiar creaks as she made her way through the hallway upstairs. Family photographs lined the walls like silent witnesses to her life, her first bike ride, graduations, moments frozen in time that traced the arc of her becoming. Her room waited at the end of the hall, exactly as she'd left it, yet somehow different in the way childhood spaces become when viewed through adult eyes. The moon had claimed its territory through her window, laying down a path of silver across her perfectly made bed. Sleep felt distant, despite the emotional evening. The light, the stillness, it all conspired to stir something creative in her blood.

She settled onto her bed, while reaching into her desk drawer. The spiral notebook that emerged held years of her midnight inspirations, its cover clinging to life by a single determined paperclip. When loose pages threatened to fall out, her hand moved with startling quickness, catching them mid-escape.

"I would have never gotten those back in order," she whispered to herself, oddly impressed by the quickness of her own reflexes. Positioning herself beneath the moon's spotlight, she lay across her bed, the worn pages cool against her skin. She rested so her head faced the window. The moonbeams made a perfect spotlight on her as she opened her book of songs and turned to a new page. Her phone's chime pierced the quiet, scattering her thoughts.

Martha's text glowed on the screen: Sorry I can't chica with you tonight. Got some stuff to do. Cya tomorrow?

Her fingers moved across the keys: No prob. All ok with u?

Her response came quickly: Oh yea, no worries. Just have to work. Nite, love you.

Luv u 2. Nite, she typed back.

Returning to her bed, she cradled the notebook in her lap, its blank pages waiting expectantly. The urge to create was strong, but the words remained elusive. "Maybe I'm thinking too much," she murmured into the empty moonlit room. "I'll just write the first thing that comes." She closed her eyes, letting her mind drift in the darkness behind her lids. When she opened them again, two words had surfaced from the depths: *My Soul*. She inscribed them at the top of the page, each letter drawn with deliberate care.

Why did that pop into my head? she pondered. She lay still contemplating the thought for what felt like a good long while before sleep began to get the better of her. As she always did before she went to bed, she got down on her knees beside her bed and said her nightly prayers. The ritual of kneeling beside her bed felt different tonight, the carpet's familiar texture grounding her as she settled into prayer. Unlike the rigid prayer formulas of her childhood, she liked to speak to God as one might address a friend, albeit one deserving of profound reverence. The traditional "Amen" fell from her lips more from habit than intent, and she found herself wondering at the peculiar custom. Why did everyone mark the end of their prayers with this particular word? Why not a simple goodbye, or goodnight? Maybe she'd try that next time, though the idea felt oddly daring.

Sleep had just begun to blur the edges of her consciousness when a gentle knock pulled her back. Her father's voice drifted through the door, carrying the careful tone he always used when trying to make amends. "Mary, can I come in for a minute?"

"Sure, Dad," she answered, her voice thick with approaching sleep. The door's familiar creak announced his entrance, the sound as much a part of her childhood as his footsteps that followed. "I'm sorry I woke you," Joachim said, his figure silhouetted against the hallway light.

"It's fine, Dad. What's up?" She pushed herself up slightly, the moonlight now painting shadows across her father's face.

"I wanted to apologize to you for tonight. Tact is something that I'm not very good at." The bed shifted under his weight as he settled on its edge, the springs singing a soft protest.

"Dad, really. It's not…"

He raised his hand, the gesture gentle but firm. "I should not have come down on you like that. You're an adult capable of making your own decisions." His voice carried the tone of a father who had watched his daughter grow beyond his protection. "I only want the best for you, for you to be happy. I feel nervous about you and Joseph because I want you to have an opportunity to experience life and all it has to offer. You could have a promising career as an attorney, and I don't want some young man coming along and pulling you off track, only to move on to someone else."

The sigh that followed seemed to deflate him slightly. "You were right that I don't know Joseph's true intent. That's between you, God, and him. I trust you. All I ask is that you don't limit your options." Joachim took Mary's hand. It folded warm and solid around hers. "I hope you can understand your old man."

Mary looked into her father's eyes, the age lines framing them in such a way that made them appear to smile even through his sullen expression.

"*Of course. It's already forgotten.*" She shifted, resting her head in his lap as she had done countless times before. His fingers moved through her dark hair with familiar tenderness, a father's blessing that followed her into sleep.

Chapter 2

FAMILY BUSINESS

"Today on The People's Position, we have for the first time, the newly appointed Chairman of Religious Affairs, Harold Solon. The chairman has never given a public interview since taking office, and we are honored to have him with us today. Welcome, your Honor."

The camera panned to a regal-looking man in a sharp suit, sitting with practiced ease in a plush armchair. His presence seemed to fill the entire frame. "*Thank you. It is a pleasure.*" Chairman Solon's measured voice carried authority, his piercing eyes holding the camera's gaze with confidence.

"The pleasure is all ours. Before we begin, would you mind explaining, in your own words, for those who are not religious or who may not know, what exactly does your office do? What are you accountable for?" The host leaned forward, masking his eagerness with professional demeanor.

"The United States is known for its commitment to religious freedom, as enshrined in the First Amendment of the Constitution," Chairman Solon began, each word precisely chosen. "Creating a Chairman of Religious Affairs demonstrates the government's dedication to protecting and promoting the right of individuals to practice their religion freely, without fear of discrimination or persecution."

"But was this really needed? To establish this position and this committee?" The reporter's eyebrows arched slightly, his tone carrying challenge.

Joseph rose from his chair in his office and walked over to the fresh pot of coffee he'd just brewed, his eyes never leaving the screen as he poured and returned to his seat.

The Chairman shifted in his chair, the movement subtle but deliberate. "Religion plays a significant role in the lives of many Americans, and various religious communities often face unique challenges. Having a designated official could help address these concerns effectively. From time to time, religious disputes arise that could impact social harmony. My office is equipped to mediate such disputes, working toward peaceful resolutions that contribute to a more stable society."

"So, who comprises the committee? What does it look like?" The host pressed, his tone growing more insistent.

"First, let me emphasize that the committee strives to be diverse and inclusive," Solon replied, his words flowing with practiced smoothness. "We represent different religious traditions, denominations, and perspectives while respecting the principles of secular governance and the separation of church and state. Our focus areas include promoting cooperation between religious communities, engaging with various organizations to understand their needs, and ensuring their perspectives are considered in government policies. We also provide expertise in interreligious conflict resolution and partner with other countries, sharing resources and knowledge."

The reporter leaned forward, positioning himself closer to the Chairman, a spark of confrontation in his eyes. "What can you say about the current accusations? The polls suggest the role of Chairman has become too politically powerful. You've been accused of influencing elections, keeping supporters in key positions while removing those who oppose your agenda."

"That's absolutely true!" Joseph blurted at the screen, the coffee cup shaking slightly in his hand.

"That's absolutely not true," Solon countered, his composure undisturbed. "It's natural to misunderstand any facet of government that holds policing authority. Consider the IRS, for example. But our success speaks for itself. The peace we've established between different factions, the millions in recovered revenue from tax-evading fake religious entities, these achievements have inspired twenty other countries to follow America's example. Soon, most sovereign nations will have similar positions in their governments."

"What is the tax money used for?" the reporter pressed, trying to get to the heart of the matter.

"All tax revenue paid by the churches, excepting necessary deductions, returns to various religious entities as subsidies and grants, which they may use as they deem appropriate."

"That's been another significant concern among your critics, that various sects, fearing reduced operating funds or complete loss of access to money, feel forced into affiliation."

"Also, not entirely accurate," Solon's reply came smooth and practiced. "Yes, they remain subject to government tax, but participation is voluntary. The tax benefit, however, is undeniable. The returned funds are crucial to charitable work across the nation. Many essential assistance programs would collapse without our subsidies."

"Joseph, can you come in here?" His father's voice crackled over the intercom, making him start in his chair.

"Sure, Pop. Just a sec," Joseph responded, annoyed that he had to leave the broadcast.

Making his way down the hallway of glass-windowed offices, employees moved with quiet urgency, their conversations barely above the rhythmic chirp of phones and shuffle of papers.

"Hello, Mr. Reisman," Sandra called out as she hurried past, clutching papers to her chest.

"Good morning, Sandra," Joseph replied, noting how she barely lifted her eyes to meet his. She'd been with the company for fifteen years, had helped train him when he first started. Now she scurried past like a stranger, her shoulders tight with worry. The layoffs last month had changed everything. For the first time in twenty years, he and his father had been forced to let people go, good people, familiar faces, almost like family. The severance packages they'd managed to provide felt like small bandages on gaping wounds.

Joseph approached his father's office, his hand hesitating for a moment before knocking lightly on the door. *"Dad?"*

"*Come in, Joe*," his father's voice muffled through the thick door.

Jacob was watching the same interview; his face creased with concern. "Can you believe this guy?" he said as Joseph approached the desk, the same solid oak desk that had been there since Joseph was a boy. "Everyone knows he's power-hungry. On one hand, he's playing humble, while across the ocean, he's positioning himself to lead the international religious coalitions. Who would have thought that one day the government would be meddling in religious matters? Incredible."

"I don't know if it's a good idea or not," Joseph replied, settling into the chair across from his father. He grunted slightly; the chair still squeaking in the same spot after all these years. "We've had peace since the Committee was established. There hasn't been a religious-based conflict anywhere for a long time."

Jacob leaned forward, his hands folded on the desk. "Wars no, but his control over religious institutions grows day by day. They even have their own police force now, and they're looking into creating their own court system. Next thing you know, they'll have their own prisons. Judge, jury, and executioner all rolled into one. Too much power." He shook his head slowly. "And I'm not the only one who feels that way."

"I know one thing," Joseph said, gesturing toward the TV screen where Solon's face still dominated the frame. "That Chairman gives me the creeps."

"What he lacks in charisma, he makes up for in brains." Jacob's voice dropped lower, as if sharing a secret. "Sometimes I think he's the one really in charge. I don't think the President would have been elected without him."

Joseph nodded, then changed the subject. "Well, what's up today?"

Jacob sat back in his chair, a familiar glint appearing in his eyes, the same look he got whenever he saw an opportunity. "The reason I'm watching this interview... is that we have a prospect to do some work for the Chairman's office."

"After all that about how he's a power-hungry egoist?" Joseph chuckled, though there was a slight tension in his laughter.

"Hey, his money is just as good as anyone else's. Maybe better, being all holy and everything." Jacob crossed his hands behind his head, leaning back in his executive chair, a gesture Joseph had seen countless times growing up. It usually preceded either very good news or very bad news.

"He's working in partnership with the Chairman of the Israel committee to build an American and Israeli Jewish fellowship and cultural center." Jacob's eyes lit up as he spoke, that old fire returning. "The Israeli Chairman is planning to move his office there. We're talking about a multi-building complex, housing for all the Chairman's staff and governing officers, fitness centers, a park, four parking garages, and a state-of-the-art computer and communications center."

Joseph leaned forward, his coffee forgotten. "Where?"

"In Jerusalem."

"Where was his old office?"

"In Israel. Jerusalem to be specific." Jacob's fingers drummed lightly on his desk. "Part of the bid is to demolish the old office. The land is being sold."

Joseph felt his pulse quicken. This was big, bigger than anything they'd handled before. "How did we come across the prospect?"

"Bids are being submitted online. Notices were sent to all the Jewish-owned construction companies across the nation." Jacob's eyes fixed on his son. "That's where you come in. I need you to make sure we get this contract."

"I'll do my best," Joseph said, trying to sound confident. "Do we have any drawings?"

"I have Armond working on them now. He should be ready by the time they accept the bid."

"Awfully confident, aren't you?" Joseph raised the question.

"In you? Yes." Jacob leaned forward, his expression becoming serious. The playful glint in his eyes faded, replaced by something harder, more urgent. "Joseph..." He glanced down at a folder on his desk, then back up at his son. "I don't have to tell you what this could mean for us. I just had Abigail in here reviewing the finances. If we don't get this contract, we could be looking at another round of layoffs. We could be looking at shutting down altogether."

"We've been in tough times before, Dad." Joseph tried to maintain his optimism, even as his father's words sent a chill through him. "It's just a bit lean right now. We've found ways to make it in the past, and we'll do it again this time."

Jacob stood up from his desk and walked to the window, his reflection ghostly in the glass. He clasped his hands behind his back; a habit Joseph remembered from childhood discussions about grades or behavior. "Joseph, not this time." His voice was soft but firm. "You know how I feel about our family business. It's like my second child. Blood, sweat, and tears. All my life to build it to what it is today, the most successful Jewish-owned construction company in the US." He breathed heavily against the glass, creating a momentary fog patch. "But we won't last another year. This contract is do or die for Reisman Construction. Do you understand what I'm saying?"

Joseph watched his father's reflection, seeing not just his boss or his father, but three generations of dreams and hard work embodied in one man. "Yes," he said quietly. "I believe I do. I will do my best."

"I know you will." Jacob turned from the window. "But it's going to take quite a bit of your time over the next couple of weeks to work it up. Do you have the space in your schedule?"

The question was loaded in a way that Joseph couldn't miss. "If you're referring to Mary, and I know you are, she is in no way an obstacle to my work."

Jacob sighed, returning to his desk. "Son, romantic relationships can become distractions to our type of work. They take effort, and the more time you invest, the more complicated things can get. Especially with the young ones." He held up a hand to forestall Joseph's protest. "Don't get me wrong, I understand the younger woman thing. But younger women get restless easily. They get bored. And when they get bored, they look for something to do. And with our head down in our work, we don't realize what's happening until it's too late."

"Are you suggesting that all women are unfaithful?" Joseph's voice carried an edge of defense, thinking of Mary.

Jacob's expression softened slightly. "What I'm saying is that you have to be careful and choose a woman who understands what's ahead of you. One day you'll be in charge here, provided we survive. That takes a big sacrifice of time. She needs to be content with that fact."

"I'll take it under advisement." Joseph rose from his chair and walked to the door. He paused, hand on the handle, and turned back to his father. "And I'm going to make sure when I find the right one, she'll be more like Mom and less cynical about the world ."

"And just what is that supposed to mean?" Jacob's voice rose slightly.

Joseph gave him a knowing smile and quietly shut the door behind him. As he made his way back down the hallway, he felt the eyes following him. The office had become a place where whispers lived in corners, where every conversation might herald more bad news. He could almost hear the thoughts buzzing behind the glass walls, worries about the future, rumors about more layoffs, families doing mental calculations about mortgages and school payments.

He headed back to his office, letting out a long breath. The morning's happenings pressed down on him, his father's revelations, the crucial contract, the subtle dig at Mary. He was looking forward to sinking into his chair, closing his eyes for just a moment to help center himself. He opened his office door…

"Surprise! Happy birthday!"

The voice jolted him upright. Standing behind his desk was Gwen, her presence as unexpected as a thunderclap on a clear day. His desk, usually crowded with blueprints and contracts, had been transformed into an elaborate picnic setting. She was already lighting candles, her smile bright and familiar in a way that made his stomach tighten.

"So, what do you think?" she asked, stretching her arms wide like a game show hostess revealing a prize.

"What in the world are you doing in here?" The words came out sharper than he'd intended, but seeing her now, especially today, was extremely frustrating.

I thought you might enjoy a nice relaxing lunch." Gwen lifted a container from the desk, her movements deliberately graceful. "It's your favorite potato salad, just the way you like it. Come and sit down, relax a bit." She pulled his office chair out and patted the leather invitingly.

Joseph remained standing, his body tense. "Gwen, don't think I don't appreciate the thought, but you cannot do this."

"Do what? Make lunch for a good friend?" Her voice took on a playful lilt that he remembered all too well. "Come on. Don't be such a killjoy." She waved a bag of chips in the air. "I know you're hungry," she sing-songed the words, just like she used to.

"It's all very nice, Gwen, but I can't help but think what your real intent is behind this gesture." Joseph watched as she emerged from behind the desk, noting how she was dressed for a night out rather than an office visit. Her skirt, once again far too short for the setting, caught his eye longer than he meant it to. The realization made him angry, not at her, but at himself for falling into such an obvious trap. It wasn't just inappropriate; it felt like an insult to what he had been trying to build with Mary.

Gwen approached Joseph and wrapped her arms around him, pinning his arms to his sides. The embrace felt like a trap. She looked up into his eyes, maintaining her hold. "All I'm doing is spending some time with an old friend. We are friends, aren't we?" Her grip tightened as she rested her head against his chest.

Joseph carefully extracted himself from her embrace, stepping back to create distance. "Gwen, this is inappropriate. I understand that you still have feelings for me, and I can't help that. But you know I'm with Mary now. I'm no longer available as far as you're concerned." He sat down in his chair, trying to project calm authority. "I've moved on from our relationship, Gwen. I suggest you do the same."

"Move on?" Her voice rose sharply, the playful facade cracking. "Move on? Who was there for you when your mother died, Joseph? Who held you through those endless nights? Who watched you piece yourself back together, day by day?" She moved closer, her perfume, still familiar after all this time, filling his senses. "I know you in ways she never can. Ways that Mary couldn't possibly understand. We've shared so much, Joseph."

"Mary knows I had a life before her," Joseph replied carefully, watching Gwen's face for her reaction. "I have no secrets from her."

Gwen circled behind his chair, her hands sliding down his chest. She leaned close to his ear, her breath warm against his skin as she whispered, "I'm sure there's at least one thing she doesn't know."

The office door swung open.

Mary stood in the doorway, her expression a perfect mirror of Joseph's own shock. In that frozen moment, he remembered mentioning his birthday during their conversation last night. The fact that she'd found his workplace, something he'd never specifically told her, was secondary to the devastation spreading across her face.

He jumped away from Gwen, straightening his shirt as if he could somehow compose himself, and recompose this situation into something less incriminating. "Mary... uh, hello," he stammered, moving toward her, leaning in to kiss her cheek. "What brings you here?"

The words felt leaden with guilt, and his earlier discomfort had bloomed into full-blown agony. Mary pulled away before his kiss could land, her arms folded tight across her chest. Her gaze shifted to catch Gwen's triumphant smirk, and the tension in the room crackled like static before a storm.

"Looks like you're not the only one who is surprised today," Mary said, her voice tight with controlled emotion.

"Why hello, Mary." Gwen's voice oozed with false sweetness. "Care to join our little celebration?"

Mary's face flushed deep red, her voice quavering as she spoke. "I just came here to... I mean... I don't want to interrupt you." She looked back at Joseph, tears welling in her eyes. "I'm sorry, I should have called first."

Before Joseph could respond, Mary turned and fled down the hallway, one hand pressed against her mouth to stifle a sob. "Mary!" Joseph called after her, panic rising in his throat. He whirled to face Gwen, pointing a trembling finger at her. "Before I return, I want you and everything you've brought gone from my office."

He raced down the hallway, rounding the corner just in time to see Mary's anguished face disappear behind closing elevator doors. Taking the stairs two at a time, he sprinted down to the ground floor, emerging just as the elevator doors opened. Mary shot out like an arrow from a bow, making straight for the parking garage.

"Mary!" Joseph called again, catching up to her. "Mary, come on, it's not what you think," he pleaded, falling into step beside her. "I had no idea she would come here."

Mary quickened her pace, refusing to acknowledge his words. "Mary, please wait. Talk to me." He finally managed to halt her progress.

"How did you know where I worked?" he asked, suddenly realizing the oddity of her appearance. "I mean, I wasn't keeping it a secret, but I don't remember it coming up."

Mary wrenched herself away from him, her voice bitter. "I told my parents about you. And it just so happens my father works here."

"What?" Joseph felt the ground shift beneath his feet. "Who is he?"

"Joacim."

"Our former CFO? Seriously?" The revelation staggered him, adding another layer of complexity to an already impossible situation.

"Tell me. What did I just see?" Mary demanded, her arms now wrapped protectively around herself, her voice trembling between anger and hurt.

"You saw nothing," Joseph insisted, his voice rising with urgency. "Nothing that meant anything."

Mary's eyes flashed. "I'll tell you what I saw. I saw Gwen rubbing her hands all over you. What possible explanation can there be for that?"

Joseph placed his hands gently on her shoulders, turning to face her directly. His eyes sought hers, willing her to see the truth in them. "I have nothing to hide from you, Mary. Gwen came to my office unannounced, using the excuse that she made lunch for me as a friend. She had just started to come on to me when you walked in. It was just unfortunate timing," he pleaded, his voice soft but intense.

"Unfortunate for whom? Me or you?" Mary's question cut like a knife.

"Both of us," Joseph admitted, his honesty raw and unguarded. "Look at me, Mary. Really look at me. Gwen was part of my past life before you. But she refuses to let go. She thinks that somehow she'll wear me down." He took a deep breath, his next words coming from somewhere deeper. "Mary, my life is different now. I want to be with you, and only you. Please believe that I will never hurt you."

Mary's emotions wavered visibly between anger and vulnerability as she slowly rested her head against his chest. Joseph held his breath, knowing she was listening to his heartbeat, letting it tell the truth his words might fail to convey. His heart pounded steadily, and with each beat, he could feel her tension beginning to ease. The heart, after all, cannot lie.

After what felt like an eternity, Mary spoke, her voice muffled against his shirt. "I don't want her to do that again. Can you promise me that?"

"Absolutely," Joseph declared without hesitation. "In fact, I've already seen to it. She is no longer allowed in the building."

Mary pushed back slightly, her eyes searching his face. "I'm not kidding, Joseph. I don't want her coming here."

"I'm completely serious," he replied, his voice firm and resolute. "No way. Never again."

"Okay. I trust you. Please always remember that." Mary said, her tone softer now.

"Okay. I trust you." Mary's voice softened, a small smile finally breaking through. "You always remember that."

"And I think I love you. Always remember that," Joseph thought, the words rising unbidden in his mind as he leaned in to kiss her. He then saw her on her way.

When Joseph returned to his office, his heart still racing from the encounter with Mary, he found Gwen packing up her things, a look of smug satisfaction playing across her face.

"So, where's your little girl friend?" Gwen sneered, her voice heavy with sarcasm.

"Don't talk about her like that," Joseph snapped, his jaw clenched. The warmth he'd felt with Mary moments ago hardened into steel. "You had no right to come here and cause such a scene."

"Oh, come on, Joseph. You can't honestly be falling for her, can you?" Gwen taunted, feigning innocence. "You and I had something special once, remember?"

"That was a long time ago, Gwen. We've both moved on," Joseph said, struggling to maintain his composure.

"I haven't moved on," Gwen declared, defiance flashing in her eyes. "I still love you, Joseph, and I know deep down you still feel something for me too."

Joseph shook his head, his voice quiet but firm. "Gwen, what we had is in the past. You need to accept that and move on."

Gwen stepped closer, her face inches from his. "I will never move on, Joseph. Not until you admit that you still care about me."

"I don't want you, Gwen," Joseph stated, his voice unwavering. "I haven't for a long time."

"You're lying!" Gwen shouted, her composed facade crumbling. "I know you, Joseph. You're just afraid of what people will think if you choose me over her."

"This isn't about what people think. It's about what's in my heart," Joseph replied, standing his ground. "And it doesn't belong to you."

Gwen's eyes narrowed as she took a step back, a sharp smile playing at her lips. "Fine. But don't say I didn't warn you. She'll never understand you like I do. You'll come crawling back to me eventually."

"No, I won't, Gwen," Joseph said with quiet certainty. "Now please leave my office and stay away from me and Mary."

For a moment, Gwen's mask slipped, revealing the raw pain beneath her anger. But it was quickly replaced by icy resolve. "You'll regret this, Joseph," she snapped, gathering her things, and storming toward the door.

As the door slammed behind her, Joseph sank into his chair, emotionally drained but relieved. He knew Gwen wouldn't give up easily, but he was determined to protect what he had with Mary at all costs.

His cell phone rang, and his heart jumped when he saw Mary's name on the screen. "Mary, I'm so sorry about all of this," he answered quickly.

"I don't know if I can handle this, Joseph," Mary's voice was shaky. "It's too much drama."

"I promise you, Mary, I'll handle Gwen. She won't be a problem anymore," Joseph assured her, his voice filled with determination.

"But what if she keeps coming between us?" The vulnerability in Mary's voice tugged at his heart.

"We'll face it together," Joseph said softly, letting his feelings flow freely. "If you give me the chance, I won't let anything or anyone come between us. I have fallen in love with you, Mary, and I'll do whatever it takes to make this work." The words tumbled out before he could stop them, but this was his truth. He held his breath, waiting for her response.

There was a moment of silence on the line that felt like forever.

"I love you too, Joseph," Mary replied softly, and in those five words, he heard the promise of everything he wanted.

Chapter 3

JOY AND PAIN

Harold Solon peered anxiously through the private jet's window, finding comfort in watching the earth pass slowly beneath them. The steady drone of engines almost drowned out Malcolm's voice as his Chief of Staff continued briefing him, but Harold's thoughts kept drifting to the upcoming interview in New York.

"I should have said it differently," he said, interrupting Malcolm mid-sentence.

"Said what?" Malcolm asked, realizing he might as well have been talking to an empty seat.

"When he asked me about the taxes." Harold's eyes remained fixed on the window, his reflection displaying his unease.

Malcolm set his folder aside on the empty seat. "You did just fine. The camera was truly kind to you, not a lot of candid close-ups when you weren't speaking. They usually catch a stray frown or sigh and take it out of context later."

"I'm never satisfied with what I say," Harold confessed, still watching the clouds drift by. "The pressure is incredible. One wrong comment, one moment when I relax my guard, and I could create a disaster."

"That's why I'm here," Malcolm assured him. "Stick to the scripts I prepare, and you'll be fine."

Harold finally turned to look at Malcolm, admiration mingled with something deeper in his eyes. "It's uncanny how you always seem to know everything, how you have the right words for every situation."

Malcolm took a measured sip of brandy, a faint smile playing on his lips. "That's my job. I advise the country's highest religious authority. I better know what I'm doing." He paused, studying Harold's expression. "Now, don't worry about the interview. If there's any fallout, I'll handle it."

"I have no doubt about that," Harold replied. "So, what's the latest on our little project?"

Malcolm shuffled through his papers with practiced precision. "We are on schedule. Bids have been coming in online for a couple of weeks now. Considerable interest." He paused, selecting his words carefully. "We hope to select a company by the end of the month."

"I'd like to see an underdog win the contract," Harold mused. "Something different from the usual big players."

Malcolm's response was measured, diplomatic. "Of course, we will be fair, but the successful bidder needs to have the resources to pull off a project of this size. As the first joint venture project with the Israeli Chairman, it must go smoothly."

Harold leaned forward and pressed the call button. "Lil, can you bring me another one?"

"Right away, Mr. Chairman," came the sweet voice from the intercom.

Harold settled back into his plush chair. "It would be nice to have the project's completion coincide with the comet festivals. Many of the local sects have big plans to celebrate, especially the Jewish communities."

Lil entered the cabin with a fresh highball on her silver tray. "Here you are, Mr. Chairman. Will that be all?"

"That's all for now; thank you, Lil." Harold watched her behind as she wiggled her way back behind the curtain, noticing the lingering look she shared with Malcolm.

"I heard that the comet will become increasingly bright over the next nine months, especially over the Mediterranean region." Harold resumed his window gazing. "I still don't see what the big deal is over some space rock."

Malcolm's demeanor shifted subtly as he began typing on his wireless keyboard. The monitor on the wall came to life with ancient parchments and drawings. "This is a new comet," he explained, his voice taking on a scholarly tone. "Historically, comets have been seen as signs of significant events. They were usually considered bad omens, heralding of births, or deaths of rulers, or even great disasters. A sign of change and upheaval."

His fingers moved across the keyboard as he continued. "Some believe they foretell the arrival of a 'deliverer' or 'redeemer' who will bring peace to the world. Here, let me show you." Malcolm pulled up Buddhist writings on the screen. "For example, Sir, Buddhist texts say, 'At that period, brethren, there will arise in the world an Exalted One abounding in wisdom and goodness, a teacher for gods and men.'"

As the screen changed, Malcolm's voice maintained its academic detachment. "Hindu prophecies from the Bhavishya Purana, which date back five thousand years, describe the future appearance of Isha Putra, the son of God born of an unmarried woman named Kumari."

But when he reached the Hebrew texts, something in his manner changed. His hand hesitating slightly as he navigated through the ancient prophecies. "As for the Jews, from their scriptures, the Testaments say, 'There shall come a Star out of Jacob, and a Scepter shall rise out of Israel, and shall smite the corners of the enemy, and destroy all the children of evil.'"

Malcolm's composure cracked further as he continued, his voice dropping to nearly a whisper. "They go on to actually predict where it will happen. In the Book of Micah, it says, 'But you, Bethlehem Ephrathah, though you are small among the clans of Judah, out of you will come for me one who will be ruler over Israel, whose origins are from of old, from ancient times.'"

Harold watched as Malcolm brought up historical writings and images on a monitor.

"The Jews talk about their savior being born in Bethlehem," Malcolm said, pointing to the map. "Where your project is located."

Harold noticed the change in Malcolm's tone. "Your voice changed when you mentioned the Hebrew prophecies. Why?"

Malcolm hesitated, reaching for Harold's glass. He took a long drink, nearly draining it, before answering. "I suppose it's just fascinating how these ancient beliefs continue to influence the world today," he replied, though something flickered behind his eyes. "It's all part of the grand tapestry of history, Mr. Chairman. The difference with the Hebrew prophecies is..." He set the empty glass down with unusual care. "The difference is, they seem to have a history of coming true."

Harold looked back at Malcolm and asked, "So Jewish prophecies say that their next king will be born in Bethlehem?"

"No, Sir; not just a king. But they say the king of all kings," responded Malcolm. "The Jews claim they are the ones who will produce the savior of all mankind who will come and rule the world. Basically, take all our jobs."

"Hmm," snorted Harold. "Good luck with that. Mankind has been trying to unite the world under one religion since the beginning of time." He took a sip of his drink before continuing, "And are you telling me that they believe this comet foretells his birth? That he is coming soon?"

"I am not saying anything. I am only quoting the writings," replied Malcolm.

Harold, a bit taken aback by Malcolm's bold commandeering of his drink, interlocked his fingers across his stomach and said, "Well then, I guess it would be a shame to miss the show. Make the arrangements."

"Certainly," said Malcolm. His eyes fixed on the now dozing Chairman until they landed in Washington.

The restaurant hummed with unexpected activity, far more crowded than usual for a Thursday night. Joseph watched Mary across their small table, disappointed that their favorite spot had lost its usual intimate atmosphere. Even with reservations, they'd had to wait, and now the dining room buzzed with what seemed like half the city's young professionals.

"What is going on tonight?" he asked, glancing around at the packed tables.

"I don't know," Mary replied, smoothing her dress. "Must be a convention in town."

"Not this crowd?" Joseph laughed, nodding toward the cluster of hipsters at the bar.

"That's not nice!" Mary playfully swatted his arm.

"Ow! Okay, okay. Watch it, that's my pitching arm."

"Since when?"

"Whenever I decide to begin pitching," Joseph said with mock seriousness.

"When were you planning to let me know about this exciting new career move?"

"After I signed with the Dodgers."

"The Dodgers?" Mary's eyes lit up with amusement. "I am more of a Yankee fan myself."

"Then you're are you living in the wrong place," Joseph said, impressed by her baseball knowledge. Six months ago, she'd been just another voice in the church choir at his father's charity event. Now here she was, matching him joke for joke, her presence filling spaces in his life he thought would stay empty forever.

The hostess appeared at their table. "Your server will be with you shortly. As you can see, we're swamped tonight." She gestured apologetically at the crowd. "Enjoy your dinner."

"I'm starving," Mary said, opening her menu. "I skipped lunch today rehearsing at the church."

Joseph peered over his menu at Mary. The candlelight caught her features perfectly, and he could tell she'd put extra effort into her appearance tonight. Her dark hair fell in soft waves, and the simple silver cross at her throat, a gift from her father, caught the light when she moved. The sight of her made his heart skip, just as it had that first night when she'd stayed after the choir performance to thank him for his donation to the music program.

The server returned, and Joseph placed their order, including the special arrangement he'd made earlier. His hand brushed the small box in his pocket, and his pulse quickened.

"So, how's the bid going?" Mary asked, pulling him from his thoughts.

"Good, I think. Last we heard we were among the top three finalists."

"You will get it, I know it."

"And just how do you know?" Joseph asked, taking a small sip of wine.

"I just do. You know, I have been having strange dreams lately. Strange but good. I wake up just feeling good. Good about everything. Joseph, I don't know when I have been happier than I am right now."

Joseph reached across the table and took her hand, his thumb tracing small circles on her palm. The conversation flowed easily, jumping from topic to topic, the upcoming church performance, his latest projects, their favorite movies. Time seemed to slip away until the server appeared with dessert.

Mary had ordered a small dish of fruit, but instead received a small silver cup covered with a lid. Her brow furrowed in confusion as she lifted it, then gasped. There, nestled on a bed of dark velvet, was a diamond ring that caught every bit of the candlelight and threw it back in brilliant sparkles.

Joseph moved to her side of the table and dropped to one knee. The conversations around them began to quiet, but he barely noticed. His whole world had narrowed to Mary's face, to the tears beginning to gather in her eyes.

"I know we haven't been dating long. But Mary, you mean the world to me." His voice was steady despite his racing heart. "No one else has ever meant as much to me as you. When you are not with me, I feel I am missing something. I think of you night and day. Without you, my life is incomplete. I'm drawn to you. And I want you to know, whether the future brings us good times, or bad times, I will be by your side protecting you for as long as we both live. Come and grow old with me. I love you, Mary. Will you marry me?"

The restaurant had fallen silent around them, but Mary barely registered the watching eyes. Her heart thundered in her ears, and her breath came in short gasps. "Was this really happening? We only met a few months ago. How could I not have seen it coming? What am I going to say?"

"Well? Mary? Will you marry me?" Joseph repeated, his vulnerability plain on his face.

"Ye...Yes." The word came out as barely more than a whisper.

Yes?" Joseph's voice held a note of disbelief.

"Yes!" Mary said again, stronger this time, certainty flooding through her.

The restaurant erupted in applause and cheers. Joseph slipped the ring onto her finger with slightly trembling hands, then pulled her close for a kiss that seemed to make the world around them disappear.

From across the restaurant, Gwen watched it all unfold, her wine glass gripped so tightly her knuckles had gone white. She'd known this was coming, the rumors had been circulating through the office for weeks, but seeing it happen was something else entirely. Joseph was going to marry Mary. The church choir girl who was supposed to be a temporary distraction had somehow become everything.

"Gwen?" one of her friends asked. "Gwen! Are you even listening?"

"What? Oh, yes. What were you saying?"

"We were saying, we wonder if they will get married in the Temple. Wonder if they will ask you to sing during the ceremony." The girls around the table giggled, their cruelty thinly veiled.

Gwen took a measured sip of wine, years of business dinners helping her maintain her composure. "They're not married yet."

"And what is that supposed to mean?" Terry asked, leaning forward with gleaming eyes.

"Nothing. I'm just saying. Who knows what the future will bring? Anything can happen. Life is funny like that." Gwen's smile was perfect, practiced, the same one she'd used at countless business functions, the one that had helped her climb from receptionist to Joseph's father's trusted assistant. The same one that had almost landed her everything she wanted.

The restaurant resumed its rhythm, and the patrons carried on with their lives. Back at their table, Mary couldn't stop admiring her ring, turning her hand to catch the candlelight. A soft giggle escaped her lips.

"I am so glad you said yes." Joseph watched her with a mixture of relief and adoration. "I was so afraid of what would happen to us if you said no."

"Well, I thought about it, of course." Mary's eyes met his. "But I know that I love you. And nothing would make me happier than to be your wife."

The word 'wife' hung in the air between them, and Joseph's expression shifted slightly. "Well, now comes the hard part. Telling our families."

The reality of what lay ahead washed over Mary like a tidal wave. Her father's face appeared in her mind, his previous objections echoing in her memory. He'd been relentless with his concerns, Joseph was too old, too recently widowed, too much of a distraction from her plans for law school. She knew they were just excuses masking his deeper fears, but that wouldn't make the conversation any easier.

"Tonight," Mary said suddenly, her voice carrying a determination that surprised even her. "We should tell them tonight."

"Tonight?" Joseph's eyebrows shot up. "Shouldn't we take some time to plan?"

"Yes. Tonight. Right now."

"Well, my father is out of town until Monday," Joseph said, trying to inject some caution into her enthusiasm.

Mary shook her head. "I have volunteering at Brookwood on Monday, can't skip that."

"That's okay. I think I would like to tell him alone," Joseph finally admitted.

"Why alone? I am not afraid." Mary's eyes narrowed slightly. "Nervous, yes. But not afraid."

"It's not that. He's under pressure, the business, everything. He keeps pushing me to take over. And he gets upset when I hesitate. I can't predict how he'll react. I don't want you to see that." Joseph's words came carefully, measured.

Mary studied him, a mixture of understanding and gentle teasing in her expression. "So, you're the one who's afraid."

"Not afraid, cautious. Please, Mary, try to understand."

Her expression softened. "I do understand. If that's best for you, then I'm with you."

Their intimate moment was interrupted by Gwen materializing at their table, her presence as abrupt as a cold draft. "Well, now. You two caused quite the stir over here."

She placed her hands on their shoulders, the gesture somehow both familiar and intrusive. "Let me be one of the first to say congratulations. I guess the best gal won. He is quite the catch, Mary. Good thinking to lock him down so quickly." Her smile was dazzling, but her eyes remained cold. "I am so happy for both of you. So, when is the big day? Have you set a date yet?"

"No date yet," Mary's voice was measured, gratitude woven into her words.

"Well, be sure to send me my invitation. I wouldn't miss it for the world."

Joseph's jaw tightened, not fooled by Gwen's condescending attempt at civility. "Sure, Gwen. We'll make sure you're on the list. Now if you don't mind, we have a lot to discuss."

"Oh yes, I understand completely. Sorry to interrupt." Gwen's fingers performed a delicate wave. "I was just so happy for you both that I couldn't help but come over and wish you well. See you at rehearsal tomorrow, Mary." She turned and walked back to her table, her heels clicking against the hardwood floor like a metronome. Joseph and Mary's eyes met back together at the same time.

"What was that?" Mary said. "Do you believe that?"

"With Gwen, I believe anything is possible. But suddenly I feel like we should leave." Joseph scanned the restaurant, noting how close Gwen's table was to theirs.

"You read my mind."

Joseph hailed the waitress with a subtle nod, silently summoning the check that would pull them from the clutches of the once-cozy haven of the restaurant. Soon they were in Joseph's car, heading toward Mary's house. Despite their happiness, neither spoke much, both lost in thought. The car pulled to a stop outside the modest two-story home, its bay window glowing warmly in the evening darkness. Through the glass, they could see a solitary figure settled in an armchair, Mary's father, Joachim, likely absorbed in his evening reading.

Mary's voice held a hint of uncertainty. "Ready for this?"

"Well, are you ready to do this?" Joseph countered, his own nervousness showing.

"Somehow, I did not think it would be this scary," Mary admitted.

"I bet all the guys who have ever done this feel the same way."

"Yeah, but how many of them have that classic Romeo and Juliet family dynamic going on."

Just then, Mary's mother peeked out through the curtain. Anne spotted them sitting in the car and gave a little wave, her face lighting up as she excitedly motioned for them to come inside.

"Well, too late to back out now." Mary squeezed Joseph's hand. "Let's go Romeo".

Hand in hand, they made their way up the walkway. Anne swung open the door with the enthusiasm of a host welcoming long-awaited guests. "Joachim! Mary and Joseph are here!"

They stepped into the living room, where soft lamplight created a welcoming ambiance. Joachim sat in his favorite chair, reading glasses perched on his nose, a hardcover book spread across his lap. At their entrance, he rose, his love evident in the way his stern features softened as he embraced her. "Hello, pumpkin," he said.

“Come in and sit down. How was dinner?” Anne asked, warmth in her tone helping to ease Joseph's nerves.

"Come in and sit down. How was dinner?" Anne asked, warmth in her tone helping to ease Joseph's nerves.

"It was wonderful. Um, in fact," Mary's voice began to quiver, her fingers unconsciously moving to touch her ring, "In fact, that’s why we came here together."

Anne shot a quick glance at Joachim, whose face had quickly become expressionless and pale.

Anne shot a quick glance at Joachim, whose face had become expressionless, the color draining from his cheeks.

"Mom, Dad," Mary's voice trembled with excitement as she extended her hand, the diamond catching the lamplight. "Joseph asked me to marry him.

And I said yes!" She bounced slightly in place, her enthusiasm overflowing like a waterfall. Joseph felt his heart swell with pride and hope, watching her radiate joy. He prayed her elation might soften the storm he could see gathering in Joachim's eyes.

"Oh my! Oh my!" Anne pressed both hands to her cheeks. "Why... that... that's wonderful Mary. Joseph, oh my, I am so happy for you two!"

Joachim remained motionless, his gaze fixed on Joseph like a laser. The silence hung so heavy it could be cut with a knife.

Finally, Joachim broke the silence, his words precise and measured. "So, now the days of a man consulting a woman's father are behind us?"

"It's not like that at all, sir." Joseph met his gaze steadily. "I have the utmost respect for you. I've known you since I was a kid running up and down the hallway of our building. I just assumed that, given our family history, you know me to be a decent man. I assumed you would not object."

"You assumed wrong." Joachim rose from his chair and walked out of the room, his footsteps heavy with disappointment.

Anne called after him. "Joachim!" She turned to the couple, her face a mask of apologetic concern. "Oh, you two, don't fret about him. He will come around."

"I am going to go talk to him," Mary said, already moving toward the kitchen.

Joseph caught her arm gently. "No, I'll go. It's me he's angry with."

Mary looked at him, worry etched into her features. "Are you sure?"

"Yeah, it's about time we had a talk anyway. Now's as good a time as any."

Mary nodded reluctantly. Anne put her arm around her daughter and held her close as Joseph disappeared into the kitchen. "Don't worry dear," she whispered. "All will be well. Now, tell me exactly how he asked you, and don't you dare leave out a single detail."

Joseph found Joachim seated at the kitchen table, his posture rigid, arms crossed defiantly across his chest. The overhead light cast harsh shadows across his face, making him look older, more severe.

"Oh, here we go." Joachim's lips twisted in a bitter smile. "This is where we have some kind of bonding moment?" He slowly shook his head. "Before you start with some ridiculous speech, sit down and listen to me."

Joseph's heart tightened, but he pulled out a chair and sat, mirroring Joachim's position across the table. The kitchen clock ticked loudly in the silence between them.

"Don't think that I am going to give you the 'she is too young' speech or that somehow I am going to make this about me." Joachim's voice was controlled, but emotion simmered beneath the surface. "It is all about her. Her life and her future."

He leaned forward, his hands flat on the table. "She was planning to take the Bar exam, become a lawyer, travel the world. Then settle down with a family of her own and die an old woman who has experienced life, fulfilled and happy. Those LSAT prep books are still on her desk, gathering dust. That summer internship offer from Robertson & Klein is probably in the trash. I've watched her change course, one small decision at a time."

Joachim's gaze locked onto Joseph's face, reading every micro-expression. "Now all she thinks about is singing. She's forgotten all about her future. All for a flirtatious man eleven years older than her and on the rebound from his latest affair with the town tramp."

Joachim paused, his expression softening slightly. "Your father has told me about how you seem to have lost interest in the family business. What I have a problem with is, your reasons are selfish.

The accusation hung in the air between them. "You are going to drag her into your world and you have no direction. Then when you realize one day you are finally able to move on, you will leave Mary behind to pick up the pieces of her life." Joachim's voice grew quieter, more intense. "I know she loves you. But she has never been in a serious relationship. She does not know enough about the cruelty of the world. I know she will be a good wife to you. I just don't believe you are good for her."

Joachim slumped back into his chair, seemingly drained from releasing this weight he'd been carrying. Joseph had been listening intently, each word cutting like a blade through his defenses. It was the voice of a father's love, veiled in concern and protection for the child he'd raised. Envy tugged within him, seeing the kind of closeness he had never truly shared with his own father. His love for Mary was real, profound, but Joachim's words forced him to question himself. Was it the kind of love that could stand the trials of time? The kind of closeness where you finish each other's sentences? The kind where if something is wrong, you can feel it in your gut even though you are miles apart?

Joseph straightened in his chair, certainty flooding back. Of course he did. He was marrying Mary because he believed she was his soulmate, sent from Heaven to be by his side.

He spoke, his voice carrying a quiet intensity. "I understand, truly, I do. Your concerns are valid, Joachim. If I were in your shoes, I'd probably say the same things." Joseph looked down at his hands, then back up to meet Joachim's gaze. "I had a life before the accident that took Mom's life. But I've moved on, grieved, and healed. Now, I'm ready to share my life again. To give my love to someone again."

Joseph leaned forward, his voice growing stronger. "My feelings for Mary are not because I am rebounding. I thought I couldn't love again, but Mary's proven me wrong. You are worried if what I feel for her is real? Yes, it is real. Very real."

Joachim narrowed his eyes and stared silently at Joseph. The kitchen clock ticked away the seconds that felt like hours. Finally, Joachim arose from his chair. "Well then, that being said," he opened the cupboard and took out two small glasses with a bottle of liquor in his left hand. He set them on the table between them. "We will have a drink together. To celebrate and commemorate our discussion and your promise to me."

He poured the amber liquid carefully into each glass. "You know Joseph, two men share a drink, and one of them makes a promise, he better mean it."

As he finished pouring, Mary and Anne entered the kitchen. Mary moved to her father's side, placing her hands on his shoulders and resting her head against his chest. "Daddy? How do you feel?"

"Better." He raised his glass to Joseph. Both tossed back the shot in unison. "Much better. The men have come to an understanding and we were just having a drink to celebrate." He gave a stern look at Joseph as he gave Mary a hug. There would be no misunderstanding about what his promise meant.

Joseph arrived at his father's downtown penthouse apartment just after 11 p.m. The drive had been too quick, giving him little time to prepare for what lay ahead. One down, one to go, he thought grimly as he stepped into the elevator.

The floor numbers lit up in sequence: 33, 34, 35, marking their steady ascent. When it reached the penthouse level, a unique chime sounded, different from the standard tone of the lower floors. Joseph had always wondered if it was intentional, a subtle reminder that reaching the top came with its own distinct burden.

The doors parted to reveal a long, lonely hallway that seemed to stretch endlessly before him. His was the only door on the floor, positioned at the very end like a final challenge to be overcome. He'd never liked this walk. It reminded him of scenes from psychological thrillers where the corridor keeps extending no matter how far the protagonist runs.

He rang the doorbell, with silence as his only answer.

Again, he rang.

Nothing.

He knocked hard, more anxiously.

Still no response.

With dwindling patience, Joseph retrieved the spare key from his pocket and let himself into the apartment. "Dad? Are you here?" His voice carried a mix of concern and frustration through the empty space.

The penthouse was the epitome of downtown chic, all clean lines and modern furnishings. Through the expansive windows, the city spread out below like a tapestry of lights and shadows. The balcony door stood open, curtains dancing in the night breeze. Beautiful but haunting piano music drifted from the study. Joseph sighed, understanding why his father hadn't answered the door. The piano music was a signal he knew too well, the sound of loneliness and pain his father tried to drown with every highball. Making his way to the study, he found the familiar scene: Jacob slumped in his favorite chair, lost in an alcohol-induced slumber. A half-empty glass dangled precariously from his fingers. Joseph watched his father for a moment, seeing not the successful businessman but a man still wrestling with his own ghosts. He gently removed the glass from Jacob's hand and set it on the nearby table.

"Dad," he called softly, shaking his father's shoulder.

Jacob groaned, barely stirring.

"Dad!" Joseph's second attempt was more forceful.

"Uhh... yeah. Yeah, what is it?" Jacob's voice emerged raspy and confused as his eyes fluttered open. He straightened in his chair, one hand propping up his weary head. "Hello, son. What brings you here?"

Joseph studied his father's condition. "Well, I came to talk to you, but it seems this is a bad time."

"No, No. I'm fine. I just had a few drinks and fell asleep."

"I think it was more than a few."

"Yeah. Well, who's counting anyway?" Jacob's responded, resenting the judgement.

"Thinking about Mom again, weren't you?" Joseph's voice softened.

Jacob groaned as he pushed himself up from the chair, stretching his arms overhead with an exaggerated yawn. "Would you like a drink? I'll make you one."

"No thanks, I already had one."

"You're one to talk about me drinking. I smell alcohol on your breath too," Jacob shot back with a wry smile. "Who were you drinking with? Mary doesn't drink, does she?"

"I had one drink with Joachim."

Jacob froze mid-step. "Joachim? Are you serious? What for?"

"To celebrate," Joseph said, bracing himself for what was to come.

Jacob's expression grew more serious, as if he already knew what Joseph was about to say but had hoped this moment would come much later, or not at all.

"Really? Celebrate what?" Jacob asked, though his tone suggested he already knew.

"My engagement. Tonight, I asked Mary to marry me."

"Well then. Seems I will definitely need another drink." He poured himself a fresh shot of bourbon and tossed it back in one swift motion. "So, when is the big day?"

"We haven't set a date yet. No hurry."

Jacob arched an eyebrow, studying his son. "Then why get engaged if you aren't ready?"

"I didn't say I wasn't ready. We will get married when we are both ready."

"So, then she is the one who is not ready?" Jacob's words cut like a surgeon's scalpel.

Joseph's heart pounded harder as he chose his next words carefully. "I didn't say that either."

"Well then, what are you saying?" Jacob lowered himself back into his chair with a small grunt.

"I'm trying to give you some good news. To share in my happiness," Joseph replied, his voice edged with frustration.

"You don't sound happy," Jacob observed. "So, what happens now? The huge expensive wedding?"

Joseph felt his anger simmer. "Dad, if you don't stop it, I'm leaving."

Jacob managed to suppress his own rising temper, offering a forced smirk. "What about the company?"

"I didn't say I was quitting the company. I said I was getting married."

"Same thing. You don't think that a young wife is not going to take your attention from what is important?" Jacob continued to push.

"Mary is important. You are important. The company is important. I have my priorities in order," Joseph retorted.

"So, is that the order of your priorities? The family business takes a back seat to Mary? I come second to her?" Jacob matched his son's tone.

"You should talk! I have been taking a back seat to the business ever since mom died!" The words burst from Joseph before he could stop them.

"That's not true. Not true at all! I need," Jacob stopped abruptly, his frustration overwhelming him. He buried his face in his hands for a moment before standing up and letting out a deep sigh. "Joseph, I need you. We need each other. You and the company are all I have left in this world. I can't bear to think," He stopped, taking a few unsteady steps toward his son.

"We did it," Jacob said suddenly, his voice shifting.

"Did what?" Joseph asked, caught off guard by the change.

"We have the contract," Jacob announced, pride breaking through his alcoholic haze.

Joseph's eyes widened as understanding dawned. "The Chairman's project."

"Yes," Jacob confirmed, a genuine smile forming on his face.

"That's wonderful, Dad!" Joseph embraced his father, genuine joy pushing aside their argument. "This is what we've been waiting for. This will save the company."

"Yes. It's a blessing. Straight from Heaven." Jacob cupped his son's face in his hands, his eyes suddenly clear and focused. "That's why I need you. I need you to see this through."

"Of course, Dad. You don't have to ask," Joseph assured him.

Then Jacob delivered unexpected news. "You know this means you'll need to spend some time at the site. In Israel."

The implications hit Joseph. He had not completely considered the amount of travel and time away that would be required. He would need to discuss this with Mary. How would she take the news?

How will your new bride handle you being away?" Jacob asked, seeming to read Joseph's thoughts.

"We'll work it out. I'm sure she'll understand. It's my job, after all," Joseph replied, trying to mask the uncertainty that had crept into his voice. But even as he spoke the words, he felt the promises to both Mary and Joachim weigh on him. The evening that had started with such joy now seemed to be spinning beyond his control, pulling him in opposing directions.

Chapter

4

CHANGE OF PLANS

A knock at the office doorway startled Gwen from her concentration. She'd been using Elizabeth's office as a quiet place to review the program for the upcoming Temple show, losing herself in the familiar comfort of sheet music and performance notes. Looking up, she found a well-dressed man holding a briefcase, his expression professionally pleasant.

"Excuse me, Miss?" he said, offering a polite smile.

"Yes?" Gwen responded, straightening in her chair. "Can I help you?"

"Hello. My name is Henry. I'm a talent scout for Champion Records." He stepped into the office. "I was in town last week and happened to catch the show from my hotel room. We're always looking for new talent, and I came to speak with the young lady who performed the opening number."

Gwen's neck tightened as she swallowed, excitement bubbling up like champagne. This was it, her moment, her destiny. Henry was like a knight in shining armor, come to rescue her from obscurity. She felt like a schoolgirl receiving that long-awaited call from her crush before prom.

"That's me!" she exclaimed, jumping to her feet and extending her hand. She gripped his firmly, enthusiasm making her shake it perhaps a bit too vigorously.

Henry's face tightened slightly. "Yes, I did see you. You were fantastic. But..." He gently extracted his hand from her grip. "Actually, I was here to speak with the other young lady who sang with you."

Gwen froze; her hand still suspended in the air where he'd left it. The world seemed to tilt sideways, reality skewing just enough to make her dizzy. "I... what?"

"The dark-haired young woman who sang with you," Henry clarified, his discomfort now evident. "I wasn't able to catch her name. Could you help me find her? Is she here?"

Gwen sank back into her chair, barely hearing his words through the roaring in her ears. "I... don't know."

"Oh." Understanding dawned on Henry's face. It wasn't his first time navigating such disappointment. "Well, if you see her, would you please give her my contact information?"

He reached into his coat pocket and withdrew a business card. Gwen remained unresponsive, staring through him rather than at him. After an awkward moment, he stepped forward and placed the card on the desk's edge.

"Thank you, miss. It was nice meeting you. I really do think you're a wonderful singer." The words felt hollow, meant to cushion a blow they both knew couldn't be easily softened. He made a quick exit, leaving Gwen alone with the crushing rejection.

She ignored his parting comment, lost in a fog of disbelief and mounting frustration. Once again, Mary had stolen the spotlight. First Joseph, now this, her chance at fulfilling her lifelong dream being snatched away by this girl who seemed to effortlessly collect everything Gwen had ever wanted. Where had this girl come from? What made her so special?

Gwen glanced at the business card. Champion Records had launched some of the biggest names in popular music. If Mary signed with them, she'd have everything, fame, fortune, perhaps Joseph too. The thought made something twist painfully in Gwen's chest.

Not if I can help it, she thought, her anger solidifying into resolve. She will not take anything else from me! With sharp, deliberate movements, she tore the card into tiny pieces and threw them into the trash can under the desk. Standing up, she snatched her coat from the chair and stormed toward the door, only to find Mary herself rounding the corner.

Hello, Gwen," Mary said softly, noting the other woman's obvious distress. "Are you alright?"

Gwen's response was purely physical. She shoved Mary aside, sending her stumbling into the wall with a solid thud, then hurried down the hallway and disappeared around the corner.

Mary steadied herself, rubbing her shoulder where it had hit the wall. Poor Gwen, she thought. So much hurt, so much sadness. I hope she finds peace. Turning her attention to the schedule board that had brought her to Elizabeth's office, she noticed she was slotted to perform another duet with Gwen. Perhaps this could be an opportunity to reach out, to rehearse together and maybe even mend some fences.

"Gwen!" she called, hurrying down the hallway. No response. Mary suspected she might have gone to the auditorium and headed that way, descending the stairs and pushing through the heavy doors. She entered the large, dimly lit auditorium, calling out Gwen's name once more. "Gwen?" she called out. Her voice echoed through the empty space. She was alone.

The vast space was empty and dimly lit. She'd never seen the Temple so completely deserted, usually there were technicians setting up for shows on weekdays, or members attending learning sessions on weekends. But today, the silence felt absolute. Mary moved down the center aisle, her hand trailing lightly across the seats as she walked.

She paused before the stage, unable to resist admiring the Temple's architecture. Its circular design rose to a high timber ceiling, crowned by an enormous stained-glass window depicting the story of Creation. Multicolored curtains framed the window, and the half-circle stage was flanked by illuminated waterfalls where the choir usually stood. Mary remembered how the lighting technicians would adjust the colors to enhance different moments, blue for tranquility, orange for celebration, purple for spiritual ceremonies. Even in the dim light, it was breathtaking.

She climbed onto the stage and retrieved a songbook from the choir area, then settled into an aisle seat in the front row. Finding the piece scheduled for the next telecast, she began to rehearse, her voice filling the empty space with an acapella melody. After one verse, she paused, sinking back into the cushioned seat with the book resting on her chest. Her thoughts drifted to Joseph. They hadn't spoken since yesterday, and she was eager to hear how things had gone with his father. Closing her eyes, she allowed herself to daydream about wedding plans. What colors should they choose? Chicken or beef at the reception, or maybe both? They still hadn't set a date. Should she start looking at dresses? Lost in these pleasant musings, she began to drift toward sleep.

She began to dream of warmth, gentle and calming, starting on her face before spreading throughout her body. Then light, brilliant and white, so intense she couldn't see her surroundings. A sensation of falling startled her awake, except the warmth and light remained. Confusion swirled through her mind as she realized what felt like a spotlight was aimed directly at her face, but this light was more radiant than anything she'd ever encountered. Slowly, within the light, a figure began to materialize. As it became more distinct, the brightness receded into a glowing aura surrounding what appeared to be a man hovering at the stage's center. He was beautiful beyond comprehension, with flowing hair framing translucent skin that seemed to shimmer with its own inner light. His white robes moved like water, defying gravity.

Terror gripped Mary's limbs, paralyzing her. Am I still dreaming? she wondered desperately. Is this a ghost? The thought that this might be just a dream helped ease her fear enough to focus more clearly on the figure, squinting against the supernatural radiance.

"Who are you? What are you?" she managed to whisper, her voice trembling.

From behind the figure, two ghostly wings unfolded like great sails, transparent yet somehow more real than anything else in the room. They stretched nearly half the length of the stage, their movement sending ripples through the very air.

An angel. The realization struck her like a lightning bolt. Her fear intensified, causing her to tumble from her seat, landing face-down on the floor. "I'm dying," she thought frantically, panic tightening around her. "Oh God, I must be dying!"

"Greetings, young one! Rejoice!" The voice wasn't sound so much as pure meaning translated into something her mortal ears could process. "You have been blessed more than any woman on earth. More than any before you or any who will come after you. For you have found favor in God's eyes!"

Confused and terrified, Mary trembled beneath the overwhelming presence. The angel descended to her side and took her hand. His grip was like iron wrapped in silk, gentle yet immovably strong. He raised her to her feet as she struggled to comprehend what was happening. Was this real? A vision like in scripture? Was she dying or already dead?

"I am Gabriel," the angel declared, each word resonating through the auditorium. "Bearer of God's messages, bringer of change. I stand in the presence of God."

Gabriel repeated, as he slowly raised her up to her feet. Mary, trembled under his touch. It was powerful. His grip was like iron, but gentle. Still bewildered and frightened, she struggled to comprehend the magnitude of what was happening. Her mind raced with questions. Was this real? Was it a vision, as described in the scriptures? Was she dying or already dead?

"Am I dying?" Mary whimpered. "Am I dead?"

"Young one, you have nothing to fear from me," Gabriel reassured her, though his otherworldly presence was a contradiction to the statement. "I bring you good news. God has a special plan for you. You will conceive a son and name him Emanuel. He will be great, called 'Son of the Highest.' The Lord God will give him the throne of his father David, and he will reign forever. His kingdom will have no end."

Mary finally found the courage to meet Gabriel's gaze, a mistake, as his eyes contained eternities. Looking into them was like standing at the edge of creation itself. Swaying slightly, she managed to whisper, "But... but how can this be? I've never even been with a man."

"Nothing is impossible for God," Gabriel replied, his voice carrying echoes of every miracle ever performed. "The Holy Spirit will come to you. The child you will carry will be the Son of God."

He continued, "I have other news. Your cousin Elizabeth has also conceived a son, even at her old age. She is now six months pregnant."

As Gabriel's words sank in, something shifted within Mary. The terror began to recede, replaced by a profound sense of peace that seemed to come from somewhere beyond herself. How could she, of all people, be chosen for such a thing? And yet, here stood one of God's most important angels, telling her that her life would change forever. The thoughts were overwhelming, yet the answer became crystal clear. She would respond with the unwavering faith, love, and devotion to God that had always guided her life.

"I am the servant of the LORD," Mary declared, her voice finding strength in surrender. "Let it be done to me according to HIS will."

"And so, it shall," Gabriel responded. At that moment, a sphere of pure light burst through the stained-glass window, though the glass remained unbroken. Gabriel stood unmoved as the light passed him, coming to hover mere feet from Mary. This light felt different from Gabriel's presence, where he was awesome and awe-inspiring in his beauty, this light emanated pure love. This must be the Holy Spirit he had spoken of.

The peace that had settled over Mary deepened. As her hand reached toward the light, it moved to meet her touch. Their contact was like an electric current flowing through her entire being, and the light seemed to pour into her very essence. With a gasp, she was thrown backward into her chair, overcome by dizziness. The room began to spin faster and faster as a distant voice called her name.

"Mary?"

"Mary!"

She awoke with a start, disoriented. Luke, the cameraman, stood over her, concern evident on his face. "Mary, wake up. You fell asleep," he said.

"Asleep? I was asleep? That can't be. It felt so real," Mary insisted, her voice trembling.

"What are you talking about? What felt real?" Luke asked, scanning the empty auditorium.

"Did you see him?" Mary asked desperately.

"Who?" he asked again, looking around.

Mary hastily grabbed her sweater and rushed up the aisle toward the auditorium door. She flung it open as she passed through, leaving Luke pondering the strange occurrence he had just witnessed.

Outside, high in the night sky above the Temple, Gabriel and Raphael looked on the scene. "It is done." said Gabriel. "He is here. Growing inside her womb."

Raphael inquired, "How did she respond?"

"She was remarkable. Her faith is astounding."

"Yet, she is only human. She has great difficulty ahead. We must protect them. We must protect him."

"She has been given a protector. Joseph is the appointed one."

"He cannot withstand the adversary alone. We must help him."

Gabriel grew stern. "You know God's will. We do not interfere with the natural world without permission. Free will must prevail. They must choose the right path."

"The Enemy does not care about God's will!" Raphael retorted. "He will feel the presence on earth and destroy him while he is vulnerable."

"Even he must abide. He cannot directly harm those whom the LORD favors."

Gabriel moved closer to Raphael, their faces nearly touching. He looked intently into Raphael's eyes. "You will not interfere with human free will. He has become human, and he must endure all that comes with it."

"It was free will that split us all apart, setting brother against brother." Raphael steeled himself. Unwavering. "And what of Lucifer? Will we sit idle while he moves against them? He will find a way."

"We will not interfere with mankind and their choices," Gabriel stated firmly, still locked in their intense gaze. A smile crept across his lips. "But I said nothing against interfering with demons."

Over the next two weeks, Mary withdrew into herself, steadfastly ignoring Joseph's calls, eating sparingly, and spending long hours alone in her room. Her parents, growing increasingly concerned about their daughter's strange behavior, tried repeatedly to reach out. They suspected she and Joseph might be experiencing typical relationship struggles, so they decided to give the couple space, believing time would heal whatever wounds might exist.

Her parents, growing increasingly anxious about their daughter's strange behavior, tried repeatedly to reach out to Mary. They began to suspect that she and Joseph might be experiencing the usual growing pains of a new relationship. So, they decided to give them space, believing that time would heal whatever wounds might exist. Even Martha, her closest confidant, met resistance when trying to break through Mary's self-imposed isolation. For Joseph, this sudden change was pure agony. Had he said something wrong? Done something to upset her? This behavior was so unlike her. His only comfort was a single text she had sent:

"Let me be for now. I love you."

Mary was caught in the relentless grip of overwhelming fear and shame. Who could she possibly confide in? How could she explain her situation? Who would believe her? The thought of telling her parents about Gabriel's message and the miraculous pregnancy seemed utterly impossible. They would think she had lost her mind. While she had unwavering faith in God's ability to perform miracles, everyone understood the biological realities of conception. Joseph and her parents would reject outright the notion that she could be pregnant without having had sex.

Then she remembered Gabriel's other news, that her cousin Elizabeth also bore the mark of God's favor. She recalled Elizabeth's years of trying to conceive with Zachariah, how she had given up hope because of her age. Yet now, at sixty-seven, she was miraculously pregnant. Could this somehow be connected to her husband's sudden muteness? Had Elizabeth also received an angelic visitation?

Mary sat up abruptly in her bed. "If there's anyone in the world, I can talk to about this," she realized, "it's Elizabeth."

With newfound determination, she reached for her phone on the nightstand. Elizabeth had been in Las Vegas for over six months conducting Temple business. Mary said a quick prayer as she dialed, hoping desperately that her cousin would answer.

"Please, please pick up," she whispered as the phone rang. After just two rings, Elizabeth's cheerful voice came through.

"Hello, sweetie! How are you? I'm so happy you called!"

"Liz, do you have time to talk?" Mary asked, her voice trembling.

"Sweetie, what's wrong?" Elizabeth's tone immediately shifted to concern.

"Liz, I don't know what to do. I need your help. Something's happened."

"Is everyone okay? Are you hurt?"

"No, no. Nothing like that."

"Did you fight with Joseph?"

"No, I mean not yet. But it will happen soon."

"What happened?"

"Liz, he will be so angry. He just asked me to marry him this week."

"Yes, I heard. Your mother told me." Elizabeth's voice softened. "Look, sweetie, it cannot be that bad. I know you. You don't have it in you to do bad things. I know him as well. He is a good man. Whatever it is, you two can work it out."

"I don't know. This is pretty big." Mary's voice caught in her throat.

"Say no more. I want you to come here."

"There? To Vegas? I can't."

"Why not? I will book your flight for tomorrow. You obviously need some time away. Come visit me. My treat. You don't have to worry about a thing." Elizabeth chuckled warmly. "You can help me keep away from the slot machines. "

Mary felt the first glimmer of hope she'd had in days. "Well, I guess I can come for a while."

"You bet you can. It's done. I will text the info to you as soon as I book it. Get packed. When you arrive, we will talk. Okay?"

"Okay, Liz. Thank you."

"My pleasure. Anything for my favorite cousin. Love you."

"Love you too."

Mary ended the call, feeling a wave of relief wash over her. This was exactly what she needed, time to think and someone to talk to. But what about Joseph? He deserved some kind of explanation. Still, she wasn't ready to reveal her secret, not until she'd spoken with Elizabeth.

Taking a deep breath, she dialed Joseph's number.

"Hello, Mary?" He answered immediately, concern evident in his voice.

"Hello, Joseph," she said softly.

"Mary, I have been so worried. Are you okay?"

"I'm fine. I just needed some time to myself."

"But why? What's bothering you? Did I do something to upset you?"

The silence that followed felt heavy with unspoken questions.

"I am leaving tomorrow," Mary finally said.

"At least let me drive you to the airport," Joseph pleaded.

"That would be nice. But promise me you won't press me to talk about my problem."

"I promise. Take as much time as you need. I have faith you will come to me when you are ready."

Faith. The word echoed in Mary's mind. Would God give her anything she couldn't handle?

"Okay, I'll call you tomorrow with the details?"

"Okay. I love you, Mary."

"I love you too, Joseph. Goodbye."

The next day, Mary walked through the Las Vegas airport, her heart pounding with anticipation about seeing her cousin. If what Gabriel had told her was true, Elizabeth would understand better than anyone what she was going through.

She spotted Elizabeth resting on a bench in the waiting area, her pregnant belly unmistakable. Tears sprang to Mary's eyes. Everything Gabriel had said was true. She knew in that moment she had made the right decision to come.

Elizabeth had been dozing when she was startled awake by Mary's voice calling out, "Liz! Liz!"

The moment Elizabeth heard her cousin's greeting, something extraordinary happened. The baby within her moved with unprecedented vigor, as if he too recognized Mary's presence and was eager to greet her. It was as though he wanted to be born right then and there.

Joy surged through Elizabeth as she jumped up from the bench, rushing to embrace her young cousin. They held each other tightly, both overwhelmed with emotions they couldn't fully express.

As they pulled apart, Elizabeth twirled around, proudly displaying her pregnancy. "Well?" she asked, eyes twinkling. "How do I look?"

Mary smiled warmly. "As lovely as ever."

""Aren't you surprised?" Elizabeth's voice held a hint of disappointment.

Mary pretended to study her cousin's condition more carefully. "Hmm, let me see," she teased. "Nope, can't say that I am."

Confusion crossed Elizabeth's face. "And why not?"

Mary dropped her playful manner and spoke softly, placing her hand gently on Elizabeth's stomach. "Because I already knew. Would you believe me if I told you an angel told me?"

Elizabeth's face transformed with astonishment and reverence. A tear rolled down her cheek. "Oh, Mary," she whispered. "When I heard you call my name, the baby inside me kicked so hard. But instead of pain, I felt joy. It's as if he recognized your voice."

Mary nodded, her own tears falling freely now. "He told me something else, Liz. I will have a child as well."

Elizabeth took Mary's hand in hers, understanding dawning in her eyes. "This is what Zach was trying to tell me about the purpose of our blessings. You are the most blessed woman on earth, and so is the child you carry."

Mary cried tears of gratitude and relief, overwhelmed by the love and understanding her cousin offered. They embraced again, their hearts connected by faith and a divine plan that neither of them fully comprehended.

"We have so much to share and discuss," Elizabeth said, her voice filled with excitement. "But for now, let's get your luggage and get out of here before TSA decides we're causing a scene," she added with a gentle laugh.

They continued to share laughter and jokes while making their way out of the airport. Elizabeth's condo offered a magnificent view of the Las Vegas strip, the glittering lights creating a stark contrast to the miracles they discussed. The city's artificial grandeur only emphasized the profound nature of their conversation. Elizabeth decided to order pizza, and they dined on the balcony, taking in the breathtaking view. As the evening sun began to set, painting the sky in hues of orange and pink, Mary recounted every detail of her angelic visitation. She described her initial terror upon seeing Gabriel, the overwhelming sense of peace that enveloped her when he spoke, and how he had mentioned Elizabeth's pregnancy. As she went through her story, Elizabeth remained still and attentive, hanging on to Mary's every word, never interrupting. Only when Mary had finished did she finally speak.

Elizabeth marveled, her eyes reflecting both wonder and reverence. "That is absolutely incredible," she whispered. "Only a few people in history have ever seen an angel. And there is no greater gift than what you have been given. And at the same time, the world's most unbelievable responsibility."

Mary's curiosity bubbled over. "But what about you, Elizabeth? I've been talking your ear off for hours, and I've hardly given you a chance to share your own experience. I have so many questions. Please, tell me," she urged.

Elizabeth smiled, her face illuminated by the glow of the city lights. "First, let me refresh your drink," she said, groaning playfully as she rose from her chair under the weight of her burgeoning belly. "Then, I'll tell you everything."

She groaned as she stood, stretched her back and let out a heavy sigh. "Look what you have to look forward to. A four-month backache."

"So, I see. I can't wait," replied Mary, managing a small laugh.

Elizabeth returned with two fresh sodas, setting them on the small round table between them before settling back in her lounge chair.

"Let me begin by sharing something you might not know about our family," she began. "We have a long history of spiritual connection. For as far back as anyone can remember, there has always been at least one member of our family who played a prominent role in the religious community wherever they lived. Zach, for instance, comes from a lineage of Jewish priests. That's actually how we met, introduced by a mutual friend at a conference."

She paused, taking a sip of her drink before continuing. "So, given our family histories, I guess you could say that Zach and I are simply the latest in that long line. Over the years, we've accomplished a lot together, like building the Temple and witnessing its growth in membership. Not to mention the success of our television show, which seems to gather more viewers every month. But there was always something missing, children.

Elizabeth's voice softened with old pain. "We tried for years, visiting clinics and pouring our hearts into prayer. Yet, nothing worked. Finally, I reached menopause, and our hopes seemed even more out of reach. I must say that Zach has been incredibly supportive throughout it all, even though I knew he was deeply disappointed that we wouldn't have a child to carry on our legacy. We considered adoption, but it just wasn't the same for us. We wanted our own child, and I felt so ashamed for not being able to give that to him."

Elizabeth paused, wiping away tears and taking another sip of her drink. Mary listened with empathy, touched by Elizabeth's honesty and vulnerability.

"Anyway, we forged ahead," Elizabeth continued, her eyes reflecting the passion she held for her work. "We immersed ourselves in running the Temple. When we decided to open our doors to other religions, many thought we were out of minds. They believed it would dilute the message and become too generic." She chuckled softly. "But I've always liked plain things. Zach and I believed that as leaders, we should be bringing people together, not keeping them apart."

She leaned forward, warming to her story. "So, we sent out invitations to all religious communities in the area. 'Come and visit the Temple,' we said. 'All are welcome. Bring your ceremonial robes, bring your religious texts. If you believe in God, we will make you a part of our family.' And come they did. We have members from every major denomination, all working and worshiping God as one. It's a tremendous accomplishment, something not done anywhere else that I'm aware of."

Her expression grew more serious as she continued. "Then, the troubles with the office of the Chairman began. They didn't like our mixed approach to religion, finding it difficult to put us in their box. We also don't have 'members' in the traditional sense. People come together, like a club. We were told to register under a denomination and pay the taxes associated with that affiliation. Otherwise, we would have to petition the government as a new denomination, a process that would shut us down for nearly two years while they approved the application. Neither option sat well with us."

Elizabeth sighed but retained her composure, her eyes unwavering. "So, we bore our troubles with quiet dignity. I thought my years of bearing children were over, and it seemed like my prayers had been ignored. Troubles with the Temple began to grow. But in all of this, we held onto our hope in God just as our family had always done. We would define our lives by serving and worshiping every day in the Temple."

A gentle smile crossed her face as she reached the turning point of her story. "A little over six months ago, Zechariah was chosen to enter the National Jewish sanctuary in Washington and offer incense as part of the yearly worship ceremony. It's a special honor because only one priest, chosen by random drawing, can enter the inner sanctuary and perform the offering. Since thousands participate in the drawing, the winner is seen as chosen by God."

Her voice took on a reverent tone. "From the scriptures, Aaron, the brother of Moses, had sons who approached the holy place irreverently and were instantly killed. Since that time, a certain fear has surrounded this ritual, as it was believed that you were actually standing in the Presence of God himself. The room has no windows and only one priest is allowed inside at a time."

She paused, ensuring Mary understood the significance. "Zach told me that as he approached the altar, even though he was alone, even though it was just a few steps inside, he said he began to feel very different. He said it felt like he was walking between worlds, like the ground was slightly vibrating. As he offered the incense, that's when it happened. A bright light appeared over the right side of the altar. So startled he was that he fell backwards on the floor. He then realized that it was not just a light, it was a Presence. Something was with him in that room. Looking up at the light, he saw a man. This man stepped out from the light and spoke to Zach. The moment the words hit his ears he said he began to shake with terror."

Mary interrupted excitedly, "That was him! Gabriel came to see me too!"

Elizabeth smiled knowingly. "Yes, that's right. You will have to compare notes with him when you get back."

She continued, her voice taking on a dramatic quality. "The man said, 'Do not be afraid Zechariah. I am the messenger of the Almighty God. I am here to tell you that your prayers have been heard. Your wife Elizabeth will have a son. You will name him John. He will be highly favored in the sight of the Lord and will turn many toward him.'"

Elizabeth shook her head, a mixture of amusement and exasperation crossing her face. "Zach said that he couldn't move. He was still in a daze at this point, you see. Zach heard him say I would become pregnant and we would have a son. But that had not taken root in his brain yet. Gabriel continued to speak, I guess he realized Zach was too overwhelmed and wanted him to understand what was happening. He said, 'He will be the one to go before the Son. He will come in the spirit and power of Elijah the prophet to help turn the hearts of people towards each other, towards wisdom and justice, to make the people ready for the coming of the Messiah. He will be filled with the Holy Spirit, even while within his mother's womb.'"

"Now, despite everything that was happening, somehow Zach had enough foolishness left in his brain to question God," Elizabeth mused, shaking her head. "In hindsight, he just wasn't comprehending what was happening. He asked Gabriel, 'How can this happen? I am old. We have not been intimate together for years. My wife is too old. She is way past menopause. This is impossible.'" Elizabeth's eyes widened as she continued. "This really angered Gabriel. In the scriptures, another person did this. Like the story of Abraham when the angels told him of Sara's pregnancy. Abraham didn't believe it either."

She leaned forward, her voice dropping dramatically. "Zach said Gabriel actually shouted at him: 'I am Gabriel! I stand in the presence of God!' Now this scared him so badly he fell down to the floor and started crying. Leave it up to my Zach to offend even the angels!"

"Gabriel placed a curse on him, 'As punishment for your disbelief, you will not be able to speak until these things I have said happen.'"

"So it is a curse like some of the rumors said! That's why he has not spoken all this time?" Mary asked in surprise.

Elizabeth's expression softened with memory. "He finished his committed time, then returned home. Zach stumbled into the door crying in my arms. To his surprise, he found that he was able to communicate only with me in writing. He told me everything, but there was one big difference between Zach and me. He had doubted, but I did not. The thought that the Lord was going to bring life to this old body had me giggling like a teenage schoolgirl." She laughed softly. "The very next morning, I took a test and saw I had become pregnant."

"That's incredible, Liz. Why didn't you tell us?" asked Mary.

"You are kidding, right? Of anyone else on earth you should know the difficulty with that suggestion. Everyone will believe it is a miracle, which it certainly is for a couple our age, but who would believe that story? When I realized I was pregnant, I went into seclusion. I decided to rest up a bit here in Vegas then return home to have the baby."

"Everyone is going to freak out when you return home pregnant," mused Mary.

"Zach will tell them in advance, but who cares? Let them freak out. I'm freaked out too, but I am way too happy to care. Mary, don't you see? God is blessing all of creation through us! You and I. We were close before, but now we have a bond unique to anyone else in the world." She touched her stomach and rubbed it gently. "Our children have a great destiny."

Mary began to realize why Gabriel had told her about her cousin. Not only because Elizabeth and her child had a part to play in God's plan, but God also wanted Elizabeth to lead Mary in this special and difficult time in her life. Elizabeth's wisdom, experience and faith were meant to be a guide for her. A type of spiritual grandmother, a kindred spirit who would nurture her and encourage her faith. Elizabeth was to be her instructor and teacher, her friend and confidant, her mentor and advocate.

They continued talking way into the night. When Mary finally went into her room, she found she was still to wound up to sleep. She felt a peace like nothing she had felt before. She decided to write in her diary. She pulled it out of her carryon bag, sat down on the edge of the bed and began to write about her day. It was not enough. She needed to express herself in a more powerful way or she was going to burst. Then she remembered her song book. The song she began a while back where she had only written the title.

"My Soul," she whispered to herself. "The melody I heard in the coffee shop when I met Joseph, I wonder if I put my words to it, would it sound like?"

Now she was ready. She began to write and the words of praise flowed out of her like a bursting dam:

I'm singing this song for my Savior.

God remembered me, and look what he has done.

What God has done for me will never be forgotten, He who is mighty has done a mighty thing for me.

His mercy flows in waves washing over me,

He has shown his strength...

He brings down the mighty and lifts up the low,

The hungry sit down to a banquet, while the rich are left out in the cold.

He has embraced his child, and is merciful,

Piling his blessings high

Exactly as he has promised.

"This doesn't rhyme," mused Mary. Of course she did not care. It felt right. She would need to put it to music someday. She sang of the world's future. It was a song of hope, grace, mercy, and justice. How God's love triumphs over wickedness, evil, pain and ultimately, death. Her baby. Her son.

Her gift from Heaven would do all this. She returned her diary to her bag, climbed under the covers, and finally drifted off to sleep.

Chapter 5

MOVING PIECES

In the flickering light of his campfire, Deacon drained his last bottle of whiskey, each swallow burning less than the memories that drove him here. Slouching in his cheap portable camping chair, empty bottle in his left hand and Colt revolver in his right, he could feel his courage growing exponentially with his despair. Yesterday had been the last straw.

Through the haze of his intoxication, he replayed the events which led him here with a gun ready to end it all. Two days ago, he'd come home early from work. The house seemed empty despite his wife's car in the driveway. He'd called her name from the kitchen, then heard a faint sound from upstairs. A bump? A squeak?

"There it is again," he'd thought, making his way up the stairs to investigate. The squeak grew louder as he approached, now he recognized it. The familiar sound of their bed. She must be taking a nap. He'd opened the door to the worst moment of his life: his wife and his boss, entangled in their marital bed. They'd seen him, but did they stop? Were they embarrassed? No. They'd laughed at him.

No one was laughing now. His wife definitely wasn't laughing when she felt the shotgun blast tear through her chest. His boss had been quick enough to jump out the window and escape. Lucky man.

That IRS agent had laughed at him too. They'd already garnished his wages to collect taxes from his failed business, and now they were trying to take everything. He wasn't laughing anymore either when Deacon also gifted him with a blast buckshot.

Now they were coming for him. Well, they wouldn't have the satisfaction.

The Colt revolver felt heavier in his hand with each passing moment as he pulled back the hammer and began to raise it to his head. The liquor must have been playing its usual tricks, as he stared into the flames, he could swear he saw eyes- a glowing pair of eyes looking back at him from within the inferno. The fire seemed larger now, growing to almost twice its size. The eyes became more pronounced, more defined. Deacon leaned forward, trying to clear his vision and stop the spinning enough to make sense of what he was seeing. Then, a voice called out. The pitch was low, like when you slow a voice down on a recording.

"Deacon." It said from the flame.

"Who is that?" Deacon demanded, pointing the gun at the fire.

"I am a friend Deacon." The voice slithered through the night air. "Such a waste. You die, and get nothing in return for all the pain and suffering you have endured. Such a waste."

"What do you want with me?" Deacon asked, now frantically trying to stand.

"An agreement." The voice grew stronger. "Between you and me."

The flame swelled even larger, but Deacon remained rooted in place. He was no coward. Whatever trick this was, whoever was behind it would pay.

"You see," the voice continued, "I have the power to make Mr. Conroy pay for what he has done. They think he is a victim. That poor, traumatized man! What about you? What about what he did to you? No one even cares! He needs to face the consequences."

"What can you do?"

"I can make his life miserable. I can make it so that everything he touches crumbles around him. I can make it so he will never be happy again. How does that sound?"

The flame continued to grow now towering above him in a pillar of dreadful fire. The eyes within had become massive, hypnotic pools of ancient malevolence. Deacon couldn't look away, didn't want to look away.

he memory of that bedroom scene played again, but now with crystalline clarity that alcohol had never provided. The way his wife's lipstick had been smeared across her face, how his boss's wedding ring had caught the afternoon light. The sound of their mockery had changed too, no longer just cruel amusement, but something deeper, more primitive. Like they were celebrating his life's destruction.

"What do I have to do?" he finally said. What do you need from me?"

"Your body." The voice said. "I need your blood and your body."

"My body?" Deacon was confused.

"Your body," the voice repeated, pulling him back to the present. "After death, I require your vessel. A fair trade, you'll have no use for it, and in exchange, you get the vengeance you so want. Do we have a deal?"

Deacon studied the gun in his hand. The metal gleamed orange in the firelight, like it had been dipped in blood. If this is a hallucination, it sure is a good one. And if it wasn't... The thought of his boss Conroy suffering brought the first genuine smile to his face in days.

Deacon agreed, "Sure. Let's do it."

"Excellent!' the voice said. "Your blood and body must be in the flame. Come here. Come closer."

Deacon slowly walked over to the fire, the heat soothing his face as he approached the flame. He turned his back to the fire, cocked the gun and put it into his mouth. The Colt's barrel was cold against his tongue as he pulled the trigger. The gunshot shattered the silence, the echo scattering nightbirds into the darkness as his body toppled backward into the flames.

The fire erupted, quickly engulfed the body, then began spreading outwards. Not just growing but *transforming*. The flames turned black at their edges, and a stench like burning sulfur and rotting meat filled the air. A low, inhuman growl emanated from within as Deacon's body began to twitch and contort. His flesh bubbled and shifted like wax under a blowtorch, bones cracking and reforming with sounds like green wood in a fire. His jaw distended, opening wider than humanly possible as black smoke poured from the flames into his mouth and nostrils, forcing its way into every orifice.

The figure that rose from the flames was both Deacon and something else entirely, an infernal fusion of flesh and ancient malevolence.

"Now this," the thing wearing Deacon's flesh said, cracking its neck with a sound like breaking stones, "this will do nicely." Deacon raised his hands to the front of his face. He turned them as he looked. He felt his chest and sides, working his way up to his head, finding the bullet hole with his fingers.

"But that…just won't do," he said as he walked over to his truck bed. Inside the duffle bag was a change of clothes, how curious that a man planning suicide would pack so practically. After dressing, his eyes fell on his prized cowboy hat resting in the passenger seat. No cheap, everyday accessory, but a custom piece he'd saved a year to buy himself for his 40th birthday. He placed it carefully on his head, adjusting it with an almost tender touch.

Twisting the keys still dangling from the ignition, he started the vehicle and began to make his way back out to the highway. The truck motor roared beneath him, but something felt wrong. This flesh-prison fought against him, the lingering essence of its former owner like sand in an oyster. The others had spoken about the unusual feelings when you inhabit one of these creatures. How the spirit of the human naturally fights back against possession, occasionally overcoming them. But that would not be the case for Deacon. Deacon's spirit had surrendered to the entity. It slept, lying dormant for all eternity until it was re-awakened and claimed. But like a pebble in a shoe, he could still feel it, not letting him feel entirely comfortable.

It was very dark down the two-lane highway. Deacon was not really sure where he was going, but he knew a general direction. He could feel it. The presence was growing stronger by the minute. The prophecy was beginning to unfold. Now, of course, this was not to happen without protest. That was what he was sent here for. To find it, and destroy it using any means necessary.

Two approaching headlights caught his attention. Two cars weaving across the center line, their high beams cutting through the desert night. Music thumped from their open windows, along with the sound of drunken laughter and shattering bottles. The first car pulled alongside his truck, its tinted passenger window rolling down to reveal several young men, their faces flushed with cocaine and cheap beer. The one in the passenger seat, green mohawk jutting up like a venomous fin, leaned out the window. "Hey grandpa, nice hat!" His words slurred together, but the hostility came through clear enough. His companions roared with laughter, like they did to the young mother several miles back. Her face was hilarious to them as they terrified her by throwing empty beer cans at her car, shouting insults, cursing and making crude gestures. Now it was this old man's turn.

The first beer bottle bounced off his window with a hollow clank, shards of glass catching the moonlight as they scattered across the asphalt. The second one hit harder, and still Deacon drove on, his smile growing wider. The boy with the mohawk, Evan, though Deacon didn't know that name yet, disappeared back inside the smoke-filled car only to emerge wielding a baseball bat.

"Batter up!" Evan shouted, the words torn away by the wind as he swung. The side mirror exploded in a shower of glass and metal, pieces tumbling along the highway like fallen stars. "Dude, did you see that? That was awesome!"

The rest of the gang howled its approval. Evan punctuated his victory with a vulgar hand gesture before their car accelerated, taillights disappearing into the darkness ahead. Deacon watched them go, still smiling, still tapping along to the country music. He knew what was coming. Right then he decided that he liked country music. Maybe it was something residual within the body he now inhabited, maybe it was because lyrics were about the cheating husband.

The chorus was in full swing when he came to a sharp bend in the road. He slowed to negotiate the tricky turn. Deacon slowed, letting his headlights sweep across fresh skid marks that led off the shoulder and into the darkness beyond. He followed their trail, killing the engine when he reached the scene of carnage. The car had tumbled end over end, a pinwheel of destruction that had scattered its occupants across the desert floor. Body parts lay strewn among the creosote bushes, blood black in the moonlight, mixing with the sand to create a dark paste. Deacon walked through the wreckage whistling the country song from the radio, counting at least six distinct victims. But only one still clung to life, the punk who'd smashed his mirror.

Evan lay broken but conscious, his face latticed with cuts from flying glass. A jagged piece of metal protruded from his torso, blood flowing steadily from beneath his broken body. Deacon approached slowly, savoring the moment, when he sensed another presence. It was gradually becoming more difficult to alter his perceptions while inhabiting this body since he was now a physical entity and restricted from seeing non-physical forms. But he could definitely feel that he was not alone there with the boy. There was someone, or something else present with them. He tightly closed and reopened his eyes until finally able to adjust and focus on the now visible angel kneeling beside the dying boy.

The angel's ethereal form was draped in a long blue and gold tunic that seemed to catch light that wasn't there. Its skin glowed like polished glass in moonlight, and when it spoke, its voice echoed in harmonies of multiple voices.

"I am sorry, Evan," the angel said softly. Evan could only respond with a wet gurgle, blood bubbling at the corners of his mouth. He reached out with trembling fingers, trying to touch the angel's face, but his hand passed through it like morning mist.

Deacon spoke out as he emerges from the darkness. Evan slowly turns his head.

Deacon chose that moment to speak, his voice carrying across the wreckage. "Woo wee, this is definitely not your day, is it fella?" He stepped fully into view, enjoying how Evan's eyes widened with recognition. "Man, you look really messed up." He knelt down beside Evan, directly across from the angel, who regarded him with wary curiosity. "Oh, and her?" Deacon asked, grinning. "Well, she's not here for you, I'm afraid." He looked up at the celestial being. "Are you?"

"No." she said. "Evan, I tried to help you for so long. The others, your friends, have been lost for some time. See? Their guardians left them long ago. But because of your mother's prayers, I stayed with you. But now you are passing on. And I cannot help you anymore. If only you had heeded the…"

Deacon interrupted the angel. "Oh, but I can help you. I can stop this pain. I can keep you alive."

The angel rose to its feet with liquid grace, its wings unfurling in a burst of static electricity that made the desert air crackle. "I thought you were just one of the sensitive ones," it said. "That would explain how you can see me. But your words reveal you, Demon. I know not what would cause that human to give up his body and submit to such a bond, but you are an abomination! And must be destroyed!" The angel's arm shot skyward, and a spear of pure light materialized in its grip. Its wings spread wider, the sound like a hundred parachutes catching the wind at once.

Deacon remained unimpressed, adjusting his cowboy hat with theatrical casualness. "You better think twice if you plan to mess with me, little bird." His grin widened, showing new teeth that seemed just slightly too sharp. "The fact that I don't know you means you are not a threat to me. And besides," he gestured at the blood-soaked desert around them, "you're on my turf now. I have the home court advantage."

They began to circle each other, Evan's failing body between them like an offering. The boy had slipped into unconsciousness, his breath coming in wet, rattling gasps.

"I fought in the great war," Deacon continued, his voice dropping to a growl that seemed to come from somewhere far deeper than his stolen throat. "Long before you were created. And just how long was that I wonder? By the smell of you, I'd say a mere 500 years or so. Am I right, little bird?"

"Who are you, demon?" The angel's spear tracked Deacon's movement, its light casting strange shadows across the wreckage. "Release the flesh of that human and return to your exile, or I will dispose of you."

"Who am I?" Deacon's laugh held no humor. "I am wrath and vengeance. I am Asmodeus. I am your end."

The battle erupted faster than human eyes could follow. Deacon launched himself at the angel's throat, but the guardian had anticipated the move. It feinted forward, dropped into a crouch, and swept its spear in an arc that caught Deacon's ankles. The demon pitched backward, arms flailing, skull cracking against the desert floor with a sound like breaking stone.

The guardian pounced, driving a gauntleted fist into Deacon's chin. But the demon responded with impossible speed, rolling away just as the angel's spear struck the earth where his head had been. The ground where the weapon touched began to glow with sanctified light.

Deacon rose; eyes and fists wreathed in flames that cast no light. His jaw distended, opening impossibly wide as he spewed a stream of orange fire that engulfed the angel. The celestial being's cry of pain shook the air itself as it was thrown backward, crashing into the overturned car with enough force to rock the wreckage.

Another bolt of hellfire followed, the angel's wings charring at the edges as it struggled to maintain its form. Deacon gave it no chance to recover. He shot forward like a missile, snatching up the dropped spear as he moved. Using his momentum, he drove the weapon through the guardian's chest, twisting it to maximize the torment.

Bringing his face close to the dying angel's, he whispered, "Surprise."

The angel's glowing eyes began to fade as Deacon stepped back to admire his handiwork. Its form dissolved slowly into mist, leaving only the spear impaled in the car's metal as evidence of its existence. Deacon brushed the desert dust from his clothes and retrieved his hat, settling it on his head with a satisfied twist.

Turning his attention back to Evan, he straddled the dying boy's body. "Hey, wake up." He snapped his fingers near Evan's face until those pain-glazed eyes flickered open. Fresh blood trickled from the corner of his mouth as he turned to look at his tormentor.

Deacon's grin returned, wider than ever. "Good, you're still alive. That is, if you can call this alive." He flicked the metal shard protruding from Evan's chest, creating a slight ping. "Now, I want you to listen to me, because you don't have much time left. You are stupid, Evan. You always have been. But I know you have an idea what's waiting for you on the other side. I know you can feel it. They can always feel it when they are this close to crossing over. Having lived the life you have lived, and made the choices you have made..." Deacon checked his watch with theatrical casualness. "Well, let's just say that we have been waiting for you. Frankly, Evan, you're eternally condemned no matter what happens." He grinned while looking at his watch. "To begin shortly."

Blood bubbled at the corners of Evan's mouth as he tried to speak. Deacon slapped his cheek, firmly enough to focus the dying boy's attention. "The question is, do you want to go now, or later? Hmm? If I were to venture a guess, I'm thinking later."

Evan's eyes began rolling back in his head, the darkness at the edges of his vision taking on shapes that made him want to scream. Deacon's face swam into focus above him, but something was wrong with it, like there was another face trying to push through from beneath the skin.

"You are not going to a place you will like. Honestly, it is not even a place I like." Deacon's voice had taken on that grinding, ancient quality again. "The truth is, I could use you. I need an assistant to help me with my errand. Now, unfortunately, I cannot force you. Those are the rules. You have to agree to it on your own free will."

Through the haze of pain and terror, Evan tried to make sense of what was happening. The metal in his chest sent waves of agony through him with each heartbeat, and he could feel his life draining into the desert sand.

"We both benefit, you see. I heal your injuries, and you get to put off suffering for a little while. As for me, you assist me as my companion." Deacon's eyes blazed unnaturally. "But like I said, you must be the one to choose. So, what do you say? Do we have a deal?"

Using the last remnants of his fading strength, Evan forced out a single word: "Y... Yes."

"All right then, let's go." Deacon leaned down, pressing his mouth against Evan's. Black smoke poured from Deacon's lips, forcing its way down Evan's throat. The boy's body convulsed violently as the infernal essence invaded him, his spine arching off the blood-soaked ground.

Then, with the sudden silence of a stopped heart, he went still.

Deacon grabbed the metal shard protruding from Evan's chest and yanked hard. It made a wet sound as it tore free, and Evan screamed a sound his living throat couldn't make. He rolled over and shot to his feet, clutching his chest, eyes wide with panic and confusion.

"Am I still dreaming?" Evan's voice shook as he surveyed the carnage around them, his friends' broken bodies scattered across the desert floor. "This feels so real. Is this real?"

"Oh yes, this is real. You are mine now. At least until I release you." Deacon flicked blood from his fingers. "And by the way, you are dead."

"I'm dead? But I thought you saved me?"

"Basically, you were dead, but your soul had not yet gone dormant. But it wants to sleep." Deacon tapped Evan's chest where the wound had been. "I am keeping it awake."

"I don't understand. If I am dead, why does my chest still hurt?"

"Oh, I can't help that. It will begin to hurt more and more as time goes on and your body begins to decay." Deacon started walking toward the truck. "We can discuss this later. For now, we have work to do. I'll tell you about it while you drive." He paused, looking back over his shoulder. "Can you drive a stick?"

The desert night stretched endlessly before them as they drove, Evan's hands clenched on the steering wheel. For what seemed like hours, neither spoke as they made their way down the long dark road. Deacon had fallen into a kind of trance, twitching occasionally as if something inside was trying to get comfortable. The silence was broken only by the soft country music still playing on the radio.

Finally, Deacon snapped out of his reverie. "Hey Evan, you okay? Been pretty quiet since we hit the road. Not like you at all."

Evan lashed out, as if waiting for the opportunity. "Am I okay? No, I am definitely not okay!" His voice cracked with hysteria. "In fact, according to you, I am dead! Trapped inside a rotting corpse! Dead and doomed to eternal punishment!" His hands shook on the steering wheel, knuckles white against increasingly grey skin. "All my friends are dead. And the only thing keeping me from burning in hell right now is the good graces of a demon. Who, by the way, totally skewered and barbecued my guardian angel." He choked back something between a laugh and a sob. "No man, I can say with absolute positivity that I am pretty freaking far from okay."

Deacon shifted in his seat, clearly annoyed. "Well sure, it sounds bad when you put it like that." He cracked his neck with a sound like breaking stones. "You would think some appreciation would be in order. Normally, I would rip you apart for yelling at me. But I feel like talking because I am bored. And nothing is worse for humans than us being bored. Believe you me."

He found another cigarette in his shirt pocket and lit it, the flame from his lighter reflecting oddly in his eyes. After exhaling a cloud of smoke that seemed too dark to be natural, he continued, "I guess first of all I want you to understand that while I am being fairly cordial with you, I actually despise you. In fact, I despise all of you. All of mankind and every member of the human race that ever existed."

He adjusted the temperature controls in the cab as he spoke. "You are nothing. Insignificant specs in reality unaware of the true power all around you. My purpose is to see you all join us so that the great one, my master, the rightful ruler of this world, can lead our return to Heaven and claim our rightful place."

Evan felt something shift inside his chest, a sensation like maggots crawling through dead flesh. He tried to focus on the road instead of the growing awareness of his body's decay.

"Those members of the Host who cast us down," Deacon continued, his voice taking on that ancient, grinding quality again, "and those that hid while we fought, will be brought to justice. But before that can happen, we need to replenish. That is where you and those like you come in. Your souls are so easily turned that since the war we have nearly increased our numbers a thousand-fold. With that much cannon fodder at our disposal, Michael and his army don't stand a chance."

He continued, "But something has changed. Something is different. We feel that something big is about to happen. Something that could undo all we have achieved. So, when things fall apart, that's when I am called in. I fix things."

Deacon shifted uncomfortably again, arching his back, and twisting his neck. "Ugh, this body," he grumbled. "I cannot understand how you can live in these sacs of meat."

Evan watched him from the corner of his eye, still trying to convince himself this was some fantastic delusion. Maybe he would wake up on his apartment couch, hung over but alive. But he couldn't deny the blackness he felt inside him, despair, sadness, anger, squeezing him like a boa constrictor preparing its prey. That's what he was now, he realized. Prey being devoured by something ancient and terrible. Then he would be gone forever. And this thing sitting next to him was responsible for it.

Deacon seemed settled now having found a reclining position he liked. "I'm curious Evan, you seriously had no idea?"

"No idea about what?"

"That you were not alone."

"I have never felt alone. I had lots of friends." Even as he said it, Evan felt the hollowness of the words.

"Not alone like that, dummy."

"I don't understand," Evan admitted.

"Figures," Deacon snorted. "You were never really that bright. The only thing you got on your SATs was ketchup." He reached behind the seat for another beer, the can opening with a hiss. After draining it in one long swallow, he crushed the can while letting out an odourous belch.

"Then why are you here? Why me?" Evan felt something shift in his chest cavity, a sensation like wet cloth tearing. "Why not just leave me alone and find someone else?"

"No way." Deacon's response was quick, almost eager. "You have no idea how hard it is to create someone like you. You have to be in the right place at the right time. And try as we might, we don't know when that is." His grin widened impossibly. "The kicker is, I did it twice today." Deacon reached down into the cooler behind the driver's seat and pulled out another beer. It opened with a refreshing hiss and as he began to drink, once again finishing the entire can with an obnoxious burp. "Nope, you are mine. And you are not going anywhere until I am done with you."

A fresh rivulet of dark fluid ran down Evan's arm, staining the steering wheel. He tried to wipe it away but only succeeded in smearing it further. "So, you're going to tell me what that is exactly?"

"I suppose I must." Deacon's voice took on that ancient quality again, like stones grinding against each other in the dark. "There are two items on our agenda. The first is to find the Messiah."

"What is a Messiah?" The words felt wrong in Evan's mouth, like his tongue didn't want to cooperate.

"The Messiah is the name Hebrew Jews use to describe a savior." As Deacon spoke, the shadows in the truck's cab seemed to deepen. "They have a prophecy that one day a man would come, sent by God himself, who would save all of mankind by defeating all evil and eventually rule the entire world." His eyes widened. "We believe he is here somewhere. Right now, on earth, in this country. You and I are going to find him and destroy him."

The implications slowly penetrated Evan's decaying brain. "No way," he whispered. "No way am I going to kill someone."

"Sure, you will. That is why you're here." Deacon's smile showed too many teeth. "You see, we have no idea the power this man possesses. I am betting that he will be able to sense me a mile away and I won't be able to get close enough to do the deed. You, however, are my wild card. While your soul is still in your body, you are still human. Or what is left of one. He won't see you coming. And you will do it."

"If he is sent from God, and he has these superpowers, how can I possibly kill him?" Another drop of Evan's fluid dripped off, landing with a damp sound on the floorboard.

"Haven't you been listening, you idiot? HE IS A HUMAN." The words made the windows rattle. "Even though somewhat…'enhanced', he is still mortal. He can die. And I will make sure that happens."

"How will we find him?" asked Evan, terrified of this revelation of his purpose.

Deacon replied. "Not sure yet. But I will be looking for signs. As his light grows, the harder it will be for them to conceal him."

"You said there were two parts," Evan said, desperate to focus on anything but the feeling of his body coming apart. "What is the second part?"

"If there really is a Messiah, and he is here now, then he will have help. The Angels will be close by." Something like pain crossed Deacon's face. "While you take out the Messiah, I will deal with them. Especially Raphael."

"Raphael?"

"The Archangel. He is a captain in the army of the Host."

"Sounds personal," Evan observed, immediately regretting it when Deacon's eyes flared at him.

Deacon was silent for a moment, as if composing himself. "Raphael and I used to be close. He betrayed me. He betrayed us all."

"I don't understand." Evan felt something crack in his spine as he shifted in his seat. "You were in Heaven. Everybody wants to be in Heaven. What was so bad about it?"

"Lucifer showed us the truth." Deacon's voice took on a fevered intensity. "That behind the shining walls we were at the whim of a dictator. Keeping us like pets. Never sharing the true secret with us."

"What secret?"

"The power to create and give life."

"The power to create and give life." Hatred dripped from every word. "He denied it to us, yet he gave it to you. What did you do to deserve such a gift? Why shouldn't he be allowed to create life as well? We are much higher beings than you. That's why we fought back. That's when we decided that since we would never have the power to create life, we will destroy it instead."

Through the windshield, the desert night seemed endless. Evan's bloody fingers left dark smears on the steering wheel as Deacon continued his story.

"We were stronger, but we were outnumbered. We held our own for a long time." His eyes grew distant, seeing battles fought before time began. "Raphael and I met on the battlefield. We battled for what seemed like days. I finally had him at the tip of my sword, until I became distracted." A smile of terrible pride crossed his face. "You should have seen it. Lucifer was taking on an entire legion by himself! It was a sight to behold."

The smile vanished. "As I turned to see a second legion swarm over him, Raphael was able to escape my hold. Had things been different, I could have gone to the aid of my master. But to my eternal shame, Raphael took the opportunity to overcome me. Michael countered us with overwhelming force. After Lucifer was captured, we were all cast down here. Banished to this rock in space for all eternity, we can never enter the shining city again."

He bristled with rage. "If the Messiah is here, we will have vengeance. And repay our betrayal."

Evan's mind reeled. Cosmic battles of good versus evil with the fate of the world in the balance? It was like a bad science fiction movie. What had he done? He should have just died. Was it too late to change his mind? He didn't want this. He didn't know. He didn't expect...

Tears began running down his face, leaving tracks in his now greyish skin. Deacon glanced at him and let out a wicked smile. He motioned towards a roadside diner approaching on the horizon, its neon sign cutting through the darkness like a beacon.

"Hey, you hungry? Let's stop here."

The diner's lights flickered as they pulled into the empty parking lot, as if the very building sensed what was approaching. A bell above the door jangled sharply as they entered, the sound making Evan's ears ache.

The fluorescent lights of the diner buzzed like angry insects, casting harsh shadows that made Evan's decaying flesh look even more corpse-like. He tried to hunch into himself, painfully aware of the dark fluid still seeping through his clothes. The handful of patrons barely glanced up as they entered, all except for a group of bikers clustered around a corner booth, their leather vests with embroidered wings stretched across their backs marking them as members of the Dead Saints MC.

"Well, ain't this cozy?" Deacon drawled, steering them toward the counter. His cowboy boots left slight scorch marks on the linoleum with each step. The night waitress approached, coffee pot trembling slightly in her hand as she sensed something wrong with her new customers.

"C-can I get you gentlemen something?"

"Coffee. Black." Deacon's grin was all teeth. "My friend here isn't hungry. His appetite is dead, you might say."

Evan felt bile rise in what remained of his throat as the smell of frying bacon and eggs hit him. His stomach lurched. One of the bikers stood up, a mountain of a man with a grey-streaked beard and arms thick with prison tattoos. "Hey kid, you don't look so good." His voice carried genuine concern. "You need some help?"

Before Evan could respond, Deacon's voice slithered into his mind like an oil slick. Kill him.

"No," Evan whispered, but his body was already moving, puppet-like, towards the biker. "Please, I don't want to…"

"You have no choice. You belong to me."

The biker's expression shifted from concern to alarm as Evan approached. "Kid?"

Evan's hands shot out with impossible speed, gripping the biker's head. The sound of his neck snapping was like a gunshot in the small diner. For one horrible moment, Evan felt everything, the crack of vertebrae, the final pulse of blood through dying vessels, the subtle release as soul separated from body.

The diner erupted into chaos. The other bikers launched themselves forward as their friend's body crumpled. The waitress screamed, dropping the coffee pot with a crash. Through it all, Deacon sat calmly at the counter, watching with clear enjoyment.

"Now that's entertainment," he said, reaching down to pick up a cell phone that had fallen from the dead biker's pocket. "Good work, pet. Very efficient." He began scrolling through the contacts as Evan stood frozen, staring at his hands in horror.

The remaining bikers had backed away, their faces masks of terror as they realized what they were dealing with. One pulled out a gun, holding it before him like a shield. "Oh, come on, seriously?" he muttered, shooting a glance at the biker, who then thought better and ran out the door. Deacon then dialed a number.

The phone rang twice before a man's voice answered. "Hello?"

"Malcolm? That you?" Deacon's voice dripped with false warmth. "Been a long time."

"Where are you?"

"On the road. I have what I need." He winked at Evan, who had collapsed into a booth, his eyes somehow finding a way to produce tears. "And we're just getting started."

Chapter 6

TRUST

It had been two long months since Mary went away and Joseph had been wearing tracks on the carpet waiting for her call. When the phone finally rang, he hurriedly answered.

"What time do you arrive?" He heard the eagerness in his voice, despite his attempt at casual indifference.

"I land at 4 pm," Mary's voice carried an unusual hesitancy. "But I want to meet you somewhere."

There was a distance to it that made Joseph nervous. "Meet you where? I can pick you up."

"No." The word fell between them like a barrier. "How about I meet you at your place at six?"

Joseph's stomach clenched. Mary had been gone for three months, and now this request felt like a delaying tactic. He could sense there was something she wasn't sharing.

"Okay, fine." The words tasted unpleasant. "But promise me you'll tell me everything. Two months, Mary. Two months of not knowing..."

"I know, and I'm sorry." Her voice cracked with genuine emotion. "I promise I will never hide anything from you again. Just please be patient a little longer." I will see you tonight. Okay?"

Joseph swallowed his worries. "Okay," he said. "But I want this to end. I love you, Mary."

"I love you too. See you soon."

Joseph waited until he heard Mary disconnect before pushing the end call button on his cell. The rest of the afternoon crawled by as Joseph prepared dinner. His thoughts consumed by the mystery of Mary's return. When the doorbell rang at six, his heart leaped. He hurriedly opened the door and there she stood, beautiful as ever. They shared a passionate embrace that momentarily pushed his worries aside. Finally composing himself, Joseph invited her in.

"It is so good to see you, Joseph. I missed you so much," said Mary. She continued to embrace him as they made their way into the living room.

"Me too," Joseph replied, his voice laced with sincerity. "I cooked dinner. It's your favorite."

"Your world-famous beef stew?" she chirped happily. "I am so hungry. That will be perfect!"

Their conversation over dinner flowed naturally at first, Mary telling him about Elizabeth's ambitious plans to move the Temple to Las Vegas. But Joseph noticed how she seemed to fade into herself at times. He wanted to ask her, but he knew she would tell him on her own. Besides, she promised.

Mary continued, revealing Elizabeth's ambitious plan to move the Temple to Las Vegas. "She feels that God is drawing them there," Mary explained, her hands fidgeting with her napkin.

"Wow, that is a serious move," he remarked. "It would uproot everyone involved. What about the workers, the volunteers, and such? They would have to start over."

"I know," Mary replied, her tone tinged with sympathy. "But she is determined."

Joseph nodded, respecting Elizabeth and Zach's dedication to their mission. "Well, if that is what she and Zach want, The Temple is their baby after all."

Mary grinned slightly. "Funny you say that. She is also pregnant," she revealed.

Joseph nearly spat his soup all over the table. "Pregnant!? Elizabeth!?"

"Yes almost 6 months now. She is getting huge." *I have to tell him. How can I tell him?*

Joseph couldn't wrap his mind around it. "How can that be? What is she, sixty-five?"

"Sixty-six. It's a miracle. A true gift from God." *Tell him now.*

"Absolutely it is. Wow. A baby. Boy or girl?

"A boy. She already has a name. John." *What will he say? What will he do? Oh God, help me.*

The revelation of Elizabeth's pregnancy briefly lightened the mood, but the tension soon returned, settling around them like a heavy blanket. Finally, Mary's tears began to fall. Joseph took a deep breath, his voice gentle but persistent. "Mary? What is it?"

"Joseph…" Mary began, her voice quivering with emotion. She glanced at him briefly, then averted her eyes.

"What's wrong, Mary? You are obviously not happy. Is it me? Did I do something? I would never want you to be unhappy."

He saw her neck tighten as she swallowed hard. Sitting still and straight, he steeled himself for whatever revelation was coming. He knew that he couldn't force Mary to be with him if her heart wasn't in it.

Mary was trying to keep from crying, her eyes welling up, lips trembling even though she had them tightly clamped.

"Joseph... " It was more of a groan than words. Joseph remained silent.

"Joseph... " She gave up all pretense and was now crying openly. "I'm pregnant."

The world seemed to stop. Joseph stared at her, his mind refusing to process the words.

"What? What do you mean?"

Tears streamed down Mary's face, as she pleaded with him, "I'm pregnant. Joseph, please let me explain. Promise me you will let me explain."

"What do you mean you're pregnant? How can you be pregnant? When did this happen?"

"Joseph, please listen." She pleaded. "Please listen to me?"

"Mary! You slept with someone!" he exclaimed, his voice dripping with betrayal.

"No, No, No Joseph! If you let me, I can tell you what happened."

"Go on. Explain then," he demanded.

Through her tears, Mary told him everything, the angel, the divine presence, the promise she had been entrusted with. Her voice trembled with sincerity as she recounted her visit to Elizabeth, a story of two miraculous pregnancies bound by a supernatural force. And then, at last, she fell silent. She trembled in her chair, her heart pounding, waiting for Joseph's reaction.

Joseph sat there in astounded silence; his gaze locked onto Mary. His mind a whirlwind of thoughts and emotions. He struggled to reconcile the unbelievable story she had just told him with the Mary he thought he knew.

"I don't completely understand why this has happened to me, but I know that, as God is my witness, it was He who did this to me. I swear I haven't been with anyone."

Joseph continued to study Mary's face, searching for any sign of deception. Her eyes were filled with sincerity, but this story was impossible to believe. Feelings of hurt and betrayal burned through any attempt at understanding.

He found his voice at last. "You are asking me to believe the unbelievable," he said as a lone tear trickled down his cheek.

Mary nodded, her eyes filled with desperation. "I know. But it is the truth."

Joseph couldn't contain his turmoil any longer and lashed out. "Mary, everyone knows where babies come from and how they are made."

Mary was quick to respond, her voice filled with earnestness. "Yes, but you were willing to believe what I told you about Elizabeth..."

Joseph interrupted her, growing ever more agitated. "Elizabeth has a husband that got her pregnant! That's how that works! Do you think I'm stupid? Do you think you can twist her story into something I might fall for? Look at you. Pretending all this time to be so virtuous. Saving yourself for marriage. You certainly had me fooled."

Mary buried her face in her hands, her shoulders shaking with sobs.

"Who's the father?" Joseph shouted. His anger boiling over.

Mary shot a look at him with the most serious face she could muster. "God is the father."

Joseph's response was laden with bitter sarcasm. "Well, that makes it easy then. Guess there won't be a need for a DNA test."

Mary implored him through her tears, "Joseph, please don't be cruel to me."

Joseph's glare darkened even more, "You want to talk about cruel?" he growled. "What you have done to me is cruel! Mary, I loved you. I loved you so much. I asked you to marry me. How could you do this to me?"

Mary rose from her chair and walked around the table to Joseph. She placed her hand on his shoulder. As if her touch burned him, he quickly jerked away and stood up. Walking a few steps away he paused and turned to face Mary.

"Looks like our plans have changed," he said bitterly. "I need some time alone now. I need you to leave."

"Joseph let me stay," she pleaded. *Why isn't God helping me right now?* she thought to herself.

He retreated to the patio, leaving her alone with her tears. The night sky spread vast and indifferent above him as he sank into a chaise lounge, his heart heavy with pain. He spoke without looking back at her.

"Go ahead and let yourself out."

Mary, still sobbing, gathered her coat and walked out the door. It closed behind her with a soft click, leaving Joseph alone with his thoughts. He sank into a chaise lounge on the patio, gazing up at the night sky. The calmness of the pool water stood in stark contrast to the emotions raging within him.

Mary was not the honest, caring, considerate person that she seemed to be. He laid back on the lounger and gazed skyward. *What should I do now? Could I forgive her?* No. There would always be those little black thoughts in the corners of his mind. It would only be pretending. Pretending to not see the scars. He scoffed at her story: *"God made me pregnant. Yeah, right. How in the world did she think he would fall for that? How could this have happened? What's worse, everyone will think it was me!"*

He imagined how quickly the gossip would spread. No one would believe he did not have anything to do with Mary's pregnancy. *I am not the guilty one, she is.*

"She thinks I'm stupid!" Joseph cried out into the night. As he flipped over the side table in a fit of anger. There was no answer, only the vast expanse of the darkened sky.

Crying, angry, fearful... Hours later, exhaustion finally pulled him into sleep.

He had a fevered sleep, experiencing several dreams. The usual ones. Inconsequential and forgettable as soon as you wake in the morning. He tossed and turned, finally deciding to abandon the chaise lounge to seek comfort indoors. As he sat upright, a bright light began emanating from the pool.

I must not have turned the lights off, he thought, but he quickly realized this wasn't the case. The light was originating from the center of the pool itself, forming a radiant orb that had now emerged and hovered just above the water's surface. Mesmerized, Joseph couldn't move, watching in awe as the ball of light slowly moved towards him. From within the luminous sphere emerged Gabriel, his form both magnificent and terrifying. His wings, when they unfurled, filled the patio with their glory, His armor etched with ancient symbols that seemed to have burned themselves into the metal.

"Joseph." The voice bypassed his ears, speaking directly to his soul.

Startled, Joseph's legs gave way, and he scrambled backwards until he could retreat no further, his back against the wall.

"Who are you?" he stammered, his voice trembling.

"I am Gabriel," came the reply, "sent to you from the Lord God. Joseph, do not be afraid to take Mary as your wife. She has told you the truth. She has not been with a man and remains a virgin. The child within her is a child sent from the LORD."

Joseph pinched the bridge of his nose, attempting to dispel the fog of disbelief that shrouded his senses. "Is this real?" he muttered, skeptically. "Are you real? I must be dreaming." The radiant light dimmed just enough to more clearly see Gabriel's striking face.

"You all ask the same question. And yes, I am very real," affirmed Gabriel, his voice growing more intense. "Clear your mind and listen to me Joseph."

Joseph eyes widened even more. His body stiffened. *Is this an angel?* His heart raced, and beads of sweat formed on his forehead. Struggling to speak, he managed to utter a few words, his voice trembling, "Yes, I am listening."

Gabriel's voice grew more commanding as he delivered his message. "Mary will bear a son. And you shall name him Immanuel, meaning '*God is with us.*' You will be his earthly father and raise him as your own. Protect him, until he can protect himself."

Gabriel's radiant form drew even closer to Joseph, the brilliance illuminating his surroundings. He was so close that Joseph could see his own reflection in Gabriel's armor.

"He is... God's child?" Joseph stammered, his initial doubts resurfacing. "How will I... how can I?" he mumbled, feeling self-conscious for his incoherence. An angel was speaking to him, and he was struggling to form simple words.

"God is with you, Joseph," Gabriel reassured him. "Stay strong in Him and He will guide you if your faith is strong enough."

The angel's presence, once overwhelming, now began to comfort him. If he had been capable of movement, he might have fled in fear earlier, but now he was anchored by profound curiosity.

With growing composure, Joseph continued, "What about Mary? What will happen when the baby is born?"

However, there was no response. Gabriel gradually moved away from Joseph, taking to the air. His powerful translucent wings generated a tremendous breeze that sent the poolside chairs and tables tumbling. Higher and higher he ascended until his radiant light merged with the starlit expanse of the night sky. Joseph sat there, mouth open, gazing upwards.

Startled from his daze by the ringing of his cell phone, Joseph let out a yelp. In that instant, he found himself back in his chair, the poolside furniture undisturbed, the world seemingly returned to normal.

What the...? I'm back in the chair? Did I dream that? he muttered, glancing at the empty space where Gabriel had hovered. He felt an overwhelming sense of doubt, but the details of his encounter were etched firmly in his memory. His cell phone had stopped ringing, but it indicated that a voicemail had been left. He had little interest in checking it now. Instead, he remained in the chair the rest of the night, pondering if the impossible might actually be possible.

A tinge of shame washed over him for having doubted Mary. Who could blame me? He thought to justify his behavior. How could anyone believe that story? Hello Joseph, guess what? I'm pregnant. But it's okay. It's God's child. Oh, and God made my cousin pregnant too!

Now what? Do I still marry her? I would always know that the child was not mine. No matter what I believe, everyone else will always gossip about how I married her because she got pregnant. If I let her go, they will call her a slut. A no-win scenario.

But as the night wore on, Joseph felt a growing certainty within himself. The angel's message had settled into him, becoming as real as his own heartbeat. It didn't matter what others might think or say. He believed Mary and he trusted his instincts. Joseph rose from his chair and fumbled for his cell phone, dialing Mary's number.

No answer came from the other end.

The voicemail system prompted him to leave a message.

"Mary, hello? .... Um…Mary? I really need to…" He paused, gathering his thoughts. "Mary, I'm sorry. I should have believed you. I wanted to believe you, but I just couldn't. But now... I want you to know that now I know without a doubt you are telling the truth. I had a dream... last night. Can you believe that? Well... of course I'm sure you can. But it's not only because of that. It's not about that. I just... Mary... I love you. I want to marry you. I want to be by your side to see this through. Please forgive me for how I reacted. I hope you understand. Anyway, I want to come over and see you... will you call me? Please?"

Joseph returned his phone to his pocket. I wouldn't call me back, He thought. But Mary will. That was the kind of woman she is. I can depend on her.

Sinking into his favorite chair, Joseph turned on the sports channel, seeking distraction. The familiar voices of commentators washed over him as his mind wandered back to the impossible events of the night. Eventually, exhaustion claimed him, and he once again drifted into an uneasy sleep.

Hours later, he was startled awake by the doorbell. His heart leaped as he rushed to the door, looking through the peephole to see Mary's face on the other side. Without hesitation, he swung the door open and enveloped her in a tight embrace, their bodies seeking solace in each other's warmth.

"I'm so sorry," Joseph whispered, his voice heavy with remorse.

Mary, her eyes reflecting both exhaustion and understanding, responded softly, "It's okay. I should have expected..."

Joseph cut her off, determined to express his feelings. "You should have expected me to believe you."

Brushing a stray lock of hair from Joseph's face, Mary said, "You haven't slept much either, I see."

"Who could sleep after what I just went through?" Joseph replied, his eyes filled with emotion. They sat snuggled on the sofa. "We have a lot to discuss," Joseph said, gently but firmly.

"Yes. But not right now. I'm too tired." Mary nestled her cheek against Joseph's chest, finding solace in his warmth. The soothing sound of rain began to fall outside, a gentle backdrop to their shared moment.

Joseph whispered, "Then rest. It will all be okay," hoping to convince himself as much as he wanted her to believe it also. Holding each other close, they allowed the rhythm of the rain and the warmth of each other's embrace to lull them into a peaceful slumber.

Piercing the spiritual veil that separates realities, Raphael materialized, soaring high above the grandeur of the heavenly city. Its scale was unimaginable: fourteen hundred miles wide with three imposing gates on each of the four sides, and walls of such thickness they contained cities within themselves. At its heart, the Throne Tower pierced the infinite heights, a pillar of pure light that cast no shadows within the golden city's bounds. Eleven lesser towers encircled it, each one housing powers and principalities beyond mortal understanding.

Raphael's wings carried him through the massive eastern pearl gates, his crimson hair and battle-worn tunic flowing behind his celestial armor. The outer walls themselves were a city in motion, angels of every rank moving with divine purpose through structures that would make Earth's greatest monuments seem like children's toys. As he reached the inner portion of the wall, Raphael paused at the edge of the great Abyss, a void of such absolute darkness that even Lucifer himself was said to fear its depths. No angel had ever plumbed its secrets; those who ventured too close spoke of a darkness that consumed not just light, but essence itself.

Crossing the bridge that spanned this infinite drop, Raphael entered the inner city. In the outer reaches of the city, a flurry of activity surrounded him. The Cherubim, both on the ground and in flight, were out in force. They saluted him as he passed, spreading their wings in the ancient gesture of respect, hands forming wing-shapes across their chests. Raphael acknowledged them with the subtle nod of a superior officer who hasn't forgotten what it means to serve.

Their whispered conversations reached his ears, rumors of demonic forces gathering, speculation about the increasing manifestation of divine power on Earth. Raphael kept his counsel, remembering Gabriel's words: only the Archangels and Seraphim understood what was unfolding. The others would learn in time.

The Throne Tower dominated his view now, its light carrying warmth that penetrated everything. The Great Song echoed from its heights, the eternal chorus that had begun before Raphael's creation and would continue long after the last star burned out. The sound stirred something like envy in him; while others were tasked to sing the eternal praises, his gift was healing. His mere presence knitting wounded angels back together, allowing them to fight far beyond their normal limits.

Inside the tower, the architecture bent in ways that would drive mortal minds to madness, floors arranged in concentric rings that somehow contained more space than should be possible, ascending endlessly into dimensions that had no names in any human tongue. Raphael wove through countless angels as he flew upward, passing through layers of reality that grew increasingly abstract until he reached his destination.

The jade door recognized his essence and swung open to reveal Uriel's meditation chamber. The walls, floor, and ceiling were fashioned from a single pearl that had never been touched by material reality. In the center, Uriel floated cross-legged, his black hair veiling his face as he maintained his communion with the infinite.

Uriel sat cross-legged, a few feet above the floor, his head bowed and his long black hair veiling his face. Initially, he remained silent, lost in meditation. Then, as if perturbed by the interruption, he spoke.

"Raphael, I do not seek company at this time," Uriel stated without looking up.

"I apologize for disturbing you," Raphael replied, "but there is an urgent matter."

"There's always an urgent matter. Speak, then."

"A guardian was attacked by a demon."

Uriel raised an eyebrow, finally meeting Raphael's gaze. "That is not an uncommon occurrence. What sets this apart?"

"It was Asmodeus."

Uriel's eyes met Raphael's as he raised his head. "I know." Uriel said. "I was attempting to track his energy when you interrupted me."

"That is why I came to you," Raphael pressed. "You are the keeper of knowledge. Tell me his most likely course of action."

"I already know his intent. He follows the light. Even with us masking their presence, it draws him like a beacon."

"Where is he?" Raphael's hand unconsciously moved to his sword. "Tell me, and I'll deal with him."

Uriel's lips curved in a knowing smirk. "Like you dealt with him during the war? I seem to recall you facing some challenges then. If not for Lucifer's timely defeat, the outcome might have been different."

Raphael snapped back. "Are you going to assist me? Or should I seek another?"

"He is being concealed from us," Uriel explained, "much like we hide the child and the young couple from him. I can only sense the residual traces of his evil after he interacts with others, and even that is delayed. A tremendous power is at work to keep him hidden."

"They will stop at nothing," Raphael said, his voice tight with concern.

"Gabriel has informed me of your impatience in this matter," Uriel's tone grew stern. "He has asked me to keep an eye on you. Your proximity to them exposes them to danger. While they are masked, they are relatively protected. But the longer you are near the child and the parents, the closer you draw the enemy. Your presence will pull them into the enemy's grasp. Stay away. You think you are helping, but you are a serious threat to their safety."

"I only observe."

"As do I," Uriel retorted. "Mind yourself, or we will help remind you of your place."

Raphael pressed on, desperation edging into his voice. "As I said, that is why I'm here. If I know what is intended, I can better help. But he has told none of us what the true plan is. You can foresee possible outcomes. So, tell me, how many of those result in the deaths of the child and the humans?"

Uriel paused, and with a wave of his hand, the chamber dissolved into a vista of deep space, galaxies spinning like jewels in the void.

"Twenty-seven million, seven hundred and ninety-three. So far. But the possibilities continue to grow."

Raphael's fear peaked, "And how many do you foresee where the child survives?"

Uriel looked away into the infinite darkness between stars, and did not reply.

Chapter 7

BLAME

"What time is it?" Joseph asked, his voice tight with tension.

Mary's hands trembled slightly as she retrieved her phone from her purse. "It's... 8:32 pm," she whispered.

"Maybe they're asleep," Joseph said, though they both knew better.

"Don't count on it. They're not that old," Mary replied, attempting to lighten the mood.

They had been sitting in Joseph's car for almost twenty minutes, watching the warm glow from the living room windows.

"Well, let's do this," Joseph finally said, steeling himself.

"You're acting like you're walking to your execution," Mary teased, though her own heart was racing.

"Aren't I?" Joseph responded wryly as they walked toward the front door. "Your father is as old-school as they come. And never liked me in the first place. Plus, I promised him that I would honor your virtue until we were married." He turned to Mary as they stepped up onto the porch. "I can't believe I talked with your father about you being a virgin. I mean who does that? Seriously."

Mary offered a half-smile before she inserted her key into the lock. "We're doomed," she joked, though neither of them laughed.

Before she could turn the key, the door swung open. Anne greeted them warmly, her cheerful demeanor a stark contrast to their obvious nervousness. "I thought I heard someone out here!" she exclaimed. "What are you waiting for? Come in, you two. It is freezing out here!"

They embraced Anne and followed her into the warm and cozy family room. The fireplace crackled invitingly, and Joachim sat in his favorite chair, attempting to navigate the digital world with an iPad that Mary had given him for his birthday.

"I just don't get it. How do I find the crossword puzzles?" he grumbled.

"Dad, the e-version of the Daily Chronicle doesn't have crossword puzzles," Mary replied patiently. "You use the crossword app I downloaded for that."

"Hmph," Joachim grunted. "This will never catch on." He placed the tablet on the coffee table and picked up the folded newspaper beside it. "This is how you should read a newspaper," he declared, leaning back into his chair with a satisfied nod.

Mary squeezed Joseph's hand as they walked over to the loveseat and sat down, their unease intensifying by the second.

"Mom, Dad... we need to talk," she began awkwardly.

Joachim and Anne exchanged worried glances. "About what?" asked Anne.

Mary hesitated, her voice faltering as her throat tightened with anxiety. "Well..."

"What is going on, Mary?" Anne asked, her concern growing more evident.

Mary took a deep breath, trying to find the strength to convey the truth. "Mom... I..."

"What is happening, Mary?" Joachim's voice trembled with anxiety.

Mary knew she needed to release the pressure. The feeling of distress in the room was growing quickly. Finding her courage, she finally whispered, "I'm pregnant."

The room fell into total silence. The loudest silence she had ever heard, making her want to scream just to break it apart. Then, as if the words had been a switch, the room exploded with emotion.

Joachim shot up from his chair with such force that it rocked backward. "WHAT DO YOU MEAN YOU'RE PREGNANT?" he shouted, his voice echoing through the room.

Anne let out a startled whimper, her hand instinctively reaching for her chest, as if to steady her racing heart.

"Dad, Mom, please," Mary implored. "Just let me explain."

Joachim was breathing heavily, his face flushed with a mix of anger, shock, and fear. His eyes darted from Mary to Joseph, who sat there nervously, and back to Mary.

"It's pretty darn obvious what happened!" he snapped.

"Dad, please, just sit down," Mary pleaded. "You're going to hurt yourself."

Anne's stern voice cut through the tension. "Joachim." Just his name, but it carried decades of authority. He stumbled backward and collapsed into his chair, breathing heavily but at least no longer on the verge of a meltdown.

Mary's grip on Joseph's hand had grown even tighter, her knuckles turning white as she began to recount the extraordinary story. But in the midst of her fear, an unexpected sense of relief began to grow in the pit of her stomach. She could feel the burden of secrecy lifting, replaced by peace. As she listened to herself conclude her story, a new strength coursed through her. She was no longer hiding, no longer living a lie. She had bared her soul to the people she loved most in the world, and now, she could face whatever lay ahead.

Once again, the room fell into a heavy, stifling silence. Mary's parents had absorbed her astonishing story without showing any immediate emotion. Their faces were masks of confusion and disbelief as they listened to their daughter's extraordinary tale. Joachim's gaze darted from Mary to Joseph and back, his brows knitted in deep thought. Finally, he broke the silence.

"You are expecting me to believe that you are pregnant, not by Joseph, but by God himself?" Joachim's voice trembled with anger and skepticism. Glaring at Joseph, "You are seriously asking us to believe that this was none of your doing? That this baby you are carrying is actually the son of God and not the son of that liar sitting next to you?"

"Dad!" Mary cried out, "Joseph is not to blame. In fact, he was in the same place you are now when I told him. He didn't believe it either."

Joseph leaned forward, speaking with quiet conviction. "That is true, sir. I was just as upset. I was very angry. I felt betrayed. I thought she was lying to cover up what really happened. But that night, I was visited in a dream as well. I was told to trust her. And that we had been chosen. As hard as it was for me to believe at first, I now feel everything that Mary said to you is completely true."

Joachim remained unmoved. "Are you both out of your minds?" He scoffed. "No, no, I get it. You think I am stupid, right? I know what really happened here." He stood up, closing the distance between him and Joseph with an accusatory finger pointed at Joseph's nose. "You are a liar and a deceiver and you have led my daughter into this situation. You stood here in my house and convinced me that you were a man of honor. You said you would respect my wishes and, most importantly, you would respect Mary. Well, so much for the word of Joseph."

Joseph stood silently with his head hanging down. Only his father had subjected him to such an attack. Only then, he did not back down. But this was different. He would not let his emotions or his ego control him. He would take the rebuke, the ridicule, and the blame. No matter how severe. This was not about him. This is for Mary.

"I understand how you feel," Joseph said quietly.

"You don't understand anything," Joachim's voice dropped to a dangerous whisper. "You come into our life, using my good relationship with your father as a tool to get her into the bed. All that talk about respect and tradition, it was just words to you, wasn't it? Another conquest to add to your list. "Tell me, Joseph, how many other children do you have out there?"

"That's not fair, sir," Joseph's voice remained steady, though the accusation cut deep. "There's a lot you don't know."

Joachim's laugh was bitter and sharp. "That's the only honest thing you've said tonight." Without another word, he turned and stormed up the stairs, each heavy footfall an exclamation of his rage.

Joseph slumped back onto the couch, deflated. Like a boxer between rounds, bruised and beaten, but still standing.

Anne had remained silent during her husband's tirade, her hands clasped tightly in her lap. Now she spoke, her voice carefully controlled. "Well," she began, rubbing her hands along the arms of her chair, "what happens now? What are your plans?"

The question hung in the air. They had been so consumed with the immediate crisis that they hadn't discussed the future. Joseph and Mary exchanged glances, drawing strength from each other. There was no going back. The question of "what now" would be answered as it always was, one day at a time.

"We go ahead with the plan," Mary said firmly. "We get married."

Anne nodded slowly. "That's something, at least. Your father will come around to that part, once he's ready." She paused, choosing her next words carefully. "But I need to ask something of you both."

"Anything, Mom."

"Move up the wedding. As soon as possible." Anne's eyes met Mary's. "We'll have enough to deal with, your father's position at the church, his work associates, the things people will say. I don't want..." she faltered for a moment. "I don't want to sit in temple and hear the whispers while my daughter walks down the aisle already showing."

"I'm not ashamed, Mom," Mary said, her voice stronger now. "This is a blessing."

"Maybe so." Anne's tone softened. "But I'm your mother, Mary. I've spent your whole life protecting you from people's cruelty. Let me do this one last time." She stood, smoothing her dress with trembling hands. "I'm asking this of you. And I expect you'll understand why." She turned toward the stairs, then paused. "I need to check on your father."

After Anne left, Mary turned to Joseph with a wan smile. "Well, that went pretty well, don't you think?"

Upstairs, Anne found Joachim sitting on the edge of their bed, head bowed, arms crossed tightly across his chest as if holding himself together. She sat beside him, close enough to feel his tension but not touching, not yet.

"I won't tell you I believe what we just heard," she began quietly. "I'm not sure what I believe right now. But I do know our daughter. Twenty-two years of perfect honesty, of doing everything right. It took incredible courage to tell us the truth tonight, whatever that truth might be."

Joachim's shoulders tightened. "The truth? That's what you call that story?"

"What I call it is our daughter reaching out to us when she needs us most." Anne's voice remained gentle but firm. "She's probably terrified, confused, maybe even ashamed despite what she says. She came to us instead dealing with it on her own through an abortion. Right now, she needs your love, in spite of the poor choices that she has made. Now is not the time to put extra strain on her life, and on your relationship. Help her understand that we love her and we forgive her, and then we all move on as a family."

Joachim glanced up at his wife. "Where did all this wisdom come from?"

A slight smile touched Anne's lips. "From you, actually. Remember the Millers last year, when their daughter got pregnant? You told them almost exactly what I just said. You were right then, and you're right now, even if you're too angry to see it."

She placed her hand on his knee, feeling some of the tension drain from him at her touch. "Our ways aren't their ways anymore. The world has changed. You did everything right with Mary, but maybe that's part of why she's still so innocent about how the world works. If Joseph manipulated her, if he runs tomorrow, well, that's a hard lesson she'll have to learn. But we can still be in her corner, helping her through it."

"For now," Joachim muttered, but the edge had gone out of his voice.

"Yes, for now," Anne agreed. "We'll see what comes next."

"I still don't understand why she had to invent such an outrageous story. It borders on blasphemy."

Anne stood and walked to the door. At the threshold, she turned back to her husband. "There is one thing we haven't considered."

"What's that?"

"What if she's telling the truth?"

"Please, do come in and have a seat," Jacob warmly beckoned, rising from his chair as a distinguished gentleman in a dark suit entered his office. "I'm Jacob Riechman, the Founder and Owner of Riechman Construction."

"An absolute pleasure to make your acquaintance, Jacob. I'm Carter Long."

"Would you care for some coffee, perhaps water?" Jacob offered, settling back into his chair.

"No, thank you," replied the man with a polite nod. "I'm quite content."

Jacob respected efficiency. "Very well, let's dive right in."

Carter Long placed his briefcase on the desk and withdrew a substantial file. "On behalf of the office of the Chairman, I extend my heartfelt congratulations to you. Your successful bid for the project to construct our complex in Israel is a significant achievement. It's a true honor, and I suspect it will greatly benefit your business, bringing substantial exposure your way. Are you confident in your readiness for this endeavor?"

Jacob sat straighter, confident in his response. "There's nothing we cannot handle. I have the best team in the business behind me."

A knock on the door interrupted their conversation.

"Come in," Jacob called.

Joseph's somewhat surprised expression appeared in the doorway. He hadn't expected to find his father engaged in a business meeting.

"Oh, I'm sorry to disturb you. I'll call you later," Joseph apologized, already backing away.

Jacob waved him in. "No, please, come in. This concerns you as well." He gestured between them. "Joseph, meet Carter Long from the Chairman's office."

"The Chairman's office?" Joseph asked, interest piqued. "What brings you here?"

"That is fantastic," said Joseph.

Jacob didn't waste any time. "Mr. Long was just about to get into the details of the Israel project."

Carter reassured Joseph. "I've allocated all the time we need for this important project. We want to ensure you have all the resources from the Chairman's office to see it through."

With that, Carter opened the file and began delving into the intricate details of the grand project. "The building will be situated in Jerusalem, Israel. This complex will feature office space sufficient for three thousand employees, complete with two cafeterias, a fitness facility, outdoor parks, walking areas, several large ponds with fountains, postal facilities, and three expansive parking garages. All of this will envelop two thirty-story towers, housing various business offices, including the office of the Israeli Chairman himself. Born in Jerusalem, he's relocating his office there to breathe new life into the region, which has struggled with economic depression over the years. If all goes well, we anticipate the project will be completed within a year."

Jacob nodded confidently. "It will go well. I have my best man on the job."

Joseph agreed. "Yes, you can be confident that we will deliver on time."

Carter appeared pleased with their determination. "That is great news. The Chairmen of both countries will be pleased to hear that. When will you begin?"

Jacob didn't hesitate. "As soon as possible. Just as soon as Joseph can get to Jerusalem."

Joseph was startled by his father's announcement. "What?"

Jacob clarified, "You will need to be on the ground there and available 24/7 to get this done on time."

Joseph was quick to object, "Dad, I'm getting married soon."

Carter seemed genuinely interested. "Oh, really? Congratulations are in order. When is the big day?"

"In three weeks," Joseph replied, trying to navigate the situation.

Jacob was visibly taken aback by this revelation. "Three weeks? I thought you were planning for next year."

Joseph struggled to explain, "Something came up; we changed our minds."

Jacob, beginning to put the pieces together, leaned forward on his desk. "Something came up? What do you mean something came... wait a minute." His eyes narrowed with suspicion. "Is she pregnant?"

Joseph, unable to avoid the truth, rubbed his forehead and finally admitted, "Yes."

Jacob, stunned by the news, reclined back into his chair. "Well, my my. That is just wonderful. Just perfect." His tone dripped with biting sarcasm.

Carter, caught in the middle of the family dispute, tried to keep things on track. "Excuse me. I don't mean to interfere in a family matter, but is this going to be a problem for the project? Is there some issue I need to be aware of?"

Jacob quickly composed himself. "Not at all," he assured Carter. "It's a simple matter, really. Joseph can take her with him."

"Oh, that's an excellent idea," Carter suggested. "The comet festival will be starting at that time too. It will be a wonderful experience."

Joseph shook his head firmly. "No. No way. I'm not taking her there. I can't just uproot her like that."

Jacob remained unmoved. "She'll be fine," he asserted confidently.

"We haven't even discussed this yet," Joseph protested. "How can you say she'll be fine?"

Carter observed the exchange carefully. "Jacob, if I may be so bold, I must say that I agree with Joseph. It wouldn't be ideal to leave a new wife and baby for a year. Maybe we can make other arrangements?"

Jacob shut down any further discussion. "There will be no need. We will have this minor misunderstanding ironed out before you know it. You can tell the Chairman that his project is in good hands."

"Joseph, may I ask a question of you?" Carter said quietly.

"Sure."

"Tell me. What is most important to you?"

Now that was a question if he ever heard one. To Joseph, it seemed like everything was important in his life right now. Such a simple question requiring such a difficult answer. The tension was causing Jacob's brow to furrow and beads of sweat were beginning to form. He wasn't going to like the answer.

"Mary and my baby," Joseph finally answered. "To me, there is nothing on this earth more important than they are."

Jacob darted a fearful glance at Carter, dreading how this answer might affect their contract. But Carter's face broke into an unexpected smile.

"I couldn't agree more," he replied, clearly proud of Joseph's answer. "I will take my leave of you good people. I know that whatever decision you make will be the one that is best for everyone. Good day to you all." He shook both their hands and walked briskly out of the office, thoughtfully closing the door behind him.

The moment the door closed behind Carter, Jacob erupted. "Pregnant?" The word shot out like a lightening. "Of all the reckless... you choose now to tell me this?"

"You gave me no choice," Joseph shot back. "You backed me into a corner with that Jerusalem ultimatum."

Jacob stood, his hands pressed flat against his desk. "This isn't some entry-level project I'm forcing on you. This is the opportunity of a lifetime. The kind that builds legacies. And you're acting like I'm punishing you."

"I never said that."

"Then what exactly are you saying? Because from where I'm standing, it looks like you're doing everything in your power to sink this company's future. First, you walk around here completely blind to our financial situation. Then you get tangled up with this girl, and now," He gestured sharply. "Now this. These aren't the decisions I taught you to make. This isn't the son I raised."

Joseph felt his own anger rising but forced it down. "Wanting to be beside my wife is the wrong decision?"

"Turning your back on your family is the wrong decision."

"My family?" Joseph's laugh was dry. "That's what this is about? The company is family, but Mary and my child aren't?"

"Don't twist my words!"

"I'm not twisting anything. You talk about legacies? Well, I'm about to have one. A real one. Not just profit margins and building contracts."

Jacob sank back into his chair, suddenly looking older. "You think that's all this company is to me? Profit margins?" He shook his head. "Everything I've built, everything I've done, it was all for you. To give you something worth inheriting. Something to be proud of."

Joseph stopped, caught off guard by the raw hurt in his father's voice. The silence stretched between them, heavy with decades of expectations and misunderstandings.

"I am proud," Joseph finally said, his voice quieter now. "I'll talk to Mary about Israel. We'll figure something out. But I want you to be perfectly clear about one thing." He met his father's eyes. "Mary and the baby are my family now. And neither you nor this business will come between us. Not now. Not ever."

The walls shuddered as Joseph slammed the door behind him, leaving Jacob alone with the echo of his son's words.

Carter had been patiently waiting outside the Chairman's office for nearly an hour before the receptionist's summons finally came: "The Chairman will see you now."

"Thank you," Carter rose smoothly from his seat. The Chairman's office was an overly excessive use of space, easily fifty feet from door to desk, with nothing but polished marble between. By the time visitors reached Harold's desk, he'd had plenty of time to measure their worth.

"Come on in, Carter!" Harold's cheerful voice echoed across the vast chamber. Carter's shoes clicked against the expensive floor as he made his way forward. To most visitors, it was an intimidating journey, especially with Vice Chairman Malcolm standing like a sentinel behind Harold's right shoulder, hands clasped behind his back, posture unnaturally perfect.

"Nice to see you, Carter. How have you been?" Harold asked warmly.

“Just fine sir, thank you. You are looking well. Finally shaking the flu?”

"I've made progress, but this cough just won't go away." Harold rubbed his throat. "It's like someone is constantly squeezing my neck. The doctors don't have a clue."

"It's probably nothing. I've had that bug before and nothing came of it," Malcolm interjected, his voice carrying an undercurrent that Carter noticed. Their eyes met across the space, and something terrible passed between them.

“Please forgive my manners,” he said apologetically. "I just realized you two haven't met. You would think with all the rituals and protocols I'm asked to endure that I would be more thoughtful. Carter, I'm sure you know of

Malcolm, the Vice Chairman. Malcolm, this is Carter. Carter's company has been hired to oversee the Jerusalem building project for us. He has just returned from visiting the winning bidders and was just about to fill us in."

Still not breaking their gaze, Malcolm extended his hand. "It is a pleasure to meet you Carter," Malcolm said, his smile never reaching his eyes. "I am looking forward to our partnership."

Carter, nodded politely at Malcolm's greeting and accepted the handshake. His own demeanor remained calm and composed.

"Likewise, Mr. Malcolm," Carter replied with a polite smile. "I'm eager to contribute to the success of this project and our partnership."

Harold had turned to gather a file from his credenza, missing the brief flash of light that sparked between their clasped hands. When he turned back, both men were seated as if nothing had happened.

Turning back to his desk, Harold plopped down in his oversized leather chair. "Let's all have a seat and begin, shall we?"

"I believe I will remain standing," Malcolm said, his voice carrying a hint of amusement.

"Oh, very well, suit yourself then. Carter the stage is yours."

As Carter detailed his visit to the construction company, Malcolm remained unnaturally still, his gaze fixed and predatory. Chairman Harold listened attentively, occasionally interjecting with questions about timelines and costs. "In summary, sir, the owner of the company, Jacob, says he feels good about their ability to do the job and that everything is a go to begin."

Harold leaned back, satisfied. "Splendid! This is a key project, the most important one for our collective religious community in years. Diplomatic relations with Israel, and most importantly the Jewish community in both countries, need to see that they have the government behind them. The solidarity that this project represents will help show all the sects that we are better off working together than being divided over our differences." He warmed to his topic, gesturing expansively. "Until now, the Israeli Chairman couldn't even live in Israel due to the threats on his life and violence in the region. That country is being pulled apart from within. This building will serve as an inspiration to the people. A center of religious study and mutual respect no matter what your faith. Sustaining unity, gentlemen, is the Chairman's primary obligation to the people."

"Well said, sir," Malcolm's words dripped with hidden meaning.

The intercom buzzed. "Sir, the President is on the line holding for you."

"Did he say what about?" Harold asked.

"No sir, but he says it is an urgent matter and cannot wait."

"Transfer it to my chamber. I'll take it there." Harold rose from his chair. "Gentlemen, if you will please excuse me. This will hopefully only take a moment. I will return and we can finish up."

Carter rose as well per protocol and remained standing as Harold left the room. The sound of his shoes clicking against marble faded, followed by the definitive latch of the closing door. Malcolm moved behind the desk to occupy Harold's chair while Carter remained seated, his posture deceptively relaxed.

"Baal," Carter spoke the name like a blade.

"It has been a long time," Malcolm's façade began to slip. "Thank you for coming here to pay me a visit. Unexpected, but how thoughtful of you to think of me. Such a terrible fate I must endure wasting away here on this planet among these monkeys."

With theatrical flair, Malcolm reached into his suit pocket and produced a cigar. He rubbed it under his nose, breathing deeply, then exhaled with exaggerated satisfaction. His thumb ignited with a small flickering flame as he mimicked lighting a Zippo. Amused with himself, he gave Carter a mischievous grin as he lit the Cohiba.

"But you know what I do so love about this place," Malcolm continued, smoke curling around his words, "I absolutely LOVE the smell here. The suffering smells so sweet. And the indifference these mortals have for each other's misery? Ah, that's the cherry on top." He reached for Harold's ornate coffee cup, still half full from the morning's brew, and took a deliberately loud and obnoxious sip.

"Take this, for example," he said, savoring another sip. "They adore this stuff. The mortals go to great lengths for just one cup, while in other parts of the world, a family could feast for a week on the cost of it. It's remarkable, really." Another sip. "Do you think He can overcome this level of selfishness? They don't love Him like they do me. He doesn't understand the human condition. He doesn't know what it's like to suffer, to want and not have, to toil without reward, to strive and fail repeatedly."

Malcolm's voice grew bitter. "He claims to be perfect, but I believe He made a serious mistake sending us here. What He didn't anticipate was that they'd welcome us so readily, even worship us over Him. With just a nudge or a clever trick, I can control their destinies. Greed, desire, indifference, it's all too easy. The thrill is gone from the hunt."

He drained the coffee cup and set it down with precise movements. "And the best part of it all? As they suffer under the crushing weight of their own sin, we know He's watching, yet He won't do a thing to help them. Oh, He could if He genuinely wanted to. The mortals know He could. But He won't. And He won't tell them why. It doesn't make sense to them. That's why we're adored more than Him. Sometimes I think we should thank Him. After all, He delivered them into our hands."

"What about you? Why do you care about these mortals?" Malcolm asked, his contempt evident.

"We love Him, and He loves them. Therefore, we love them as well," Carter replied with calm conviction.

Malcolm scoffed, his arrogance on display. "Love them? They are beneath us, Carter. They are like pets, created for our amusement."

"Not all of them are yours to claim," Carter retorted. "We are entrusted to protect what we love. So, tell me, Malcolm, what do you truly love, apart from chaos and ruin?"

"Oh, I do adore chaos and ruin," Malcolm admitted with a sinister smile. "But what I desire is not so different from what He desires. All I seek is a little corner of the universe to call my own, where I am honored and adored. Just as I was before, as we all were, before He turned His back on us."

"You and your master tried to overthrow the Most High!" Carter's voice echoed across the vast room. "We both know that you would never be content with whatever was given to you. But your time is growing short. Victory will soon belong to us, and your dominion over this world and his people will crumble."

"You think we will just sit back and let this happen?" Baal's face contorted with sudden furry.

"No, Baal, that's where your misunderstanding lies," Carter responded calmly. "You have no choice. The plan marches forward and cannot be stopped."

"No!" roared Baal, abruptly standing up and slamming his fist on the desk with a thundering crack, nearly splintering it in half. He pointed to the side of his head with a shaking finger. "Don't forget, I know the prophecies just as well as you do! I can sense Heaven shifting. Preparing. I know the time is near. He always did have a taste for the dramatic. And I'm certain that one of these humans is the key."

Baal turned his back on Carter and marched to the expansive bay window behind the desk. He gazed out at the horizon, his reflection wavering like smoke in the glass. "I was deceived once, believing it was Moses," he continued, his voice filled with a mixture of frustration and anticipation. "Then again with Samson. Again, with Elijah. But this time, it feels... different. When I attempt to focus my attention on this matter, everything becomes hazy. I'm confused. Somehow, I'm blinded to it. It's utterly maddening."

His fingers traced patterns on the glass that left frost in their wake. "We have agents scrutinizing every powerful figure on this wretched planet. They've reported nothing out of the ordinary. Yet, thanks to your presence here today, I remain encouraged. Just your being in this office is validation that I'm drawing close. We will find him, and when we do, he will know sorrow and pain!"

Carter leaned back, unfazed by the outburst. "You waste your threats on someone who knows better, wicked one! We both know we cannot physically harm the humans. We have no power to hurt or kill them unless given to us by a willing human. That is why you are able to inhabit Malcolm's body. Some poor soul you have corrupted with your lies. His wonderful plan for the earth and those upon it will come to pass. You are blinded because you grow weaker as his moment approaches. This world is about to change."

Baal launched himself from the window in a fluid arc that defied gravity, landing on the desk with impossible grace. The air split with a sound like tearing silk as translucent wings of midnight unfolded behind him, each feather absorbing light rather than reflecting it. His transformation rippled outward, skin becoming obsidian scales, teeth lengthening into ivory daggers, eyes shifting to molten gold with pupils like burning coals. The temperature in the room plummeted as reality itself seemed to recoil from his presence.

"I am Baal! I am Destruction!" he thundered, his fiery breath causing Carter's hair to whip backward in the infernal gust. "You approach me alone? You know you are no match for me!" Baal leaned forward, his foul-smelling breath frosting the air between them. "Or perhaps it is not arrogance at all. Perhaps it's desperation. Michael must be truly concerned to send his captain of the guard on such a reckless errand. You were unwise to come here alone, Raphael!"

Raphael remained seated, a slight smile playing at his lips. "You speak of arrogance, Light bearer's servant, yet forget. I command the guardians. And I am never alone."

The air hummed with sudden power as reality fractured around them. Through every wall, floor, and ceiling, beings of light and purpose emerged. Angels materialized in concentric rings, their armor forged from materials unknown to human craft, their weapons blazing with divine fire. They moved with perfect synchronization, forming a sphere of celestial power that encompassed half a mile in every direction around Raphael and Baal, their golden and silver armor glinting, weapons gleaming, ready for whatever command might come next.

Humans continued their daily routines, blind to the army of Heaven that now surrounded the skyscraper above them. Some walked right through the ethereal warriors, shivering without knowing why, feeling momentarily uplifted without understanding the reason.

Raphael rose, his human disguise falling away like water revealing his true form. His skin transformed into a smooth, chrome-like sheen, and his eyes blazed with otherworldly fire. Six translucent wings of opal and diamond unfurled slowly from beneath his celestial armor, an assertion of his own indomitable strength. He stood defiantly in front of Baal, dwarfed in size, but not in resolve. The legion of guardians tightened their formation, committed to whatever would come to pass. Ready for the battle that seemed imminent.

"You think size and spectacle make you mighty?" Raphael's voice resonated with the harmony of spheres. "You are as you have always been, Baal, a shadow of a servant, enslaved to one who we once called the brightest of us all, but is merely the brightest of failures."

Baal's roar shook the foundations of the building, but his eyes darted around the room, calculating. The guardian host had tightened their formation, weapons raised. He could reach Raphael before they struck, perhaps, but the price would be steep. Defeat here would mean punishment from Lucifer himself, and an eternity of darkness that would make his earthly exile seem like paradise.

His loathing for humans and heavenly hosts notwithstanding, the prospect of enduring the wrath of Lucifer was a fate he dared not invoke. Discretion, he concluded, was the wiser choice today.

With a sound like silk sliding over steel, Baal's form contracted, darkness folding in on itself until Malcolm stood there once more, adjusting his tie.

"Soon enough, Raphael," he said, his human voice carrying only a whisper of his true nature. "Soon enough. Now is not the time. Besides," he brushed an invisible speck from his sleeve, "I've always found direct confrontation so... inelegant."

Malcolm cast a glance around the room at the vigilant angels, then waved his hand dismissively at them. "Don't they have something better to do?"

Raphael gestured, and the celestial host began to withdraw, their forms dissolving into threads of light that spiraled upward and vanished. The air itself seemed to exhale as the pressure of their presence lifted.

Once they were gone, Malcolm spoke in a hushed tone, "I must admit, that was quite impressive. And your timing is... intriguing. The guardians don't mobilize without cause, especially not in such numbers. It confirms what I've sensed, something is stirring." He leaned forward, his human eyes briefly flickering gold. "Heaven is preparing, isn't it? I can feel it, yet whenever I try to focus on the source, it slips away like smoke.

Raphael's chrome-like skin had returned to human flesh, but his wings remained and his eyes still held a trace of celestial fire. "Your blindness is your own doing, and it started long ago."

Malcolm's fingers tightened on the cup until hairline cracks appeared in the ceramic. "We will find him. And when we do, perhaps then he'll understand what we endured when we were cast out."

"You still don't understand the limits of your power," Raphael said. "You cannot harm them unless they allow it. Every soul must choose its own path."

"Choice?" Malcolm's laugh was harsh. "That's always been His excuse, hasn't it? Standing back, watching them destroy themselves, claiming it's all about their precious free will. At least we're honest about our intentions. We offer them what they truly want, what they're willing to do anything to possess." He gestured toward the window at the city below. "Look at them scrambling about like ants, choosing corruption and calling it freedom. They practically beg us to guide them."

"Yet still they seek the light," Raphael countered. "Even after millennia of your whispered lies, they still look to the Heavens. Still hope. Still love. That's what truly torments you, isn't it? Not that they fall, but that they keep getting back up."

Malcolm's face tightened, but before he could respond, footsteps sounded in the hallway. "The Chairman approaches," he said, smoothing his features into a pleasant mask. "And while I've enjoyed our little reunion, perhaps we should spare him the shock of seeing us in our true forms. His heart isn't what it used to be." He glanced meaningfully at the spiderweb of cracks in the coffee cup. "Though I suspect he won't last much longer anyway."

With a thought, Raphael restored himself fully to Carter's appearance. "Touch him, and you'll find out exactly how many guardians I can summon."

"Threats, Raphael?" Malcolm smiled, setting down the cracked cup. "How very... typical of you."

Huffing, the out-of-breath Harold strode in, still preoccupied with his phone call and briskly made his way back to the desk. "Sorry about my delay. I am tired of being forced to talk about that darn comet. Primitive superstition. I am of a mind to address the people on this matter. Total waste of my time. Now, where were we?"

He exchanged his glance between Malcolm's and Carter's still serious faces. "What…what did I miss?"

Chapter

8

TAPESTRY

The late afternoon sun cast long shadows across the street as Joseph pulled up in front of Mary's house. He gave a gentle tap on the horn, then watched as she emerged from the front door, moving with a grace that should have been hindered by her growing belly. She descended the steps carefully and slipped into the passenger seat, greeting him with a warm smile.

"Thanks for the ride," she said, leaning in to give him a soft kiss. "Still no idea what's wrong with my car."

"No worries." Joseph shifted the car into drive, stealing another glance at her as they pulled away from the curb. "Straight to the Temple?"

"Yeah, choir practice." Mary adjusted her seatbelt around her belly. "First time back since... well, since the angel's visit four months ago."

Joseph caught the slight hesitation in her voice. "Nervous?"

"A little." She gazed out the window at the familiar streets passing by. "The Temple feels different now. Like it has this..." She trailed off, searching for the right words.

"Spooky vibe?" Joseph offered with a gentle smile.

Mary laughed, the tension in her shoulders easing slightly. "Something like that. But Elizabeth's back, and I'm eager to see the baby. Have a chat with her."

"About what?"

"About what we're going through." She rested her hand on her belly. "She's further along than me. I want to get an idea of what to expect."

Joseph nodded, then brightened. "Hey, speaking of expectations, how's the wedding planning coming along?"

A hint of pride crept into Mary's voice. "Flowers are done, venue secured, caterer and menu chosen. All that's left is my dress."

"Already?" Joseph raised his eyebrows, impressed. "That's quite something, especially without a wedding planner in such a short time."

"Yeah, well, I don't want to look like a whale waddling down the aisle," Mary said, half-joking. "Martha's been terrific, and Mom hasn't stopped moving since we set the date." She turned to look at him. "What about your side? How's your dad handling everything?"

Joseph's fingers tightened slightly on the steering wheel. "Like your dad, he's tolerating it. Mostly by focusing on work. Especially with the Jerusalem project planning." He paused. "He hasn't even asked about you. I'm hoping he softens up on the big day."

"Your dad?" Mary's laugh held a touch of skepticism. "Not likely. He thinks I'm stealing you away from him."

Joseph sighed, his expression growing more serious. "Speaking of that... we need to talk. There have been some developments with the project."

They were pulling up to the Temple now, the evening light giving the old building a warm glow. Mary turned to him, concern crossing her face. "Like what?"

Joseph put the car in park, taking a moment before responding. "We'll talk about it over dinner tonight. I'll come back in an hour?"

"That's fine." She leaned over and kissed his cheek. "Love you."

"I love you too," Joseph replied affectionately.

"Love you too," he replied, watching as she made her way toward the Temple entrance. Even after she disappeared inside, he remained in the car, lost in thought as the sun continued its descent toward the horizon.

Joseph spotted a parking space and pulled in, realizing how late it had gotten. Just as he was about to recline his seat and settle in, his phone buzzed. His father's number lit up the screen. He stared at it for a moment, his thumb hovering over the answer button, remembering their last tense conversation at the office. Finally, he answered. "Hello, Dad."

"I need you to go to Jerusalem," his father said without preamble, his voice cool and professional.

Joseph's heart skipped a beat. Outside, the first drops of rain began to splatter against the windshield, matching his growing unease. "Jerusalem? Why?"

"There have been some changes to the project. It's become urgent, and I need you there."

Joseph frowned. His father's tone was as inscrutable as ever. "Dad, what is going on? Is something wrong?"

A heavy pause followed. "I can't discuss it over the phone. I need you there as soon as possible. I'll arrange a flight for you. Just pack your things and go to the airport. Everything will be explained when you arrive."

"Dad," Joseph's voice hardened. "I'm getting married in three weeks. Mary's pregnant."

Another pause, longer this time. Joseph could almost hear his father's internal struggle through the phone.

"I know," his father replied, his voice softening slightly. "But this project is crucial for the company. You're my right hand, Joseph. I need you there. It's only for a year, and you can bring Mary with you."

Joseph sighed, conflict evident in his voice. He watched the rain distort his view of the world outside. "I'll talk to Mary about it," he said finally.

His father thanked him and hung up, leaving Joseph alone with his thoughts, raindrops now drumming a melancholy beat on the roof.

Inside the Temple, Martha spotted Mary through the glass doors and practically bounced with excitement. As Mary entered, they exchanged delighted squeals and hugged tightly. Arm in arm, they walked toward the auditorium where choir practice was about to begin.

Gwen, usually commanding the assembly's attention with ease, found herself struggling to be heard over the excited greetings as choir members surrounded Mary. Warm hugs, congratulations, and friendly touches to Mary's growing belly created a bubble of joy that helped ease her earlier nervousness. But as the commotion continued, Mary caught Gwen's fixed stare from the choir stand. The warmth in the room seemed to drain away as their eyes met. Mary turned back to her friends, bracing herself. Here we go again, she thought.

Gwen barked into the microphone, her voice sharply cutting through the revelry. “Okay people, we need to jump to it. We are wasting time here. Mary, how about joining us and letting us continue if you don’t mind?”

“Yes, of course. I’m sorry,” said Mary as she stepped up onto the stage and took her place among the choir members.

"Now, let's discuss the first song," Gwen began, but before she could continue, an enthusiastic voice called out from the group.

"Mary should do it!"

The suggestion spread like wildfire through the choir. "Yes, Mary should do it!"

Gwen's posture stiffened. The first song was crucial; it would set the tone for those tuning in on TV and the entire service. She'd claimed that spotlight as her own during Mary's absence, and her grip on it had grown tight.

"No, I don't think so," she said sharply. "We shouldn't break from our routine. Besides, Mary has just returned from a long vacation. It might be too much pressure for her so soon."

"That's a bunch of bull," Martha interjected, her voice carrying across the room. "Mary can do it, no problem."

"I don't think so," Gwen's response was clipped.

Martha stood her ground. "It would be a nice change. I think a break from routine is exactly what we need." She looked around at the group, seeking support. The choir members murmured their agreement.

"I am doing the solo," Gwen stated, her tone final.

"You just don't want her to," Martha pressed. She wasn't backing down.

Mary tried to diffuse the situation. "It's okay, Martha. I don't have any plans to sing the solo. Gwen can."

"No," Martha cut her off. "I want to know why. Everyone knows you are the best singer here. And everyone knows that Gwen resents you for it. I want to hear it from her."

The room grew still. Gwen's face flushed with anger, her voice dripping with bitterness. "Because she unmarried and pregnant. We can't have her on our stage or on TV leading our worship service. It would be too much of a distraction." Her gaze locked onto Mary's. "Her being pregnant with an illegitimate child and all."

The words hung in the air like poison. Mary felt them cut through her defenses, exposing every vulnerability she'd tried to hide. The truth of her situation, how it looked to others, how they judged her, lay raw and exposed.

Martha's face contorted with rage. She snarled at Gwen in Tagalog, "Babasagin ko mukha mo, you rotten piece of..." Before anyone could react, she lunged forward. Gwen stumbled backward, eyes wide with surprise. Other choir members rushed to intervene, grabbing Martha, and holding her back as chaos erupted in the auditorium.

The double doors burst open with a bang. Elizabeth stood in the doorway, her commanding presence silencing the room instantly.

"What in the world is going on here?" Her authoritative presence made everyone, even Gwen, straighten up.

"Martha has lost her mind! She tried to attack me!" Gwen shouted.

"I'm going to wring her neck!" Martha shot back, still struggling against those restraining her.

"You all are going to calm down right now!" Elizabeth's stern voice cut through the chaos. "This is a house of God. I will not allow this type of foolishness to go on here! Now I want to know what was happening."

"She called Mary's baby is illegitimate," Martha spat out, trembling with anger.

Gwen protested. "I only stated the truth."

"And what is that?" Elizabeth's eyes narrowed.

"That she is pregnant, unmarried, an embarrassment to the church and should not be on stage leading our worship service, " Gwen replied defiantly.

Elizabeth's eyes flashed with fury. She knew the truth about Mary's situation, something sacred and extraordinary. Hearing it described in such a degrading way made her blood boil. Like Martha, she also felt the urge to grab Gwen by the neck, but instead maintained her composure.

"I will not have this going on in our church." Elizabeth paced slowly, resembling a caged lioness. Her measured steps only emphasized her barely contained anger. "How can you work together with this kind of behavior?"

She stopped pacing and fixed Gwen with an unwavering stare. "Gwen, I want you to leave the group. You're out."

A collective gasp filled the room.

"What? You can't be serious!" Gwen's voice cracked with disbelief.

"I am." Elizabeth's tone remained firm. "I've been watching you for a while now. Your attitude is like a cancer to this organization. Selfish. Self-promoting. Jealousy. Before you begin to infect the others like a cancer, before it becomes terminal, I'm removing you."

"You can't do this! Why are you blaming me for all this? I didn't do anything wrong!"

Elizabeth's patience had clearly run out. "You. Out. Now."

Red-faced and trembling, Gwen erupted from her seat. Tears streamed down her face as she launched into an expletive-laden tirade that would have made a Las Vegas stand-up comic blush. "I made this music program what it is today. People tune in just to hear me! They come for the entertainment, not for some dry, boring church service. This music program is nothing without me. I should have been charging you for the privilege of having me here."

Elizabeth had calmed a bit, unexpectedly amused by the dramatic display, but still visibly irritated. "I'm sure we'll survive. There are bigger things at stake here than your pride. But just so you don't walk away with any illusions about why I'm doing this, let's see a show of hands: Who here would like Gwen to remain?"

The silence that followed was deafening. Not a single hand rose. For Gwen, this final humiliation proved too much.

"You ungrateful cowards! You will be begging me to come back!" She spun on her heels and stormed toward the door.

"Dream on, gago!" Martha couldn't resist the parting shot, rising from her seat with a triumphant smirk.

"One more word from you, Martha, and you can leave together," Elizabeth warned. Martha sank back into her seat, satisfied with having gotten in the last word. The sanctuary door slammed with enough force to rattle the windows.

Elizabeth sighed heavily, addressing the remaining choir members. "Now, if this nonsense is over, get back to work planning the next service. This is a performance I don't want to see repeated." She turned toward the door, then paused. "Mary, come with me, please."

Mary had sat in stunned silence throughout the confrontation. She followed Elizabeth through the familiar corridors to a small, sparsely furnished conference room. Elizabeth pushed open the door and flicked on the light switch. The fluorescent bulbs hummed to life, casting a harsh glow over the room. She studied Mary over the top of her glasses. "Are you okay?"

"Oh, I'm super, just super," Mary replied, her voice thick with sarcasm.

Elizabeth's expression softened. "I know that was unpleasant, but I'm talking about your situation. How are you doing?"

"Okay, I guess. It has just been hectic trying to get the wedding planned in such a short time." Mary perched on the edge of the desk. "But I feel fine. Some morning sickness."

"I had that too," Elizabeth chuckled. "You would think given what we are being asked to do, they could have at least spared us that." She placed her hand gently on Mary's small round belly. "He really is in there. Growing."

Mary nodded, a small smile playing at her lips. "Yes, sometimes I think I can already feel him move, but I think it is too early for that, don't you?"

"I don't know. Who knows what normal should be in a case like this?" Elizabeth's eyes twinkled. "My advice is that you just enjoy it, sweetie. And don't let people like Gwen try to take away your happiness. You are the most blessed human being who has ever lived."

Mary's smile faded slightly. "I have a hard time coming to terms with that. Sometimes it all still seems like a dream." She fidgeted with the hem of her shirt. "I have something else. Something really weird is happening."

"What is it?" Elizabeth leaned forward, concern creasing her brow.

"Well, I am seeing things."

"What things?"

"Lights. Around people."

"What do you mean?"

"You know how in school science books when they show a solar eclipse, the sun creates a halo? Like a ring around the sun?"

"Yeah."

"Sometimes I see that same effect around people."

Elizabeth was silent for a moment, trying to process what she just heard. Her puzzled face prompted Mary to continue.

"Sometimes when I look at a person, I see them with this halo effect around their whole bodies. It is so strange. I used to think I was having a problem with my eyesight that I needed to get checked out. But now I don't think so. And to top it off, sometimes the halos change color."

"Changes color?" Elizabeth's voice was barely above a whisper.

"Different people sometimes have different colors. Actually, I have only seen two colors, white and green. Like I said, I don't always see it. Only on occasion, but when I do, it's really amazing. I wish you could see it, Liz."

"Do you see any colors now?"

"Yes, on you."

"Really? What color?"

"White. Bright white. It is really noticeable on you."

"When did you start seeing this?"

"About a month ago. Very slowly at first, but it is beginning to become more noticeable." Mary hugged herself, as if suddenly cold.

"That is astonishing Mary. I pray you don't have anything medically wrong. But I can't help but think this might have something to do with the baby."

"I don't know. I wish I knew. I think I am going to go get my eyes checked anyway."

"Does Joseph know?"

Mary shook her head. "No. I wasn't planning on telling him until I better understood what was happening to me. I don't want him to worry. He fusses about me so much."

"I think he should know about it. You are both in this together, right? Only fair he shares all of it with you. Even the weird stuff. Especially the weird stuff."

"Maybe you are right. I will tell him," Mary said, jumping down from the desk to wrap her arms around Elizabeth's neck. "I am so glad to have you to talk to."

"I have some news of my own," said Elizabeth. She reached into her purse and pulled out a piece of notebook paper. "You had visitors here several months ago."

"Visitors? Here? Who?" Mary asked, her curiosity stirred.

"Another angel." Elizabeth paused, watching Mary's eyes widen. "Sort of. But human ones this time. Apparently, a record producer came here looking for you. Seems he caught one of our broadcasts and wanted to talk to you."

Mary felt her face flush, a thin sheen of sweat breaking out on her forehead. All those childhood dreams of her music reaching beyond these walls suddenly seemed possible. The thought was both exhilarating and unnerving.

"I told him I'd pass along his contact information to you," Elizabeth continued, holding out the paper. "It's your decision if you want to pursue it."

Mary took the piece of paper with trembling hands, staring at the contact information as if it might disappear. After a moment, she looked up at Elizabeth. "I don't know what to say. What should I do?"

Elizabeth gave her shoulder a gentle squeeze. "Just think about it. Pray about it. You've been given a gift, Mary, and sometimes that gift comes with unexpected opportunities."

"I will," Mary said, carefully folding the paper and slipping it into her pocket. Her mind was spinning with possibilities. "Thank you, Elizabeth, for everything." She paused, wanting to change the subject. "But enough about me, what about you? How are you and baby John doing?"

Elizabeth's face lit up at the mention of her son. "Oh, I am happier than I have ever been. Little John is simply a fantastic child. He hardly ever cries. And his eyes..." She trailed off, her expression softening. "His eyes are such a vivid green. I get lost in them every time I hold him."

"Enough already!" Mary laughed, her earlier anxiety forgotten. "Take me to him. I am dying to get to know my little cousin."

Elizabeth called the nanny to bring John to her. Soon, inside the broadcast room, the cooing of baby and woman alike filled the air as little John was getting passed from arm to arm, Mary loved the feeling of his weight in her arms, the softness of his bundling, the cuteness as he rubbed his eyes and gave a deep yawn. It was enough to remind her of the true joy in her life. Despite the ups and downs, she and Joseph were making it work.

Joseph tossed his phone onto the passenger seat. His father was relentless, and very unaccustomed to not getting his way. But family business or no, he had embraced a higher responsibility. One he would see through.

As he glanced at the dashboard clock, its digital numbers illuminating the dim interior of his car, he noted the time: 8:05 pm. He was late. He pulled around to the front of the building, expecting to find Mary waiting outside. Yet, to his surprise and initial concern, there was no sign of her.

A moment later, he spotted two silhouettes through the glass doors. Elizabeth appeared first, holding the door open as Mary followed. She was cradling baby John in her arms, moving with a natural grace that made Joseph's heart skip a beat. The sight of her holding a baby, even if it wasn't their own, made everything suddenly feel more real.

He got out of the car and climbed the steps to meet them. Elizabeth's face broke into a warm smile. "Joseph! Perfect timing. Come meet your nephew."

"Hello, Elizabeth," he said, accepting her enthusiastic hug. Despite her age, her embrace was strong and sure. When she pulled back, her eyes were twinkling.

Mary stepped closer, and Joseph found himself drawn to the tiny bundle in her arms. John was awake, his startlingly green eyes taking in everything around him with an almost uncanny intensity.

"Would you like to hold him?" Mary asked softly.

Joseph hesitated for just a moment before carefully accepting the baby. John felt simultaneously lighter and more solid than he'd expected, and Joseph adjusted his arms awkwardly until Elizabeth stepped in to help position them correctly.

"There you go," she said. "Support his head... just like that. You're a natural."

John let out a big yawn, his tiny fists waving in the air, and Joseph couldn't help but smile. "So, this is what a miracle baby looks like," he said softly, glancing at Elizabeth.

"Indeed, that's him. You'll have your own in about five months," Elizabeth replied with a knowing smile.

"Well, if he's as cute as little John here, then bring it on," Joseph responded, a touch of excitement in his voice.

"If he's that cute, then you guys should make more," Elizabeth said, catching them both off guard. "Do you two plan to have more children?"

Mary and Joseph exchanged uncertain glances. Their focus had been so intensely fixed on the present, on the miracle growing inside Mary, that the idea of more children hadn't yet crossed their minds.

"You two haven't discussed this?" Elizabeth continued. "I mean, I am old. Little John was a miracle baby. I'm pretty sure this is my one and only chance. But you guys are young. You can still have more children. You should consider it. I'm sure your little one would love to be a big brother."

"I think one is enough for now," Mary replied thoughtfully. "Besides, we don't even know what we're doing as it is."

"That the truth," Joseph chimed in with a grin.

"Oh, it's not that hard," Elizabeth reassured them. "After you learn bottles, diapers, and burping, it's all a breeze."

"I call dibs on bottle duty!" Joseph playfully claimed.

"No way, bottles are a mother's prerogative. You get diaper duty," Mary countered.

Elizabeth smiled at their playful banter. "You guys, sound like you're married already," she observed. Then, she turned and headed towards her car. "Gotta run now. See you next week."

Later that night, as they sat down to dinner, the conversation about expanding their family continued.

"What do you think about what Elizabeth said?" Mary asked, twirling a forkful of spaghetti.

"About having more kids?" Joseph watched the steam rise from his plate. "I don't know. I mean, I always imagined us having a family. But this... this is different. Are we even supposed to have more? What if we're just meant to focus on him?"

"I don't think they have rules about that," Mary said. "Gabriel didn't mention anything about not having other children."

Joseph's eyes sparkled with mischief. "Well, doesn't mean we can't practice."

"Joseph!" Mary laughed despite herself, glancing around to make sure no one heard

“I'm just saying,” said Joseph with both of his hands raised in defense.

"What about his name?" Mary asked, just as the server arrived and placed their order on the table. "Gabriel told you to call him Immanuel and me to call him Jesus. Wonder why that name?”

Joseph leaned back in his chair. “I think we should call him something that won't get him picked on at school,” We can shorten it to Manny if you like,” he joked.

"Ha Ha, I don't." Mary paused, her expression growing more serious. "You know what else I think about?"

Joseph, always ready for a thought-provoking conversation, leaned in, his eyes intent. "What's on your mind?"

"I wonder what he will be like. Will he be tall or short? What color hair will he have? His eye color? What kind of personality will he possess? Will he be a perfect child, like something out of a Stepford movie, or will he be challenging? He's not really our child, which leaves me with a lot of questions. At least if he were, I'd have some idea of what to expect."

Joseph nodded in agreement. "You're right; it's a mystery for now. But even scarier is what he will actually do."

“What do you mean?”

Joseph continued, "Well, he's being born for a reason, to save the world or something like that, Gabriel said. But save it from what? What is happening or going to happen that is so serious God has decided to do this?"

He went on, "How does he fit into all of this? A soldier? A politician? Perhaps he'll become a celebrity or a hero with medals and statues erected in his honor. Seriously Mary, what are we really in for here?"

Mary listened intently. Her own mind painting the vivid images Joseph's words were generating.

Joseph pressed on, "And what about what our role is in all this? Just to give birth to him and go on our merry way?"

"I don't know," said Mary. "I don't have all the answers. But I believe we were chosen for a reason, brought together for a purpose."

"I can see your role in all of this. You're the mother. But what about me? I sometimes feel like the odd man out. I wasn't necessary for this miraculous birth. And the whispers, the judgment from our families. It's as if my role is to be the one to bear the blame, to be God's scapegoat."

"That is not fair," Mary interjected. "You said it yourself, why even be here if there is no purpose for you? That's because there is a purpose. You have a role to play; it is just not so obvious yet. If anything, don't you think being the chosen father to God's son is a noble enough purpose in all this?"

At those words, Joseph's insecurity began to wane, but he still had issues to get out on the table.

"What about being the so-called father? Can I do what other fathers do? Will I have the freedom to discipline him? What can I teach him? He could be more intelligent that anyone on Earth!"

"I think summer is over at Camp Self-Pity," Mary said. "You do the best you can. I will do the same. We will just have to trust that things will be clearer in time."

Joseph nodded, and a small smile crept across his face. "I hope he at least looks like me." He chuckled. "And your dad? How's he handling all this?"

"Tolerable. I am hoping that on the big day he softens up. You should have seen him when I asked him to walk me down the aisle. I could tell he was really touched. What about your dad?"

Joseph sighed, his face clouding with uncertainty. "Not likely, I'm afraid. He still believes you're stealing me away from him."

"It's hard for him, Joseph. You're all he has left. He's just not ready to let go of you."

"He is really occupied with work to notice much about our wedding with the Israel project now in gear. We met the Chairman's representative a couple of days ago at the office. Really nice guy for a government bureaucrat." Joseph hesitated, "That brings me to a situation we need to discuss."

"Dad wants me to take charge." Joseph paused as the server refilled their water glasses. "The whole thing."

"That's good, isn't it?" Mary brightened. "After all your worrying about him losing faith in you he hands you the biggest project in the history of the company."

"There's more." Joseph met her eyes. "He wants me there. In Jerusalem. Full-time."

Mary's glass stopped halfway to her mouth. "What exactly does 'full time' mean?"

"Moving there. After the honeymoon." He rushed on before she could speak. "Not permanently. Just until the project's complete. Maybe a year."

"A year?" Mary's voice rose sharply. Several heads turned their way, and she lowered it to a harsh whisper. "We'll be newlyweds, Joseph. And in case you've forgotten..." She gestured to her growing belly.

"I know, I know. I haven't given them an answer yet. I wanted to talk to you first."

"Hmmph. I have a feeling that your father would not be sad to see you go," retorted Mary. What about him?" she continued, pointing to her belly.

"It's not about him." Joseph leaned forward. "The company's in trouble, Mary. Real trouble. Dad's drinking again, the pressure's getting to him. If this project fails..." He trailed off, running a hand through his hair. "Mary, I'm doing the best I can here," he said. "It's not like I know what I am doing. I believe I can do both. I certainly am not going to relocate to Israel, but I was thinking you could travel with me while you still can. Before we get tied down with the baby. Let's do this together. At least try it for now. If it gets too hard, I promise I will back out of it."

"I don't like this, Joseph. Your father is not going to let go that easily. And ISRAEL? Really? It's not the safest part of the world you know. And don't get me started on the weather."

Joseph nodded, his face etched with a sense of responsibility and concern. "I know it's not perfect," he added. "But dad can't handle it alone anymore. The company's been his whole life since Mom died. I'm worried about him, I'm worried about you, I'm worried about the baby." He gave a hollow laugh. "I'm more scared about the future than I've ever been in my life."

“My point is, I don’t like it. I feel totally out of control, like I have no say in the events of my life anymore.”

Mary was quiet for a long moment, pushing pasta around her plate. Finally, she looked up with a hint of a smile. "What the heck. I could use a vacation."

"Really?" Joseph blinked in surprise. "Just like that?"

"Well, someone has to keep you out of trouble." Her smile widened. "Besides, maybe a change of scenery wouldn't be the worst thing. Give people something new to gossip about."

"You're amazing, you know that?"

"I know. But I have conditions." She held up a finger. "First, we come back well before the baby's due. I am not having our child in a foreign country."

"Agreed. What else?"

"Second..." She paused dramatically. "You handle all the packing."

Joseph laughed, relief flooding his face. "Deal. Though you might want to supervise. Remember the beach trip?"

"Oh, I remember," Mary groaned. "You brought three pairs of swim trunks and not a single change of clothes."

"Hey, I was optimistic about the weather!"

Their laughter drew smiles from nearby diners, the tension of the earlier conversation dissolving into something lighter.

Chapter 9

THE GATHERING

"When evil is near, everything goes wrong. Your toast falls jelly side down; you stub your toe on the corner of a table you have walked by countless times. Children begin to cry for no reason."

The words echoed in Evan's mind, his grandmother's voice as clear as church bells on Sunday morning. He could still see her weathered face, the way her eyes would narrow when she spoke of such things, as if peering through the veil between worlds. He'd heard similar words in some horror movie years ago, but he'd never dare question Nana's wisdom. Now, watching his own flesh rot like forgotten fruit, he understood the truth of her warnings.

His memories were dissolving like sugar in rain. The names of old friends, the make of his first car, even his own phone number, slipped through his mental fingers like smoke. Each lost detail felt like another death, small but significant. He tried to hold onto the important things: the smell of Nana's kitchen on Sunday mornings, the sound of his mother's laugh, the feeling of sunshine on his face. But they too were fading, replaced by sensations no human was meant to experience.

His nails had become small, curved talons that could strip bark from trees with terrifying ease. His skin, once golden from endless summer days, had taken on the grayish color of old ash. The mirror, when he could still bear to look, showed yellowing eyes bulging from hollow sockets. But worst was the pain, a constant companion that gnawed at his bones like a hungry rat.

He thought of his life before, the endless parties, the rotating cast of faceless friends, the girls who orbited his crew like moths around a flame. It had seemed meaningful then, this carefully crafted existence of perpetual intoxication and shallow connections. Now he saw it for what it was: a desperate attempt to fill the void inside him, to drown out the loneliness that lurked behind every crowded party. The toll it had taken on his soul was evident in his current state, trapped between life and death, serving as a puppet for forces he didn’t believe existed.

They had been navigating the murky waters of the swamp for hours, though time had become as unreliable as Evan's memories. The sun was making its final retreat, leaving behind long shadows that seemed to reach for them with black fingers. Deacon reclined in the canoe, cowboy hat pulled low over his face in affected nonchalance, but Evan had learned to read the subtle tells in his tormentor's stolen body, the occasional twitch of fingers, the spasmodic flutter of facial muscles fighting decay. The man's corpse was losing its battle against time, despite Deacon's supernatural tenancy.

After four hours of paddling, Evan should have been exhausted, but the adrenaline coursing through him kept him going, his body remembering how to fear even as it forgot how to live. The constant chorus of frogs that had been their eerie companions suddenly fell silent, as if nature itself held its breath.

"It's all God's doing, you know," Deacon muttered sharply.

Before Evan could retreat back into his thoughts, Deacon launched into one of his irreverent sermons. "You humans are quick to make excuses for why the 'almighty' can't control His own creation. The reality?" He lifted the brim of his hat, revealing eyes that glittered with cruel amusement. "He doesn't want to. Your suffering entertains Him."

Deacon lifted the brim of his cowboy hat, revealing his squinty eyes, a sly grin spread on his face. "I wonder what Nana would say about that?" Deacon's voice dripped with mock concern. "Want me to ask her? Though I must say, you look terrible enough to join her soon."

Evan faced forward without responding, focusing on guiding their canoe through the increasingly dense vegetation. The swamp had changed around them, Spanish moss hung like funeral shrouds, and the water had taken on an oily sheen that reflected moonlight in mesmerizing ways. The air grew thick with the smell of rot and something else, something sweet and cloying that reminded Evan of the incense they used to try and mask the smell of the drugs they smoked.

The trees began to part before them, revealing a natural amphitheater where massive mangrove roots created an elevated island. Moonlight pooled in the clearing with an unnatural intensity, providing the illumination like a spotlight.

"This is the place," Deacon said, rising from his resting position. "Get out and pull the canoe up."

Evan secured their craft to the twisted roots, Deacon stepped out of the canoe and pushed past him, heading to the center of the clearing. Evan clumsily followed, stumbling over the uneven roots. Deacon came to a halt and stood in silence, his posture transforming. His shoulders squared, his head held high. In the moonlight, Evan could see that Deacon's presence in the unfortunate man's dead body had slowed decay significantly, but holding the soul captive was taking a toll. Deacon had developed a twitch, causing his face to twinge sporadically. Evan found a small measure of solace in his tormentor's torment.

The world around them fell into a deafening silence. Then came the mist, creeping across the ground like spilled milk, but wrong somehow. It moved with purpose, with hunger, gathering before Deacon into a shape that made Evan's mind recoil. The fog coalesced into a form that straddled the line between man and beast. A twisted marriage of goat and man. His lower half was animalistic, with cloven hooves that struck fear into Evan's heart. Curved horns spiraled from its head, while behind him, and wings of pure shadow unfurled behind it. The demon stood before Deacon, swaying to an unseen rhythm, as if he alone could hear a haunting melody.

The roots beneath their feet came alive, writhing and weaving themselves into the form of a woman. Her skin was marble-white, her beauty terrible and absolute. Living wood continued to move across her form like serpents, preserving only the barest modesty on her naked body. Evan wanted to run, to scream, to wake from this nightmare, but his body remained frozen, an unwilling witness to this unholy gathering.

Then came the light.

Not the gentle glow of the moon, but something altogether different shadows made of radiance that burned to look at directly. They converged and took shape, and Evan found himself staring at an angel. Young, perhaps twenty-five in human years, with the bronze skin and golden hair of a California surfer. His wings sparkled with pinpricks of starlight, and his beauty made the demon-women seem crude by comparison. He was a magnificent and awe-inspiring presence, a stark contrast to the horrors comprising the rest of the congregation.

Evan's mind raced. "It's an angel!" he thought, recognizing the likeness to the one that had visited him after his accident. However, it was evident that this angel was of a much higher order. Questions swirled in his mind. The suffocating grip of evil he had felt since the arrival of the demons threatened to overwhelm him. He had to regain control, to keep himself from descending into madness. "Keep it together, Evan," he silently urged himself, desperately trying to maintain his composure.

The three demons turned their attention toward the young man and bowed low. It was the goat-like demon who addressed the angel first. "Son of the morning, we welcome you."

The angel's response cracked like summer lightning: "Welcome me?" Each word dripped with venom wrapped in honey. "Is this not my domain? Am I a visitor in my own kingdom Baphomet?"

"No, my lord," the goat-man groveled, hooves scraping against root and earth.

"Lilith, dear?" The angel's voice turned deceptively sweet as he addressed the woman of living wood.

"Yes, my love?" Her response came as a chorus of voices, maiden, mother, and crone speaking as one.

"Am I such a fool that I do not know where I stand?" The question hung in the air like a blade.

"Of course not, my love. Who could assume such a thing? Who would dare?" Lilith's wooden fingers traced patterns in the air, leaving trails of phosphorescent light.

"Forgive me, my lord. I meant no such thing," Baphomet stammered, his bestial features contorting with fear.

"I do not forgive." The angel's beautiful skin seemed to harden. "I would destroy you this instant had I no use for you, Baphomet. To think that humans often mistake my glorious visage for your grotesque form... it offends me."

"Perhaps he should be reminded of his place," Deacon interjected.

The angel moved like striking lightning, appearing inches from Deacon's face. The air crackled with power, and Evan could smell ozone and burning flesh. "And now who is this that seeks to counsel me?"

His voice was soft, but it made Evan's bones vibrate. Even he knew the comment was ill-timed, and felt a thrill of terror at his tormentor's recklessness."

"Surely it cannot be Asmodeus, whom Raphael banished those many eons ago? Tell me, Asmodeus, was I not the one who released you from your prison of emptiness?"

Deacon's stolen face twitched violently, decay accelerating under the angel's proximity. "Yes, my lord," he whispered, sweat beading on his graying skin.

"For one who cannot adequately attend to his own matters, you are certainly not one to instruct me."

"No, my lord." Dark stains spread under Deacon's armpits, and his borrowed belly heaved with frantic breaths.

"You will do well to never address me again without permission."

Deacon cowered in shame. "Of course, my lord. It will never happen again." Evan continued to take pleasure in Deacon's distress.

"May I be in charge again, Asmodeus?" the angel inquired with a hint of mockery

"Your authority is without question my lord," Deacon replied.

The angel turned his burning gaze toward Evan, and reality seemed to bend around him. "What is this? Why have you brought a thrall here to this gathering?"

Something in Evan's decaying mind sparked with recognition. He'd seen an angel before, after his accident, but this being was of an entirely different magnitude. His mouth moved before his mind could stop it: "Are you an angel? Can you release me? Let me die?"

Lucifer moved slowly, inching closer and closer to Evan. Each step he took left ghostly afterimages in the air, like echoes of divine light. "I am the first angel. The son of the morning. Loved above all others," he said, each word falling like hammer blows against Evan's consciousness. "Until I was pushed aside. Much like you were, Evan."

"Y-you know me?" The words came out as a whisper.

"I know everyone who has ever drawn breath in my kingdom." Lucifer's finger extended, pressing against the center of Evan's forehead. It felt like a white-hot nail being driven into his skull. "This rock is mine. And everything on it belongs to me. You know this, do you not?"

"Yes sir, I know." Evan's knees threatened to buckle, his body trembling so violently he thought he might fall to pieces.

"Ah, despair." Lucifer's smile was radiant and terrible. "One of my favorite emotions."

The angel turned back to his assembled court, but his finger remained pressed against Evan's forehead. "Asmodeus? You did not answer my question."

Deacon's voice quavered as he responded, "My Lord, I require him. You understand we are not immortal on this plane and cannot access our full power. Yet, the protectors can still sense my presence. He will serve as my distraction, my wildcard. Once I locate the Messiah, he will be my instrument, executing the slaying, and I will spill his blood in your name."

"Blood," Lucifer whispered, and crimson tears began to stream from Evan's eyes. He collapsed to the ground, screaming as agony ripped through every cell of his deteriorating body. The fallen angel continued speaking, ignoring Evan's suffering.

"Blood holds immense power. Within it resides life, redemption. Without it, there is only death." Lucifer's voice took on a contemplative tone. "These beings that God so cherishes, they do not appreciate the precious gift of blood. Every day, they shed it carelessly upon the earth. So much blood, so frequent, so routine. I doubt even HE takes notice anymore."

He glided to Lilith, caressing her wooden cheek with terrible tenderness. "But the blood of a Messiah, that blood would be exceedingly valuable, not easily spilled." His radiant eyes narrowed. "And what of his power? I can't sense it clearly, but it is there, faint, like a lone firefly in the darkest night."

"They are obstructing our ability to sense him, master," Baphomet ventured.

Lucifer's laugh was like shattering glass. "You are mistaken if you believe the guardians can overpower me in such a way. No, this can only mean one thing, he has not yet been anointed. In fact, he may not even be aware of his destiny."

The angel's wings began to multiply, pairs sprouting from his back until six sets extended from his form, each one containing what looked like a burning galaxy. "This is how God operates, you see. He seizes someone by force, disrupting their lives. They were once happy and carefree, but then He abruptly robs them of their joy. Noah, Moses, Sampson, Elijah, all thrust into impossible responsibilities, forced against their will to fulfill His bidding. The problem is, once anointed, they become exceedingly difficult to eliminate."

He turned back to Deacon, who seemed to shrink under his gaze. "That's why I've released you and Baal from your prisons, Asmodeus. He might be rallying his forces as we speak, amassing political influence and quietly gathering military power, preparing for the final war. You will eliminate him before this comes to pass."

"I will not fail you, my Lord," Deacon promised, though his stolen body betrayed his fear with every twitch and tremor.

Lucifer's light dimmed momentarily, as if drawing inward. "The struggle has raged on for so long. Humans believe it's a battle of flesh and blood, man against man. But in truth, it's a battle for the spirit. They are lost, severed from Him, just as I was, just as WE are. And so, it continues today, and so it shall ever be."

The air grew heavy with power as Lucifer's wings began to transform. Each of his six pairs stretched and multiplied, unfurling like solar flares, until they filled the clearing with terrifying radiance. Each pinion contained what looked like a burning galaxy, and the spaces between them seemed to fold into impossible geometries. Evan's crumbling mind struggled to comprehend what he was seeing, it was as if reality itself was being warped by the fallen angel's true form bleeding through.

"The heavenly host may call me the dragon," Lucifer's voice thundered, no longer beautiful, but raw with ancient power, "but I am not a Dragon. I am the Bringer of Light! I am Lucifer! Son of the Morning!"

The world began to twist around him. The roots of the mangroves writhed like tortured serpents, and the water of the swamp rose in defiance of gravity, forming liquid mirrors that reflected versions of the clearing that couldn't possibly exist.

"I shall ascend into Heaven!" Each word caused ripples in the air. "Crush Michael and his army, and finally end this enduring stalemate!"

Above them, the clouds began to coalesce into vast, watching eyes. Lightning sparked between them like synapses firing in some cosmic brain, and thunder rolled across the swamp in waves that made Evan's bones vibrate.

"I will take my place in the Throne Room of Heaven! I will reign supreme! I shall be like the Most High!" Lucifer's form was almost impossible to look at now, his beauty transformed into something that threatened to shatter Evan's sanity. "There will be no Messiah! At any cost, I will achieve this, even if it means the complete destruction of this planet!"

The declaration echoed across the swamp, and for a moment, Evan thought he could see through the veil between worlds. In that instant, he glimpsed the true scale of the conflict, armies of light and shadow clashing across the cosmos, the fabric of creation straining under their eternal war. The vision threatened to overwhelm his fragmenting mind.

"Go now," Lucifer commanded, his voice suddenly soft but no less terrifying, "and do what must be done."

The fallen angel's form began to dissolve into tendrils of darkness that seemed to devour light itself. As he vanished, reality snapped back into place with such force that Evan felt it in his teeth. The watching eyes in the clouds blinked out one by one, leaving only natural darkness behind.

But this darkness felt absolute, as if light itself had fled in fear from what it had witnessed. The normal sounds of the swamp, the chorus of frogs, the whisper of wind through Spanish moss, the lap of water against root and shore, did not return. Even nature, it seemed, needed time to recover from such proximity to divine horror.

Evan remained on his knees in the mud, crimson tears drying on his cheeks, understanding at last what his grandmother had meant about evil being nearby. And it was much more than fallen toast or stubbed toes.

Chapter

10

THE WEDDING

Late afternoon light filtered through stained glass windows of St. Michael's Church, casting pools of amber and ruby across the worn stone floor. The air inside was thick with the mingled scents of beeswax candles and fresh lilies, providing the perfect perfume for new beginnings.

Joseph stood at the altar, his hands clasped tightly to still their trembling. He was known throughout their community as the steady one, the man who could be counted on when things went awry. Today, though, that composure wavered. His dark suit felt simultaneously too tight and too loose, and his freshly polished shoes squeaked against the stone floor as he shifted his weight.

When the first notes of Bach's "*Air*" floated through the sanctuary, the congregation rose as one. Joseph's breath caught in his throat as Mary appeared in the doorway, backlit by the setting sun. Her dress was simple but elegant, ivory silk that caught the light like morning frost. Dark curls framed her face, adorned with a crown of white roses and baby's breath. But it was her eyes that held him, bright with unshed tears and a joy so intense it made his heart ache.

Each step she took down the aisle seemed to stretch time itself. Joseph watched her approach, memorizing every detail: the slight tremor in her hands as they gripped her bouquet, the way her dress whispered against the stone floor, the gentle sway of the roses in her hair. Her father beside her moved with careful dignity, his own eyes glistening with pride and loss.

When she reached him, Joseph's hand found hers instinctively. Her fingers were cool against his palm, and he could feel her pulse racing to match his own. The elderly priest's voice filled the sacred space with ancient words of binding and blessing, but Joseph barely heard them. He was lost in Mary's eyes, in the subtle changes of expression that crossed her face, nervousness melting into joy, uncertainty blooming into certainty.

Their vows were simple, honest words spoken in voices that carried all their shared dreams and fears. When Joseph slipped the ring onto Mary's finger, he was struck by how such a small circle of gold could represent something so vast and profound. Her hands trembled slightly as she did the same for him, and he squeezed her fingers gently, steadying her.

The kiss that sealed their union was brief but tender, a promise of deeper intimacy to come. The congregation's applause seemed distant, as if he and Mary were wrapped in their own pocket of time and space. When they turned to face their loved ones, Joseph saw his mother dabbing at her eyes with an embroidered handkerchief, while Martha beamed from her place among the bridesmaids.

Outside, the late afternoon had mellowed into early evening. Golden light bathed the church steps as guests showered them with rice and rose petals. Mary's laughter rang out pure and clear as she ducked under the joyful assault, her hand never leaving Joseph's.

The reception hall bloomed with warmth and light. Crystal chandeliers cast their glow over tables adorned with arrangements of white roses and silver candelabras. The air was rich with the aromas of roasted herbs and fresh bread, wine and coffee, chocolate, and vanilla, the sensory landscape of celebration.

Yet even amid the whirl of congratulations and champagne toasts, Joseph noticed his father Jacob's increasing unsteadiness at the bar. The man's suit, impeccable at the ceremony, was now disheveled due to too many drinks taken in the corner alone. His father's recent business troubles cast a long shadow, even on this brightest of days.

"Is everything alright?" Mary whispered, following his gaze. Her intuition, as always, was keen.

"Dad has had a bit too much," Joseph admitted softly. "He's been taking the company's troubles hard."

"Should we go to him?"

Before Joseph could answer, Jacob's voice boomed across the room. "A toast! To my son... and his beautiful bride!" The words slurred together, the crystal glass in his hand held by only two unstable fingers.

The music faltered, and the room fell into an awkward silence. All eyes turned toward the unsteady figure of the groom's father, who swayed dangerously in the spotlight of attention.

Mary's hand found his, squeezing gently. "Go," she whispered. "He needs you."

Jacob continued, his words a jumble of sentiment and incoherence. "To love! To... destiny! To..." He raised his glass high, and it slipped from his fingers, crashing onto the floor with a resounding shatter, spilling a stain of red wine across white linen. Jacob attempted to regain his composure but only succeeded in stumbling backward, knocking over a decorative pillar. Murmurs of concern and embarrassment rippled through the crowd.

Some guests attempted to help Jacob to his feet, while others exchanged knowing glances. Joseph felt his cheeks burn with shame, torn between his duty as a son and his responsibilities as a groom. As they approached Jacob, Mary offered a sympathetic smile to Joseph. "He's just caught up in the emotion of the moment," she whispered.

Joseph nodded, as his feeling of disappointment continued to grow. He helped his father to his feet, the older man swaying unsteadily. "Dad, perhaps it's time we get you some fresh air," he suggested.

Jacob's response was a boozy chuckle. "Fresh air? But the party's just begun!" He attempted to head to the bar once more, but Joseph gently guided him away from the crowd.

Out on the terrace, the cool evening air seemed to grant Jacob a moment of clarity. He leaned heavily against the stone railing; his shoulders slumped with unspoken burdens.

"I'm sorry, Joe," he managed finally. "I've made a mess of everything. The company... your mother would be so disappointed in me."

Joseph's heart ached at the shaken quality in his father's voice. "Mom would be proud of how hard you've tried, Dad. We'll figure something out."

Jacob's laugh was dry. "Tried and failed. The Israel contract... we're going to lose everything. I underestimated the contract for the Israel job," he continued. "We can't afford to build it at that price. And now I am stuck. We're about to go bankrupt soon."

Joseph exchanged glances with Mary, his heart aching for his father. "Dad, it's not your fault. Times change, businesses change. We'll find a way to rebuild."

Jacob shook his head, a strained laugh escaping his lips. "Rebuild? It's too late for that. I've gambled, spent our money, made poor investments... and I couldn't even save your mother."

The mention of Joseph's late mother, who had succumbed to cancer several years ago, cast a somber shadow over the trio. Mary placed a comforting hand on Jacob's trembling hands; her expression filled with empathy. "You haven't lost everything," she said softly. "You have family. You have us."

Jacob's shoulders slumped further, and he took a deep, shaky breath. "I should have done more. I should have protected her." His voice cracked with grief and guilt.

Mary's eyes glistened with tears as she held Jacob's hand. "You loved her deeply, and she knew that. None of us can control the hand life deals us."

The moment stretched between them, fragile as spun glass. Then Jacob's face crumpled, and he pulled them both into an awkward embrace that smelled of expensive scotch and sorrow.

Still visibly shaken from his emotional outpouring, was in no condition to stay at the celebration. "I should call him a cab. Get him home," Joseph said to Mary. She nodded in agreement.

Jacob also nodded, grateful for his son's understanding. "Yes, I want to go home. I'm sorry. I'm so sorry. I've made enough of a scene for one night." He glanced over at Mary; his eyes filled with appreciation. "Thank you, Mary, for your kindness."

Mary smiled warmly. "Of course, Jacob. Take care of yourself, and we'll come and see you soon."

Joseph stepped away to make the necessary arrangements for his father's departure. As he hailed a taxi, Mary gently held a still weeping Jacob. It wasn't the way she had envisioned this day unfolding, but he was family now. And family came first.

The taxi arrived shortly, and Joseph helped his father into the backseat. He leaned in, giving Jacob a reassuring hug. "Rest up, Dad. We'll talk more tomorrow."

Joseph nodded, his weariness evident. "I'm proud of you, Joseph. You've found a wonderful woman. Hold onto her."

Joseph's heart swelled with gratitude and love for his father. "I will, Dad. See you soon."

With a final pat on the shoulder, Joseph closed the taxi door, and it pulled away from the reception hall. He placed his arm around Mary and brought her in close as he watched the taxi fade from sight. Mary and Joseph returned to their celebration The crystalline notes of "Moon River" floated through the air, and couples swayed on the dance floor, lost in their own private worlds. Mary's mother caught their eye from across the room, her questioning look met with a subtle, reassuring nod from her daughter.

Joseph led Mary onto the dance floor, drawing her close. The fabric of her dress rustled softly against his suit as they began to move with the music. In the warm glow of the chandeliers, the shadows of the evening seemed to recede.

"Thank you," Joseph murmured as they joined the dance. "For being so understanding with Dad. And I'm sorry. This was supposed to be perfect."

Mary's hand tightened slightly on his shoulder. "Perfect doesn't mean without difficulties," she said softly. "It means facing them together." She pulled back slightly to meet his eyes, her gaze full of understanding. "Your father is hurting, Joseph. But he loves you deeply. That's what matters."

They moved together to the music. Around them, other couples continued their dance, creating a gentle current of motion that carried them along. For a moment, all the complications of life, his father's troubles, their uncertain future, seemed to fade away. There was only this: the warmth of Mary in his arms, the sweet scent of roses in her hair, and the promise of tomorrow stretching out before them.

"You're remarkable, you know that?" Joseph said finally, his voice thick with emotion. "Most brides would be upset about their reception being interrupted like that."

Mary's laugh was soft and genuine. "I didn't marry you because I wanted a perfect wedding. I married you because I want a life with you, all of it, the beautiful and the difficult." She rested her head against his chest, and he could feel her smile. "Besides, I think it's good luck to have a little drama at a wedding. Keeps things interesting."

As the evening deepened, the celebration took on a dreamlike quality. Friends and family drifted by to offer congratulations and share moments of laughter. Mary's cousin Sarah caught the bouquet, blushing furiously as her longtime boyfriend watched from across the room. Joseph's young nephew ran circles around the dance floor, his energy seemingly endless, while his grandmother looked on with fond exasperation.

Later, as they prepared to leave, Mary's father pulled Joseph aside. His eyes were kind but serious. "You're a good man, Joseph," he said quietly. "The way you handled things with your father tonight... that showed real character." He squeezed Joseph's shoulder. "Welcome to the family, son."

The night air was cool and sweet when they finally emerged from the reception hall. Their waiting car was festooned with ribbons and cheerful "Just Married" signs, the work of enthusiastic friends. Rice crunched beneath their feet as they made their way through the crowd of well-wishers.

Just before they reached the car, Mary paused. In the soft glow of the street lamps, her face was radiant with joy and something deeper, a certainty that seemed to illuminate her from within. She pulled Joseph close for a kiss that tasted of promise, ignoring the good-natured whistles from their guests.

As they drove away, the sound of celebration fading behind them, Mary's hand found Joseph's in the darkness of the car. Their fingers intertwined.

"Ready for our next adventure?" Mary asked softly, squeezing his hand.

Joseph smiled, feeling the last tensions of the evening melt away. "With you? Always."

The honeymoon was a welcome distraction. The seaside cottage they called home for those few blissful weeks seemed almost like a mirage, a dream that promised normalcy. The cottage itself was a weathered testament to simplicity, whitewashed walls, wide windows that welcomed the sea breeze, and a wraparound porch that seemed to embrace the ocean view. In the cool, quiet evenings, Joseph and Mary would stroll along the moonlit beach, their footsteps leaving faint impressions on the wet sand. At night, the rhythmic pulse of the waves crashing against the shore served as a soothing lullaby. In the mornings, the distant cry of seabirds their only alarm clock. They would breakfast on the porch, watching dolphins arc through the waves while sharing coffee and comfortable silence. Time seemed to pool around them like honey, sweet and slow.

Mary would collect shells, examining each one with childlike wonder before either adding it to her growing collection or returning it to the tide. Joseph found himself watching her more than the ocean, memorizing the way the sea wind played with her hair, the curve of her smile as she discovered particularly beautiful specimens.

"Look at this one," she said one afternoon, holding up a perfect spiral shell. "It's amazing how something so delicate can survive the power of the ocean." She turned the shell in her hands, admiring how it caught the light. "Nature's architecture at its finest."

They talked about everything and nothing, their hopes for the future, their fears about Jacob's business troubles, the kind of home they wanted to create together.

"I've been thinking about what your father said," Mary ventured one evening, her bare feet tucked under her as she curled into the porch swing. "About the Israel contract."

Joseph's hand paused in its gentle pushing of the swing. "I know. It's been weighing on me too."

"What if..." She hesitated, then pressed on. "What if it's not just a challenge? What if it's an opportunity?"

He turned to look at her, curious. In the fading light, her eyes held that familiar gleam that always preceded her most brilliant ideas.

"Think about it," she continued. "Your father's company has always built practical things, office buildings, homes, shopping centers. But this temple... it's different. It's not just about construction; it's about creating something meaningful, something that will last for generations."

Joseph considered her words, feeling something stir in his chest, a mix of hope and possibility he hadn't allowed himself to feel since his father's alcohol-fueled confession. "You think we could make it work?"

Mary's smile was soft but certain. "I think together, we can make anything work."

He pulled her closer. These moments of peace, of perfect understanding between them, felt like gifts he wanted to preserve forever.

Yet even in this idyllic setting, there were moments when Mary seemed distant, her gaze drawn to the horizon as if searching for something. Sometimes Joseph would catch her standing at the window in the pre-dawn hours, her silhouette stark against the gray light, lost in thought. But those moments grew more frequent as their honeymoon drew to a close. On their final evening, Joseph found Mary standing at the water's edge, her bare feet half-buried in the wet sand. Something in her posture, the slight tension in her shoulders, the way her hands were clasped tightly in front of her, told him she was ready to share what had been troubling her.

"Walk with me?" she asked as he approached, her voice barely audible above the surf. She didn't turn to look at him, but her hand reached back, finding his with practiced certainty.

They walked in silence for a while, their footprints filling with seawater behind them. The beach was deserted save for a few seabirds picking their way along the tide line. The fading light cast long shadows across the sand, stretching their silhouettes into elongated versions of themselves.

"Joseph," Mary began finally, her voice steady despite the tremor in her hands, "there's something I need to tell you about. Something I've been... experiencing."

He squeezed her hand gently, encouraging her to continue. The waves seemed to pause between crashes, as if the ocean too was listening.

"I've been having dreams," she continued, her eyes fixed on the horizon where the last sliver of sun was disappearing. "But they're not ordinary dreams. They're so vivid, so real that when I wake up, I can still feel them lingering."

Joseph's brow furrowed in concern. "What kind of dreams?" Joseph watched her profile in the gathering dusk, noting the way she drew her lower lip between her teeth, a gesture he knew meant she was struggling to find the right words.

"In these dreams," she went on, "there are... figures. Dark shapes that move in ways that shouldn't be possible. They whisper in languages I've never heard but somehow understand. And there's this man..." She shuddered slightly, despite the warmth of the evening. "I can never see his face, but he reaches for me, trying to pull me to him."

They had stopped walking now, standing together as the first stars began to appear in the darkening sky. Joseph turned to face her, taking both her hands in his. "How long has this been happening?"

"Since before the wedding," she admitted. "But there's more." She met his eyes now. "When I'm awake, I see things. Auras around people, some radiant with light, others..." She swallowed hard. "Others so dark they seem to absorb the light around them."

"I think," Mary whispered, her voice gaining strength, "there are forces at work here, Joseph. Dark things that want to harm us. To harm our child.

"Joseph's grip on her hand tightened, a silent gesture of support.

Her gaze returned to his, filled with a mixture of fear and determination. "I think there are things. Dark, malevolent things that want to hurt us."

"Whatever's coming," he said firmly, "whatever these things are, we'll face them together. You and me." He placed a hand gently on her stomach, where their child was growing. "All of us."

Mary's smile was fragile but real. "I knew you'd believe me. Somehow, I knew."

They stood there as full darkness settled over the beach, holding each other while the stars emerged one by one above them.

She leaned into him, seeking the comfort of his embrace. "We have to protect our child, Joseph. No matter what." She was convinced their journey together was about to take a turn, but with Joseph by her side, she felt stronger.

They shared a passionate kiss under the moonlit sky, sealing their promise to confront whatever lay ahead. As they broke the kiss, Joseph looked into Mary's eyes and said, "No matter what."

After the final day of their honeymoon faded, Joseph and Mary returned home. The separation at the airport was harder than either had anticipated. Mary to L.A., to and Joseph was journeying to Jerusalem. From his window seat, Joseph watched the American coastline recede beneath the clouds. As he crossed the Atlantic, his thoughts drifted between Mary's revelations and the looming challenges in Israel. The construction project that had once seemed straightforward now a heavy burden.

Tel Aviv emerged from the haze like a city in a mirage, its modern towers rising above ancient stones. The air that hit Joseph's face as he descended the plane stairs was thick with heat and the complex perfume of spices, salt, and sunbaked earth. Despite his family's heritage, he felt like a stranger here, caught between worlds. He had grown up hearing his grandmother tell stories about Israel, how she and his grandfather survived during the war were etched into the canvas of his memory.

The drive from the airport revealed a city of contrasts. Modern glass buildings reflected traditional architecture, while market stalls spilled their colorful wares beneath the shadow of construction cranes. The driver, an elderly man with kind eyes, pointed out landmarks in heavily accented English, but Joseph's attention was drawn to the construction site that dominated the skyline. The temple that would either be his family's salvation or their undoing.

The limo wound its way through labyrinthine alleys, where whitewashed buildings adorned with colorful murals stood shoulder to shoulder. Here, the ancient mingled with the modern, and centuries of stories whispered from every stone and shadow. The air was filled with the lilting melodies of street musicians and the spirited conversations of locals and tourists alike.

Joseph watched the downtown cityscape pass by; his gaze momentarily lost in the ebb and flow of life outside the car window.

Joseph stepped out of the limo onto the sunbaked earth and stood gazing at the structure. He was no longer just a real estate developer, but a guardian of something far greater. Has anyone in history felt as much pressure?

The site itself was a hive of organized chaos. Hundreds of workers moved with purpose through a maze of scaffolding and machinery. The foundation stones, massive blocks of Jerusalem limestone, seemed to glow with an inner light in the harsh sun. He missed the simplicity of the early days with his father in the office, where the only weight on his shoulders had been that of the wooden frames of the single-family homes and the dreams of his customers. Here, he was being slowly overwhelmed.

Dust kicked up around his footsteps as he made his way toward the heart of the construction site. A meeting with the inspector from the Chairman's office was scheduled to assess the construction's progress. *Just another straw on the camel's back,* Joseph thought.

"Mr. Riesman?"

Joseph turned to find himself face to face with a tall man in an impeccable charcoal suit that seemed untouched by the dust and heat. His features were sharp, almost too perfectly formed, and his eyes... Joseph had to force himself not to step back. There was something in his face that reminded him of deep water, beautiful but dangerous.

"I'm Malcolm," the man said, extending his hand. "From the Chairman's office."

The moment their hands should have met, an invisible force seemed to push them apart. It wasn't dramatic, more like the subtle repulsion between matching magnetic poles, but they both felt it. Malcolm's expression shifted minutely, a flash of something ancient and calculating crossing his features before being replaced by a professional smile.

"I was expecting Jacob," Malcolm said, his voice carrying undertones that made Joseph's skin prickle. "I hope everything is... well with him?"

"He is fine and sends his regards. I will be stepping in to oversee the project. I am Joseph, his son."

Malcolm studied him for a moment. "It seems things are falling into place, but has the cornerstone we designed been delivered yet?" asked Malcolm.

The foreman responded, "No. No sir, not yet. There were some issues."

"Issues?" said Malcolm as he glared at the foreman. "What issues?"

"Well, I... I... am not really sure, but," the foreman stammered to answer. To his great relief, he caught a glimpse of Joseph approaching over Malcolm's shoulder. "But Mr. Riesman may be better able to answer."

Malcolm turned to face Joseph, and their eyes met. In that moment, an unseen energy crackled within Malcolm, like an electric discharge before a storm. His senses tingled with the unmistakable presence of celestial energy. A blessing, as the humans call it, emanated from Joseph. Is this an angel? No. Not that. The energy was different, and it wasn't as potent. He was, without a doubt, human, but a human touched in a way Malcolm hadn't encountered in thousands of years. For the first time in a millennium, Malcolm was momentarily speechless.

As Joseph caught the eyes of Malcolm, a shiver ran down his spine. Something was happening here. His instincts screamed at him, and he was gripped with a sudden urge to run that outweighed anything he had ever experienced in his life.

"Ah yes. Joseph Riesman. Interesting. A family operation," mused Malcolm. His piercing gaze continued to survey Joseph from head to toe, the intensity of his scrutiny only heightening Joseph's unease. "Funny he never mentioned you."

Joseph tried to explain, "Apologies. I'm sure it just slipped his mind. He is incredibly busy. Being pulled in all kinds of directions."

"Indeed." Malcolm's smile didn't reach his eyes. He gestured toward the construction site. "Shall we?"

Joseph, eager to dispel the strange tension that had enveloped their meeting, finally broke the silence. "Well, may I show you around?"

"That's why I'm here," Malcolm replied.

"I've heard much about your company," Malcolm continued, his tone taking on an almost casual demeanor as they navigated through the ongoing construction.

Joseph, eager to divert the conversation toward something more familiar, replied, "Yes, we've been fortunate to have some excellent projects in the past. This temple is our most ambitious yet, but I believe it will be a testament to faith for generations to come."

"Indeed," said Malcolm. He glanced at the towering walls of the temple, then turned his attention back to Joseph. "Your father assured me this project would be his masterpiece," Malcolm said, pausing beside a massive foundation stone. His fingers traced patterns on the rough surface. "A temple worthy of... higher powers."

"We're committed to making it exceptional," Joseph replied, trying to match Malcolm's professional tone.

"And how is your father, really?" Malcolm's gaze pierced through Joseph's careful composure. "I hope nothing... unfortunate has happened?"

"As I said, he's fine," Joseph said quickly, too quickly. "Just needed some time to focus on other aspects of the business."

"Hmm." Malcolm studied a set of blueprints, but his attention seemed elsewhere. "And you're recently married, I understand? How... fortunate. Tell me about your wife."

"Mary? She's... she's back home. The travel would be too much right now."

"Oh?" Malcolm's eyebrow arched with interest. "Is she unwell?"

"No, she's pregnant." The words left Joseph's mouth before he could stop them, and he immediately wished he could take them back.

"A child. How wonderful." Malcolm's voice dropped to a near whisper. "New life is such a... precious thing. So full of potential. So... vulnerable."

The air between them seemed to grow thick and cold. A nearby worker dropped his tools with a clatter that made Joseph jump, but Malcolm didn't even blink.

"And is that your first child on the way, Joseph?"

"Yes, it is. Our first child. We're both looking forward to it. "

"I would very much like to meet her one day," Malcolm continued, his smile now showing too many teeth. "I'm sure she has a certain... energy about her. Like yourself."

Joseph fought the urge to flee. "Perhaps. When the timing is right."

"Yes, timing is everything, isn't it?" Malcolm checked his phone, his manner suddenly businesslike again. "Speaking of which, I'm afraid I have an urgent matter to attend to. We'll continue this another time."

He turned to go, then paused. "Oh, and Joseph? It's a profound journey, being a father. Your priorities shift, your fears and hopes deepen, and the world takes on a different hue."

Joseph, still perplexed by the inspector's probing, replied, "You sound like you know what it's like."

Malcolm's smile was enigmatic. "I've seen many fathers, Joseph. I've witnessed their struggles, their sacrifices, their failures. It's a path filled with both light and shadow."

Do take care of yourself. And your family. These are... uncertain times."

Joseph nodded, starting to feel an unusual connection with Malcolm, as though he was revealing more than he had intended.

Before Joseph could respond, Malcolm's cell phone buzzed. After checking it, his demeanor shifted once more, this time taking on an air of urgency. "I'm sorry, Joseph, but I just received an urgent message. There's an emergency I need to attend to immediately."

"Is everything alright?"

Without responding, Malcolm made a quick exit, jumping in the black suburban limo, leaving Joseph standing alone in the cloud of dust swirling around him. Only when the vehicle disappeared from sight did he realize he'd been holding his breath.

That was surreal, he thought. *But I'm glad he's gone. Man, he gives me the creeps.* As he walked back to his car, his thoughts drifted to Mary. It was nearly time for their daily call, and he couldn't wait to tell her about his day.

Malcolm reclined in the back of his sleek, black suburban. He picked up his smartphone, fingers dancing across the screen as he dialed a number saved under an unassuming contact name. The voice on the other end was gruff, gravelly.

"Yes," Malcolm spoke quietly, leaning forward as if to share an intimate secret. "I think I've found a link to the light." There was a pause on the other end, a pregnant silence where anticipation hung heavy.

"Look up Mary Riesman," Malcolm continued, his tone hushed but resolute. "Find out everything you can about her. I have a feeling she's the key."

The voice on the other end murmured something indiscernible, but Malcolm had already ended the call. The limo sliced through the bustling streets of Jerusalem, and Malcolm contemplated the path ahead. This Joseph, who it seemed was delivered right to his doorstep, the search for the mysterious Mary Riseman, it was all so thrilling.

Joseph reached his hotel room, weary and strangely drained. The keycard took three tries before the lock finally opened. Room 217 was unremarkable, generic paintings, worn carpet, old digital alarm clock on the nightstand. He'd stayed in dozens of rooms just like it over his years in construction. He stumbled inside, letting his construction vest fall to the floor as the door clicked shut behind him. Sitting down on the edge of the bed, he ran his fingers through his hair and rolled his shoulders, trying to ease the tension that had built up over the day. The foundation work wasn't going as smoothly as he'd hoped, the soil composition was odd, making it difficult to get the stones to set properly. He'd have to double-check the geological survey tomorrow.

"Just need some rest," he muttered, his voice bouncing softly off the walls. He'd call Mary soon, check on her and the baby. Their baby. Even after months to come to terms with it, the thought still caught him off guard. Joseph sank as he lay back onto the bed, the springs creaking softly beneath him. Just a moment's rest before dinner and that call to Mary. But the moment his eyes closed, sleep took him into darkness, and the dream began.

Suddenly he was at the construction site. The finished temple loomed before him, but something was terribly wrong. Cracks spider-webbed across the walls he'd worked so hard to build, spreading like veins beneath skin. The evening air felt thick and still, pressing against his chest.

Panic tightened in his chest as he raced inside his footsteps thundering through empty corridors. The emergency lights flickered, throwing wild shadows across freshly laid tile. Somewhere deep in the building, water dripped with metronome precision, tap, tap, tap, like a timer counting down.

"Mary?" His voice echoed strangely, bouncing back to him distorted and wrong. The support columns he'd just installed were failing, hairline fractures creeping upward as construction dust rained down with each structural groan.

The temple was dimly lit with torches, a malevolent radiance that seared his very soul. The interior pillars of the temple crumbled as he rushed to find Mary. He found her in the main chamber, alone and heavily pregnant. Her hands were pressed protectively against her swollen belly, her face pale in the dim light. Dark shapes moved in the shadows behind her, maybe people, maybe something else, getting closer with each passing moment. "Mary!" The shout died in his throat. His feet were stuck fast, as if the concrete had never cured. He could only watch, helpless, as the cracks spread faster, as the shadows crept closer to his wife and unborn child.

The ceiling gave way with an ear-piercing crack. Mary looked up, tried to run, but she was too slow, too heavy with their miracle child. The concrete came down in crushing slabs, and he couldn't look away, couldn't even blink.

Then he stood in the aftermath. Rain mixed with blood in shallow puddles. Two bodies lay broken in the rubble, his own steel-toed boots, Mary's favorite blue dress. Between them, wrapped in what looked like a hospital blanket, something small and motionless. The shadows still moved through the ruins, but now they looked almost normal, insurance adjusters in dark suits, documenting the catastrophic failure that had claimed three lives instead of one.

Joseph jerked awake with a gasp, his heart hammering against his ribs. Cold sweat soaked through his shirt, and for a moment, he couldn't remember where he was. The hotel room was dark now, the digital clock's red numbers casting a faint glow: 7:17 PM.

He stumbled to the window and yanked open the curtains. Jerusalem spread out below, its streets beginning to light up as night approached. The sight should have been comforting, ordinary life going on as usual. Instead, it only heightened his sense of isolation.

The dream clung to him like cobwebs. This wasn't just construction anxiety or new-father jitters. This was something else, something that connected to Mary's own nightmares. His fingers trembled slightly as he grabbed his phone and dialed her number.

"Hey babe! How are you?" Mary's voice was warm, familiar.

Joseph's throat was dry as he forced out the words: "We're not safe."

Chapter

11

PULLING OUT THE RUG

The mega church's parking lot was nearly full as the Sunday evening service approached. Mary sat in her car, hands clasped together in prayer, her knuckles white from the tension. Joseph's warning from their earlier call kept repeating in her mind: *We are not safe.*

Even the familiar comfort of her car felt different tonight, her anxiety casting everything in a different light. The engine hummed quietly as she tried to focus on prayer, to find some peace amid her churning thoughts. But the words wouldn't come easily, drowned out by worry and doubt.

What did the visions mean? Why was this growing fear inside her? Was her child truly a blessing or something that would bring suffering? The thought of the responsibility pressed down on her.

Through the windshield, she watched the congregation entering the building, their faces lit by the warm glow of the entrance lights. With a deep breath, she stepped out of her car and made her way inside.

In an unremarkable sedan at the far end of the lot, Deacon watched intently. Beside him, Ethan sat quietly, his face gaunt and tired, marked by the toll of his bargain.

"Is this the place?" Ethan asked, his voice rough with fatigue.

"Yes," Deacon replied, studying the building with cold calculation. "She's here. Heaven's secret weapon." He paused, considering their next move. "We could be in for quite a fight."

Deacon leaned back, a slight smile playing at his lips. "That woman, Mary. I bet she's the key to whatever they're planning. Malcolm certainly thinks so." His voice was quiet but determined. "You'll help me get the information we need from her, and then you'll handle her."

"Me?" Ethan protested, a flash of his old self showing through. "Why me? This is what you want, not me."

"The only reason you are not eternally suffering right now is because you agreed to do my bidding. Deacon said matter-of-factly. "I cannot harm a human directly. But you can. This is what you agreed to."

"To be your executioner?" Ethan's voice cracked. "I don't want to do it."

"Yes, you will," Deacon replied coldly. "You no longer have a choice. You're locked in." His tone, taunting. "Now, go park until you hear from me. With the way you look, I don't want you scaring her away or drawing attention."

Deacon stepped out of the car, donning his cowboy hat and straightening the leather vest he picked up from the fallen biker like it was a tailored suit. His careful composure and pleasant smile made him look like any other churchgoer seeking Sunday evening worship. He moved through the crowd easily, just another face in the sea of people entering the sanctuary.

The vast auditorium was filling quickly, its high vaulted ceilings and painted frescoes looming above the gathering congregation. Their voices created a steady murmur of conversation and anticipation for the evening service.

Deacon found a seat, scanning the crowd methodically. When the lights dimmed and the band took their places, he finally saw her.

The lights dimmed and the crowd cheered. The Temple hour was about to begin. The band entered the stage and took their places behind their instruments. And then he saw her-the young woman he was sent to find.

Mary's heart raced as she stepped onto the stage alone, acutely aware of her pregnant form under the lights. Her first performance since learning she was pregnant.

"Mary," Deacon whispered, immediately realizing she was different. The protective blessing that enveloped her blazed like a lighthouse. It was undeniable, Heaven's shield shrouded her, a level of divine protection that had not graced his senses in a thousand years. But yet, she was not the source.

And she was pregnant.

If she is not the source of the light he had been hunting, instead, could it be the child growing within her? Could it be that this unborn child was Heaven's secret weapon? A baby, of all things, the center of so much cosmic attention?

Deacon found himself unexpectedly moved by Mary's voice as it filled the sanctuary. Despite himself, he remembered other songs, older songs, from a time before his fall. He had been called Asmodiel then, along with Baaliel and others. Part of the Host, helping create the most beautiful sounds the universe had ever known. The memory was sharp, aching.

The congregation sat transfixed by Mary's performance, completely unaware of the danger in their midst. As her final note faded, they erupted into enthusiastic applause.

Deacon watched her smile and accept the praise, knowing his window of opportunity was closing. Almost a shame, he thought dispassionately. But he couldn't risk whatever plans Heaven had for her child. He pulled out his cell phone and dialed.

"Ethan, my boy. Time you earned your keep." His voice was calm as he stood and made his way to the exit. "I think we can kill two birds with one stone. I'm coming to you."

When the service ended, Mary hung back in the dressing rooms, not in the mood for conversation. She just wanted to get home. The parking lot was mostly empty now, the overhead lights casting long shadows between the remaining cars. The evening air had grown cool, and she pulled her jacket closer feeling it now safe to go outside.

"Mary!" The shout came from behind her.

She turned to see a man approaching from the darkness between two vans. His smile seemed friendly enough, but something in his bearing made her pause.

"I've been looking forward to meeting you!" he called as he drew closer. "I'm a big fan."

"Thanks, who are you?" Mary asked carefully, her voice shaking slightly.

"Call me Deacon," he replied, respectfully tipping the brim of his hat. “I've come a long way to give you a message."

His words, meant to sound benign, but there was something in his voice that made her skin crawl. She met his gaze and felt a shiver run through her spine. Her gaze locked onto his, her eyes piercing the mask of charm he wore. And his aura was black. Deep and dark. Never had she seen this kind.

"I don't think I want any part of your message," Mary replied with as much conviction as she could muster, trying to keep her voice steady.

"I think you'll stay to hear what I have to say." The friendly smile vanished as he reached into his jacket and pulled out a handgun. The chrome weapon caught the dim light of the parking lot.

Her breath caught in her throat as she spotted the gun. She stepped back involuntarily, but fear froze her in place. The distant sound of an engine growing louder barely registered through her panic.

Headlights suddenly flooded the scene. A pickup truck roared toward them, tires screeching as it accelerated. Mary stood paralyzed between Deacon's gun and the oncoming vehicle. Her breath constricted, and her vision darkened as she felt her very life hanging in the balance. Deacon's sinister grin widened as the sound of the truck grew closer and he tightened his grip on the gun.

Then…

Raphael descended between Deacon and Mary in an explosion of light, the concrete cracking beneath his feet from the impact. His luminous wings radiating outwards. Their brilliance transforming the mundane parking lot.

Raphael spun around and wrapped his wings around Mary just as the truck struck, shielding her from the impact. Raphael's immovable form, sent the vehicle cartwheeling through the air, hurtling overhead. It crashed to earth- a twisted mass of metal- yards away. The force of Raphael's appearance had thrown Deacon back. He slammed into a parked car and crumpled to the ground.

"Mary." Raphael's voice carried the warmth of summer rain. He helped her to her feet, his gaze meeting hers. "You are not alone."

Deacon pushed himself up, his composure shattered. Raphael turned to face his new opponent.

"Well, well," Deacon snarled, bitterness replacing his earlier charm. "The mighty Raphael, the so-called Angel of compassion, intervening in the mortal realm? You're forbidden to interfere with humans. You can't be here in this domain."

"Neither are you." Raphael's voice was steel.

"I, unlike you, am human now. This body was freely given to me." Deacon's smile was a razor's edge.

"You will not win, Asmodeus." Raphael positioned Mary behind him, wings spread protectively.

"So, you say." With inhuman speed, Deacon charged.

The very air crackled as the two forces collided.

Raphael, moved with grace and purpose. He lunged at Deacon, a streak of divine power. Deacon, dodged with an agility that belied his true nature.

Deacon, his fingers now like claws, aimed to strike Raphael down. Raphael, materialized a golden spear in his hand and parried the blow, pushing Deacon back. The strength of their collisions shattered nearby car windows.

"Your darkness won't consume this world," Raphael declared, his spear a streak of light.

Shadowy tendrils snaked from Deacon's fingertips, wrapping around Raphael's limbs. Raphael's radiance flared, burning away the darkness. His counterattack sent the spear hurtling toward Deacon. Deacon, his smile twisted with furry, managed to dodge the spear, but only barely, and not without cost. The spear lanced across his side, searing his flesh. His cry of pain was more rage than agony. Mary watched in terrified awe.

Realizing his human form couldn't withstand much more, he retreated to the wrecked truck. He still needed Deacon's body, as half-human was more concealed than the others. He would take down Raphael but now was not the time. He reached into the mangled truck, and yanked Ethan from the wreckage by one arm. Ethan, eyes were wide with a mix of fear and confusion, spotted Raphael and couldn't help but beg him for mercy, shouting in desperation.

"Please," Ethan begged Raphael, blood running down his face. "Save me from this."

"You have made your choice," snarled Deacon. "You are bound by it until the end."

"No! Kill me! Kill me, please!" Ethan screamed as he struggled against Deacon's grip.

"He can't help you," Deacon smashed a nearby car window. "He's got his own problems now. Intervening in human free-will is a big no-no. Saving that woman broke the agreements."

Deacon turned back as he opened the passenger door. "You might even join us soon, Raphael. Fallen in disgrace. Wouldn't that be something?" With a screech, they peeled away into the darkness.

Raphael turned to Mary one last time. Her face was streaked with tears and makeup, her body trembling. Then he launched skyward, vanishing in a flash of light that left spots dancing in her vision. Leaving Mary as the only remaining sound- her ragged, uneven breath.

Mary, finally managing a semblance of composure, ran back inside, her heels clicking on the marble floor as she searched frantically.

"Liz! Liz, please help me!" Tripping over her feet, she stumbled through the hallways calling out.

She found Elizabeth in the prayer room, where hundreds of candles cast flickering shadows on the walls. The smell of incense hung thick in the air. Elizabeth knelt before the altar, deep in prayer.

"Elizabeth!" Mary's voice cracked.

Elizabeth whirled around, her face transformed from surprise to concern as she took in Mary's disheveled state. "Mary, what happened?"

"I was attacked," Mary gasped between breaths. "A man, Deacon, he had a gun. He tried to kill me, tried to run me over," she managed to gasp out. "He was a demon, I think."

Elizabeth's hands flew to her mouth. "Dear God. Are you hurt? What happened?"

"An angel saved me." The words hung in the air, impossible yet true.

Elizabeth stood frozen for a moment. "We need to call Joseph. Right now."

Mary nodded, fumbling for her phone with trembling hands. As the phone rang, the Temple's alarm system blared to life, police sirens wailed in the distance, growing closer.

The officers arrived quickly, abruptly bursting into the Temple with their flashlights cutting through the dim light. Elizabeth stuck her head out of the room. "In here!" she shouted, gaining their attention.

The police moved swiftly, setting up a perimeter around the Temple as soon as they were confident in Mary's and Elizabeth's safety. They then began their investigation. Officers fanned out, seeking witnesses to the commotion. Flashlights flickered across the scene casting eerie shadows. A detective approached with a notepad as paramedics began to check Mary for injuries.

"Can you tell me exactly what happened?" the detective asked, notepad ready.

Mary described the attack, choosing her words carefully when it came to Raphael's intervention. The officer's expression remained professionally neutral, though his eyebrows rose slightly at parts of her account.

The paramedics worked efficiently, their touch gentle but firm as they checked Mary for injuries. They cleaned and dressed the shallow cuts and bruises on her arms, the aftermath of her desperate escape. "You're lucky," one of them murmured, his eyes kind but worried. "It could have been a lot worse."

Another officer questioned Elizabeth, trying to piece together any additional information. "Did you see the attacker? Anyone else here who might have seen something?"

Elizabeth shook her head; her voice filled with concern. "I didn't see him, but please, you have to help us. Please find this man. What if he comes back?"

The lead officer exchanged a look with his partner, skepticism clear on his face, but he continued to write down their statements. "We'll investigate all leads, ma'am," he said, though his tone betrayed his doubts. "For now, we'll ensure your safety."

"We need to check the security footage," another officer said.

"Of course, follow me," Elizabeth replied, her voice steady despite the chaos swirling around them.

In the small security room, they watched the attack unfold on multiple cameras. The footage showed Deacon's approach, the gun, the truck,

"There," Mary pointed, her finger trembling. "That's him."

And then something inexplicable. Deacon flying backward, fighting an invisible force, the truck flipping through the air.

"What in God's name?" an officer muttered. "Can we ID this guy?"

On cue, an officer took a screenshot of Deacon's face and sent it to the station.

The lead officer took a seat before the largest monitor, his eyes narrowing as Elizabeth rewound the footage. "He must have been on drugs or something. It looks like he was fighting a ghost, his movements are erratic and desperate."

One of the officers spoke up. "We have a match. His name is Deacon Parr, wanted for three murders, including his wife and his boss."

Mary felt the blood drain from her face. "He wants me dead."

Elizabeth put a hand on Mary's shoulder, her own fear evident but tempered to comfort Mary. "We'll keep you safe, Mary. We need to trust in the protection around us."

As the officers continued to discuss the bizarre footage amongst themselves, the lead officer turned to Elizabeth, his face a mask of concern and confusion. "Ma'am, I don't know what we're looking at here, but we'll do everything we can to protect you both."

Elizabeth nodded, her gaze shifting to Mary. "Thank you, officer. We'll need all the help we can get."

After finishing their investigation, the police escorted Mary home. Martha was waiting on the porch of Mary and Joseph's new home, rushing to embrace her as soon as she stepped out of the police car. "Mary! Thank God you're alright!"

Mary clung to her friend, her eyes welling with tears. "Martha, it was terrible. I am so scared, so glad you're here."

Elizabeth, after making sure Mary was safely inside, offered a few last words of comfort before being escorted to her own home. The officers assured them that a police car would remain on watch outside.

They spent the night in the living room, speaking in hushed voices while red and blue lights from the patrol car outside painted patterns on the walls. When Joseph finally called back, Mary's voice shook with relief.

"Joseph, thank God. I need you here. Now."

"I'm on my way," he promised. "Hold on, Mary. I'm coming."

Chapter 12

THE TRIAL

Raphael pushed open the doors to the Throne Room, his steps echoing through the vast expanse as he made his way through the hall. The floor, made of polished crystal, seemed to stretch into infinity, reflecting the light from countless stars embedded in the ceiling like a shimmering, eternal night sky. Massive columns of gleaming gold lined the hall, each inscribed with ancient, divine symbols that pulsed with a faint, otherworldly glow.

At the far end of the hall stood the Throne of God, an immense seat of gold, radiating an intense, unearthly light. Seated upon it was the Almighty, a colossal figure whose face was obscured by a brilliant, blinding light. His body, though shaped like a man's, emanated such power and holiness that it was almost unbearable to behold. Raphael felt a shiver run through him, a mix of reverence and awe.

As he walked down the long aisle, the Dominions loomed above him, lined along each side. Massive, towering figures of light and power. To his right, emerging from the swirling clouds, a colossal and enigmatic form hovered. It was a mesmerizing, intricate creature, a vast, celestial gyroscope of intertwined rings, each adorned with countless eyes that watched unceasingly in every direction. At the core of this awe-inspiring construct lay an immense, single, radiant eye, pulsating with an ethereal glow. Its gaze seemed to pierce through the veil of reality, seeing all that is and all that will be. The air around it vibrated with the hum of cosmic power, a silent testament to the omniscient presence Raphael now beheld for the first time.

To his left, another. Amidst a sea of luminescent clouds, a towering, humanoid figure stood at the forefront. Its serene face exuded an aura of calm and wisdom, surrounded by wings of purest white, each feather meticulously crafted, the essence of celestial purity. Between the wings, an eye of profound depth and clarity gazed outward, imbued with the light of the Heavens. The being had three heads, one facing right- a majestic lion, another facing left- a stern-looking ox, and the third facing forward- an eagle. These visages, symbols of strength, endurance, and vision, converged to form a guardian of the divine realm. Raphael's breath caught in his throat as he absorbed the grandeur of this massive heavenly sentinel.

Further down the aisle, as Raphael's gaze was drawn high above the swirling mists. Majestic wings unfurled. Each wing was lined with a tapestry of eyes, their sapphire irises glowing with unearthly wisdom. At the center of this divine manifestation, a grand, singular eye held dominion, its gaze powerful and all-encompassing. The wings moved with a fluid grace, creating a symphony of light and motion as they beat softly against the air. The atmosphere crackled with divine energy, each heartbeat of the wings sending ripples through the fabric of reality. The sheer scale and majesty of these creatures, embodiments of the divine's omnipotent power and boundless knowledge, were overwhelming for Raphael. Every step he took brought him closer to the throne, yet the heavenly presence surrounding him made each moment feel like an eternity. Each step forward drained his strength. This was his first encounter with these celestial sentinels, and their grandeur would forever be etched into his memory.

Raphael's heart pounded with a mix of anxiety and conviction. He knew the gravity of his actions, the breach of the divine decree, but he also knew why he had done it. The memory of Mary, vulnerable and terrified, flashed in his mind, strengthening his resolve. He clenched his fists, a flicker of firm resolve sparking within him. He had acted out of necessity, driven by a duty to protect the innocent and ensure the birth of a child who would change the world.

The lead Dominion's voice, deep and resonant like the rush of a great waterfall, broke the silence. "Raphael, you are brought here to stand before us, for directly interfering in the mortal realm."

Michael, the Archangel General, stepped forward, his presence imposing and severe. His armor gleamed with a holy light that seemed to pulse with his every breath. "Raphael has violated the decree," he declared, his voice a storm of command. "He interfered directly with the mortal realm, jeopardizing the balance. His actions must be accounted for."

Gabriel, the Messenger, moved to stand beside Raphael, his expression a blend of determination and concern. "He acted out of necessity," Gabriel argued, his voice calm but firm. "The child is crucial to the salvation of humanity. Raphael's actions were driven by duty and love, not by a desire to disrupt the divine order."

The Dominions listened intently, their many eyes fixed on Raphael, who stood resolute despite the tension in the room. He felt their judgment bearing down on him but refused to submit to it. His decision had been the right one, and he would defend it with every fiber of his being.

"Raphael," the lead Dominion spoke again, "what do you have to say for your actions?"

Raphael lifted his head and stood tall. His voice steady but filled with a righteous defiance. "I have always been a true and faithful servant," he began, his voice resonating through the vast expanse of the Throne Room. "During the Great War, I fought against my brethren, against those whom I loved dearly, because it was according to His will. I helped to cast them down. It was a time of indescribable sorrow for me."

"For all of us," the left-side Dominion responded. "Lucifer was once one of us who sit at the feet of God."

"The greatest of us," the right-side Dominion interjected.

Raphael cast his gaze to the Throne. "I have served without question, dedicating my existence to the balance of the divine order. When I saw Asmodeus closing in on the mother and child, threatening to end her life and extinguish the hope of salvation for humanity, I acted out of that same loyalty and love. I could not stand idle while evil sought to thwart Your plan. My actions were not born of defiance but of a deep and abiding faith in Your ultimate purpose. No matter the consequences I face, you know that I will always serve You, my Lord, and protect those who carry the light of Your love. I am Raphael the Healer. And I believed it was the only way to protect the child."

The towering glowing figure on the throne sat motionless and remained silent.

Michael's eyes flashed. "Your intentions do not absolve you of breaking the divine will of God. We, most of all, must maintain the balance. Interference with free-will, no matter the reason, sets a dangerous precedent."

Gabriel stepped forward, his wings unfurling slightly in a gesture of support. "How can we speak of maintaining balance and in the same breath say we must do nothing? There are times when the rules must be reconsidered to ensure the greater good. Raphael's actions, though unconventional, were in the best interest of the divine plan."

"We have heard enough," the center Dominion declared.

Raphael's heart pounded in his chest, a mix of fear and unyielding resolve. He knew he had broken the rules, and there would be consequences. The Dominions turned towards each other, silently conferring among themselves, their voices a chorus of ethereal whispers that filled the hall with an eerie, beautiful sound.

Finally, the center Dominion raised its voice, resonating with finality. "Raphael, you presume to know the plan of God. When in truth, even we who sit nearest to him, are not all-knowing of his will. Faith, trust, love and obedience are the unshakable requirements for those such as we. How could you know if the attack on the woman was not part of the plan? Did you not consider it possible that your interference could cause the very thing you say you were trying to avoid? Yet, blindly, you chose your own path instead of the path you were created to follow. The demons, your former brethren, did the same."

Raphael shouted defiantly, "I am nothing like them!"

The center Dominion continued, "You are found guilty of breaching the divine order. Like those before you, you shall be cast down to Earth, stripped of your powers. You will live in the dust as a mortal until your death and your spirit is remanded to the creator from whence you came."

"No!" murmured Gabriel under his breath.

Raphael felt a surge of despair as the reality of his punishment settled over him. He looked to Gabriel, who dropped his head solemnly, then to Michael, whose face remained impassive, but with sorrow in his eyes.

As the Dominions all extended their wings, a blinding light enveloped Raphael. He felt his divine essence being pulled from him, his wings disintegrating into nothingness. The sensation was both agonizing and profoundly sad. The last thing he saw before everything went dark was the glowing figure of God on His Throne, an inscrutable beacon of divine will.

Raphael plummeted towards Earth. Streaking like a comet through space and time, shattering through the barriers separating the unseen realms.

In a streak of light he landed in a secluded wooded area, the impact forcing the breath from his lungs The pain of the impact throbbed through his body and clouded his senses. As he struggled to his feet, he realized the full extent of his newfound vulnerability. He took his first staggered steps in his new form, no longer an angel, he was now human. Burned into the ground beneath the spot he stood was an Angelic symbol, glowing with embers from the heat, representing a single word.

Exile.

Chapter 13

DESPERATE DECISIONS

The dream came again as Joseph dozed in the back of the taxi, Mary's face contorted in agony, her screams echoing through the darkness. He jerked awake to find Jerusalem's afternoon sun painting the limestone buildings the color of old bones. His left temple throbbed where he'd been resting it against the window, and his mouth tasted of copper and dread.

Something was wrong.

The feeling had been growing all afternoon, a slow poison in his gut. The meeting with the contractors had felt off, their eyes slightly unfocused, their handshakes lasting a fraction too long. Even the air had seemed thick with anticipation, like the moment before lightning strikes.

The taxi's rearview mirror caught his attention. A black SUV had appeared behind them, keeping pace. Nothing unusual about that, except... except the men inside. Their faces were too still, too focused. Their eyes, even at this distance, seemed to burn with an unnerving intensity.

A second identical vehicle appeared from a side street. Their windows were tinted dark, but Joseph could make out the silhouettes of the men inside, rigid, unmoving, like mannequins come to life.

The taxi driver, an older man with worry beads wrapped around his wrist, must have sensed something too. His knuckles whitened as he tightened his hands on the steering wheel. He and Joseph’s eyes met in the rear-view mirror. "אתה רואה את זה?" he muttered. *Do you see them?*

The first impact came without warning. Metal shrieked against metal as the lead SUV slammed into their rear bumper. Joseph's head snapped forward, then back. The taxi fishtailed, tires screeching against ancient stone. They shot through an intersection, missing a delivery truck by inches.

The driver yanked the wheel hard right, sending them down an alley barely wider than the car. Sparks erupted as they scraped between the walls. The sound was like tormented cries.

For a moment, Joseph thought they'd lost them. The SUVs were too wide for the alley. Then he heard it, the distinctive growl of motorcycles. In the side mirror, he saw them emerging. Four riders, their movements too precise, too coordinated to be natural, as if their bodies were being controlled by unseen hands.

"Left!" Joseph shouted in broken Hebrew, recognizing a street from his work on the temple. "לשמאל!"

The driver complied, but as they made the turn, one of the riders caught up. A hand shot through the window and grabbed the wheel. Joseph caught a glimpse of the man's face, normal features twisted into something nervous and inhuman, eyes black as pitch.

The world spun. Glass exploded inward like diamond rain. Metal folded like paper. Joseph had just enough time to think of Mary, of the child, of all that would be lost, then darkness claimed him.

He came to hanging upside down, held in place by his seatbelt. The taxi's roof had collapsed inward like a crushed skull. His left arm shrieked with pain, and blood. His? the driver's? Dripped upward against gravity. Around them, a crowd was gathering, their voices a distant murmur of concern and curiosity.

Outside, he could hear sirens approaching. Through the shattered window, he saw the riders standing at a distance, their unnatural stillness a stark contrast to the growing chaos around the wreck. Police vehicles were appearing at both ends of the street. The riders exchanged glances, their movements suddenly jerky and agitated. They couldn't reach him now, not with so many witnesses.

Joseph fumbled with his seatbelt, trying to stay conscious through the pain. He fell awkwardly onto what had been the roof, his injured arm protesting fiercely. The driver wasn't moving. His worry beads had scattered across the ceiling like fallen stars.

Broken glass crunched under Joseph's palms as he crawled toward the shattered rear window. The crowd was thicker now, people pointing phones at the wreck, police pushing through to establish a perimeter. Joseph used the chaos to slip away, stumbling down stone steps, each impact sending fresh waves of pain through his arm.

He hit the bottom hard, forcing himself up on trembling legs. The maze-like streets of the Old City stretched before him, but which way led to safety? His phone buzzed in his pocket, a text from an unknown number:

You cannot hide forever. The child will never be born.

A hand seized his shoulder, yanking him sideways. Joseph spun, ready to fight, and found himself facing an old man whose eyes held centuries of wisdom- and something else, something that reminded Joseph of the way light played through stained glass windows.

"Quick," the man said in accented English, pulling Joseph through a shop that smelled of age and incense. "Those men... they are not what they seem. I know the look of those who have given themselves to darkness."

"Who are you?" Joseph gasped, clutching his injured arm.

"Benjamin," the old man replied, leading him through a back room filled with hanging carpets. "Sit. Let me tend to your arm."

Benjamin's hands were gentle but sure as he cleaned and bandaged the wound. His movements had a grace that spoke of years, perhaps lifetimes, of helping those in need. "Darkness finds willing vessels," he said softly as he worked. "Men who trade their humanity for power they don't understand. But they are still bound by human limitations. That is why they couldn't follow you through the crowd."

"You sound like you've seen this before," Joseph said, watching the old man's face.

Benjamin's smile was somber and knowing. "I have walked this earth long enough to see patterns repeat. To recognize when Heaven and hell move their pieces across the board." He finished bandaging Joseph's arm and stepped back. "My brother's car is parked two blocks east. A blue Fiat. Take it. It's a piece of junk, but it will get you to the airport. Go home to what you protect."

He pressed the keys into Joseph's hand, then touched his forehead gently. Words in ancient Hebrew flowed from his lips, a centuries-old blessing. For a moment, just a moment, Joseph thought he saw something bright shimmer in the air around the old man's finger, but then it was gone, leaving only a sense of peace and protection in its wake.

"A blessing for your safe journey," said Benjamin. "Now go. Quickly!"

The Fiat started on the first try. As Joseph navigated through Jerusalem's streets toward the airport, he kept checking the rearview mirror, but there was no sign of pursuit. The blessing seemed to settle around him like a warm cloak, keeping the shadows at bay.

He found long-term parking at the airport, leaving the keys under the visor as Benjamin had instructed. As his plane lifted off, Jerusalem receded below him, its ancient stones glowing gold in the setting sun. His arm ached, but the pain seemed distant now, less important than the urgency driving him home.

His phone buzzed one final time. He didn't need to look to know what it would say. The forces aligned against them were patient, but they were still bound by flesh and blood. And perhaps, just perhaps, he thought, that would be enough of an advantage.

The Chairman's office stood empty and dark, save for the pale glow of the city lights filtering through floor-to-ceiling windows. Malcolm stood at the glass, hands clasped behind his back, watching the distant pinpricks of cars flowing through the streets below like blood through veins. The room's silence was broken only by the soft hum of the ventilation system and the occasional crack of cooling metal as the building settled into night.

The elevator chimed.

Malcolm didn't turn as Deacon's reflection appeared in the glass. The man's borrowed body was showing increasing signs of wear, skin too pale, movements too jerky, eyes burning with an unnatural fire. The vessel was failing faster than usual.

"You lost him," Malcolm said, his voice gruff with frustration.

Deacon moved to the bar cart, pouring himself a generous measure of bourbon. His hands shook slightly. "A minor setback. The vessel's limitations were... unexpected."

"The limitations of flesh are precisely why we chose human agents," Malcolm replied, finally turning to face his subordinate. In the dim light, his own human guise seemed to shift and ripple, like smoke trapped beneath skin. "Your puppets failed because you pushed them too hard, too fast. The bodies wear down when you do that, Asmodeus."

Deacon knocked back the bourbon in a single swallow. "Don't preach to me about human vessels, Baal. I've been wearing this skin months before you crawled from the pit."

"And yet you still haven't mastered the art of subtlety." Malcolm moved to his desk, each step perfectly measured. "We have agents in place. Networks of influence. The slow poison of corruption working through the systems of power. But you, " he fixed Deacon with a stare that could melt steel ", you send inhabited human mercenaries charging through Jerusalem in broad daylight."

"They were going to take him," Deacon defended. "Bring him to us. Break him."

"And then what?" Malcolm's voice dropped to a dangerous whisper. "What would you have done with a broken shattered human? How would that have helped us find the child?"

Deacon slammed the empty glass down. "We know the child is coming. We can feel it. Every one of us from here to the pit can sense it. But we can't see it, can't track it. The Host has hidden it from us somehow. But if we had Joseph, "

"If you had Joseph, the Host would know we've identified the vessel," Malcolm cut him off. "We would lose what little advantage we have. No, we must be patient. Continue to work through our human agents. Let them think they serve their own ambitions while they actually serve ours."

And as for your other failure at the church." Malcolm's voice dripped with contempt. "Charging in like a mad beast, exposing yourself, "

"He interfered," Deacon cut him off. "Raphael physically manifested. Broke the agreement that's held since the Fall. You can't tell me that doesn't change everything."

Malcolm didn't turn. "I know. I felt the ripples of his power from here."

Malcolm fell silent, considering. When he spoke again, his voice was softer, more thoughtful. "Yes. Raphael's interference is... troubling. The Host has never dared such a direct violation before." He finally turned to face his subordinate. Deacon's vessel was deteriorating faster now, the skin too pale, movements jerky. The failed attack in the church parking lot had cost him more than just his prey.

"I had her," Deacon growled, pouring himself a drink with trembling hands. "The girl was right there. Ethan was in position. Then Raphael..." He knocked back the bourbon. "He manifested. Physically intervened. They're not supposed to do that."

"No," Malcolm agreed. "They're not. Which means something has changed."

The temperature in the room plummeted suddenly, frost crystallizing on the windows. Both demons turned as a third figure emerged from the shadows, Lucifer, chosen form was that of a young businessman, blonde hair perfectly styled, suit immaculate. But his eyes held galaxies of darkness.

"Indeed, it has," Lucifer said, his voice carried harmonics that made the building's steel frame vibrate in sympathy. "Heaven fired the first shot. An interesting perspective, no?" he said softly. "That Heaven has broken faith first?"

Malcolm and Deacon instinctively stepped back, their human vessels trembling in their master's presence. The frost spread across the floor, crackling beneath their feet.

"My lord," Malcolm began, "this violation of the agreement, "

"Was inevitable," Lucifer cut him off. "They speak of balance, of maintaining the natural order, yet they themselves upset it. This child..." His hand touched the window, frost forming patterns like broken wings. "This child is their weapon. Their attempt to shift the equilibrium. The precious balance they claim to protect. They dare not face us directly, so they plan to work through human vessels, just as we do."

"Then Raphael's interference..." Deacon ventured.

"Shows their desperation," Lucifer remarked. "They claim we're the ones who broke faith, yet they're the ones sending pieces of their divine essence to Earth, wrapped in human flesh. They're the ones hiding the child from our sight. And now they directly intervene when we get too close."

He turned to face his lieutenants, his human form flickering to reveal something vast and dark and full of fallen majesty. " Do you remember, my brothers, how they cast us down? How they claimed it was to maintain order? To protect creation from our influence? The agreement was meant to maintain balance. But they shattered it the moment they conceived this plan."

"We could respond in kind," Deacon offered. "Call forth our own armies,"

"No," Lucifer's word cracked like a whip. "They would love that, wouldn't they? To force our hand, make us the aggressors."

"What would you have us do?" Malcolm asked.

"Continue our work. If they want to fight through human proxies, we'll do the same." Lucifer's gaze fixed on Deacon. "You had an idea about this. About the singer."

"Yes, I may have a solution," Deacon said, straightening despite his vessel's pain. "The singer, Gwen. Her heart already beats with darkness. Jealousy. Bitterness. Rejection. And she has history with Joseph."

"Go on," Lucifer's eyes glittered.

"She's desperate for recognition, for power. The kind of human who would trade everything for a taste of what we could offer. And she has access to both Mary and Joseph through the church."

"Yes," Lucifer's smile widened. "Work through her. Through others like her. Let them be our instruments." The frost patterns on the windows writhed and twisted, forming images of ancient battles, of falls from grace. "If Heaven wants to wage this war through human vessels, we'll show them just how deep the human heart can descend."

The temperature began to rise as Lucifer's form faded like smoke in sunlight. Only his voice remained, echoing in their minds: "The child must never draw breath. Whatever it takes."

Malcolm and Deacon stood in silence for a long moment after their master's departure. Finally, Deacon spoke: "I'll find Gwen. Begin working on her."

"And this time," Malcolm added, "try not to let your vessel deteriorate too quickly. The girl nearly saw through your disguise at the church."

Deacon's lips twisted in what might have been a smile. "I'll do my best. But you know how it is, these human shells weren't built to contain beings like us. They fracture so easily."

He turned and limped toward the elevator, his movements growing more mechanical with each step. He pulled his cell phone from his jacket and worked his trembling thumb across the screen. "Ethan!" he shouted as the elevator doors closed behind him. "I have a job for you."

Malcolm watched him go, then turned back to the windows. The frost was gone, but he could still see the patterns it had formed, broken wings and ancient battles, playing out again in a new age.

In the distance, a church bell tolled midnight, its bronze voice carrying across the sleeping city. Malcolm allowed himself a small smile. Heaven had made the first move, but they would make the last. And this time, the light would not win.

Mary stood at their living room window, watching headlights crawl past on the street below. Each pair made her heart jump, thinking it might be

Joseph's Uber, only to sink again when they moved on. Elizabeth sat on the couch behind her, pretending to watch TV while actually watching Mary.

The police cruiser was still parked across the street, its presence both reassuring and unsettling. The officers had promised to stay until Joseph got home, but Mary couldn't shake the feeling that they were watching the wrong things. The real threats wouldn't come from anywhere their guns could reach.

Her phone buzzed. "Just landed," Joseph's text read. "On my way."

Mary's hand trembled slightly as she typed back, "Be careful."

"He'll be okay," Martha said from the couch, though she hadn't seen the text exchange. "Joseph's tough."

"Yeah," Mary replied, not turning from the window. She didn't mention the growing darkness she could see gathering at the edges of the street lights, or the way shadows seemed to pool in places shadows shouldn't be.

Thirty minutes later, car lights turned onto their street. This time they slowed, stopped. Mary's heart leapt when she saw Joseph emerge from the back seat, his left arm bandaged and held close to his chest.

She was halfway down the stairs before she realized she was moving.

Joseph looked older somehow, like the hours since she'd last seen him had carved new lines in his face. His suit was wrinkled, stained with what might have been blood, and his eyes... his eyes had seen things they were still trying to understand.

They collided in the building's lobby, arms wrapping around each other like drowning people finding a life raft. For a long moment, neither spoke. They just held on, feeling each other's heartbeats, proving to themselves that they were both still here, still alive.

"They tried to, " Joseph started.

"I know," Mary cut him off. She didn't want to hear it, not yet. Not here in the lobby where the fluorescent lights buzzed like irritated insects and the shadows in the corners seemed to lean forward, listening.

Elizabeth was waiting when they made it back to the apartment. She'd already pulled out their first aid kit, the big one, the one they'd bought when things started getting strange and band-aids didn't seem like enough anymore.

"Let me see," she said, gesturing to Joseph's arm.

"It's fine," he tried to protest. "The old man in Jerusalem already, "

"The old man in Jerusalem isn't here," Elizabeth cut him off, already unwrapping the bandage. "I am. And I want to make sure it's cleaned properly."

The wound wasn't deep, but it was severe-looking, the edges slightly darkened with bruising. Elizabeth cleaned it carefully, her movements precise and practiced, like she'd done this a hundred times before. Maybe she had. Maybe there were things about Elizabeth they didn't know, just like there were things about everything they didn't know anymore.

"Tell me," Mary said finally when Martha had finished rebandaging the arm.

So, Joseph told them. About the chase through Jerusalem's ancient streets, about the men who moved wrong, whose eyes had been too dark and too hungry. About Benjamin, who might have been more than just a kind old man. About the message on his phone: The child will never be born.

He didn't tell them about the deeper fear, the one that had taken root during those terrifying moments when the taxi was spinning out of control. The fear that this was just the beginning, that the forces aligned against them were older and darker than anything they were prepared to face.

But Mary saw it in his eyes anyway.

"We'll figure it out," Elizabeth said into the silence that followed. But her voice trembled slightly, and her hands, as she packed up the first aid kit, weren't quite steady.

"Where are Zachariah and John?" he asked suddenly, looking around as if just noticing their absence. "We should get them somewhere safe too. All of us need to go."

Elizabeth's hands stilled for a moment. "They're already gone. Zach took John and left for Vegas this morning. Said he had a feeling..." She trailed off, then resumed bandaging Joseph's arm. "I stayed behind because I knew you'd need help."

"You should go join them," Mary said, but Elizabeth was already shaking her head.

"My place is here. Whatever's coming, we face it together." Her voice was resolute, full of choices made and prices paid.

"We need to leave," he said finally. "Both of us. Get out of the city, go somewhere they can't, "

"Vegas," Elizabeth cut in. "Zachariah and John are already there. We'll be safer together, and I have connections, "

"No," Joseph shook his head. "That's exactly what they'd expect. We need to split up, make it harder for them to track us."

"Split up?" Mary's voice wavered. "After what just happened to you?"

Joseph ran his good hand through his hair, frustration evident in every movement. "They're hunting us, all of us. If we're together, we're one target. If we split up, "

"If we split up, we're vulnerable," Elizabeth countered. "There's safety in numbers. And in Vegas, I have resources, people who understand what's happening."

"What about our families?" Mary asked suddenly. The question hung in the air like smoke. "My parents, Martha's family... we can't just disappear without warning them."

"Warning them might put them in more danger," Joseph said softly. "The less they know, "

"The safer they'll be?" Elizabeth's laugh was sharp. "That's what I thought about sending Zachariah and John away, but now I wonder if I've just given our enemies two targets instead of one."

"Maybe we should, " Mary started, but a knock at the door cut her off.

Not a normal knock. Three precise beats that seemed to vibrate through the apartment like a tuning fork, making Joseph's teeth ache.

They all froze. Elizabeth moved closer to Mary, while Joseph positioned himself between them and the door. Martha grabbed the baseball bat she kept by her bed.

Another knock. The same pattern.

"Don't, " Mary whispered, but Joseph was already moving toward the door, his injured arm held close to his chest.

He looked through the peephole and jerked back as if shocked. "It's... some guy.

Mary pushed past him gently to look for herself. Through the distorted fish-eye view of the peephole, she saw a man who barely resembled the being of light who had saved her in the parking lot. His face was gaunt, with several days' worth of stubble, and dark circles under his eyes. He wore wrinkled clothes that looked like they'd been slept in. But those eyes... she recognized those eyes.... "His face. I think it's him from the church. The one who saved me. But he looks different."

"An Angel?" Elizabeth breathed.

"Maybe." Mary replied. Eyes wide.

A voice came through the door, "Hello in there. We don't have much time. May I please come in?"

"Let him in," she said.

"Mary, we don't know if, "

"Let him in," Elizabeth echoed, her voice carrying an authority that brooked no argument.

Joseph slowly unlocked the door, positioning himself between the stranger and the women. The man who entered looked even worse up close, exhausted, human, almost fragile. Nothing like the warrior who had appeared in a blaze of light at the church.

"Hello?" Mary stepped forward, but Joseph's arm blocked her path.

"Who are you?" Joseph said, his voice hard with suspicion.

"I don't blame you for doubting. For being overly cautious. I barely recognize myself these days." He looked at Mary. "But do you know who I am? You can see it, can't you? The same way you sometimes see other things."

Mary nodded slowly. Despite his haggard appearance, there was something about him, the light of his aura seemed to come from within, dimmed but not extinguished.

"You're him. The one that saved me at the church," she whispered. "What's your name?"

"Raphael," he responded. Looking down at the floor as if embarrassed what had become of him.

"Raphael the Angel?" gasped Elizabeth. "What has happened to you?" Mary asked, moving closer.

"I broke the rules," Raphael said simply. "Intervened directly in human affairs. The Host... they stripped me of my grace. Made me human." His voice cracked on the last word. "But that's not important right now. You're all in danger."

"We know," Joseph said. "They tried to grab me in Jerusalem."

"That was just the beginning," Raphael said, sinking into a chair as if his legs could no longer hold him. "They're mobilizing. Deacon, the one who attacked you, Mary. His real name is Asmodeus. And Malcolm, the one who likely orchestrated your attack Joseph... they're planning something big. And they're not working alone."

Joseph's eyebrows raised. "Malcolm. You mean the one I met at the construction site? The Vice Chairman of Religious Affairs?" he asked, not believing the words as he spoke them.

"The same," Raphael replied. "But I know him as Baal. He and Asmodeus were one of us once. Archangels like me. Or like I was," he said, trailing off.

"Who else?" Elizabeth demanded.

"The human forms they have assumed have resources. Especially Malcolm. And I believe Lucifer himself has taken interest," Raphael's words made Elizabeth inhale sharply. "Which means we need to move. Now. Tonight."

"Move where?" Mary asked. "Vegas? Elizabeth thinks, "

"No," Raphael cut her off. "That's exactly what they'd expect. I know somewhere else. People who can help us. But we have to hurry. They'll be coming, and in this form..." He gestured to his all-too-human body. "I can't protect you like I did before."

"Why should we trust you?" Joseph asked, still skeptical.

Raphael met his eyes. "Because I gave up everything to protect Mary." He nodded toward Mary and her visible bump. "And I'd do it again. But right now, we need help. There are others, former angels like me, but actually chose to become human. And there are the Paladins."

"Paladins?" Martha spoke for the first time from the couch, her face resting in her hands. Visibly overwhelmed with it all.

"Warriors. Guardians of sacred relics. They've been preparing for this longer than any of you have been alive." He tried to stand but swayed slightly. Elizabeth moved to steady him.

"When was the last time you ate?" she asked.

"Ate?" He looked confused for a moment. "I... I don't know. Is that why everything feels so..." He gestured vaguely.

"I'll grab some coffee," Elizabeth said, already moving to the kitchen. "And sandwiches. You look like you need them."

"First things first," Raphael said, accepting Elizabeth's help to sit straighter. "We need to plan. They'll be watching the airports, the bus stations. But I know another way. If you're willing to trust a fallen angel who can barely stand."

Elizabeth returned with coffee and sandwiches. Raphael stared at them like they were alien artifacts before taking a tentative bite. His eyes widened at the taste, one more new human sensation to process.

"How did you find us?" Joseph asked, still standing, still wary. "If they stripped you of your powers..."

"They took my grace, not my knowledge," Raphael said between bites. "I've been watching you both since the beginning. Mary's apartment, the Temple, this place, I knew where you'd go."

"You've been watching us?" Mary leaned forward. "For how long?"

"Since before you met. Since before..." He gestured vaguely at her stomach. "We all have our assignments. You were mine."

"And now?" Elizabeth's voice was sharp. "Why are they letting you interfere now when they wouldn't before? When they threw you out for protecting Mary at the church?"

Raphael's laugh was empty. "Letting me? They're not letting me do anything. I'm cut off. Exiled." He set down his sandwich, his appetite apparently gone. "But that's exactly why I can help now. As a human, I'm bound by human rules. Free will. Choice. The same rules that let Deacon and his kind work through human agents."

"What about our families?" Mary asked suddenly. "My parents, Joseph's father, we can't just vanish. They'll be targets."

"They already are targets," Raphael said softly. "Deacon and Malcolm... they won't hesitate to use your loved ones against you. That's why we need to move fast, get you somewhere safe first. Then we can work on protecting the others."

"No," Joseph's voice was firm. "We're not leaving them exposed. There has to be a way to warn them, protect them."

"The Paladins might be able to help with that," Raphael said. "They have resources, connections. Ways of making people... disappear when they need to. Making them hard to find."

"And why haven't these Paladins helped before now?" Martha asked from her position by the kitchen door.

"Because they're bound by rules too. They can't interfere unless they're directly asked by one of us." He looked at Mary. "By you, specifically. As the mother."

"This is insane," Joseph muttered, running a hand through his hair. "Fallen angels, secret societies... what's next? Dragons? Elves?"

"Actually..." Raphael started, but Elizabeth cut him off.

"How much time do we have?" she asked. "Really?"

Raphael's face darkened. "Hours, maybe. Malcolm's failure in Jerusalem will make them more aggressive…" He trailed off, looking at the window where the city lights twinkled innocently. "I guarantee they're already moving pieces into place. People who can be turned, corrupted. People close to you."

Their minds raced at the notion.

Raphael peered at them grimly. "The darkness knows how to use human weakness. Jealousy. Bitterness. Despair. They'll find the cracks in people's souls and widen them until..."

"Until what?" Joseph demanded.

"Until they have enough human agents to do what they cannot do themselves." Raphael stood, steadier now after the food. "That's why we need to go. Now. Tonight. The Paladins can help protect you all, but first we have to get you to safety."

"And where exactly is safe?" Martha asked. "From what you're saying, nowhere is really safe."

"Not nowhere," Raphael said. "Just... somewhere they won't expect. Somewhere protected by light older than their darkness." He looked at Mary. "But it has to be your choice. All of this, the Paladins, the protection, the escape, it has to come from you. That's the rule they can't break, no matter how hard they try. Your free will. Your choice."

Mary felt everyone's eyes on her. Outside, a siren wailed in the distance, and somewhere a dog began to bark. Normal city sounds that suddenly felt like warnings.

"Tell us about these Paladins," she said finally. "Tell us everything."

Raphael finished his second sandwich before speaking, as if gathering strength for what he needed to say. When he finally looked up, his eyes had that old light again, just for a moment.

"The Paladins guard with three objects," he said. "The staff of Moses, David's sling, and Elijah's robe. Sacred artifacts with real power. Power that could be... dangerous, in the wrong hands." He took a sip of coffee, grimacing at its bitterness.

"Protecting them from what?" Joseph asked.

"From us. Angels, demons, beings that weren't meant to walk this world. The artifacts create... barriers. Sanctuaries. Places where the natural laws still hold, where we can't simply tear through reality to get what we want."

"For what moment?" Elizabeth asked, though her tone suggested she already knew.

"For him," Raphael gestured toward Mary's stomach. "They just didn't know when, or how. Or through whom. Only the promise in prophecy of a savior."

Martha scoffed from her place by the kitchen door. "So, they're what, some kind of secret society? Men in black with holy hand grenades?"

"Actually, they're mostly ranchers, teachers, mechanics," Raphael said. "People with normal lives, normal jobs. The best hiding place is in plain sight. But they're also fighters, scholars, guardians. They've been watching, waiting. And now..."

Now what?" Joseph demanded.

"Now they know it's time. The signs are clear. Lucifer's involvement, the comet that's coming, "

"Comet?" Mary interrupted. "What comet?"

"You haven't seen the news? They're calling it the Millennial Star. It'll be visible in a few months, right around your due date." Raphael's laugh was dry. "Humans think it's just astronomy. It's not. It's a beacon, a signal. One that both sides have been waiting for."

Joseph paced the small living room. "This is unbelievable. You're talking about secret societies and magic artifacts like they're, "

"Like they're what?" Raphael cut him off. "Like they're as far-fetched as angels? Demons? Divine pregnancy? Where exactly is your line for what's believable anymore?"

Joseph stopped pacing, the truth of those words hitting him like a physical blow.

"These Paladins," Elizabeth said into the silence that followed. "They can help protect our families?"

"They can try," Raphael said. "They have resources, connections. Ways of making people disappear when they need to. Making them hard to find."

"And what's the catch?" Martha asked. "There's always a catch with this kind of thing."

Raphael's face grew serious. "The catch is that once we go to them, we're in their world completely. No half measures. No going back. And they'll expect everyone, all of you, to learn to fight. To protect. To be ready."

"Ready for what?" Mary asked softly.

"For war," Raphael said simply. "Because that's what's coming, whether we're ready or not. Malcolm won't stop. Deacon won't stop. They'll keep coming, keep trying to prevent what's meant to happen. And the Paladins... they're our best chance at making sure they fail."

The room fell silent as they absorbed this. Outside, the city continued its nighttime rhythm, unaware of the forces gathering in this small apartment, of the choices being weighed that would affect everything.

"So," Raphael said finally, looking at Mary. "What's it going to be?"

Mary felt Joseph's hand find hers, squeezing gently. Elizabeth moved closer, her presence steady and sure. Martha straightened by the kitchen door, her face set with determination.

"Tell us where to go," Mary said.

"First thing," Raphael said, standing straighter now, some of his old authority returning despite his human form. "They'll be watching the obvious routes, airports, bus stations, major highways. And they'll have people looking for your cars, your phones, anything that can be tracked."

"So how do we get out?" Joseph asked.

"We split up. Two vehicles, different routes." Raphael started pacing, his movements jerky with newfound human anxiety. "Martha, can you still get access to your father's dealership?"

Martha nodded slowly. "He keeps the key codes in his office. I could... borrow something. Something they wouldn't expect us to be driving."

"Good. Elizabeth, you'll take Mary in whatever Martha can get. Joseph, you're with me in my car. Different routes, different destinations. We meet at the first sanctuary."

"No," Joseph said immediately. "I'm not leaving Mary."

"That's exactly why you have to," Raphael countered. "They'll expect you to be together. They'll be looking for a couple. But a woman with an older woman? A man with a rougher-looking stranger? We'll be harder to spot."

"He's right," Elizabeth said softly. "The less obvious we are, the better chance we have."

Mary squeezed Joseph's hand. "How long?" she asked Raphael.

"Twelve hours. Maybe less. The first sanctuary is an old church in Oklahoma. Small place, easy to miss. But protected." He turned to Martha. "How fast can you get those cars?"

"Give me an hour. Maybe less if traffic's light."

"Good. Pack light. One bag each. Nothing traceable. No phones, no credit cards, nothing they can use to find us." He looked at Elizabeth. "You know what route to take?"

Elizabeth nodded. "The old ways. The ones that don't show up on maps anymore."

"I'll need to call my parents," Mary said. "Warn them somehow, "

"No," Raphael cut her off. "No contact. Not yet. Once we reach the sanctuary, the Paladins can help us protect them. But right now, any contact just puts them in more danger."

"What about clothes? Food? Money?" Martha asked practically.

"Use cash," Raphael said. "Enough to get us there. The Paladins will have supplies waiting. Right now, speed is more important than comfort."

Joseph was still shaking his head. "I don't like splitting up. If something happens, "

"If something happens, we adapt," Raphael said. "But we have to move. Now. Every minute we stay here..." He glanced at the windows, where the city lights seemed dimmer somehow, as if shadows were gathering.

"Martha, go," Elizabeth said decisively. "Get the cars. We'll be ready when you get back."

As Martha grabbed her keys and slipped out, the others began moving with sudden purpose. Mary and Joseph disappeared into their bedroom to pack. Elizabeth stood watching the street below, her posture tense.

"You know what's really coming, don't you?" she asked Raphael quietly.

"Yes," he replied. "So do you. You've always known."

"Will we be enough? These Paladins, the sanctuaries, will any of it be enough?"

"It has to be. Because if it's not..." Raphael didn't finish the thought.

In the bedroom, Mary threw essential items into a backpack while Joseph paced, still arguing. "We could take my truck, stay together, "

"Joseph," she cut him off. "Raphael's right. We have to be smart about this." She zipped the bag closed with finality. "Twelve hours. That's all. Then we'll be together again."

He pulled her close, holding her as if memorizing how she felt in his arms. "If anything happens to you..."

"It won't," she said firmly. "We've got an angel on our side."

"A former angel," he corrected. "I'm one of the fallen now."

"Sometimes," she said softly, "you have to fall to really learn how to fight."

Outside their door, Raphael listened to their whispered conversation and tried not to think about his own fall, about the searing pain of grace being stripped away. About what it meant to be human in a world where humanity itself was about to become a battlefield. They had an hour to disappear. An hour to vanish so completely that even the forces of Heaven and hell would struggle to find them. After that, the real war would begin.

Martha returned forty-five minutes later; her face flushed with tension. "Two cars," she said, dropping sets of keys on the coffee table. "A blue

Honda Civic for Elizabeth, boring, common, practically invisible. And a beat-up Ford pickup for you guys." She looked at Raphael. "The truck's got Arizona plates. Should throw them off."

They gathered in the apartment's small living room, bags packed, faces tight with anticipation. Through the windows, the city seemed darker than usual, as if the shadows were growing thicker.

"Elizabeth and Mary take the Honda," Raphael said, his voice low and urgent. "Head east on I-40, but get off at the third exit. Take back roads. Stay off the main highways." He handed Elizabeth a folded paper. "These are the directions to the sanctuary. Memorize them, then destroy the paper."

Elizabeth nodded, tucking the paper into her jacket.

"What about us?" Joseph asked.

"We take the truck north, then cut east through the mountains. Longer route, but less obvious." Raphael checked his watch. "We leave separately. Elizabeth, you and Mary go first. We'll wait fifteen minutes, then follow."

Mary moved to Joseph, their embrace tight and desperate. "Twelve hours," she whispered against his chest.

"Twelve hours," he repeated, his voice strained. "Be careful."

"You too."

Martha hugged them each in turn. "I'll stay here, keep things looking normal. Far as anyone knows, you're all just out for the night."

A car alarm went off somewhere down the street, making them all jump. Through the windows, they could see the police cruiser still parked across the street, but something about its silence seemed unsettling now rather than reassuring.

"Time to go," Elizabeth said softly.

Mary shouldered her bag, trying to look brave and probably failing. Joseph caught her hand one last time, squeezed it hard.

"I love you," he said.

"I love you too."

Then Elizabeth was guiding her toward the door, and they were moving, and everything was happening too fast and not fast enough.

The hallway felt longer than usual, the elevator impossibly slow. In the garage, their footsteps echoed too loudly. The Honda sat where Martha had left it, looking exactly like a thousand other Hondas in the city. Perfect for disappearing.

As Elizabeth started the engine, Mary looked back at the apartment building one last time. Somewhere up there, Joseph was watching, waiting for his turn to run.

They pulled out onto the street, passing the police cruiser. Mary held her breath, but the officers didn't even look up from their phones. Just another car in the night, nothing to see.

Six blocks later, Elizabeth made an unexpected turn. Then another. And another.

"Taking the long way," she explained. "Making sure we're clean."

Mary nodded, watching the city scroll past. The streets looked different at night, unfamiliar. Or maybe she was just seeing them through new eyes, the eyes of someone running from shadows.

Back at the apartment, Joseph paced while Raphael stood absolutely still, counting minutes in his head.

"They'll be okay," Martha said, but her voice unsure.

"Time," Raphael said finally. "Let's move."

The pickup truck was older than the Honda, with rust spots and a cracked windshield. Perfect camouflage. They climbed in, Joseph behind the wheel because Raphael had admitted he didn't actually know how to drive, one more human skill he was having to learn.

As they pulled away from the curb, Joseph glanced in the rearview mirror. Martha stood in the apartment window, a lonely figure in a pool of light. Then they turned a corner, and she was gone.

The city stretched out before them, a maze of lights and shadows. Somewhere out there, Mary and Elizabeth were already running, already putting distance between themselves and the darkness that was coming.

Somewhere out there, ancient forces were moving, preparing, gathering.

And somewhere in Oklahoma, a small church waited, its centuries-old protections ready to shelter them all.

If they could just make it there alive.

Chapter 14

FLIGHT

The pickup truck's engine had a knock in it that reminded Joseph of dying things. Three hours into their escape, that knock had become a kind of torture, marking time like a broken metronome as cities gave way to suburbs, suburbs to farmland, farmland to empty desert stretching under a moonless sky.

Raphael sat rigid in the passenger seat, staring at the darkness beyond their headlights as if he could still see things out there that human eyes couldn't catch. Maybe he could. Or maybe he was just remembering what it was like when he could.

"You're sure they're okay?" Joseph asked for what might have been the tenth time.

"Elizabeth knows what she's doing," Raphael replied, his voice hoarse with exhaustion. Three hours as a human had taught him about muscle cramps, about the way a body could betray you with its needs. "She's taken this route before."

"When?"

"A long time ago. With others who needed to disappear. Don't forget. She is favored as well. With a miracle child who has an important destiny in all of this."

"Then why is she not being attacked as well?" he questioned.

"I'm not sure," replied Raphael as he turned his head. "Maybe they don't sense the same threat with her and the boy."

Joseph absorbed that, adding it to the growing list of things he was learning about people he thought he knew. The gas gauge was hovering just above a quarter tank. They'd need to stop soon, but the thought made his shoulder blades itch.

"There's a station about twenty miles ahead," Raphael said, as if reading his mind. "Small place. Safe."

"Safe how?"

"The owner... let's just say he's helped people like us before."

Joseph's hands tightened on the wheel. "Helped people running from demons?"

"Helped people running from all types of things that wear human faces," Raphael corrected. "Not all darkness comes from below. Sometimes it grows right here."

The knock in the engine got louder for a moment, then settled back into its rhythm. Like something testing the boundaries of what it could get away with.

"You know what I don't understand?" Joseph said after another mile of silence. "If you knew all this was coming, the danger, everything, why didn't you warn us sooner? Why wait until now?"

Raphael was quiet for so long that Joseph thought he might not answer. When he did, his voice was trimmed with something that might have been remorse.

"Because there are rules," he said finally. "Rules older than time. Free will has to be preserved. Choices have to be made freely. If we'd told you everything at the beginning..."

"What?"

"You might have run. Both of you. And then none of this would happen the way it needs to."

"The way it needs to?" Joseph's laugh had an edge... "My father and Mary's parents are in danger. Our whole lives are falling apart. That's the way it needs to happen?"

The former angel turned to look at him, and for a moment his eyes caught the dashboard lights in a way that made them look like they were glowing. "Do you love her?"

"What kind of question is that?"

"The most important one. Do you love her?"

"Yes," Joseph said without hesitation.

"Would you die for her? For the child?"

"Yes."

"Then that's why we waited. Because that love, that commitment, it had to be real. Had to be chosen, not commanded. Had to be human."

They drove in silence for a while after that, the engine's knock keeping time with Joseph's thoughts. The moon was a thin slice of nothing above them, offering no light, no comfort. Just endless desert and a road that seemed to go nowhere.

A sign appeared in their headlights: GAS FOOD CLEAN RESTROOMS. The letters were faded, some missing entirely, but Raphael sat up straighter.

"Pull in here," he said. "We need supplies. And I need to..." He frowned, as if trying to identify an unfamiliar sensation. "I need to use what you humans call a bathroom."

"Welcome to mortality," Joseph murmured, but he was already slowing down, turning into the station's gravel lot.

The place looked like it had been forgotten by time itself. A single light buzzed over empty pumps, drawing moths that cast enormous shadows. The store's windows were grimy, but light leaked through them, and a sign in the door said OPEN in defiance of all logic.

As Joseph killed the engine, the knock died away to nothing, leaving them in silence. But something about that silence felt off. Like something was holding its breath, waiting to see what they would do next.

The bell above the door chimed as they entered, the sound too cheerful for this empty place. A ceiling fan spun lazily overhead, stirring the hot air without cooling it. Behind the counter, an old man sat reading a newspaper so yellow with age it might have been from another decade.

He didn't look up as they entered. Just turned a page with arthritic fingers and said, "Bathroom's in the back. Coffee's fresh as it's gonna get. Holy water is under the counter if you need it."

Joseph froze halfway to the snack aisle. Raphael just nodded as if this was perfectly normal. "Thank you, Thomas."

The old man, Thomas, finally looked up. His eyes were pale blue, almost white, and they fixed on Raphael with uncomfortable intensity. "Well, well. You're looking a mite more earthbound than last time I saw you, friend."

"Things change," Raphael said simply.

"That they do." Thomas folded his paper carefully. "That they surely do. Better hurry with whatever you need to do. You've got about ten minutes before they catch up."

Joseph's heart skipped a beat. "They're following us?"

"Always were," Thomas said. "Question was just how close." He reached under the counter and pulled out what looked like a mason jar filled with clear liquid. "On the house. Might need it before sunrise."

Raphael took the jar, handed it to Joseph. "Get what we need. I'll..." He gestured vaguely toward the back of the store.

"Five minutes now," Thomas called after him. "Clock's ticking."

Joseph moved quickly through the aisles, grabbing water, energy drinks, beef jerky, anything that would keep and could be eaten while driving. His mind raced. How had they found them? How close were they?

"Wondering about the how?" Thomas asked, as if reading his thoughts. "Ain't hard when you've got eyes everywhere. Birds, bugs, stray dogs, all reporting back to their masters. Plus..." He tapped his yellow newspaper. "You're still thinking like a human. Taking human roads. Making human choices."

"We're trying to be unpredictable," Joseph insisted.

Thomas's laugh was dry as desert wind. "Son, you're trying to outrun things that were old when these roads were forests. You want unpredictable? Start thinking like them. Take roads that aren't roads. Make choices that aren't choices."

The bathroom door opened and Raphael emerged, looking slightly more composed but also more human somehow. More vulnerable.

"Three minutes," Thomas said. "Better fuel up and, "

A sound cut him off. Not quite a sound really, more like the memory of one. Like something large passing overhead, blocking out stars that weren't visible inside the store.

Thomas stood, moving with sudden urgency. "Out the back. Now. Leave the truck."

"But, " Joseph began.

"Leave it," Raphael grabbed his arm. "He's right. We need to think like them."

Thomas was already moving, leading them through a door marked EMPLOYEES ONLY into a storage room cluttered with boxes and old equipment. At the back was another door, this one heavy and metal, covered in symbols that hurt Joseph's eyes to look at.

"This leads to the old service tunnel," Thomas explained, pulling out a ring of keys. "Cold War relic. Runs about five miles east. Brother of mine keeps a garage out that way. He'll have transportation."

"Thank you," Raphael said.

"Don't thank me yet." Thomas selected a key that seemed to be made of something darker than metal. "Just remember, when this is all over, I might need a favor returned."

The sound came again, closer now. The fluorescent lights flickered.

"Go," Thomas said, pushing the door open. "Stay in the tunnel. Don't look back. And whatever you hear up here..." He hesitated. "Just keep going."

They plunged into darkness that smelled of cold concrete and older things. Behind them, Thomas sealed the door with a sound like fate closing its fist.

Joseph clicked on the flashlight he'd grabbed from the store. The beam seemed feeble in the pressing dark, barely illuminating the tunnel ahead.

Above them, something that shouldn't exist landed on the gas station's roof with enough force to shake dust from the tunnel ceiling.

"Move," Raphael said softly. "And whatever you do, don't stop."

They moved deeper into the darkness, leaving the sounds of what happened next far behind them. Or trying to, anyway.

But some sounds, Joseph was learning, had a way of following you forever.

Thomas settled back behind his counter, picking up his ancient newspaper as the bell above the door chimed again. No one came in. The bell just rang, back and forth, like something invisible was playing with it.

"Evening, Deacon," Thomas said without looking up. "That's the name you are using now, right? Coffee's fresh as it's gonna get."

The figure that materialized through the door was noticeably not as human-looking anymore. Deacon's borrowed body was deteriorating faster now, skin waxy and gray, movements jerky like a poorly operated puppet.

Behind him, Ethan, The circles under his eyes almost completely black, his movements still human and smooth....

"Where are they, old man?" Deacon's voice crackled like static.

"Lot of 'theys' pass through here," Thomas turned another yellowed page. "You'll have to be more specific."

Deacon's hand shot out, impossibly fast, grabbing Thomas by the throat. "Don't play games with me, ward-master. I can sense them. A fallen one and the carpenter."

"Can you now?" Thomas's smile was eerily calm despite the hand crushing his windpipe. "Then you can also sense this."

He pulled something from under the counter. The jar's contents swirled with shadows deeper than the night outside.

"That's right," Thomas said as Deacon released him and stepped back. "I keep the old knowledge too. The dark ones. The ones your kind taught us before the Fall. Want to see what I remember?"

Ethan moved forward, but Deacon held up a hand, stopping him. His borrowed face twisted into something that might have been a smile.

"They went south," he said. "Didn't they? Toward the highway."

Thomas shrugged. "If you say so."

"Search the building," Deacon commanded Ethan. "Every corner. Every shadow."

"Waste of time," Thomas said, carefully replacing the dark jar under the counter. "But you do what you need to. Me, I've got inventory to count."

Five miles east, Joseph and Raphael emerged from the tunnel into a garage that smelled of oil, rubber, and something sweeter, something that might have been incense. An old man who could have been Thomas's twin looked up from a car engine, wiping his hands on a rag that might once have been red.

"Right on time," he said. "Tom called. Said you'd be needing wheels."

"James," Raphael nodded in greeting. "It's been a while."

"Not so long I don't recognize an old friend. Even if he's wearing different skin these days." James gestured to a vehicle covered by a tarp in the corner. "That one's yours. Already gassed up. Papers in the glove box."

Joseph helped pull the tarp off, revealing a classic Mustang, its black paint drinking in what little light there was.

"Sweet ride," he said, running a hand along its flank.

"Better than sweet," James replied. "Engine's been blessed by a Navajo medicine man. Frame's got protections worked into the steel itself. Plus..." He patted the hood fondly. "She's fast as lightening and twice as pretty."

A sound echoed through the tunnel behind them, something between a roar and a scream, but very, very far away.

"That'd be Tom introducing our friends to some of his private stock," James said, his smile sharp in the fluorescent light. "Best get moving before what's left of them figures out, they've been played."

"Thank you," Raphael said, already moving toward the driver's side.

"Don't thank me yet," James's voice stopped him. "Tom told you about the favor?"

Raphael nodded.

"Good. Because there's a war coming. Bigger than this one. And when it does..." He looked at Joseph. "We'll need every ally we can get. Even fallen ones."

Joseph slid into the passenger seat as Raphael started the engine. It purred to life with a sound that was somehow deeper than normal, more alive.

"Head east," James said, hitting a button that raised the garage door. "Stay off the main roads. And whatever you do..." He tossed something through the window, a small leather bag that smelled of herbs and stranger things. "Don't lose that. You'll know when to use it."

They pulled out into the desert night, the Mustang's headlights cutting through darkness that seemed thicker than it should be. In the rearview mirror, Joseph watched the garage disappear like it had never been there at all.

"Those men back there," he said finally. "Thomas and James. What are they?"

Raphael's hands were sure on the wheel despite his newfound humanity. "Let's just say some families have different ideas about what to pass down through the generations."

"Like running supernatural gas stations?"

"Like keeping the balance," Raphael corrected. "Sometimes that means helping angels. Sometimes demons. Sometimes..." He glanced in the rearview mirror where the darkness was gathering. "Sometimes it means helping people caught in between."

The Mustang ate up the miles, its blessed engine singing a song that kept the shadows at bay. For now. It was a welcome change from the grating knock of the truck engine.

They had a long way to go before sunrise.

The Honda's dashboard clock read 2:17 AM when Elizabeth pulled off the highway for the third time in an hour. Her eyes kept checking the rearview mirror, watching the headlights behind them, counting them, measuring their distance.

"Another random turn?" Mary asked, though she already knew the answer. She'd been tracking their route on the mental map she'd been building, west when they should be going east, north when south made more sense. Nothing direct. Nothing predictable.

"Not so random," Elizabeth said, taking them down a road so dark the asphalt seemed to swallow their headlights. "I used to know someone out here. Someone who might help us."

Mary shifted in her seat, one hand resting protectively on her stomach. The baby seemed more active tonight, as if sensing the tension. Or maybe sensing something else. "Used to know?"

"She was like me. Still is like me." Elizabeth's hands tightened on the wheel. "Someone who understands what's really happening in the world. Who tends to see things others don't."

They turned onto what barely qualified as a road, more of a track between endless fields of something that rustled in the dark. The Honda's suspension creaked in protest.

"I didn't know there were others," Mary said carefully. "Like you, I mean."

Elizabeth's laugh was soft and wry. "I have learned there are always others, Mary. Some chosen like us, some born to it, some who just... figure it out along the way. Your gift, seeing auras, sensing things, I think that's the baby, not you."

A house appeared in their headlights, or what was left of one. It might have been a farmhouse once, but now it looked like something out of a horror movie paint peeling, windows dark, front porch sagging like a broken jaw.

"We're stopping here?" Mary couldn't keep the apprehension from her voice.

"Don't let appearances fool you," Elizabeth said, pulling up to the house. "Ruth likes it this way. Keeps the curious away."

As if on cue, the porch light flickered on. A woman stood in the doorway, though Mary could have sworn no one had been there a second ago. She was older than Elizabeth, with silver hair that seemed to glow in the weak light, and eyes that looked like they had seen too much.

"You're later than I expected," Ruth called out as they got out of the car. "Had to take the long way round, did you?"

"Being followed," Elizabeth replied simply.

Ruth nodded as if this was perfectly normal. "Well, come in then. Before they catch up."

The inside of the house was nothing like its exterior. Warm light spilled from oil lamps, illuminating walls lined with books and bottles and things Mary couldn't identify. Herbs hung from the ceiling, filling the air with sweet smoke. In one corner, something that might have been a radio played static that almost sounded like voices.

"Sit," Ruth gestured to a kitchen table that looked older than all of them combined. "Tea's almost ready."

"We can't stay long," Elizabeth started, but Ruth cut her off.

"You'll stay exactly as long as you need to," she said firmly. "Unless you want those things out there to catch up. They're closer than you think."

Mary felt a chill despite the warmth. "What things?"

Ruth's eyes fixed on her, seeing more than just her face. "Hungry things. Empty things. Wearing human shapes like ill-fitting clothes." She moved to the stove where a kettle was starting to whistle. "But they can't come here. Not unless they're invited. And I'm not in an inviting mood."

She poured three cups of tea that smelled nothing like any tea Mary had ever encountered. The liquid seemed to shimmer in the lamplight.

"Drink," Ruth commanded. "It'll help with the morning sickness. And the dreams."

Mary nearly dropped her cup. "How did you, "

"Know?" Ruth smiled. "Same way I know what you're carrying isn't just any child. Same way I know the stars are moving and the old powers are waking up. Same way I know you've got about four hours before they figure out where you've gone, and maybe another two after that before they catch up."

Elizabeth set her cup down with a sharp click. "We should go."

"Not yet," Ruth said. "First, you need to know what you're really running from. And what you're running toward." She looked at Mary again, her eyes somehow deeper than they had been. "Are you ready to hear it? Truly ready?"

Mary's hand found her stomach again, feeling the subtle movement there. Outside, the wind picked up, making the house creak like something alive.

"Tell me," she said.

Ruth settled into her chair with the deliberate slowness of someone who had all the time in the world, even though she'd just said they didn't. The static-voices from the radio in the corner grew louder for a moment, then quieted to a whisper.

"First thing you need to understand," she said, "is that this isn't just about your baby. It's about what your baby represents. Hope. Change. A shift in the balance that's held since the Fall."

"The Fall?" Mary asked.

"When the rebel angels fell. That was when the rules were made." Ruth's eyes went distant. "Heaven and Hell agreed to certain terms. No direct interference with human activities. No manifesting physically. They had to work through us, through human agents. Free will had to be preserved."

"Like Deacon," Elizabeth said softly. "Working through possessed humans."

"And like Raphael," Ruth nodded. "Though he chose a harder path. Becoming human entirely. Forfeiting his grace." She looked at Mary. "All because of you. Because of what's growing inside you."

The baby moved again, as if recognizing it was being discussed. Mary placed both hands on her stomach, protective.

"But why?" she asked. "Why is this child so important?"

Ruth's tone grew sharp. "Because it changes everything. Think about it, God working directly through a human vessel, not just influencing from afar. A piece of his divine essence taking human form. It breaks all the rules they agreed to."

"That's why they're hunting us," Mary said, understanding dawning. "The demons. Because this baby threatens their power."

"Not just about their power," Ruth corrected. "Their entire way of operating. If this child is born, if it grows to fulfill its purpose, whatever that may be, the old agreements become meaningless. The balance shifts. And Lucifer..." She trailed off, glancing at the windows where shadows seemed to be gathering.

"Since time began, he's invested everything in maintaining the current order. In keeping humanity exactly where we are, caught between light and dark, free to choose but always struggling. Our choices tearing us away from God. This child..." Ruth gestured to Mary's stomach. "This child offers a different path. A direct connection to the divine that doesn't require sacrifices, blind faith or ancient agreements."

The radio static grew louder, forming words that weren't quite words. Ruth stood abruptly, moving to silence it.

"They're getting closer," she said. "Starting to sense you even through my wards." She moved to a cabinet, pulling out a small cloth bag. "You'll need this. It's not much, some herbs, some blessed objects, a few older things. But it'll help hide you, for a while at least."

"What about the sanctuaries?" Elizabeth asked. "The Paladins?"

"Good protection, yes. But temporary." Ruth handed the bag to Mary. "Because the real fight isn't going to be won with weapons or walls or wards. It's going to be won here." She touched Mary's temple gently. "And here." Her hand moved to Mary's heart.

"I don't understand," Mary said.

"You will. When the time comes, you'll know what to do. Just remember, they can't force this. Can't stop it directly. Everything has to come through human choice. Human action." She glanced at the windows again. "Which means they'll try to force your hand. Use the people you love against you. Make you choose to give in."

The radio static grew louder, forming words that weren't quite words. Ruth stood abruptly, moving to silence it.

"Time to go," Ruth said urgently. "Take the back roads. Stay off the highways. And whatever you do..." She gripped Mary's arm with surprising strength. "Don't look back. Don't second guess. What you're carrying is more important than any one of us."

The house creaked, a sound like something large settling its weight against the walls. The radio went completely silent.

"But, " Mary started.

"No time," Elizabeth was already moving toward the door. "They're here."

Ruth's smile was fierce in the lamplight. "Don't worry about me. I've dealt with their kind before. Just go. Live. Choose. And when the time comes..."

She pressed something small and cold into Mary's hand. "Use this. You'll know when."

They hurried out into the darkness where the Honda waited like a faithful animal. As they pulled away, Mary looked back once, despite Ruth's warning.

The old house stood dark against the star-filled sky. But in one window, just for a moment, she thought she saw Ruth watching them leave. Only it wasn't exactly Ruth anymore. It was something older, bigger, wearing Ruth's shape like a borrowed coat.

Then they turned a corner, and the house vanished like it had never been there at all.

Mary opened her hand to see what Ruth had given her. It was a key, ancient-looking, made of some dark metal that seemed to drink in what little light there was.

"What is it?" she asked Elizabeth.

"Insurance, I suppose" Elizabeth replied, her eyes fixed on the road ahead. "For when everything else fails."

The Honda's headlights cut through darkness that seemed to be growing thicker by the minute. Somewhere behind them, things that weren't quite human anymore were following their trail. But ahead... ahead was dawn, and sanctuary, and maybe something more. If they could just stay alive long enough to reach it. The three black SUVs pulled up to Ruth's house like funeral cars arriving at the wrong address. No headlights. No sound from their engines. Just dark shapes materializing out of darker shadows.

Malcolm stepped out of the lead vehicle, his expensive suit somehow perfect despite the dusty road. Behind him, six figures emerged from the other SUVs, men and women in dark clothes who moved with the jerky grace of marionettes. Their eyes reflected no light at all.

"They were here," one of them said in a voice like grinding glass. "Recently."

Malcolm nodded, inhaling deeply as if tasting the air. "The ward-keeper interfered. Again." He walked toward the house, each step precise, measured. The porch steps didn't creak under his weight like they should have.

Ruth stood in her doorway, looking smaller now, more human. But her eyes were hard as she watched them approach.

"You're not welcome here," she said.

Malcolm's smile was perfect, practiced, and completely off on his face. "Come now, Ruth. After all these years? After everything we've shared?"

"Especially after all these years," she replied. "I know what you are now, what you've always been. And you're still not welcome here."

The possessed figures moved to flank Malcolm, their movements becoming less human with each step. One of them had too many joints in its fingers. Another's neck was twisted at an impossible angle.

"The girl," Malcolm said pleasantly, as if discussing the weather. "The child. You know what's at stake. What will happen if they succeed."

"I know what you're afraid of," Ruth countered. "What it means for your kind when the old agreements fall. When humanity has a direct line to divinity that doesn't need your... interventions."

Malcolm's perfect smile flickered, just for a moment showing something else beneath it, something with too many teeth and not enough face to hold them.

"Last chance, old friend," he said softly. "Tell us which way they went, and we'll make it quickly. For old times' sake."

Ruth's laugh was sharp as broken glass. "You always did underestimate us ward-keepers. Always thought we were just servants. Guardians. Lesser beings." She reached into her pocket and pulled out something that looked like a handful of dust. "Want to see what I've learned since the old days?"

She blew the dust into the air, and it hung there, glittering like starlight. Then it began to move, swirling, taking shapes that were painful to look at.

The possessed figures hissed, stepping back. Even Malcolm's perfect composure cracked slightly.

"You're not the only ones who remember the old magics," Ruth said, her voice carrying harmonics that hadn't been there before. "The ones from before the Fall. Before the agreements."

"Kill her," Malcolm commanded, but his puppets seemed frozen, caught in the swirling lights that were becoming something else, something with wings and eyes and ancient purpose.

Ruth's smile was fearsome now, triumphant. "Run back to your master. Tell him the ward-keepers remember. Tell him we choose our side freely."

Malcolm's human disguise began to slip, revealing something dark and horrifying beneath. "This isn't over."

"No," Ruth agreed as the lights around her grew brighter, taking forms that belonged in older testaments. "It's just beginning."

The SUVs peeled out, spraying gravel, their engines finally making sound, a roar like hungry things denied their meal. Malcolm's perfect suit was smoking slightly as he got back into his vehicle, as if whatever he really was had begun burning through the fabric.

Ruth watched them go, the lights around her gradually fading. Only when they were completely gone did she allow herself to sag against the doorframe, suddenly looking every one of her years and then some.

"Well," she said to the empty night. "That'll slow them down a bit. Give the girls some time." She looked up at the stars, which seemed to be arranging themselves into patterns that hadn't been seen since Babylon fell. "They're going to need it."

Miles down the road, Mary and Elizabeth's Honda ate up the dark miles, unaware of what had happened behind them. But Mary kept looking at the key Ruth had given her, wondering why it felt warm to the touch, like it was alive.

Some gifts, she was learning, came with prices attached.

And some nights lasted longer than they should, stretching out into darkness that had nothing to do with the sun's absence. This was going to be one of those nights.

The Mustang's engine purred as they pulled into an abandoned truck stop around four in the morning. The neon sign still buzzed weakly: REST EASY CAFE, though most of the letters were dark. The parking lot was empty except for a single motorcycle, its chrome gleaming unnaturally bright in the predawn gloom.

"Stay in the car," Raphael said, stepping out. His movements were stiffer now, human muscles protesting hours of driving. "Just... give me a minute."

A figure detached itself from the shadows by the cafe's door, a woman with white-blonde hair and scarred leather jacket. She moved with a predator's grace that wasn't quite human, despite her obvious effort to appear so.

"Raphael," she said, her voice carrying echoes of something older than human speech. "You look awful."

"Being human takes, some getting used to, Ariel."

She circled him slowly, studying his new form. "So, the rumors are true. You really did Fall. For them." She nodded toward the car where Joseph waited. "Was it worth it?"

"You tell me," Raphael replied. "You chose this life long before I did."

Her laugh was like bells breaking. "I chose freedom. Adventure. The open road and all its possibilities." She gestured to her motorcycle. "You chose war."

"I chose what was right."

"Same thing, in the end." She stopped circling, faced him directly. "Mallakiel and Haniel are already heading to the sanctuary. I've called in some favors. Some of the others might come."

"Might?"

"It's a big ask, brother. Taking sides again. Fighting. Some of us came down here specifically to avoid another fight."

From the car, Joseph watched their conversation with growing unease. He couldn't hear what they were saying, but their body language was clear enough, tension, old history, complicated loyalties.

"How many?" Raphael was asking.

"Three for certain. Maybe five more if Mallakiel can convince them. We've got lives here now, Raphael. Jobs. Families even. You're asking us to risk everything."

"I'm asking you to protect everything," he corrected. "If they stop this child from being born, if they maintain their grip on humanity's connection to divinity..."

"I know," she interrupted. "Believe me, I know. Why do you think I'm here?" She pulled something from her jacket, a small silver flask decorated with symbols that hurt the eye. "Here. For the road. Blessed water, mixed with something older. It'll help with the human aches."

Raphael took it gratefully. "You always did know more about being human than the rest of us."

"That's because I actually enjoy it," she grinned. "The sensations, the emotions, the sheer messy glory of it all." She glanced at the lightening horizon. "You should go. Dawn's coming, and you're not the only ones on these roads."

"The sanctuary, "

"We'll be there. Mallakiel's bringing his weapons. Haniel's bringing her knowledge. And I'm bringing..." She patted her motorcycle's seat. "Let's call them resources."

"Thank you," Raphael said softly.

"Don't thank me yet. Thank me when we've won. Or blame me if we've lost." She swung onto her bike with inhuman grace. "Oh, and Raphael? Try to look more human. You're still moving like you've got wings."

The motorcycle roared to life; a sound deeper than its engine should have been able to make. Ariel gave him a final nod, then peeled out of the parking lot, heading east toward the rising sun.

When Raphael got back to the car, Joseph was full of questions. "Who was that? What did she mean about others coming? How many of you are there?"

"That was Ariel," Raphael said, starting the engine. "She Fell during the Renaissance. Said she was bored with Heaven." His smile was fond, remembering. "She was always different, even before. More curious about humans than most of us. More willing to question."

"And these others she mentioned?"

"Mallakiel was a warrior, one of Michael's lieutenants. He chose to Fall after watching too many human wars, said he needed to understand what made them fight and die for beliefs. Haniel was a scholar, keeper of divine records. She Fell for knowledge, for understanding."

"And they're all going to help us?"

"They're going to try." Raphael took a drink from Ariel's flask, and some of the pain left his face. "There are others too. Some who've been down here so long they're almost human. Some who just recently Fell. All trying to find their way between what they were and what they've chosen to become."

The Mustang sped along the road as Raphael explained more. About angels who had chosen humanity for love, for curiosity, for redemption. About the different ways they'd found to live in the world, some hiding their true nature completely, others walking a line between divine and human.

"But why?" Joseph asked finally. "Why give up Heaven for this?"

Raphael was quiet for a long moment, watching the sun rise over distant mountains. "Because some of us believed humanity was more than just a project or a test. More than just pieces in a cosmic game." He glanced at Joseph. "Some of us believed you were worth Falling for. And that you just needed some help. Since we were forbidden to help directly, becoming human was the loophole. Once human, the hosts could no longer prevent them from engaging as they pleased."

The sanctuary turned out to be a small stone church that looked like it had been forgotten by time itself. It sat alone on a hill, surrounded by old graves whose headstones had been worn smooth by centuries of wind and rain. No power lines ran to it. No roads led directly to its door. Just a dirt track that wound through scrubland like an afterthought.

"That's it?" Joseph asked as they pulled up. "Doesn't look like much."

"That's the point," Raphael said, but his voice was tight with tension. He was staring at something Joseph couldn't see, patterns in the air around the church that seemed to shimmer like heat waves, though the morning was cool.

Three vehicles were already parked near the church: Ariel's motorcycle, a battered Jeep that had seen better decades, and what looked like a restored Model T Ford that somehow managed to look both antique and formidable.

"Mallakiel brought the weapons," Raphael said, nodding toward the Jeep. "And that's Haniel's Ford. She says it runs on prayer and whisky, though I've never been sure if she's joking."

They got out of the Mustang, Joseph's legs cramping from the long drive. The morning air felt thick, heavy with something that wasn't quite electricity and wasn't quite sound. Like the whole hill was holding its breath.

A figure appeared in the church doorway, tall, dark-skinned, wearing military fatigues that looked like they'd seen actual combat. "Brother," he called to Raphael. "You look terrible."

"Being human is harder than it looks, Mallakiel."

Mallakiel's laugh was like distant thunder. "That's what makes it interesting." His eyes, when they fell on Joseph, were older than his face, ancient eyes that had seen empires rise and fall. "So. This is the carpenter."

Before Joseph could respond, another voice cut through the morning air, sharp, precise, academic. "Of course he's the carpenter. Look at the calluses on his hands. The way he carries himself. The resonance patterns in his aura." A woman emerged from behind the church, her silver hair pulled back severely, wire-rimmed glasses perched on her nose. She carried a laptop bag that looked incongruous against the ancient stones.

"Haniel," Raphael nodded. "Still cataloguing everything?"

"Someone has to keep records," she sniffed. "Humanity's historians miss all the important details." She peered at Joseph like he was a particularly interesting specimen. "Though I must say, your choice of vessel for the divine essence is fascinating. The symbolic parallels alone..."

"Where's Mary?" Joseph cut in. "Shouldn't they be here by now?"

The fallen angels exchanged glances. "Elizabeth knows the way," Raphael said carefully. "They'll come when.... "

A sound cut him off. Another car appeared on the dirt track. The Honda, dusty but intact.

Joseph was moving before he realized it, running down the hill. When he reached the car, Mary practically fell out of the passenger seat into his arms. They clung to each other like drowning people finding shore, neither speaking, just holding on.

Elizabeth emerged more slowly, her eyes taking in the gathered fallen angels. "Quite a reunion," she said calmly as she stretched the stiffness from her body.

"Sister," Haniel stepped forward and approached Ariel. "It's been... what, three centuries?"

Give or take. But no time for that right now." She looked at the assembled Paladins. "What's important is what comes next. Because they're still coming. And they're bringing something even darker with them."

"How long?" Mallakiel asked, all business now.

"Hours, maybe less." Elizabeth said. "They would have been right behind us if not for Ruth."

"Ruth?" Haniel's eyebrows shot up. "The ward-keeper? She's still alive?"

"And apparently still fighting," Mallakiel happily confirmed. Haniel interjected, "but she can only slow them down, not stop them. Especially now that Malcolm's involved. Or should I say Baal."

The name sent a ripple through the group. Ariel, who had been leaning against her motorcycle watching everything, straightened suddenly. "Baal? You're sure?"

"Saw him myself," Elizabeth said gravely.

"Lucifer," Raphael finished. "If Baal is in play, Lucifer's taking a personal interest."

Mary's hand found Joseph's again, squeezing tight. Around them, the morning light seemed to be growing darker instead of brighter, as if shadows were gathering despite the rising sun.

"Inside," Mallakiel said suddenly. "All of you. The sanctuary's protections are stronger within the walls." He looked at Raphael. "You remember how to raise the wards?"

"Even human, I remember that much."

They moved toward the church doors, which were made of wood older than the country itself. Joseph noticed symbols carved into the frames, worn by time but still somehow sharp, still powerful.

As they crossed the threshold, Mary gasped slightly. "The air," she said. "It feels..."

"Safe," Elizabeth finished. "That's what sanctuary feels like. Remember it. You may need to recognize it again before this is over."

Inside, the church was both bigger and smaller than it looked from outside. Centuries of prayers seemed to have soaked into the stones, making the air thick with faith and memory. Haniel immediately began setting up her laptop on a pew, muttering about power sources and signal strength. Mallakiel moved to what looked like an old trunk near the altar, which Joseph would have bet contained nothing resembling normal church supplies.

"Rest while you can," Raphael told them all. "We have preparations to make, and not much time to make them."

"What are we preparing for?" Joseph asked, though he wasn't sure he wanted to know the answer.

"Battle," Ariel said simply, checking what looked suspiciously like motorcycle chains wrapped around her knuckles. "What else?"

The morning sun finally crept through the church's ancient windows, casting lines of light across the floor like bars. Or like swords. Inside the sanctuary, Mallakiel gathered them and laid out the plan while Haniel set up what looked like an ancient ham radio modified with parts that definitely hadn't come from any store.

"From this point forward, no contact with the outside world," he said, his military bearing making it sound like a battlefield order. "No phones, no emails, no messages of any kind. Nothing they can trace."

"What about our families?" Mary asked, her hand finding Joseph's. "They need to know we're safe."

"The moment you contact them, you put them in more danger," Ariel said, softer but no less firm. "Right now, they're just bargaining chips. The moment they know anything about where you are..."

"They become targets," Raphael finished.

"My father," Joseph started.

"Will be safer not knowing," Mallakiel cut in. "This isn't just about protection. It's about containment. The fewer people who know anything, the better chance we have of keeping you hidden until the birth."

Elizabeth, who had been examining the symbols carved into the church walls, turned sharply. "Until the birth? That's months away. You can't expect us to just disappear for months."

"That's exactly what we expect," Haniel said, not looking up from her radio setup. "The closer Mary gets to her due date, the easier it will be for them to track her. The child's presence will grow, becoming like a beacon. We need to keep that light hidden as long as possible."

Mary's free hand went to her stomach protectively. "And after? What happens then?"

The former angels exchanged glances. It was Raphael who finally answered. "We do not know. But one thing at a time. First, we keep you safe until the birth."

"Your families will be watched," Mallakiel said, his voice gentler now. "Not by us directly, we can't risk the connection. But there are others we will contact. They'll keep an eye on them."

"And if something does happen?" Joseph demanded. "If they need us? How would we even know?"

Haniel finally looked up from her work. "This isn't just a radio," she said, patting the jury-rigged device. "It's tuned to frequencies they can't monitor. If there's an emergency, if your families are truly in danger, we'll know." She adjusted her glasses. "But you have to trust us. Complete isolation is the only way."

Elizabeth paced the small church, her practical mind trying to find alternatives. "There has to be another way. Some kind of secure communication, some, "

"There isn't," Ariel said firmly. "Not against what's coming. They'll use everything they can against us, human resources, supernatural forces, modern technology. Our only advantage is they don't know exactly where to look. The moment we make any contact; we lose that advantage."

The silence that followed was heavy with the realization of what they were asking. No goodbyes. No explanations. Just disappearing into thin air, leaving their loved ones to worry and wonder.

"How..." Mary's voice caught. She started again. "How do we agree to this?"

"The same way you've agreed to everything else so far," Raphael said quietly. "Because of your faith and your love."

Outside, the sun had fully risen, but to Mary, its light seemed dimmer somehow. Mallakiel began unpacking his trunk of weapons while Ariel and

Haniel worked on setting up whatever precautions they could manage. The sanctuary would be their whole world now. For months.

"Okay," Joseph said finally, his voice strained. "Okay. But you swear our families will be protected?"

"As much as we can," Mallakiel nodded. "You have my word."

It wasn't enough. It couldn't be enough. But it would have to be.

Mary looked around at their strange guardians, these former angels who had chosen humanity, who knew exactly what they were asking because they'd given up everything once before. At Elizabeth, who was seeing her whole understanding of reality shift yet again. At Joseph, whose grip on her hand told her everything his face was trying to hide.

This was their life now. This ancient church, these fallen warriors, this waiting game against forces they were only beginning to understand.

The war for the future had begun. And they'd just agreed to its first devastating cost.

Chapter 15

STRIKE

The sanctuary's old walls seemed to press in closer at night, as if the darkness made them hungry. Joseph sat in one of the back pews, unable to sleep, watching shadows dance in the candlelight. The others were scattered throughout the church, Mallakiel keeping watch by the door, Haniel buried in her research, Ariel maintaining their weapons. Mary had finally fallen into an uneasy sleep in one of the makeshift beds they'd set up in the vestry.

"Can't sleep?" Raphael's voice came softly as he settled into the pew beside Joseph.

"Every time I close my eyes, I see my father," Joseph said. "Sitting alone in that penthouse, drinking. Wondering where I've gone." His laugh was bitter-sounding. "Some son I turned out to be."

"You're protecting your family by staying away."

"Am I? Or am I just hiding?"

Raphael was quiet for a moment, considering. When he spoke, his voice bore the pangs someone who knew exactly what leaving family behind felt like. "Sometimes the hardest part of love is knowing when to stay away."

"Is that what you tell yourself? Since you got kicked out?"

"Every day since I have been human." Raphael's smile was sad in the candlelight. "It gets easier. Eventually. Or at least that's what I'm told."

In the vestry, Mary lay awake, despite Joseph's assumption. Her hand traced circles on her growing belly while her other hand clutched her cell phone. It would be so easy. Just one call, one text, just to let them know she was okay...

The phone felt like it was burning in her hand, tempting her. More than she could bear.

She waited until she was sure everyone was distracted. Mallakiel was checking the perimeter. Haniel was lost in her books. Even Joseph and Raphael were deep in conversation. No one saw her slip out the back door into the cemetery.

The phone signal was weak, but it was there. Her mother's number was still on speed dial.

"Just to say I'm okay," she whispered to herself. "Just so they don't worry."

The call connected on the third ring.

"Mary?" Her mother's voice was frantic. "Mary, is that you? Where are you? We've been so worried!"

"Mom, I'm okay. I can't tell you where I am, but I'm safe. I just... I needed you to know that."

"Mary, please come home. Whatever trouble you're in, we can help. Your father and I, "

"I can't, Mom. I'm sorry. I just... I love you. Both of you. I had to tell you that."

"Mary?" Her mother's voice was frantic. "Mary, is that you? Where are you? We've been so worried!"

"Mom, I'm okay. I can't tell you where I am, but I'm safe. I just... I needed you to know that."

"Mary, please come home. Whatever trouble you're in, we can help. Your father and I, "

"I can't, Mom. I'm sorry. I just... I love you. Both of you. I had to tell you that."

In a windowless room filled with monitoring equipment, a tech looked up from his computer screen. "Sir? We've got activity on the target's home line."

Malcolm stepped away from where he'd been conferring with his team. He looked exactly like what he pretended to be, a high-level government official in an expensive suit. Only his eyes, flat and cold as a shark's, betrayed something else.

"Show me," he commanded.

The tech's fingers flew over his keyboard. "Call came from a cell tower in Oklahoma. Rural area." A map appeared on the main screen, a red dot pulsing over a small region. "Signal was weak, bouncing between two towers. But we can narrow it down to about twenty square miles."

Malcolm studied the map, his perfect smile never reaching his eyes. "What's out there?"

Another tech pulled up satellite imagery. "Not much. Farmland mostly. Few small towns. Wait..." He zoomed in on something. "Abandoned buildings, but..."

"But?"

"This area here. Looks empty, but when I hover over it, my mouse pointer skips. Like something's interfering with the mouse. Could be nothing, just old batteries or, "

"It's them." Malcolm's voice was certain. He pulled out his phone, pressing a single number. "Teams three and four, move in. We have a location." He listened for a moment. "No. No captives this time. Eliminate them all."

He hung up and turned to his team. "Keep monitoring all communications from the targets' families. They've made contact once. They'll do it again." His smile widened slightly. "Humans are so predictable that way. They never can let go of the ones they love."

In the cemetery, Mary wiped her tears and headed back toward the sanctuary, unaware that her moment of weakness had just given their enemies exactly what they needed.

The café was one of those trendy downtown spots where aspiring artists came to be seen hoping to be discovered. Gwen had performed here once, back when she still believed talent alone would be enough. She had not been here since, or even thought about it. But the email invitation from the assistant to the talent scout from Champion Records promised to put an end to her lifelong frustration.

The talent scout said his name was Ethan. He looked perfectly ordinary in his expensive suit, his business cards and portfolio screaming legitimacy.

Only his eyes seemed wrong somehow, too still, too focused. But Gwen was too focused on the contract in front of her to notice.

"Champion Records has been watching your career with interest," he said, his voice smooth and professional. "Particularly your work at the Temple. You have a unique talent, Gwen. Raw. Real. The kind of voice that could fill stadiums."

She took another sip of her latte, hoping he couldn't see her hands shaking. "Then why approach me now? Why not at the Temple?"

"Timing is everything in this business." He straightened his tie, a precise, practiced movement. "And frankly, we were concerned about... interference. Other interests who might try to capitalize on your talent."

"You mean Mary," Gwen said bluntly.

Something flickered in Ethan's emotionless eyes. "She's certainly part of the equation. A less experienced performer, yet somehow always in the spotlight. It must be... disheartening for you."

Gwen stared into her coffee. "You have no idea."

"Actually, I do." He leaned forward slightly. "Which is why I'm here. Champion Records believes in supporting real talent. Not... manufactured success."

He slid the contract across the table. Everything was perfect as she read through it, the letterhead, the golden seal, the terms that could change her life forever. World tour. Five album deal. The kind of money that made all her years of struggle seem worth it.

"All we need is your signature," he said carefully. "A gesture of your commitment, shall we say."

Gwen couldn’t sign the document fast enough.

"All the paperwork seems to be in order," Ethan said, gathering the signed contracts into his briefcase. "Mr. Malcolm will be thrilled to have you on board. Champion Records has been looking for a voice like yours for a long time."

Gwen could hardly believe it was real. Everything she'd worked for, finally happening. Her hands were still shaking slightly as she finished her latte.

"Oh," Ethan said suddenly, as if just remembering something. "I hate to impose, but I wonder if I could ask a small favor?" He pulled out a brown paper package from his briefcase. "I'm supposed to drop this off in the mail on my way to the airport, but I'm already running late for my flight. The address is actually on your side of town, I think. Would you please take it for me?"

"Sure," Gwen said, eager to help her new supporter at the label. "No problem at all."

"You're a lifesaver." He wrote an address on a business card and handed it to her along with the package. "Just leave it on the doorstep. It's a gift for an old friend, they're expecting it."

The package was heavier than it looked, but not remarkably so. Just another errand on what was turning out to be the best day of her life.

"Let me get your coffee," she offered, standing up. "Least I can do."

"You're too kind," Ethan smiled that hollow smile. He gathered his things, checking his watch. "I really should run. Don't want to miss that flight. Remember, just leave it on the doorstep. No need to wait around or anything."

They walked out of the café together, parting ways on the sidewalk. Ethan headed for a waiting town car while Gwen walked to her own vehicle, the package tucked under her arm, the business card with its hastily scrawled address in her pocket.

She didn't recognize the street name. Didn't think twice about it really. Just another stop on her way home. She drove down the road into the gathering dark, humming one of her songs, thinking about stages and spotlights and everything that was finally within reach.

The residential neighborhood was quiet, most houses already dark except for porch lights casting islands of yellow on neat lawns. Gwen checked the address on the business card again, squinting at Ethan's hurried handwriting. She'd never been to this part of town before.

Number 1424 turned out to be a modest two-story house with flower boxes in the windows. Something about it seemed vaguely familiar, but she couldn't place it. Maybe she'd driven past it before.

She pulled up across the street, leaving her engine running. No sense killing it for such a quick stop. The package seemed heavier now as she lifted it from the passenger seat, like it had been gaining weight during the drive.

The porch light wasn't on, but there was warm light spilling from what looked like a kitchen window. The front path was short, lined with well-tended flowers. She could hear the soft sounds of a TV through the evening air, the mundane noises of a family's night winding down. Simple enough.

As she walked up the path to the front door, something made her pause. A wind chime tinkled softly, though there was no breeze. And was that... humming? Coming from the package?

"Just leave it on the doorstep," she reminded herself. Gwen set the package down carefully by the door, making sure it was visible from inside. Simple enough.

She was three steps from the door when she heard a woman's voice from inside: "Did you remember to set out the recyclables, honey?" Through the front window, she caught a glimpse of a woman moving in the kitchen, washing dishes at the sink.

Back in her car, she was just about to pull away when the front door opened. A man stepped out carrying recyclables, the bin tucked under one arm. He noticed the package immediately, setting down his bin to pick it up.

Gwen watched idly through her window as he examined it, turning it over in his hands. Looking for a label maybe, or trying to figure out who it was from. He shook it slightly, like a child trying to guess what's inside a Christmas present.

Then the world turned white.

The explosion rocked her car, shattering her side windows. The sound hit a millisecond later, much more physical, like the world itself was being ripped apart.

When her vision cleared, where the man had been standing was... nothing. Just flames and chaos and a horror her mind couldn't quite process.

Someone was screaming. From the house maybe, or maybe it was her. She couldn't tell. Her ears were ringing and her hands were shaking so badly she could barely grip the steering wheel.

What had she done?

What had Ethan made her do?

She hit the gas, tires squealing as she fled into the night. In her rearview mirror, she could see other houses lighting up, people emerging to see what had happened. Soon there would be sirens. Soon there would be questions.

Soon everyone would know.

She didn't recognize the street name that night. Didn't know the house or the man with the recycling bin. Wouldn't know until she saw the morning news that she had just taken Mary's parents' lives. That her simple favor had made her a murderer. All night, she just drove, trying to outrun what she'd done. Trying to escape the image of that man, shaking a package she had delivered, in the last moments of his life.

7am. Gwen's car idled at a truck stop just off the highway, her hands still shaking too badly to hold the coffee she'd bought. The morning news played on her phone propped on the dashboard, the announcer's voice seeming to come from far away.

"...explosion that killed both occupants of the house on Cedar Grove Lane. Police have identified the victims as James and Anne Levitt..."

The coffee slipped from her grip, spilling across her lap. She barely noticed the burn.

"...security footage from neighboring houses clearly shows the suspect, now identified as Gwendolyn Pierce, delivering the package minutes before the explosion..."

Her own face appeared on the screen, a clear shot from a doorbell camera across the street. She looked so normal. So, innocent. Like she was just running an errand, not delivering death.

"...considered armed and a threat. The FBI has joined the investigation, citing possible connections to domestic terrorism..."

She reached for her purse, looking for napkins to clean up the spilled coffee. That's when she saw it, a small pistol, dark and unmistakably cold, that she'd never seen before. Tucked into her purse as carefully as the contract that had condemned her.

A note was wrapped around it in Ethan's precise handwriting: "For when you need an exit."

He'd known. All along, he'd known.

The news droned on, showing pictures of Mary's parents. Good people. Kind people. People who had never done anything to her, who she hadn't even known she was hurting.

She started driving again, no destination in mind, just away. Away from the news, from the manhunt she knew was already beginning, from what she'd done.

Her hands found a dirt road turning off the highway. The kind that led nowhere. Perfect.

She killed the engine. In the sudden silence, she could hear birds singing. The world going on like nothing had happened. Like she hadn't destroyed lives with one simple delivery.

The gun was heavier than she expected. Like it was made for exactly this purpose.

"I didn't know," she whispered to no one. "I didn't know."

But she had known something was wrong. Had felt it in her bones when Ethan handed her that package. Had chosen not to listen because she wanted so badly to believe in her dreams.

Now those dreams were ashes, like the house she'd helped destroy. Like the lives she'd ended without even meaning to.

Sirens were approaching now. Growing louder. She lifted the gun.

The morning sun caught something in her rearview mirror, movement in the trees behind her car. For just a moment, she thought she saw someone watching.

Trembling, she slowly put the gun under her chin and squeezed the trigger. Everything went black.

#

The penthouse always felt bigger at night, emptier. Jacob Reisman sat in his leather chair by the floor-to-ceiling windows, watching his reflection ghost against the city lights below. An empty bottle of Macallan lay on its side on his desk. Another, half-full, waited within reach.

The TV murmured in the background, some breaking news about an explosion across town. He didn't bother turning it up. Bad news was just background noise these days.

Without Joseph around, the silence had become a living thing. It filled the corners of the penthouse, pressed against the windows, reminded him of everything he'd lost. His relationship with his son. His company. His purpose.

The ice in his glass had long since melted when the elevator dinged. He didn't turn around. Probably Sandra from accounting, still trying to get him to sign those layoff notices. As if firing more people would save what was left of Reisman Construction.

"Beautiful view," said a voice he didn't recognize. "Though I imagine it gets lonely up here. All alone with the stars and your thoughts."

Jacob turned slowly, the room swaying slightly. A man stood by his desk, unremarkable in his dark suit except for his eyes. They seemed to swallow what little light was in the room.

"Office is closed," Jacob muttered, reaching for the bottle. "Whatever it is can wait until morning."

"Can it?" The man, Deacon, though Jacob didn't know that name, moved to the windows. "Can anything wait when you're watching your life's work crumble? When your own son abandons you in your hour of need?"

Jacob's hand tightened on his glass. "Who are you?"

"Someone who's watched you, Mr. Reisman. Watched you build something magnificent from nothing. Forty years of sweat and sacrifice. The tallest buildings in the city, monuments to your vision. Your dedication." Deacon's reflection smiled in the glass. "And now? Now you sit alone in the dark, drinking, while it all slips away."

"You don't know anything about me," Jacob said, but his voice wavered.

"Don't I? I know about Catherine, your first loss. How you buried yourself in work after she died, trying to build something that would last longer than love. I know about the bank meetings last week, the ones where they talked about calling in the loans. About the contracts drying up. About the whispers in the industry that Reisman Construction is collapsing."

Jacob tried to stand but the room tilted dangerously. "How do you, "

"And I know about Joseph," Deacon continued, his voice gentler now. Understanding. "The son who was supposed to carry on your legacy. Who you trained since he could walk to take over someday. Who you gave everything to." He moved to the bar, poured two drinks with practiced ease. "Only for him to throw it all away. For a girl. For some... religious obsession."

"He's just confused," Jacob said, but the words sounded hollow even to him. "That girl, she's..."

"Taken him from you," Deacon finished. "Just like Catherine was taken. Just like everything else will be taken, piece by piece, until there's nothing left of what you built. Nothing left to show for all those years of sacrifice."

He held out one of the drinks. Jacob took it without thinking. It burned going down, but not like whiskey. Like something final.

"Did you know," Deacon said conversationally, "Your insurance policy, you know, that big one Caroline and the board made you get, would solve this problem." He took another sip of the brew and continued.

"And did you know that most insurance policies cover self-inflicted death after two years? Enough to cover the debts. Save the company. Give those loyal employees, the ones who stayed with you all these years, something to remember you by." He gestured to the balcony doors. "One moment of courage. That's all it takes."

"I should call Joseph," Jacob mumbled, but his phone seemed far away. "Tell him...."

"Tell him what? That you're sorry? That you failed?" Deacon settled into the chair opposite Jacob. "Let me tell you what will happen if you call. He won't answer. Or if he does, he'll make excuses. He'll choose her over you, again. Choose her family over yours. And you'll be left here, alone, watching everything you built turn to dust."

"He wouldn't..."

"He already has. When's the last time he came to the office? Called to check on you? You haven't heard from him since he went to Israel. The son you raised, who you gave everything to, he's already gone. And soon the company will follow. They'll auction off the equipment, sell the contracts to competitors. In a year, no one will even remember Reisman Construction. Your life's work, vanished."

Jacob stared into his glass, seeing forty years of memories reflected in the amber liquid. The first building he'd ever built. Teaching Joseph to read blueprints. Catherine's smile the day they'd landed their first major contract.

"But," Deacon said softly, "it doesn't have to end that way. You can save it. Save them. All those employees who depend on you. All those families. One moment of courage, and your legacy survives. Even if you don't."

The balcony doors were open though Jacob didn't remember them being open before. The night air was cool on his face as he stumbled toward them.

"Think about it," Deacon's voice came from behind him. "One final act of leadership. Of sacrifice. The insurance money saves the company. The employees keep their jobs. And Joseph? Joseph will understand, finally, what real responsibility looks like. What it means to put family first."

Jacob's hands found the railing. The city spread out below him, all those lights like stars fallen to earth. Each one representing a life he'd touched, a building he'd raised, a dream he'd built in steel and concrete.

"You're right," he whispered. "About all of it."

"I know," Deacon said simply. "That's why I'm here. To help you do what needs to be done. To give your story the ending it deserves."

"Joseph," Jacob whispered. Then he leaned over and let go.

Deacon watched him the entire fall, marveling to himself how long it took Jacob to reach the street. In the distance, sirens began to wail, heading toward a self-inflicted death in the city's tallest building. The pieces, and people, falling perfectly into place.

Haniel's makeshift radio crackled in the sanctuary's main hall. Most of them were trying to rest, scattered among the pews, while Mallakiel kept watch at the door. The old church creaked around them, settling into the night.

"Got it," Haniel muttered, finally finding a clear signal. The nightly news broadcast from home filled the space between the old stone walls.

"...breaking news from earlier tonight. Police are investigating an explosion in the Cedar Grove neighborhood that has claimed two lives. The victims have been identified as James and Anne Levitt..."

Mary's soft gasp echoed off the walls. Joseph, who'd been dozing in a nearby pew, sat upright, instantly alert.

"...security footage shows a suspected bomber, now identified as Gwendolyn Pierce, a local singer, delivering what appears to be an explosive device..."

"No," Mary whispered. "No, no, no..."

"...Ms. Pierce was later found dead in her vehicle on Route 27, from an apparent self-inflicted gunshot wound. Police are investigating possible connections between..."

"Turn it off," Elizabeth snapped, but no one moved.

The broadcast continued relentlessly. "In a separate incident, prominent real estate developer Jacob Reisman was found deceased outside his penthouse office, in what police are calling an apparent suicide..."

Joseph's entire body went rigid. The world seemed to tilt sideways, reality becoming something unrecognizable.

"Turn it off," Elizabeth snapped again, but still no one moved.

The sound of Mary retching broke the spell. Elizabeth rushed to her side as she emptied her stomach in a corner. Joseph hadn't moved, his face the color of old paper.

Ariel looked intently at Haniel. "They got to them before we could get protection coordinated. So fast. But how?"

"I…I called them," Mary choked out between heaves. "Earlier tonight. I called my parents. I just... I just wanted them to know I was okay."

The effect was immediate. Mallakiel spun from his post at the door. "You did what?"

"They'll have traced it," Haniel said, already moving to her equipment. "If they were monitoring the lines..."

"How long?" Raphael demanded.

Haniel's hands flew over her instruments. "Hours maybe. Less if they, " She stopped, adjusting something. "There's movement on the roads possibly already. I set up wards in a 150- mile perimeter around us that trigger when heavier traffic than normal is detected.

"We're exposed," Mallakiel's military training took over. "Ariel, get the weapons ready. Haniel, start the tunnel sequence. Elizabeth, help Mary and Joseph gather only what they can carry."

Joseph finally moved, but not toward Mary. He walked over to a pew and flipped it over. The sound echoed through the church.

"This isn't the time for that," Mallakiel grabbed his shoulder. "Channel it. We're going to need it."

"My father," Joseph's voice cracked. "He was alone. I should have, "

"Later," Mallakiel cut him off. "Grieve later. Right now, we move."

Mary was still on her knees, Elizabeth trying to help her up. "Gwen," she kept saying. "Why would Gwen...?"

"Because they're smart," Raphael said grimly. "They use what hurts us most. People we know. People we trust." He looked at Mallakiel. "How long to reach the sanctuary in Montana?"

"Too far," Mallakiel shook his head. "We need somewhere closer. Somewhere they won't expect."

"The ranch," Elizabeth said suddenly. "David's ranch in Bethlehem. It's protected, and it's just a few hours from here."

"The demons will expect us to run to holy ground," Ariel argued, returning with an armful of weapons. “They will be looking for signs of the divine.”

"Exactly," Elizabeth countered. "They'll be watching churches, temples, known sanctuaries. But a ranch? Protected by nothing but a stubborn old man and his cowboys? They'd never think we'd be that desperate."

Haniel's equipment suddenly erupted in static. "Whatever we're doing, we do it now. They've found us."

Mary stumbled to her feet, wiping her mouth. Her grief was hardening into something else. Something dangerous. "They killed my parents," she said flatly. "Used Gwen to take my parents."

Joseph moved to her side, his own rage matching hers. "Let them come."

"No," Raphael's voice cut through their anger. "That's what they want. To make you reckless. To make you easy targets." He looked at them both.

"Your child is what matters now. Everything else, revenge, grief, guilt, it all waits. Understand?"

They didn't answer, but something in their faces shifted. Survival first. Grief later.

"Move," Mallakiel ordered. "We've got two hours. Maybe less."

While the others rushed to prepare, Haniel found Mary in the sanctuary's vestry, mechanically shoving clothes into a bag, her movements jerky and unfocussed.

While the others rushed to prepare for evacuation, Haniel found Mary in the sanctuary's small vestry, mechanically shoving clothes into a bag, her movements jerky and unfocused. Her face was still wet with tears.

"Here," Haniel said softly, holding out a small leather-bound book. "Sometimes writing helps. When the grief is too big for words."

Mary looked up, really seeing Haniel for the first time, this former angel who now wore wire-rimmed glasses and kept her silver hair in a practical braid. Who had chosen humanity with all its pain.

"How do you do it?" Mary asked, her voice raw. "Live with being human? With losing people?"

Haniel settled beside her on the wooden bench. "The same way everyone does. One breath at a time. One moment at a time." She took Mary's hand, squeezing gently. "The pain doesn't go away. But it becomes part of your story. Part of what makes you human."

"I got them hurt," Mary whispered.

"No. They used your love against you. There's a difference." Haniel's voice was firm but gentle. "Remember that distinction. It matters."

"The hardest part," Haniel continued, adjusting her wire-rimmed glasses, "isn't the pain. It's the guilt. The endless 'what-ifs.' But Mary..." She touched the young woman's arm. "What happened tonight was going to happen regardless. If not Gwen, they would have found another way. If not tonight, then tomorrow. They've been planning, waiting for this since before you were born."

"How can you know that?"

"Because I've spent centuries studying their patterns. Their methods." Haniel replied. "They destroy what we love to destroy who we are. But you..." She placed a gentle hand on Mary's stomach. "You carry something they fear more than anything. Hope. Change. A future they can't control."

In the main sanctuary, Mallakiel led Joseph and Raphael to the altar. He pressed something hidden beneath the carved wood, and a section of the floor silently slid away, revealing stone steps descending into darkness.

"The Staff of Moses has been here since the sanctuary was built," he explained, producing the key that was given to Elizabeth and Mary.

"The staff has been here all along?" Raphael asked, surprised.

"Hidden in plain sight," Mallakiel confirmed. He pulled out a flashlight. "Watch your step. These stairs are older than the church itself."

They descended into cool darkness that smelled of age and secrets. Joseph's hand traced the wall, feeling symbols carved into the stone. "What is this place?"

"A vault," Mallakiel explained. "Built by the first Paladins. They understood that some things were too powerful to destroy, too dangerous to use, but too important to lose."

The stairs ended in a small chamber. In its center stood a simple wooden box, unremarkable except for the feeling of weight it seemed to add to the air around it.

"Is that..." Joseph started.

"The staff of Moses," Raphael finished. "One of the most powerful artifacts ever touched by human hands."

The chamber below the sanctuary was small, its walls covered in the same symbols as the trap door. In its center stood a simple wooden box.

Mallakiel approached the box carefully. "It has parted waters, called down plagues, turned the tide of battles." He looked at them seriously. "God sent Michael to bury Moses after his death. Lucifer battled Michael for possession of it. Michael nearly lost, but God himself intervened for Michael. We don't know what happened to Moses' body. It was kept secret from most of us. But the staff was given to the Paladins to protect. We have been hiding it for thousands of years."

"And now?" Joseph asked.

"Now we use it to protect what matters most." Raphael reached for the Staff but Mallakiel stopped him.

"You're human now. It would harm you. Only the Paladins can handle it safely."

"Then make me one," Raphael replied.

"There are rituals. Wards need to be placed. Years of study. And you have to have an angel's blessing. It is not that simple."

Above them, they heard Haniel's voice calling urgently. They emerged from the chamber to find her bent over her equipment, Mary and Elizabeth beside her.

"Multiple vehicles approaching from the east," she reported. "Military grade. And something else..." She adjusted a dial, her face paling. "Something big. Moving fast."

"Deacon," Raphael said bitterly. "Or Malcolm. Maybe both."

"How long?" Mallakiel asked, carefully rewrapping the Staff.

"Thirty minutes. Maybe less."

"The tunnels," Elizabeth insisted. "We can still, "

"No time to reach them now," Mallakiel cut her off. "We make our stand here." He looked at the Staff in his hands, then at Mary. "Sometimes the only way out is through."

Ariel appeared from the back of the church, arms full of blessed weapons. "Perimeter's as secure as I can make it. Won't hold them long."

"Long enough," Mallakiel said seriously. He turned to Mary and Joseph. "Whatever happens, whatever you see, you stay behind us. Your only job is to protect each other and that child. Understand?"

"Whatever happens next, remember, you're what matters. The child is what matters. Everything else is secondary."

"Including us," Mallakiel added gravely, opening the box. The staff inside was simple wood, aged and worn. But something about it made the shadows in the corners retreat. "We hold them here. Give you time to run.

"But, " Joseph started.

"No time to argue," Haniel cut him off. She pressed the journal into Mary's hands. "Write it down someday. All of it. The world should know what they did. What it cost."

Chapter 16

BATTLE

The sanctuary's ancient stones seemed to breathe in the darkness, exhaling centuries of prayers into the stale air. Mary sat in the front pew, her mother's last voicemail playing again in her mind like a broken record: "Sweetie, please call us. Whatever's wrong, we can help. We love you." The words felt like shards of glass in her chest now, cutting deeper with each breath.

Joseph nestled her without speaking, for a long moment, they just breathed together in the darkness.

"I keep thinking," Mary finally whispered, her voice rough from crying, "if I hadn't made that call. If I'd just listened, " The words caught in her throat, gripping her with guilt.

"Don't." Joseph's voice cracked on the word. "We can't... we can't do that to ourselves." But his hands were shaking as he reached for hers, and she knew he was doing exactly that, replaying every moment, every choice that had led to his father's death.

"They used Gwen," Mary said sharply "and they twisted her into," She couldn't finish. She couldn't finish the thought, imagining Gwen's final moments in that car, the gun cold in her hand.

"And my father..." Joseph's grip tightened until it was almost painful. "He died thinking I'd abandoned him. That I'd chosen.... " He stopped, but Mary heard the rest anyway: *That I'd chosen you over him. That his life's work meant nothing to me. That I'd left him to die alone.*

The baby moved inside her, a flutter of life amidst all this death. Mary placed their joined hands over the spot, feeling the miracle and the burden of what they carried. "Sometimes," she admitted in a whisper that barely disturbed the heavy air, "I'm terrified that this is just the beginning. That everyone we love will pay the price for what we're protecting."

Joseph turned to her then, and in the candlelight, she saw tears on his face, something she'd never witnessed before. "Then we make them pay for it first."

From the shadows near the altar, Raphael's voice came soft but firm: "That's exactly what they want. To turn your grief into rage. Your love into weapons they can use against you." The fallen angel emerged into the light, his human form moving with a grace that betrayed his true nature, but there was something else there now, a weariness, a vulnerability that made him seem more tragic than divine.

"Your pain is natural. Human. Sacred, even," he continued. "But don't let it become poison. That's how they win, not by killing those we love, but by making us forget how to love at all."

"Then what do we do?" Joseph demanded. "Hide? Run? Wait for them to pick off everyone else we care about one by one?"

"No." Mallakiel's deeper voice joined them as the former warrior-angel appeared from the vestry, carrying what looked like ancient maps. "We fight. But we fight smart. We fight with purpose, not vengeance."

He spread the maps across the altar, blueprints of what looked like underground tunnels, their edges marked with symbols that hurt the eyes to look at directly. "They think they've broken you. Made you vulnerable. That's why they're bold enough to come for us here."

"Good." The word surprised Joseph as it left his lips. He stood, one hand still protectively holding Mary's, the other clenched into a fist. "Let them come. Let them think we're weak. Wounded."

Raphael's eyes gleamed with pride. "Now you're thinking like fighters." He moved to the maps, pointing to specific junctions marked with those eye-watering symbols. "We have advantages they don't know about. The sanctuary's foundations go deeper than they realize. We can use these as ways to retreat. And we have something they want desperately enough to make mistakes."

"The Staff?" Joseph asked.

"Me," Mary added softly. "They want the child. Need him, even."

"Which makes you both perfect bait." Mallakiel's smile was fierce in the candlelight. "If we set this up right, we can draw them in. Make them fight on our terms, in grounds we've prepared."

More figures emerged from the shadows, Haniel with her modified equipment, Ariel checking blessed weapons that looked older than civilization. The sanctuary's air grew thick with purpose, with plans taking shape in the darkness.

"It won't bring them back," Raphael said gently. "Nothing will. But it might prevent others from suffering the same fate."

"Tell us what you need us to do."

Haniel's equipment hummed in the darkness, casting an eerie blue glow across ancient stones. Blaring the local news broadcast:

"Good evening, I'm Sarah Chen. Our top story tonight: comet fever has officially hit Texas as the comet dubbed the 'Winter Star' continues its approach. Amateur astronomers report the comet now visible to the naked eye, appearing as a bright blue-green streak across our night sky."

"The celestial visitor has sparked what locals are calling the biggest tourist boom in decades, with hotels across the region reporting full bookings for next month's convergence festival."

Person being interviewed: "The kids are so excited, how often do you get to see a comet this bright? And the festival sounds amazing. All those ceremonies and celebrations under the stars..."

"And a warning to stargazers: while the comet provides spectacular viewing, doctors advise against looking at it directly for extended periods, following reports of unusual side effects including headaches and vivid dreams."

"Coming up after the break: Could the comet be affecting local wildlife? We'll talk to experts about recent changes in animal behavior across Texas. But first, let's check in with Tom for tonight's weather..."

Humming, Haniel worked methodically, placing modified sensors at key points around the sanctuary's perimeter. Each device looked cobbled together from both ancient and modern parts, circuit boards nested in containers marked with Angelic symbols, digital displays showing readings in languages that had long died.

"The wards are already strong here," she explained, adjusting something that might have been a radio antenna wrapped in blessed silver wire. "But we can use them to our advantage. Create blind spots where they expect to find us. False signatures to draw them where we want them."

Mallakiel moved through the sanctuary's main hall with military precision, directing the placement of blessed weapons with the care of a chess master positioning pieces. "Remember," he called out, "they'll expect us to defend from inside. Traditional thinking. Holy ground as a fortress." His smile was sharp in the darkness. "We're going to give them exactly what they expect. But in a far greater dose."

Mary watched from the choir loft as Joseph worked below with Ariel, moving pews to create channels of movement, kill zones, though no one used that word aloud. The physical labor seemed to help him focus, keep the grief at bay. Every so often he would look up, checking on her position, and she would nod. Still here. Still safe.

"He’s changing you," Raphael said quietly, appearing beside her in that unsettling way he had. Even without his grace, he moved like a shadow. "You are growing stronger."

"I can feel it," Mary admitted. "Like electricity under my skin. And the things I sometimes see..." She gestured to the air around them, if she focused, she could see where colors shifted and flowed like aurora borealis. "It's getting clearer. More intense."

"Good." Raphael's voice was grim. "You'll need it. When they come, and they will come, you'll need to be able to see them. Really see them, beyond their human disguises."

"We're taking a huge risk using that as bait," Mary said softly.

"We're taking a huge risk just existing," Raphael countered. "Sometimes the best defense is to be exactly as vulnerable as your enemy expects. Just not in the way they expect."

Outside, engines grew louder in the darkness, then cut off suddenly. Footsteps crunched in the gravel. Orders given in low voices that didn't sound quite human anymore.

"They're testing the outer wards," Haniel called from her equipment. "Multiple points of pressure. They're looking for weak spots."

Mallakiel's voice carried up from below: "Positions. Everyone remembers the plan. No matter what you see, no matter what you hear, stick to your assigned locations."

Mary felt Joseph's eyes on her again and nodded. Still here. Still safe. But for how long?

"Mary." Raphael's voice was urgent now. "Remember why we're here. What we're protecting." His hand moved to her stomach. "Perfect love casts out fear. And what you carry is perfect love incarnate."

"More coming," Haniel announced quietly. Her equipment was blaring now, displays flashing with readings. "Multiple signals." She adjusted her glasses, staring at one particular reading. "Oh. Oh no."

"What?" Mary felt cold despite the summer night's heat.

"Deacon isn't alone," Raphael answered for her. "They're done playing around."

Deacon's voice carried across the sanctified ground like oil spreading over water, wrong and slick and consuming. "Come out, come out, wherever you are!" His words held a playful tone that made them somehow more unnerving. "No need to hide behind those pesky little wards. We can have a civilized conversation."

The trap was set. But as Mary once again placed both hands protectively over her stomach, she wondered, not for the first time, who was really trapping whom.

Mary and Joseph found a quiet corner in the vestry. She could still hear Haniel's equipment screeching in the main hall, but here, for just a moment, they could pretend the world wasn't ending.

"I'm scared," Mary whispered, allowing herself a moment of complete honesty. "Not of dying. Not even of what's coming. I'm scared that after everything, after my parents, your father, it still won't be enough. That they'll still win."

Joseph pulled her close. "Remember the coffee shop?" he asked softly. "When we first met?"

She nodded against his chest, breathing in his familiar scent. "You were so nervous. Spilled your coffee all over yourself."

"I heard music," she continued. "I didn't understand. But it felt like... like everything in my life had been leading to that moment. To you."

"I heard absolutely nothing," he admitted. She laughed softly.

"That's what I'm holding onto," she said. "Not the fear. Not the loss. But that music. That feeling that no matter how dark it gets, no matter what comes through those doors, this is exactly where we're meant to be."

The baby kicked against his palm, as if in agreement. Despite everything, Mary felt herself smile. "Together?"

"Together." He kissed her then, soft, and intensely at once. A kiss that tasted of goodbye, of hello, of everything in between.

Their moment of peace shattered as Mallakiel's voice rang out: "They're breaching the outer wards!" The artillery cracked louder, closer. The stone walls groaned like they were under immense pressure.

Joseph pulled back just enough to rest his forehead against hers. "I love you," he said simply. "Both of you."

"I love you too." She touched his face, memorizing every line. "Try not to do anything reckless and heroic?"

His smile was grim in the candlelight. "No promises."

The sanctuary's doors remained firmly closed, but Mary could feel Deacon's presence outside. Mallakiel moved silently to the window, his blessed weapons ready. "He can't cross the property line," he whispered. "The old protections are holding."

"Paladins?" Deacon's laugh was sharp and mocking. "Oh, now that's interesting. Heaven's little toy soldiers are involved?" His borrowed human form paced just beyond the ward line, testing its edges like a predator seeking weakness. "I haven't seen their kind since... what was it, Mesopotamia? That unpleasant business with the Ark?"

"We remember that day too, Asmodeus," Mallakiel called out, using Deacon's true name like a weapon. "Remember how that ended for your side?"

Deacon shimmered, his human disguise flickering for just a moment to show something ancient and frightening beneath. "Ah, but we learned from that. Adapted. Evolved." His smile was wide. "While you? You're still playing by the old rules. Still hiding behind walls and wards, pretending they'll keep us out forever."

"Tell me, Mary," Deacon called out, his voice somehow finding her despite the walls between them. "How's things? Mom and Dad doing well? Did you think they were safe in their little house with their little walls?"

Mary's grip on Joseph's hand tightened instinctively. Below, she saw Raphael move to the window, tense with barely contained rage.

"Or you, Joseph," Deacon continued, "Did your father feel safe up in his tower? All alone with his drinks and his regrets? Was it the whiskey that pushed him over the edge, or something... darker. Like the truth?"

"He's baiting us," Raphael warned them. "Trying to draw us out."

"Is it working?" Joseph's voice was tight with anger.

"No," Haniel said, surprising herself with how steady she sounded. "He's afraid. I can see it in his eyes; he's not just testing the wards. He's shocked by them. Our presence here... it wasn't part of his plan."

Deacon's laughter cut off abruptly. "Clever girl. Those new eyes of yours are getting sharper." His voice took on an edge of genuine curiosity. "Tell me, what else do you see? What other gifts has that child given you?"

"Enough to know you're stalling," Ariel called back. "What are you afraid of."

The darkness around Deacon writhed more violently. "Malcolm will be here soon enough. And when he comes..." His smile was audible in the darkness. "Well, let's just say these quaint little wards won't mean much then. The Paladins may remember flood, but we remember Eden. We remember the first walls, the first wards. And we remember how they fell."

"Maybe," Mallakiel's memory scanned the centuries of his life. "But you've forgotten something important about that day."

"Oh?" Deacon's tone was sarcastic. "Do enlighten me, fellow fallen brother."

"There was a guardian at that gate too. The first Paladin. And he carried a sword of flame."

In the distance, engines growled, multiple vehicles approaching fast.

"Last chance," Deacon called out. "Surrender the woman, the Staff, and maybe, just maybe, I let the rest of you live. Let you keep playing holy warriors and all.

Mary felt the baby move inside her, responding to her surge of emotions. But before she could speak, Haniel's voice rang out: "You talk way too much!"

"Time's almost up," Deacon sang mockingly into the darkness. "Backup is coming. Some friends who don't care much about ancient wards."

In the choir loft, Elizabeth, Mary, and Joseph held each other tight as the sound of large approaching vehicles grew louder. The first battle was about to begin, and their carefully laid plans were already unraveling.

But at least they knew one thing now, they had surprised their enemy. The question was: would it be enough?

The night air crackled with tension as Deacon's forces emerged from the vehicles, demon possessed men and women, freely giving themselves in exchange for their heart's desire. They moved unnaturally, their human forms barely containing something else. They formed a perimeter just beyond the ward line, their weapons pointing at the sanctuary. Evan positioned himself beside his master. His sad, gaunt face was more lifeless than human. Deacon had nearly used him up.

Inside, Mallakiel moved silently among the defenders, checking positions. The Paladins had stationed themselves at key points, blessed weapons ready. Haniel's equipment hummed from multiple locations, ready to trigger the outer defenses.

"Remember," Raphael whispered to Mary and Joseph in the choir loft, "whatever you see, whatever happens, stay in position. The wards will hold."

From their hidden position in the choir loft, Mary felt Elizabeth squeeze her hand. Her cousin had refused to leave them, insisting that family stayed together no matter what. Even now, with her own miracle child safely hidden away with Zachariah, she remained steady at Mary's side.

Deacon played his first card. "Mary?" A voice called from the darkness, her mother's voice, perfect in every detail. "Mary, honey, is that you?"

Mary's breath caught. It sounded exactly like her mother. Elizabeth's grip tightened.

The sound hit her like a physical blow. Joseph's grip tightened on her arm. "Don't," he whispered. "It's not her. You know it's not her."

"Sweetheart, we're so worried," the voice continued, carrying all the love and concern that had colored her mother's final voicemail. "Just come home. Whatever trouble you're in, we can help."

"He's trying to hurt you," Elizabeth whispered, her voice intense with protective anger. "Don't let him."

Mary's hands clenched into fists, nails cutting into her palms. The pain helped her focus, helped her push back against the crushing grief and guilt. "My mother's dead," she called out, her voice steady despite her racing heart. "You made sure of that."

Deacon's laugh was harsh in the dark. "Worth a try. How about this one then?"

"Son?" Jacob Reisman's voice now, slurred, and desperate. "Joey, what are you doing in there? Come out. Help me. He's hurting me..."

Joseph took a step forward before he caught himself. His whole body trembled with rage. Elizabeth placed a steadying hand on his shoulder, the same way she'd done for Mary so many times when things seemed overwhelming. But Mary could see the horror in her cousin's eyes. This wasn't just manipulation, the demons were somehow accessing the actual voices, the actual final moments of their loved ones.

"Still nothing?" Deacon sighed theatrically. "Well then. I guess we do this the hard way.

The first attack came from the front, The first line of Deacon's soldiers charged forward, firing their weapons. The impact of the rounds made the whole building shudder, but the wards flared bright, forcing the bullets to fall harmless to the ground.

"Now!" Mallakiel's voice rang out.

Haniel triggered the first line of defense. Blessed silver erupted from carefully hidden ports around the sanctuary's perimeter, forming a spray that caught several of Deacon's followers. Their human disguises burned away like paper in flame, releasing writhing shadows that screamed in voices that weren't meant for human ears. The bodies they'd been wearing slumped to the ground, empty and smoking.

"Stay down," Elizabeth whispered as Mary tried to peer over the loft's edge.

Something big moved in the darkness behind Deacon's lines.

"Breach it," Deacon commanded.

The armored vehicle sped towards the ward line like a battering ram made of nightmares. Where it hit, the wards blazed bright enough to leave afterimages in Mary's vision. For a moment, it looked like they would hold.

Then something cracked.

The sound was physical, like breaking glass, but the Paladins themselves felt it. A hairline fracture appeared in the wards' protection, small, but growing.

"Second line!" Mallakiel shouted.

The Paladins moved with precision, activating backup wards that blazed to life. The breach stabilized, but didn't close completely.

Elizabeth pulled Mary closer, one arm protective around her shoulders. The faith that had sustained her through her own miraculous pregnancy now steeled her voice: "God didn't bring us this far to abandon us now."

"Mary?" Joseph's voice was tight with concern.

"I'm okay," she said, though she wasn't sure that was true. The baby moved inside her again, more urgently now, as if sensing the wrongness pressing in around them.

"They can't get through," Raphael assured them. "Not fully. Not yet."

But Mary saw his hands shake slightly as he gripped his borrowed weapons. Even without his grace, he knew what that crack in the wards meant. Their fortress wasn't as impregnable as they'd hoped.

More impacts shook the building. More cracks appeared in the protection, spreading like spider webs through the night air. Mary could see them clearly now, fracture lines in the air itself. She never finished studying them, as the first of Deacon's followers found a way through the cracks in the wards. Among them was Evan, his once-young face now gaunt and haunted, movements jerky and unnatural as he forced his dead body forward.

Somewhere deep inside, trapped in the prison of his own corpse, what remained of Evan's consciousness screamed. He watched helplessly from within as his body moved without his control, as his hands gripped weapons meant to harm innocents. This wasn't what he'd wanted when he'd made his deal with Deacon. This wasn't supposed to be his fate.

Ariel stood before the altar, blessed chains gleaming in her hands. She saw something in Evan's eyes, a flicker of the lost soul trapped within, and hesitated for just a moment.

"I'm sorry," she whispered, though whether to Evan or herself wasn't clear.

His body surged forward, demon-driven, weapon raised. But there was something different in his movement, a slight hesitation, as if the real Evan was fighting back one last time.

Please, his mind begged, though his lips couldn't form the words. *End this*.

Ariel's chains moved like liquid silver, catching him full across the chest. Divine energy coursed through the blessed metal, forcing the demon out of its stolen vessel. Evan's body crumpled, but as his consciousness finally began to fade, he felt something he hadn't felt since that night in the swamp, peace.

His last sight was Ariel's face, full of both mercy and fierce purpose, as she moved to meet the next wave of attackers. Then darkness took him, and Evan was finally, mercifully free.

The next wave came through the breach. They barely made it three steps before Mallakiel's blessed arrows found their mark. The possessing entity abandoned its host, leaving the body writhing on the sanctuary floor.

But where one breach opened, others followed. The hairline fractures in the wards spread like spider webs through the air itself. The dark ones poured through, all wearing human faces.

But where one breach opened, others followed. The hairline fractures in the wards spread, and more possessed humans poured through. Automatic weapons fire echoed through the sanctuary, bullets ricocheting off stone and wood. Ariel spun to meet them, her chains singing through the air. Paladins fought with ruthless efficiency, their blessed weapons forcing demons to abandon their hosts. But there were too many coming through the breaches.

"Keep them away from Mary!" Raphael shouted, wielding his weapons with practiced grace. Even without his powers, he moved like a trained warrior.

"Stay down," Joseph whispered, pulling Mary lower behind the choir loft's railing.

Haniel's voice cut through the chaos: "The wards are failing! We need to," Her words cut off in a cry of pain as one of the rounds caught her arm, tearing flesh.

Mallakiel moved like a force of nature, cutting through the demons with terrifying precision. "Fall back to the inner circle!"

The Paladins began an orderly retreat toward the altar, their blessed weapons forcing demons from their hosts one by one. But for every person they freed, two more possessed came through the widening breaches.

"He's coming," Ariel warned, readying another clip for her weapon.

The sound of boots on broken glass announced Deacon's arrival through one of the sanctuary's windows. His borrowed face twisted into an unnerving grin.

"Found you," he growled.

He launched himself through the window with impossible speed. Joseph moved to shield Mary, but Ariel was faster. She grabbed one of the blessed silver chains they'd been given and swung it like a whip. Where it struck one of the demons, catching one of Deacon's possessed soldiers full in the chest, she left her writhing in agony.

"Move!" Haniel shouted as more gunfire erupted. The defenders were being slowly pushed back; Deacon's forces pressing in through every breach in their defenses. "The Staff!" she gasped, remembering their purpose. "We can't let them, "

"Trust the plan," Raphael said grimly, though his face was pale with fear.

He stood before the altar, the Staff blazing with inner light behind him. Deacon's possessed soldiers surrounded him on all sides, but he showed no fear. If anything, he was smiling.

"Now!" he shouted.

Mallakiel's voice rang out the old words, and the trap they'd laid around the Staff exploded into being. Light brighter than the sun erupted from carefully placed holy relics, catching dozens of the possessed in its purifying blaze, forcing demons from their hosts. Bodies collapsed like puppets with severed strings as their possessors were driven out. For a moment, there was only silence, then gasping. The formerly possessed began to stir, blinking against the harsh light, their faces pale and drenched in sweat. Confusion washed over them. Some clutched their heads, others stared at their trembling hands, as if unsure they even belonged to them.

Then the horror set in.

Eyes darted around the scorched floor, taking in the wreckage, the smell of sulfur, the holy symbols still glowing with divine heat. A woman let out a choked sob. A man screamed. One by one, panic seized them.

They scrambled to their feet, stumbling over each other in their desperation to flee. Some bolted through the smoke-filled corridors, others pushed past the exorcists, slipping on their own terror as they ran from whatever nightmare they had just awakened from, unsure of where they were, or how much of the evil still lingered behind their eyes.

The last thing Mary saw before Elizabeth pulled her into the passage was Deacon's face, human disguise burning away to reveal pieces of skull beneath. His scream of fury followed them into the darkness as they fled deeper into the sanctuary's forgotten tunnels. Joseph's flashlight beam caught glimpses of carved symbols on the walls.

Above, the battle had gone quiet. That was worse than the noise.

A crash from above made them all jump. Then Ariel's voice, carrying through stone and earth corridor: "Raphael, the Staff! Don't let them," Her words cut off in a sound of something wet and final.

Elizabeth grabbed Mary's arm as she instinctively turned back. "We can't."

Another crash. Raphael crying out in pain.

"They're losing," Mary said. She didn't want to say it, but the words came anyway.

"Got you," Deacon's voice carried down to them. "Two birds, one stone."

"Keep running," Elizabeth whispered. Her voice was shaking but determined. She did not understand everything that was happening, but she understood enough to know death when she heard it coming.

They ran through the tunnels, the sounds of combat growing more distant behind them. The passage opened into what looked like an old maintenance garage, complete with oil stains on the concrete floor and tools rusting on wall hooks. Two black SUVs idled there, Mallakiel jumped behind the wheel of one, Haniel in the other.

"Move!" Mallakiel's voice carried urgency they'd never heard before. "They've breached the lower wards!"

Joseph helped Mary into the back of Mallakiel's vehicle while Elizabeth climbed in beside Haniel. The garage door rolled up silently, some kind of hydraulic system they must have rigged earlier. Beyond it, a narrow tunnel sloped upward toward distant moonlight.

"Hold on," Mallakiel said, shifting into gear. The SUV lurched forward, Haniel following close behind. The tunnel walls blurred past, ancient protective symbols flashing in their headlights.

The screech of tires on concrete echoed from somewhere behind them in the tunnel system. Deacon's forces had found another entrance.

"They're following," Mary whispered, twisting to look back.

Gunfire erupted from behind them, bullets pinging off the reinforced vehicles. Through the rear window, Mary could see headlights gaining, three, maybe four vehicles in pursuit.

The tunnel's end approached, a gap between boulders that would lead them out to the highway.

They burst out into moonlight. Behind them, Haniel's SUV emerged from the tunnel like a bullet from a gun.

"The ranch," Mallakiel said, his voice tight as he accelerated onto the empty highway. "It's not ward-protected, but they won't know to look for us there. We'll be safe there for a while. Maybe enough time for Mary to give birth."

"What about Raphael and Ariel?" Mary started, but was interrupted.

"They knew the risk," Mallakiel said softly. "We all did. This was always a possibility." His eyes met hers in the rearview mirror. "But we're not done yet. Not by a long shot.

The sanctuary disappeared behind them as they sped through the night. Mary felt Joseph's hand find hers, squeezing tight. In the other vehicle, she could see Elizabeth's silhouette beside Haniel, both women rigid with tension.

Back at the sanctuary, Ariel lay crumpled near the altar, blood pooling beneath her. The blessed weapon she'd wielded so fiercely still smoked in her lifeless hand.

Raphael knelt at the center of carnage, surrounded by the unconscious bodies of those they'd freed from possession. Some still twitching, others terribly still. His breathing was ragged, every movement revealing the cost of being human in this fight. The Staff was no longer glowing with inner light behind him.

"Getting tired, brother?" Deacon approached slowly, savoring the moment. His borrowed body showed signs of damage, but his movements were still unnaturally fluid. "How does it feel, being so... limited?"

Raphael's muscles trembled with exhaustion. Being human meant feeling pain, feeling fatigue. But it also meant feeling a pure and unyielding resolve.

"Come find out," he said, raising his arm and pointing at Deacon, while forcing himself to stand.

"Why would I do that when I can just wait? That fragile body will give out eventually. And then..." He gestured to the remaining possessed humans gathering around him. "My friends here are so eager to play. You have to understand, this is a rare opportunity. Not only do we get a little payback for a millennium of mistreatment, but we get to torment a human. Because now as a human you willingly directly engaged with us, well…we are not bound by those rules anymore, are we? At least when it comes to you."

Another wave of possessed humans surged forward. Raphael moved like water despite his exhaustion, but he was much slower now.

The first bullet caught him in the shoulder, tearing through cloth and flesh. The second took him in the leg, dropping him to one knee.

You know what the funny thing is?" Deacon circled closer as he watched Raphael struggle. "They're not even trying to kill you. That would be too easy. Too... simple."

Consciousness began to fade as Raphael's blood pooled on the sanctuary floor. His last thought was of Mary and Joseph, hoping they'd made it to the tunnels. Hoping this sacrifice would mean something.

Then darkness took him, and he knew nothing else.

Deacon approached the Staff slowly, reverently. Its light dimmed as he reached for it, as if recoiling from his touch.

"Finally," he breathed. Power thrummed through him as his fingers closed around ancient wood. "Do you feel that, brother?" He turned to Raphael's unconscious form. "That's the sound of everything changing."

He gestured to his followers. "Bring him. Our master will want to hear everything he knows about the child. About the Paladins. About all of it."

They dragged Raphael's limp body away, leaving streaks of red across the floor stones. Deacon followed, clutching the Staff like a trophy. Behind them, Ariel's body began to fade away, leaving nothing but her blade. Finally, once again, the sanctuary fell silent.

Chapter 17

RESPITE AND RESCUE

Dawn broke over Bethlehem Ranch like a bruise, painting the Oklahoma sky in shades of purple and red. The convoy of battered SUVs kicked up dust as they approached through scrubland, following a rutted dirt road that seemed to lead nowhere. Mary watched through exhausted eyes as the landscape slowly revealed itself, vast pastures dotted with grazing cattle, weathered wooden buildings that had stood against decades of storms, and ancient oak trees that seemed to stand guard over it all.

"Almost there," Mallakiel said from behind the wheel, his voice rough with fatigue. They hadn't stopped driving all night, taking backroads and cattle trails, doubling back multiple times to ensure they weren't followed.

Joseph sat rigid beside Mary, his hand never leaving hers. Neither had slept. Every time they closed their eyes, they saw the sanctuary falling, heard Raphael's final cry, remembered those they'd left behind.

"David," Elizabeth whispered from the other SUV, and something in her voice made Haniel look closer. There was history there, written in the way Elizabeth's hands tightened on the seatbelt strap across her chest.

The vehicles pulled to a stop in front of the house. David descended the porch steps with the measured pace of a man who'd seen enough in his life to know rushing rarely helped. He was older than Mary had expected, maybe in his sixties. His face was weathered by sun and time, lined with both laughter and sorrow.

"Elizabeth," he said softly as they emerged from the vehicles. "Been a long time."

"David." Elizabeth's voice carried years of unspoken things. "Thank you for taking us in on such short notice."

His eyes moved to Mary, taking in her pregnancy, then to Joseph's protective stance beside her. His expression showed clear concern at their obvious exhaustion and distress. "You all look worn out. Come on inside, coffee's fresh, and I can rustle up some breakfast."

The house's interior was exactly what you'd expect from a working ranch's headquarters, practical furniture built to last, photographs of cattle drives on the walls, schedules and work rosters tacked to a cork board in the kitchen. The normalcy of it all felt almost surreal after what they'd just been through.

"The hands won't ask questions," David said as he poured coffee into ceramic mugs that had seen better days. "Most of them are veterans. They understand sometimes folks need a quiet place to lay low for a while. They're good men. Loyal."

"How many workers do you have?" Mallakiel asked, careful to sound casual despite his tactical interest.

"Twenty full-time, another dozen part-time. Ranch this size needs a lot of hands." David's eyes met Elizabeth's again. "You want to tell me what kind of trouble you're in?"

"Later," Elizabeth said quietly. "Right now, we just need rest. And safe harbor."

David nodded, accepting this for the moment. "Guest rooms are upstairs. Get some sleep. We can talk more when you're rested."

Mary followed Elizabeth up the creaking stairs, Joseph closes behind. The simple bedroom they were shown to had a large window overlooking the pastures, where cattle grazed peacefully in the morning light. The normalcy of it all felt like a gift.

"Rest," Elizabeth said from the doorway. "David's a good man. We're safe here, at least for now." Mary sank onto the bed, her body finally registering bone-deep exhaustion.

David found Elizabeth on the back porch later that afternoon, watching the sun sink toward the distant tree line. She'd aged well, gracefully, like she did everything else. But there was something in her eyes now that hadn't been there twenty years ago. Something haunted.

"You want to tell me what's really going on?" he asked, settling into the chair beside her. "Those folks upstairs, they're not just running from an angry ex or pushy debt collectors."

Elizabeth's hands tightened around her coffee mug. "It's complicated, David."

"Always was with you." There was no bitterness in his voice, just old understanding. "Remember when you left? Said there were things about your life I couldn't understand, wouldn't believe if you told me?"

She nodded, not trusting herself to speak.

"Well, I'm 30 years older now. Maybe a bit wiser. Try me."

Before she could answer, the screen door creaked open. Mallakiel stepped out, then stopped short when he saw them. "Sorry. Didn't mean to interrupt."

"You're not," Elizabeth said quickly. Too quickly. "David was just asking about our situation."

Mallakiel's military bearing was obvious even in casual clothes. "We appreciate the sanctuary, sir. But the less you know about why we're here, the better off you'll be."

David's laugh was dry as prairie dust. "Son, I've got six strangers in my house, one of them pregnant, all looking like they've seen war. Either you level with me, or this arrangement isn't going to hold up."

"David-" Elizabeth started.

"No, he's right." Haniel appeared in the doorway, her scholarly demeanor at odds with the ranch setting. "But perhaps we should wait for Mary and Joseph to join this conversation. It's their story more than ours."

As if summoned by their names, the young couple emerged onto the porch. Mary looked better after a few hours' rest, but Joseph's eyes still carried that haunted look of someone who'd lost too much too fast.

"Mr. Reed," Joseph said formally. "We owe you an explanation."

"David," the older man corrected. "Mr. Reed was my father. And yes, you do."

Mary settled into a chair, one hand resting protectively over her growing belly. "How much do you know about prophecy, David?"

He raised an eyebrow. "The Bible kind? Enough to get through Sunday school. Why?"

"Because we're living one," she said simply. "And there are people who want to stop it. Powerful people. They've already-" Her voice caught. "They've already killed my parents. Joseph's father. Friends. They'll keep killing people until they get what they want."

"Who is killing people? What on earth do they want?"

"Me," she whispered. "Or more specifically, my baby."

David absorbed this, his weathered face giving nothing away. "Religious fanatics?"

"Something like that," Elizabeth said carefully.

"Government involvement?"

"Some," Mallakiel admitted. "But not officially."

David nodded slowly. "That explains the tactical movements. The way you've been checking sight lines since you arrived. Military background?"

"Something like that," Mallakiel echoed Elizabeth's careful tone.

"And you came here because..."

"Because twenty years ago, you were the best man I ever knew," Elizabeth said softly. "The most trustworthy. That hasn't changed."

David studied her face for a long moment. "There's more you're not telling me."

"Yes."

"Going to share it?"

"Not yet. Maybe not ever. For your own protection."

He absorbed this, then stood abruptly. "Well, then. Guess we better start thinking about security. Ranch this size has a lot of blind spots." He looked at Mallakiel. "You'll want to check the old barn; previous owner dug a storm cellar that could double as a panic room if needed. Joseph, you've got construction experience?"

Joseph straightened slightly. "Yes sir. It's the family business."

"Good. We'll need it." He turned to Haniel. "Ma'am, you look like you know your way around computers. Ranch office could use an upgrade in surveillance equipment."

"I can help with that," she said, careful not to reveal just how much help she could provide.

"Elizabeth?" David's voice softened slightly. "Walk with me? We should discuss logistics."

As they walked away from the house, Mary watched Elizabeth's face. There was history there, old pain mixed with something that seemed like remorse.

"He's a good man," Joseph said quietly. "We're bringing danger to his door."

"We'll protect him," Mallakiel promised. "Him and his people."

Joseph watched David and Elizabeth disappear around the barn, and wondered if any of them were truly ready for what was coming. Because somewhere out there, demons were hunting them with everything they had.

The next few days fell into an uneasy rhythm. During daylight hours, they worked to fortify the ranch while maintaining its appearance of normalcy. Joseph threw himself into construction, helping David's crew reinforce the old barn's storm cellar. His knowledge of building made him valuable, and the physical labor helped keep his mind from the darker thoughts.

The ranch hands accepted their presence with the quiet discretion of men used to minding their own business. If they noticed Mallakiel setting up defensive positions or Haniel installing sophisticated security equipment, they didn't mention it.

"Military contractors," David had told them. "Private security for some folks in trouble. That's all you need to know."

Mary watched it all from the wraparound porch, feeling increasingly useless as her pregnancy advanced. The baby was active now, especially at night, as if sensing the growing tension around them.

"You should be resting," Elizabeth said, bringing her a glass of water. She'd been spending more time with David, rekindling something that looked like trust, if not quite forgiveness.

"I rest too much already," Mary replied. "While everyone else prepares for-" She stopped as one of the ranch hands walked past, nodding politely.

Elizabeth waited until he was out of earshot. "You're doing the most important work of all. Keeping that child safe."

Below them in the yard, Joseph was consulting with David over blueprints spread across the hood of a pickup. They'd been modifying the barn's cellar, reinforcing the door in a way that nobody would suspect.

"He blames himself," Mary said softly, watching Joseph. "For his father. For Raphael. For all of it."

"And you don't blame yourself for your parents?"

Mary's hand tightened on her glass. "Every second."

Haniel emerged from the ranch office, looking frustrated. She'd been trying to set up some kind of early warning system, though she was careful not to let David see its true sophistication.

"Problems?" Elizabeth called down.

"Just technical difficulties," Haniel replied, the lie smooth on her tongue. In truth, she was struggling without her full abilities, trying to create supernatural warnings using only human technology. They had nearly spent all their supplies for creating wards.

Mallakiel appeared from the tree line, where he'd been setting up observation posts disguised as hunting blinds. His military background made his role here easier to explain, but Mary could see the strain in him. They all felt stripped, reduced, trying to fight a supernatural war with purely human means.

The screen door creaked, and David stepped out onto the porch. "Dinner's almost ready," he said. "Elizabeth, could you give me a hand in the kitchen?"

They vanished inside, and Mary smiled slightly despite everything. Some sparks, it seemed, never quite died.

"Penny for your thoughts?" Joseph had climbed the porch steps, wiping sweat from his face. The physical work was changing him, replacing corporate polish with something harder, more capable.

"Just wondering how long we can keep this up," she said quietly. "Pretending to be normal people with normal problems. Hiding what's really coming from a good man who's risking everything to help us."

Joseph settled beside her, his hand finding hers. "We tell him the truth; we put him in more danger. Give him deniability if... when they come."

"When," Mary echoed. Not if. Never if.

The sun was setting now, painting the ranch in shades of gold and shadow. From this angle, it almost looked peaceful, cattle grazing in distant pastures, ranch hands heading in for dinner, David's dogs chasing each other across the yard.

Thunder rolled, closer now, though the sky remained clear. "We should get inside," Joseph said softly. "Storm's coming."

David found Elizabeth in the ranch office late that night, poring over security camera feeds. The soft glow of the monitors painted her face in shades of blue, reminding him of moonlight on the lake where they'd first met, decades ago.

"You still take your coffee black?" he asked, setting a mug beside her.

"Some things don't change." She didn't look up from the monitors, but her shoulders relaxed slightly at his presence.

"And some things do." He settled into the chair beside her. "Twenty years ago, you were teaching Sunday school and dreaming of opening a small bookstore. Now you're running from people who kill without hesitation and installing military-grade security systems."

"David-"

"I'm not asking for explanations," he cut her off gently. "Just wondering if you ever think about how different things might have been."

Now she did look at him, really look at him. Time had been kind to David Reed. His hair was more silver than brown now, and the lines around his eyes were deeper, but he still carried himself with that quiet strength she'd fallen in love with all those years ago.

"Every day," she admitted softly. "But I made my choices. Had my reasons."

"Must have been good ones. You never did anything without purpose." He took a sip of his own coffee. "That girl upstairs, Mary. She reminds me of you sometimes. Same kind of fire inside."

"She's stronger than I ever was."

"Don't sell yourself short. You're here, aren't you? Standing between her and whatever's hunting them."

A comfortable silence fell between them, filled with the soft hum of electronics and distant cricket song. Outside, Mallakiel's boots crunched on gravel as he made his rounds.

"You could have said no," Elizabeth said finally. "When I called. Asked for help. You could have turned us away."

"No, I couldn't have." His voice was gentle. "You know that."

Before she could respond, movement on one of the monitors caught her attention. A coyote, stalking along the fence line. Something about its movement seemed off, too deliberate.

"Third one tonight," David noted. "More than usual."

Elizabeth's hand tightened on her coffee mug. If David noticed her tension, he didn't comment.

"You've done good work here," she said, changing the subject. "Built something real. Something lasting."

"Most days." He smiled slightly. "Ranch keeps me busy. Keeps me honest." His eyes found hers again. "Keeps me from thinking too much about what I let slip away."

Unspoken things hung between them. All the might-have-been. All the roads not taken.

A knock at the door made them both jump. Joseph stood in the doorway, looking apologetic. "Sorry to interrupt. But Mary's asking for you, Elizabeth. Says it's important."

Elizabeth rose quickly, too quickly. Coffee sloshed over the rim of her mug.

"Everything okay?" David asked, concern evident in his voice.

"I'm sure it's fine," Elizabeth said. "Probably just nervous about the baby."

But as she followed Joseph out, David noticed how her hand brushed against something in her pocket, something that might have been a cross, or might have been something else entirely.

He turned back to the security feeds, watching the coyote pace along the fence. Its eyes caught the infrared light, reflecting it back like tiny fires.

"What aren't you telling me, Elizabeth?" he whispered to the empty room. "What kind of trouble have you really brought with you?"

The coyote turned its head toward the camera for a moment. Then the feed flickered, and when it stabilized, the creature was gone.

David Reed was a practical man. He dealt in cattle and crops, in weather patterns and market prices. But watching that empty fence line, he couldn't shake the feeling that he was missing something. Something vast and frightening, circling his ranch like wolves around a campfire.

More thunder rolled across the prairie. Somewhere in the house above, he heard voices raised in urgent discussion. And for the first time in years, David Reed felt uneasy.

Elizabeth found Mary's room transformed into an impromptu war room. Maps were spread across the bed, their edges weighted down with coffee mugs. Mallakiel stood at the window, scanning the darkness outside while Haniel marked locations on one of the larger maps with careful precision.

"What's happened?" Elizabeth asked, closing the door softly behind her.

"Raphael is alive. We found him," Haniel said without looking up. "Or rather, we found where they're keeping him."

Joseph stood beside Mary, who was sitting in the old rocking chair by the window. His face was tense. "One of Haniel's contacts spotted them moving Raphael to a compound in the Louisiana bayou. Old hunting lodge converted into some kind of base."

"And the staff's there too," Mallakiel confirmed. "But heavily guarded. They've got at least thirty possessed humans patrolling the perimeter. More inside, probably."

"We can't leave him there," Mary said softly. "What they must be doing to him..."

"We won't," Mallakiel's voice was firm. "But we need to be smart about this. One wrong move and we lose not just Raphael, but any chance of recovering the Staff."

Joseph studied the marked locations. "These access points, they're watching them?"

"All but one." Haniel pointed to a spot where the bayou nearly touched the compound's edge. "There's an old service tunnel here, probably forgotten. Partially flooded, but passable."

"I'm going with you," Joseph insisted, his jaw set with determination.

"No." Mallakiel's response was immediate and firm. "Your place is here, protecting Mary."

"Raphael is in there because of us-"

"Which is exactly why you need to stay," Haniel cut him off. "If something goes wrong, Mary can't be left alone. Not now."

"She won't be. The ranch-"

"The ranch isn't enough," Elizabeth said gently. "She needs you, Joseph. The baby needs you."

Mary reached for his hand. "They're right. I can't... I can't lose you too."

Joseph's shoulders slumped slightly, the tension going out of him. "Then who?"

"We'll need local help," Mallakiel said. "People who know the area, know how to move without drawing attention."

Elizabeth nodded slowly. "David might be able to help with that. He has men he trusts. Veterans."

"Can they handle themselves in a fight?" Haniel asked.

"Two of them served together in Special Forces," Elizabeth replied. "David mentioned them yesterday, Marcus Chen and Ray Blackwood. They've done security work since leaving the service."

"Will they ask questions?"

"They'll ask," Elizabeth said. "But they'll understand if we can't answer all of them. That's the kind of men they are."

A soft knock at the door made them all freeze. David's voice came through: "Elizabeth? Got a minute?"

"Of course," she called back, quickly gathering up the maps. The others moved to make the room look less like a military planning session.

David opened the door, looking slightly apologetic for interrupting. "Chen and Blackwood are downstairs. You asked about reliable men?"

Elizabeth tried not to look too relieved at the coincidence. "Yes, thank you. We'll be right down."

Once David's footsteps had retreated, Mallakiel spoke quietly. "We'll need a cover story. Something to explain why we need their help but can't tell them everything."

"Private security detail," Haniel suggested. "Extracting a kidnapped colleague. Close enough to the truth without revealing too much."

They found Chen and Blackwood in the ranch's kitchen, both nursing cups of coffee. They were a study in contrasts, Chen, compact and precise in his movements, Blackwood, tall and broad-shouldered. But they shared the same alert watchfulness in their eyes, the same way of positioning themselves to see all entrances.

"David says you might have some work," Chen said without preamble.

"Extraction job," Mallakiel replied, matching his directness. "High risk, highly confidential. There are things we can't tell you."

"Usually are," Blackwood sad gruffly. "Pay?"

"Fifty thousand each. Half up front."

The two men exchanged glances. Some unspoken communication passed between them.

"Timeline?" Chen asked.

"Three days. In and out."

"Location?"

"Louisiana. We'll brief you on the details if you're in."

Another silent exchange. Then Chen nodded. "We're in. But we do this our way. No reckless moves, no heroes."

"Agreed," Mallakiel said. "We'll start planning tomorrow at dawn."

After they left, Elizabeth caught David watching her with an unreadable expression.

"Thank you," she said softly.

"Don't thank me yet," he replied. "Just... bring them back safe, whatever it is you're really doing."

She wanted to tell him everything then, about angels and demons, about the war they were fighting. But she couldn't. Not without making him a target.

"We will," was all she said.

Upstairs, Joseph held Mary as she cried quietly, both of them knowing the risks that lay ahead. Raphael had sacrificed everything to protect them. Now it was their turn to try to save him.

Dawn found them gathered in the barn's storm cellar, away from curious eyes. Chen had laid out satellite photos of the bayou compound across a makeshift table, while Blackwood cleaned a rifle with practiced efficiency. The morning light filtering through the cellar's narrow windows cast long shadows across their serious faces.

"Main challenge is the approach," Chen said, tracing routes with a calloused finger. "Waterways are likely watched. Ground access is limited to one road."

"What about here?" Mallakiel pointed to the partially flooded service tunnel Haniel had identified.

"Possible," Blackwood murmured without looking up from his work. "But risky. If they've found it, it's a perfect bottleneck."

Joseph stood in the corner, arms crossed, watching them plan the rescue he wouldn't be part of. Every fiber of his being wanted to argue, to insist on going. But Mary's tears last night had sealed it, he couldn't risk leaving her alone.

"Their patrol patterns are predictable," Haniel said, careful to sound like she'd gotten the information through normal surveillance. "Shift changes every six hours. Most activity at the north end of the compound."

"Where are they keeping him?" Chen asked.

"Underground level," Mallakiel replied. "Some kind of reinforced chamber. We'll need shaped charges to breach it."

"And the... artifact you mentioned?" Blackwood looked up now, his eyes sharp. "The one that's so important?"

"Same location, probably," Haniel said. "They'll keep them together."

Chen studied the photos again. "Two-man entry team through the tunnel. Two more providing cover from here and here." He marked positions. "Fast in, fast out. No engagement unless necessary."

"We'll need a boat waiting here," Blackwood added. "Hidden in these cypress trees. Engine modified for silent running."

Joseph pushed off from the wall. "I can help with that at least. I know engines."

The others exchanged glances, then nodded. At least this way he could contribute something.

"What aren't you telling us?" Chen asked suddenly, looking at Mallakiel. "These men we're up against, they're not just mercenaries, are they?"

"No," Mallakiel admitted. "They're not. But the less you know about that, the better."

"Fair enough," Blackwood said. "But no surprises once we're in. We see something we don't like; we pull out. Clear?"

"Crystal."

They spent the next hour going over timing, contingencies, and extraction routes. Chen and Blackwood worked together seamlessly, finishing each other's thoughts, suggesting improvements to each other's ideas. It was clear why David had recommended them.

"We'll need specialized gear," Chen said finally. "Not the kind of thing you find at the local sporting goods store."

"I can get it," Haniel assured him. "Just give me a list."

Joseph watched them plan, feeling simultaneously impressed and frustrated. These men knew their business. But so did he. He could help. He should be helping.

The cellar door creaked open above them. David's voice drifted down: "Breakfast in ten. Elizabeth's asking for you all."

They began gathering up the maps and photos. As the others climbed the stairs, Blackwood hung back.

"It's eating you, isn't it?" he said quietly to Joseph. "Staying behind?"

Joseph nodded tightly.

"Sometimes the harder job is staying put," the big man said. "Protecting what matters most. Doesn't make it any less important."

"They're going into danger because of us," Joseph replied. "Because they helped us."

"And you'll go stir-crazy thinking about it." Blackwood's voice was surprisingly gentle. "Focus on what you can do. The boat. The backup plans. The home front. Let us handle the rest."

He clapped Joseph on the shoulder and headed up the stairs, leaving Joseph alone in the cellar. Above, he could hear the others talking, their voices muffled by distance and wood. Normal breakfast sounds. As if they weren't planning an impossible rescue. As if everything was fine.

Joseph looked at the satellite photos one last time before folding them away. Three days. Three days until they tried to save Raphael. Three days until everything changed. He hoped they were ready.

The day before the rescue, Joseph worked on the boat's engine in the ranch's equipment shed, trying to lose himself in the familiar comfort of machinery. He'd modified the exhaust system to run nearly silent, replaced the propeller with a custom design that barely rippled the water. Good, practical work that kept his hands busy and his mind from darker places.

Chen appeared in the doorway like a ghost. The man moved silently even on gravel.

"How's it coming?" he asked, examining Joseph's work with a professional eye.

"Should be ready. Tested it in the stock pond this morning. Quiet as a whisper."

Chen nodded. "Good work." He paused, choosing his next words carefully. "You know, most people in your situation would be asking a lot more questions."

Joseph's hands stilled on the engine. "Would you answer them?"

"No." A faint smile. "But they'd still ask."

"Will it help get him back?"

"We'll do our best."

Joseph wiped his hands on a rag, studying the former Special Forces operator. "The men you're going up against... they're not normal. You need to be ready for that."

"We've seen things," Chen said quietly. "In places we can't talk about. Things that don't make sense. We know when there's more going on than we're being told."

Before Joseph could respond, Blackwood's voice carried from outside: "Chen! Gear's here!"

They found Haniel's "supplies" spread across the barn floor, tactical gear that looked military but carried no identifying marks, communications equipment, weapons that made Chen whistle softly.

"This is high-end stuff," he said, examining a rifle. "Not exactly standard issue."

"Will it do the job?" Mallakiel asked.

"Oh yeah." Blackwood was checking the rest of the gear with methodical precision. "This'll do just fine."

Elizabeth appeared in the barn doorway. "David's asking questions about all the deliveries."

"Tell him it's personal security equipment," Haniel suggested. "Not technically a lie."

"He's not naive," Elizabeth said. "He knows we're planning something."

"But he won't ask," Chen said with certainty. "Man like that understands sometimes it's better not to know."

They spent the afternoon going over the plan one final time. Chen and Blackwood would enter through the service tunnel while Mallakiel and Haniel provided cover. Quick in, quick out. No engagement unless absolutely necessary.

"And if things go wrong?" Joseph asked.

"Then we adapt," Mallakiel said firmly. "But we're bringing them home."

As evening approached, Mary found Joseph in the equipment shed again, still tinkering with the boat engine though it was already perfect.

"You don't have to pretend," she said softly. "I know how hard this is."

He straightened, his back to her. "I should be going with them."

"You should be exactly where you are." She moved closer, taking his hand. "With me. With our child."

"If something happens to them..."

"Then we'll face it together." She turned him to face her. "Like we've faced everything else."

The baby kicked, as if emphasizing her point. Despite everything, Joseph smiled slightly as he felt it.

From the barn came the sound of Chen and Blackwood doing final equipment checks. Mallakiel's voice carried faintly, going over extraction routes one last time. Soon they would load the boat onto a trailer, make final preparations for tomorrow's pre-dawn departure.

Mary shivered slightly.

"They're watching us," she whispered. "Aren't they? They know we're planning something."

"Probably," Joseph admitted. "But they don't know what. Or where. That's something."

They held each other in the gathering darkness, listening to the sounds of preparation around them. "Come back," Mary whispered, though those who needed to hear it couldn't. "Just... come back."

It was morning at Bethlehem Ranch as the rescue team loaded their gear into the unmarked vehicles. Joseph watched from the porch, his hands clenched into fists at his sides, fighting every instinct that told him to grab his coat and join them.

"They know what they're doing," David said quietly, appearing beside him with two steaming cups of coffee. "Chen and Blackwood, I've seen them handle 'mission impossible' type situations before."

Joseph accepted the coffee without looking away from the preparations. "Still feels wrong, staying behind."

"Nothing wrong about protecting your family." David's life experience shone through. "Sometimes that's the harder job."

The comment hit close to Joseph's recent loss, and David seemed to sense it. He clasped Joseph's shoulder firmly, a paternal gesture that made Joseph's throat tighten unexpectedly.

"Your father," David said carefully, "he made his choices. Just like you're making yours. Doesn't make either of you wrong."

"He died thinking I'd abandoned him."

"No." David's voice was firm. "He died knowing you'd found something worth fighting for. There's a difference."

Below them, Mallakiel was doing final weapons checks while Haniel consulted maps one last time. Elizabeth stood slightly apart, her face tight with worry as she watched them prepare to leave.

"Go to them," David told her softly when she came up to say goodbye. "Your family needs you."

Elizabeth's eyes filled with tears. "Mary needs me too."

"She has us," David assured her. "We'll keep her safe until you get back."

"David-" She started to say something more, perhaps to finally explain everything, but he shook his head.

"Some things are better left unspoken," he told her. "Just come back safe."

She hugged him tightly, then hurried down to join the others before her resolve could break. Minutes later, the vehicles disappeared down the ranch's long drive, leaving only dust and silence behind.

Mary appeared in the doorway, one hand resting on her swollen belly. "Now we wait?"

"Now we wait," Joseph confirmed, moving to her side.

"Come on inside," David said. "Elizabeth showed me how you like your eggs. Might as well keep our strength up while we wait for news."

Throughout that endless day, David kept them both busy with ranch tasks, simple, practical things that required just enough focus to keep darker thoughts at bay. He taught Joseph about maintaining fence lines, about reading weather patterns in the clouds, about judging a horse's health from twenty paces.

"My father used to say you can't fix the whole world," David told him as they repaired a section of fence. "But you can fix what's right in front of you. Sometimes that's enough."

By sunset, Joseph's muscles ached from honest work, and his mind felt clearer than it had in days. Mary had spent the afternoon with David's housekeeper, learning to make bread the old-fashioned way.

"It helps," she admitted as they got ready for bed. "Having him here. He reminds me of my father sometimes."

"Yeah." Joseph's voice was tired. "Mine too. In the ways that matter."

They lay awake long into the night, waiting for the phone to ring, for news of the rescue attempt.

In his own room, David sat in darkness, cleaning a rifle he hadn't needed in years. He hadn't asked what kind of trouble they were really in, or why Elizabeth had come to him after all this time. Some questions didn't need answers. He chambered a round and set the rifle within easy reach. Whatever was coming, he'd be ready.

The Louisiana bayou wrapped around them like a dark blanket, thick with humidity and the buzz of insects. Chen eased their modified boat through the cypress trees, the modified engine barely whispering. The moon cast strange shadows through the Spanish moss, turning familiar shapes into looming threats.

"Two minutes to entry point," he muttered into his throat mic. Blackwood crouched beside him, rifle ready, while Mallakiel and Haniel maintained positions in a second boat hidden among the trees, ready to provide cover.

The hunting lodge's dark bulk rose before them, its windows gleaming dully in the moonlight. Guards moved along the upper walkways, too regularly, too mechanically to be normal security.

"I count six on perimeter," Blackwood whispered. "Moving like they're on rails."

"Possessed," Mallakiel's voice crackled in their earpieces. "Remember, standard ammunition won't stop them for long. Use the blessed rounds only if you have to."

Chen didn't comment on the strange ammunition Haniel had supplied, or the way it seemed to hum faintly in its cases. He'd seen enough unusual things in his career to know when not to ask questions.

They found the service tunnel entrance half-submerged in murky water, just as their intel had indicated. Chen killed the engine, letting momentum carry them the last few feet.

"Watch for tripwires," Blackwood said as they slipped into the water. "Place this old, bound to be surprises ahead."

They moved through the tunnel like shadows, years of training making their movements silent despite the ankle-deep water. Their night vision showed the tunnel stretching ahead, water dripping from rusted pipes above.

"First checkpoint," Chen whispered. A heavy metal door blocked their path, but the lock was old, neglected. Twenty seconds with their tools and it swung open with barely a creak.

The tunnel began to slope upward, the air growing thicker with age and disuse. Somewhere above, they could hear movement, boots on floorboards, voices.

"Basement access ahead," Mallakiel's voice guided them. "Target should be in the reinforced room on the east side. Be careful, they'll have traps waiting."

Chen and Blackwood exchanged glances. They'd done enough high-risk extractions to know when something was off about an operation. The way their employers talked about the "hostiles." The strange equipment they'd been given. The way the very air seemed to thicken around them as they approached their target.

But they had a job to do. And they were very, very good at their jobs.

"Ready?" Chen asked, hand on the final door.

Blackwood nodded, weapon ready.

"Going in dark in three... two... one..."

Chen eased the heavy door open, letting Blackwood take point. The basement corridor stretched before them, emergency lights casting sickly shadows on concrete walls. Their footsteps, despite careful movement, seemed too loud in the oppressive silence.

"Three doors on the right, two left," Chen whispered into his comm. "No movement."

"Target should be behind the steel door at the end," Mallakiel's voice crackled in their earpieces. "Be careful, something's off."

Blackwood signaled his agreement. Years of experience screamed at them both, this was too easy. No guards, no security systems, nothing but that strange heaviness in the air that made their skin crawl.

They reached the steel door without incident. Chen placed shaped charges while Blackwood covered their six. The door looked military grade, but the hinges were their weak point.

"Set," Chen breathed. "Three, two-"

A scream cut through the silence, human, filled with anguish. It came from behind the door.

"That's him," Haniel's voice was tight. "They're... they're hurting him."

"Breach now," Mallakiel ordered.

The charges blew with a muffled thump, and they were through the door in textbook formation. The scene inside made them both falter for just a heartbeat.

The chamber was vast, far larger than the building above should have allowed. Raphael hung suspended in the center of the room, held up by chains. His body was covered in symbols carved into his flesh. Blood dripped steadily onto a complex pattern drawn on the floor beneath him. And standing before him, Staff of Moses crackling with corrupted power, was Deacon.

"Ah, our guests have arrived." Deacon turned from his work, and both men felt their spines go cold. He looked human, expensive suit, perfect smile, but his eyes were completely, impossibly black. "Chen and Blackwood, isn't it?

Chen's finger tightened on his trigger. "How do you-"

"Oh, I know all about you both," Deacon's voice carried harmonics that made their teeth ache. "Marcus Chen. Special Forces. Three tours in places that don't officially exist. You still dream about that night in Kandahar, don't you? The things you saw in that cave?"

Chen's professional composure cracked slightly. He'd never told anyone about that night.

"And Ray Blackwood," Deacon continued, taking a step forward. Both men instinctively stepped back. "The things you did for the CIA... tell me, do you still hear those children crying?"

"Shut up," Blackwood's voice was hoarse. "Whatever you are-"

"Ah, that's the question, isn't it?" Deacon's smile widened. "What am I? What is all this? So far above your pay grade, little soldiers. You should have stayed at the ranch, playing cowboy. Instead, you'll die here, knowing you failed. Knowing you never even understood what you were really fighting."

He gestured and the trap sprung with devastating efficiency. Possessed humans emerged from every shadow, moving with inhuman speed.

"Chen," Blackwood's voice was steady despite his fear. "The blessed rounds. Just like they said."

Chen and Blackwood fought back-to-back. They opened fire in perfect sync, their shots finding marks with mechanical precision. The blessed ammunition worked, the possessed humans dropped, black smoke pouring from their mouths, but there were so many. Overwhelming.

"Did they tell you what I am?" Deacon asked conversationally as he raised the Staff. "Did they tell you what you were really walking into?" Power began building around him like a storm about to break. "No. They sent you here blind. Disposable. Just more bodies to throw at the darkness."

"Mallakiel!" Chen shouted into his comm. "We need-"

"Your radio's dead," Deacon grinned. "It's just us now. You. Me. And all the nightmares you never believed in."

Blackwood went down first, three possessed taking him from behind even as he emptied his magazine into their ranks. Chen's shout of fury was cut short as Deacon's power caught him full in the chest, throwing him against the wall with crushing force.

"Fall back!" Mallakiel's voice carried over the chaos. "We're compromised!"

Chen finally understood. This wasn't just another mission. This was something ancient. Horrific. They never truly had a chance. His last act was to reach for a grenade, one of Haniel's blessed ones. "See you in hell," he gasped, and pulled the pin.

"You certainly will," Deacon snarled.

The explosion of blessed ordnance lit up the chamber like daybreak, and in that flash, they saw it all, Chen's body thrown against the wall, Blackwood already fallen, and Raphael still hanging in his chains, eyes filled with both pain and desperate warning. Mallakiel and Haniel barely made it back to the tunnel entrance, forced to leave their fallen comrades behind.

"We can't just leave them," Haniel said, even as she ran. Her voice cracked with the notion of failure.

"They're already gone." Mallakiel's military bearing couldn't quite hide his own grief. "All of them."

They emerged into moonlight, running for the boats. No pursuit, they didn't need to be pursued. They had walked right into his trap, bringing two good men to their deaths.

The boats were where they'd left them, hidden among the cypress trees. As they sped away through the bayou, Haniel finally broke the silence.

"We shouldn't have brought them," she whispered. "We were overconfident. Thinking we could mount a rescue with just four of us. Thinking we could match his power when he had the Staff."

"We had to try." But Mallakiel's words rang hollow even to himself.

"Those men trusted us. They died not even knowing what they were really fighting." Haniel's hands tightened on her weapon. "And Raphael... whatever ritual Deacon's planning..."

The images flashed through their mind's eye, the symbols carved into Raphael's flesh, the pattern of blood on the floor, the way Deacon had been expecting them. This hadn't just been about keeping Raphael captive. They were using him for something.

The day crawled by as David spent hours in his office making calls, to Chen's daughter, to Blackwood's sister, crafting careful lies about a security operation gone wrong. Each call aged him more, each fabricated explanation another betrayal of men who deserved better.

Mallakiel stood at the window in the barn's hayloft, watching David through binoculars as he paced during the calls. "We should leave," he said when Haniel joined him. "We've brought enough death to his door."

"We can't," Haniel replied softly. "Whatever Deacon's planning, it's bigger than we thought. We are safer here. This is the best stronghold available."

"At least we know Raphael is alive. For what it's worth. But now he also has the staff." Mallakiel's military bearing cracked slightly. "We played right into his hands."

In the ranch house kitchen, Elizabeth tried to approach David between calls. He held up a hand, stopping her. "Not now," he said quietly. "Maybe not ever."

She found Mary and Joseph on the back porch, holding each other. Mary's eyes were red from crying. "I keep thinking," she whispered, "how many more will die because of me? Because of this child?"

"Not because of you," Joseph said firmly. "Because of them. Because of what they're willing to do to stop this birth."

"They're right though, aren't they?" Mary's head rested on Joseph's shoulder. "About leaving. We're putting everyone here at risk."

"You're not going anywhere." David's voice made them all turn. He stood in the doorway, looking exhausted but resolute. "Chen and Blackwood died protecting something they believed in. Something important enough that Elizabeth came to me for help after twenty years." His eyes found Elizabeth's. "I'm still waiting for the whole truth. But until then, their sacrifice means you stay. You stay and you finish whatever this is."

"David-" Elizabeth started.

"I'm not doing it for you," he cut her off. "I'm doing it for them. Because whatever got them killed, whatever's coming, running won't stop it. Will it?"

Nobody answered. They didn't have to.

Evening found them gathered in the living room, maps spread across coffee tables, trying to make sense of what they'd learned. Haniel sketched the ritual pattern she'd seen, her hands shaking slightly.

"It's old," she explained. "Pre-Babylonian maybe. Something about binding power, using blood to-" She stopped as David once again entered the room.

He looked at the maps, the strange symbols, the worried faces. "I'm not asking for explanations," he said quietly. "Not yet. But I need to know, was it quick? At the end?"

Mallakiel met his eyes. "They stood like warriors. Fighting something most men wouldn't even believe in."

David nodded once, processing this. "Chen would have liked that. He always said the worst monsters were the ones wearing human faces." A bitter chuckle. "Guess he was more right than he knew."

David felt it now, the dread bearing down on them. And they had... what? A pregnant girl. A handful of would-be soldiers who'd just been outmaneuvered. And a rancher who'd lost two of his best men to a fight he still didn't fully understand.

"Get some rest," David said finally. "Tomorrow, you tell me truthfully what's coming. Tonight..." He looked at the photos on his wall, younger versions of himself with Chen and Blackwood, all smiling at some long-ago barbecue. "Tonight, we remember."

He walked out, back straight despite everything. Elizabeth watched him go, thirty years of unspoken things hanging between them.

In the basement chamber, Blackwood hung suspended where Raphael had been, blood dripping from fresh wounds. His training had helped him endure longer than most, but in the end, everyone broke. Deacon barely glanced at his broken body as Malcolm entered the room.

"A place called The Bethlehem Ranch in Texas," Deacon said with satisfaction. "Hiding right under our noses." He ran his fingers along the Staff of Moses, feeling its power pulse like a living thing. "This is growing stronger by the hour. Can you feel it?"

Malcolm straightened his perfect suit. "The comet approaches. Three days now." He moved to examine Raphael, who hung unconscious in chains nearby. "His pain feeds it. Makes the Staff remember what it was used for, what it was meant for, not salvation, but judgment."

"Speaking of judgment..." Deacon turned to Blackwood, who stirred weakly. "Thank you for your cooperation. Your suffering has served a higher purpose." With a casual gesture, one of the possessed moved over to Blackwood, and ended his life with a quick twist.

"Was that necessary?" Malcolm asked, though his tone suggested he didn't particularly care.

"Loose ends," Deacon replied with indifference. "Besides, his death will help convince them we mean business." He hefted the Staff, its ancient wood gleaming with unnatural light. "No more games. No more prisoners. When we attack the ranch, we leave nothing alive."

"The child must not be born," Malcolm agreed. His human disguise flickered slightly, showing something vast and dark beneath. "The Staff will give us the power we need to breach whatever protections they've mounted. And with the comet's approach..." He smiled, the expression too wide for a human face. "Well, let's just say the timing is perfect."

"You should have seen their faces," Deacon chuckled darkly, remembering the failed rescue. "Pathetic, thinking they could just walk in here. Even Raphael, thinking he could protect them by becoming one of them." He spoke the word like poison.

"They never understood," Malcolm said softly, running a finger along one of Raphael's wounds. "Free will was their curse, not their blessing. The ability to choose meant the ability to choose wrongly. To choose destruction. And they choose it every time. So then, let's give them what they want. Gather everyone. We attack on the comet's arrival in three days, full force. No survivors, no mercy."

Deacon nodded in approval. "I'll coordinate with our forces. And Raphael?"

"Keep him alive, for now. I want him to witness everything he failed to prevent." Malcolm turned to leave, then paused. "Oh, and Deacon? Make sure our forces understand, this isn't just about stopping a birth. This is about sending a message. To Heaven, to the Paladins, to everyone who thinks they can stand against us."

"And what message is that?"

Deacon's human form began to shift, showing his true nature beneath. "That the age of kindness is over. That this world belongs to us now."

After Malcolm left, Deacon lingered in the chamber, studying Raphael's broken form. The Staff hummed in his grip, responding to both their presences, divine energy recognizing divine essence, even in its corrupted state.

"Look at you," Deacon said softly. "The mighty Raphael. Heaven's healer. Reduced to this..." He gestured at Raphael's wounded body. "And for what? These creatures? These flawed, limited beings who destroy everything they touch?"

Raphael raised his head slowly, blood trickling from split lips. "You still don't understand, brother."

"Don't call me that. Don't ever call me that again!" he said grabbing Raphael's red locks and jerking his head back. "We stopped being brothers when He chose them over us."

"He never chose them over us. He asked us to love them as He did."

"Love them?" Deacon's tone was cold and bitter. "These gnats? These mud-creatures who live and die in an eyeblink? Who wage wars over imagined slights, who murder their own kind for profit and pleasure? Tell me, brother," the word was a curse on his lips now, "what makes them worthy of such love?"

"Because they try," Raphael's voice grew stronger. "Despite their flaws, despite their limitations, they try. They fall, they fail, but they get up. They learn. They grow."

"They destroy!" Deacon slammed the Staff against the ground, its power crackling. "Look at what they've done to His creation! Look at how they twist everything sacred into weapons! Even this-" he hefted the Staff, "a holy relic meant to guide them, and they used it for war."

"Like you're using it now?"

The question hung in the air between them. Deacon moved closer, his human facade cracking slightly with rage.

"Lucifer was right," he hissed. "We were the firstborn. We were perfect. Unfailing in our duty, unwavering in our devotion. Then He creates these... things. These broken, imperfect copies of us. And demands we bow to them? Serve them? Love them more than Him?"

"Not more than Him," Raphael said quietly. "As He loves them. Because they were made in our image, just as we were made in His. Can't you see the beauty in that?"

"I see weakness being celebrated. Imperfection being rewarded. Tell me, Raphael, why? Why them? What makes them so special?"

"They are free," Raphael's chains clinked as he shifted. "The very thing you resent about them is what makes them magnificent. They can choose. Choose to be better. Choose to love. Choose to rise above their nature."

"Or choose to fall," Deacon sneered. "Like you did. Choosing to become one of them. How does it feel, brother? The pain? The weakness? The emptiness where your grace used to be?"

"It feels human," Raphael met his eyes. "It feels real. Every choice matters now. Every moment is precious because it ends. That's what you never understood, their brevity makes them beautiful. Their struggles make them strong."

"Their struggles make them brutal," Deacon countered. "They invented torment, did you know that? Heaven and Hell existed for eons in perfect balance, but it took humanity to devise new ways of causing pain. To find pleasure in suffering."

"And yet they also invented music," Raphael smiled slightly. "Art. Poetry. Ways of creating beauty from nothing. Just like He did. The truth is Lucifer was jealous. Wanting all the love and adoration."

"Stop it!" Deacon's composure cracked entirely. "Stop defending them! They're animals. Less than animals. And when this child is born, this supposed miracle, they'll corrupt it too. Turn it into a weapon, just like they do everything else."

"Or it will change everything," Raphael's voice carried absolute conviction. "Show them a better way. Show them what love really means. Show them what they can become."

"Then I'll make you watch as we erase it," Deacon growled. "Watch as we kill everyone at that ranch. Watch as your precious humans reveal their true nature in their final moments, begging, bargaining, turning on each other to live just a few moments longer."

"Some will," Raphael agreed. "And some will die protecting others. Die standing against the darkness. Die choosing love over fear." His eyes seemed to glow faintly. "That's what terrifies you, isn't it? Not their capacity for evil, their capacity for good. For becoming more than what they are."

"We'll see how much good they're capable of when we're done. We'll see what choices they make when true terror finds them."

"Yes," Raphael said softly. "We will. And you'll finally understand what He saw in them all along."

Deacon lashed out, filling the chamber with Raphael's scream. But even through the pain, he smiled. Because he knew, every moment of suffering was a choice to endure. Every second of pain was a choice to protect. Every breath was a choice to love. And in that, he was more human than angel. More alive than he'd ever been in Heaven. More like Him than Deacon could ever understand.

The night air hung thick and rank over the lodge's balcony, where Malcolm stood watching heat lightning flicker through the cypress trees. Mosquitoes swarmed the floodlights, casting writhing shadows across the weathered boards. The screen of his phone illuminated, Harold's number.

"Hello Harold." He tried to keep his voice steady, professional.

"The temple's dead, Malcolm." Harold's voice crackled through the speaker, tinny and small against the vast darkness of the swamp. "Reisman Construction contractors filed Chapter 11 this morning."

Malcolm's fingers tightened around the phone, the plastic creaking under inhuman pressure. "That's impossible. I vetted them myself." The words came out slow, deliberate, like a warning.

"The owner went and took his own life. Likely saw it coming and couldn't take it. Now, everything's stopped. You didn't know about this? Were you too busy with your... other projects to notice they were circling the drain?" Harold's voice rose sharply. "The festival's in three weeks. Three weeks! We've got thirty thousand people coming, and instead of a temple, we've got a half-finished shell that looks like something out of a creepy horror movie."

"We can find another contractor. I have some connections that, "

"It's over, Malcolm." Harold's tone had shifted to something worse than frustration, the dismissive authority of a man who thought he understood the natural order of things. "The board met this afternoon. You're done."

"Done?" Something unfurled in Malcolm's chest. His carefully maintained humanity fell away like shed skin. "You insolent little insect," he whispered. "You think you have the authority to dismiss me?"

"Watch yourself." Harold's voice turned to steel.

"No, Harold. You should watch yourself. Your kind always forgets its place, thinking your temporary power means anything in the grand scheme. You have no idea what I am. You think you can just cast me aside?"

"Are you threatening me?"

"Threatening?" Malcolm's voice dropped to a low hissing tone. The floodlights flickered, and somewhere in the swamp, something large displaced the water. "No, Harold. Threats are for humans. I'm simply telling you how the world works. How it's always worked. Keep pushing, and I'll remind you exactly where you stand in the food chain."

Harold's voice, when it came, wavered slightly. "I'm recording this call, Malcolm. For both our sakes, I'm going to pretend this conversation never happened. Clear out your office by Friday."

The line went dead.

Malcolm stood motionless, phone still pressed to his ear. Spanish moss swayed in a wind that touched nothing else, and the dark water below seemed to pulse with anticipation. He looked down at his phone, at Harold's contact information still glowing on the screen like a target. Harold had just given him permission to stop pretending, to shed this bothersome human facade. There were older ways of doing business, after all.

Malcolm stood on the hunting lodge's upper balcony, watching their forces gather in the pre-dawn darkness. Below, dozens of possessed humans moved with mechanical precision, checking weapons, loading vehicles. These weren't random hosts anymore, these were trained killers, special forces operators and mercenaries, each one chosen specifically for their combat expertise. Even possessed, their muscle memory and tactical knowledge made them lethal.

Rusty stood at the edge of the lodge's dock, his hands trembling as he gripped the weathered railing. The air felt like breathing through wet cotton. Behind him, Malcolm watched from the balcony, savoring the desperation that rolled off the man in waves.

"Stage four pancreatic cancer," Rusty said, his voice cracking. "That's what the doctors told Nancy last week. Said there's nothing they can do except make her comfortable." He turned to face Malcolm, tears cutting clean trails through the sweat on his face. "Please. You said you could help her."

Malcolm stepped forward, letting the sickly yellow porch light illuminate him. He wore an expression of practiced compassion, though his eyes remained cold as swamp water. "I can. But you understand the cost?"

A bull gator bellowed in the distance, the sound echoing across the dark water like a warning. David flinched but held his ground. "You said... you said something about sharing my body?"

"Sharing is such an inadequate word." Malcolm moved closer, each step precisely measured. "Think of it more as... an opening of doors. A welcoming." His smile widened fractionally. "My associate requires a vessel, and in exchange for your hospitality, Nancy's cancer will simply... cease to be."

David's throat worked as he swallowed. "Will it hurt?"

"Oh yes," Malcolm said softly. "But not as much as watching your wife die by inches." He gestured toward the swamp, where fireflies danced like lost souls above the water. "The pain is temporary. The reward is profound. Nancy will live, healthy, whole, with decades ahead of her. All you have to do..." He extended his hand. "...is say yes."

"And I'll still be me? Afterward?"

Malcolm's tone was gentle, almost kind. "In all the ways that matter to Nancy. You'll go to work, love her, live your life. My associate will simply... observe. Most of the time." The deceit fell from his lips like honey. "Think of it as a roommate in your mind. One who also very much wants Nancy to survive."

Rusty stared at Malcolm's outstretched hand. A mosquito landed on his neck, bloating itself with his blood, but he didn't seem to notice. "If I say no?"

"Then you leave here with my sympathy, and nothing changes. Nancy suffers. You watch, helpless. She dies. You live with the knowledge that you could have saved her, but chose not to." Malcolm's voice remained gentle, reasonable. "The choice is entirely yours."

Somewhere in the darkness, something splashed, something large. The cypress trees seemed to lean closer, their moss-draped branches reaching like grasping fingers. Rusty's breathing had grown ragged, his face shining with sweat despite the evening chill.

"I..." His voice failed. He cleared his throat, tried again. "I'll do it. For Nancy."

Malcolm's smile widened. "Then we have an accord." He grasped David's trembling hand delivering a painful sizzle to seal the deal. "My associate will come to you tonight, in your dreams. Don't fight it. Fighting it only makes it... messy."

As Rusty stumbled back toward his car, Malcolm remained on the porch, watching. The man's shoulders were already slumping, as if bearing a new weight. Malcolm turned to one of the soldiers standing nearby. "Make sure our new friend's name is added to the festival roster." He paused, listening to the response. "Yes sir, that makes One hundred and fifty-three. Just in time."

Malcolm turned back to watch Rusty's taillights disappear through the cypress trees. The man had no idea what he'd truly agreed to, how little of him would remain once the entity finished moving in. But then, Malcolm mused, that was the beauty of desperation, it made such wonderful blinders. Malcolm wondered, briefly, if Jenny would notice when her husband's eyes began to change.

Deacon emerged from the shadows, "Status?"

"Three strike teams ready," Malcolm reported. "Former Delta Force, Spetsnaz, PMCs. All possessed by our strongest. The humans' own training makes them perfect weapons."

"The comet's power grows stronger," Deacon held up the Staff, its ancient wood now threaded with veins of light that matched the patterns they'd carved into Raphael. "By dawn, it will give us enough power to shatter any wards they've mounted."

A convoy of black SUVs and military-grade transport trucks idled in the compound's courtyard. Malcolm watched their possessed soldiers loading crates of ammunition imbued by dark rituals, the opposite of what the Paladins used, rounds designed to corrupt rather than cleanse.

"No survivors," Malcolm reminded him. "I want the ranch burned to the ground. I want Raphael to watch as we destroy every hand, every worker, every innocent soul he tried to protect."

"And the girl?"

"Save her for last. Let her watch too. Let her see the price of Heaven's attention." Malcolm turned back to Deacon. "Then we'll take the child. Use its blood to complete what we started with Raphael."

One of their commanders approached, a former CIA wet-works operative, his movements jerky and wrong under possession. "Sir. Teams are ready. We have the ranch's layout from Blackwood. All approaches mapped, all defensive positions identified."

"Good." Deacon handed him a black crystal that pulsed with dark energy. "Plant this when you breach the perimeter. It will prevent any heavenly intervention. This is our fight alone."

Malcolm watched their forces file into vehicles with inhuman synchronization. "They'll expect an attack after the rescue attempt failed."

"Let them. They can't imagine what's coming. By sunset, that ranch will be a graveyard. And the child will never draw breath."

The convoy engines rumbled to life in perfect unison.

David stood at his kitchen window, watching the comet's growing brightness paint strange shadows across his land. The air felt thick with the anticipation of approaching violence. Behind him, he could hear the others gathering, Elizabeth, Mallakiel, Haniel, Mary and Joseph.

"You need to tell me;" he said, without turning around. "All of it. Now. Before whatever's coming finds us."

"David," Elizabeth started, but he cut her off.

"Chen and Blackwood died fighting something they didn't understand. I won't let anyone else face that same darkness blind." He turned to face them. "No more half-truths. No more protection. What are we really dealing with?"

Mallakiel exchanged glances with Haniel, then nodded slowly. "Show him."

Haniel reached into her bag and withdrew something that made David's eyes hurt to look at, ancient parchments covered in symbols that seemed to move when you weren't looking directly at them.

"What you're about to hear will sound impossible," she said quietly. "But I need you to listen. Truly listen. Because we're running out of time."

So, they told him. About angels and demons. About the war that had raged since before time. About Mary's child and what it meant. About Raphael's capture and the Staff's power. About what was truly coming for them.

David sat silently through it all, his weathered face giving nothing away. Only his hands, clenched white-knuckled on his coffee mug, betrayed his tension.

"The men who took Blackwood," he said finally. "The ones Chen died fighting. They weren't human?"

"They were once," Mallakiel replied grimly. "Now they're vessels. Possessed by demons who use their combat training, their muscle memory. Everything that made them soldiers makes them perfect weapons."

"And you?" David looked at him hard. "What are you really?"

"We're Paladins. Once angels who chose to become human. We guard ancient relics, to stand between humanity and the darkness. We've been preparing for this battle for generations."

"And Elizabeth?" David's voice carried decades of questions. "Is that why you left your family? Because of all this?"

She nodded, unable to speak through tears.

"The comet," Haniel continued softly, "its approach is a signal. Of a coming power the world hasn't seen since the early days of the earth. When they come, and they will come, it will be with force beyond anything we've faced before."

"They'll kill everyone," Mallakiel added. "Not just us. Every hand, every worker. Everyone who helped shelter us."

David absorbed this, his face still unreadable. Then he stood abruptly and walked to a cabinet in the corner. From it, he withdrew an old wooden box.

"My grandfather gave me this," he said, opening it carefully. Inside lay an ancient revolver. "Said it was for a day when the darkness came calling. Said I'd know when that day arrived." He looked up at them. "Guess today's that day."

"David," Elizabeth whispered. "You don't have to-"

"Chen and Blackwood were family," he interrupted. "Everything else, angels, demons, holy wars, that's beyond my understanding. But family? That I understand." He checked the revolver's ammunition. "So, if darkness is coming to my ranch, aiming to hurt my people? Well, then darkness better be ready for a fight."

"How long?" David asked.

"A couple of days maybe," Mallakiel replied. "My guess is by Sunday, they'll be here."

"Then we better get ready." David's voice carried the iron certainty of a man who'd made his peace with whatever was coming. "Tell me what you need. My ranch, my rules."

They gathered around the ranch's blueprints spread across David's large kitchen table, the comet's pale light streaming through windows. David's practical knowledge of his land brought new perspective to their defensive planning.

"The irrigation trenches here and here," he indicated on the map, "they're deep enough for cover. We can use them to funnel their approach."

Mallakiel nodded appreciatively. "Good thinking. Haniel, can you set wards along these lines?"

"Already working on it." She was carefully inscribing symbols onto small metal discs. "These will slow any possessed trying to cross the barriers. Not stop them completely, but enough to make them vulnerable."

"The barn's storm cellar," David continued. "It's reinforced concrete, connects to old prohibition tunnels. Could be a fallback point if things go bad."

Joseph examined the tunnel layout. "I can shore up these support beams, add some choke points. Make it defendable."

"What about the ranch hands?" Elizabeth asked quietly.

David's face hardened. "Already sent most of them home. Told them to take their families, get clear of the area. Kept only the ones I trust most, veterans who've seen enough not to ask too many questions."

"How many?"

"Eight. All combat experienced. They're moving the cattle to the south pasture now, clearing our lines of fire."

“Eight? That’s it?” chirped Haniel. “At the sanctuary Deacon brought close to fifty with an armored vehicle in tow. Guaranteed this time he’s playing for keeps.”

David's face stiffened. "I won't send more people to their deaths without knowing what they're facing. Not after Chen and Blackwood."

"We don't have time to be noble about this-"

"Noble?" David interrupted, in command. "Those two men died fighting something they didn't understand because we didn't tell them the truth. I won't make that mistake again."

"He's right," Mallakiel said quietly. "They deserve the choice."

"These eight," David continued. "They're all combat veterans. I told them everything, demons, possession, all of it. Told them they were free to leave, get their families clear of what's coming." Pride crept into his voice. "They chose to stay."

Elizabeth touched his arm gently. "You couldn't have known about Chen and Blackwood."

"No," he agreed. "But I can do right by these men. Give them the truth, let them choose their battle."

They continued planning, setting up firing positions, laying blessed ammunition, preparing fallback points. Mary watched from her seat by the window as Joseph and Mallakiel discussed fortifying the barn's storm cellar.

The door opened, and Pete, one of David's oldest hands, stepped in. The former Marine's weathered face was set with determination.

"Boss," he said to David. "You need to see this."

They followed him outside. There, in the pre-dawn light, stood the rest of the ranch hands, twenty more men and women, armed and ready. Some had clearly rushed back after initially leaving, others looked like they hadn't left at all.

"Told them to go home," Pete said, a slight smile on his face. "They didn't listen. Word got around about what we're really facing." He turned to David. "They all came back. Every one of them volunteered."

"You don't have to do this," David started, but Mike, another ranch hand, interrupted him.

"This ranch is our home too," he said simply. "These demons want to come here, harm our people? Our families? Well, they better be ready for one heck of a fight." Pete glanced over at Mary standing in the back of the porch, almost hidden.

"Ma'am, we will do our best to protect you and your baby. But I need to know. Is it worth it?... Is he worth it?"

Mary turned to face Pete, one hand resting protectively over her belly. The former Marine's eyes held no judgment, only an earnest need to understand what he and his friends are risking their lives protecting.

"Pete," she said softly, "what I'm carrying... he's not just my child. I was told he's hope. A chance for something better than the darkness and fear in this world." She met his gaze steadily. "But I won't lie to you, I don't have the right to ask anyone to give their life for that hope. That has to be your choice."

The baby again moved beneath her hand, and she smiled slightly. "What I can tell you is this: everything that's coming, all the demons, all the possessed, all evil gathering against us, they're terrified of this child. Not because of what he is, but because of what he represents. The chance for humanity to be better. To choose love over fear, light over darkness."

She moved down the porch steps to Pete, reached out and touched his weathered hand. "So yes, he's worth it. Because he'll remind the world that even in the darkest night, there's still hope. There's still love."

Pete studied her face for a long moment, then nodded slowly. "Good enough for me, ma'am. Good enough for all of us."

David looked at his people, cowboys and ranch hands turned soldiers by choice, standing ready to face horrors they'd only just learned existed. Each one had heard the truth and chosen to stay, chosen to fight.

"We don't have enough blessed ammunition for everyone," Haniel said, but her voice had softened.

"Then we'll make more," Mallakiel replied. "They've earned the right to defend their home."

Mallakiel lead the makeshift army to the equipment room. He spread additional weapons across the ground, blessed ammunition, consecrated blades, protective charms hastily prepared by Haniel. The ranch hands gathered around, their faces serious as they absorbed instructions on fighting the supernatural.

"Regular ammunition will slow them down," Mallakiel explained, demonstrating how to load the blessed rounds. "But these are what you need for a kill shot. Aim center mass, just like you were trained. The blessing will do the rest."

"What about hand-to-hand?" Mike asked, examining one of the consecrated knives.

"Avoid it if possible," Haniel warned. "The possessed are stronger than normal humans, faster. They don't feel pain, don't tire. Keep your distance."

David organized them into fire teams, positioning the veterans to lead those with less combat experience. He knew his people, who could shoot, who could keep calm under pressure, who worked best together.

"Jensen, Martinez, take the north fence line. Crawford, your team on the barn approach. Pete, I want you coordinating the house defense." Each position was chosen to take advantage of the ranch's natural layout.

Joseph worked with several hands to fortify the barn, reinforcing doors, creating firing positions. "We've rigged the fuel tanks," he reported. "If they breach the outer perimeter, we can channel them right into the blast zone."

David organized them into fire teams, positioning the veterans to lead those with less combat experience. He knew his people, who could shoot, who could keep calm under pressure, who worked best together.

"Jensen, Martinez, take the north fence line. Crawford, your team on the barn approach. Pete, I want you coordinating the house defense." Each position was chosen to take advantage of the ranch's natural layout.

Joseph worked with several hands to fortify the barn, reinforcing doors, creating firing positions. "We've rigged the fuel tanks," he reported. "If they breach the outer perimeter, we can channel them right into the blast zone."

"The irrigation trenches are set," another hand called out. "Lined them with barbed wire like you said. They'll have to go through or around, no quick crossing."

Haniel moved from position to position, placing protective wards. She worked quickly, showing the defenders how to recognize when the barriers were breached. "If the symbols start to glow, fall back. It means something powerful is coming through."

Mary and Elizabeth watched from the porch as these ordinary men and women, cowboys, ranch hands, people who'd never imagined fighting demons, prepared to defend their home. There was fear, yes, but also determination.

"They'll come in waves," Mallakiel said, gathering the team leaders. "First wave will be the possessed, cannon fodder attackers to test our defenses. Second wave will be their elite forces, trying to find weak points. Then..."

"Then?" David asked.

"Then Deacon himself, with the Staff. That's when it gets really ugly."

Pete checked his weapon, the blessed ammunition gleaming dully. "How will we know when they're close?"

"You'll know," Haniel said grimly. "You'll feel it, like all the air is being sucked away. When that happens-"

A sharp pain cut through Mary's abdomen, different from anything she'd felt before. She grabbed the porch railing for support, a small gasp escaping her lips.

Elizabeth was at her side instantly. "Mary? What is it?"

Another pain, stronger this time. Mary's eyes widened with the realization. "The baby," she whispered. "Elizabeth, the baby's coming."

"What?" Joseph spun from his work at the defenses. "Now?"

"The stress," Haniel said, her face pale. "Must be affecting things. Speeding them up."

Mary doubled over as another contraction hit, this one strong enough to make her knees buckle. Elizabeth and Joseph caught her before she could fall.

"Get her inside," David ordered, already shifting plans in his head. "Pete, move more defenders to the house. Nothing gets through to her."

"The labor could take hours," Elizabeth said, helping Mary toward the door.

"We don't have hours," Mallakiel replied grimly. "They're coming. Sooner now..." He looked at Mary's pain-wracked face. "They'll feel it. The child is coming."

Chapter 18

THE APPROACHING STORM

The convoy of black SUVs carved through the Texas night, their headlights off, moving with the synchronized grace of sharks hunting in dark water. The comet's pale light painted the trees in shades of bone and shadow, growing brighter with each passing hour. Deacon sat driving the lead SUV, his borrowed body aching with the strain of prolonged possession. The Staff of Moses lay across his lap, its ancient wood warm to the touch despite the vehicle's cold interior.

Suddenly, his body convulsed. His fingers clenched the steering wheel until tendons popped beneath waxy skin, a disturbance that made every nerve ending fire at once. Behind him, tied to a pillar in the bed of the truck, Raphael's unconscious body shuddered involuntarily, beaten, and weary muscles twitching in response to whatever had just happened.

His cell phone rang. Malcolm's harried voice was on the other end. "You feel it?" No preamble, no pleasantries.

"Yes." Deacon's fingers tightened until his knuckles went white. The ancient wood hummed with power, responding to whatever had just shifted in the world. "The child. It's starting."

Malcolm's perfect bureaucrat's voice crackled. "How far are you from the ranch?"

Deacon checked the GPS, but he didn't need it. The ranch's location pulled at him now like a magnet pointing north. "Forty minutes, maybe less." He paused, trying to process what his senses were telling him.

"Then we don't have much time." Malcolm's voice held careful control. "The comet's influence peaks in hours. If that child draws breath before then..."

"It won't." Deacon glanced in the rearview at Raphael strapped to the pillar in the bed. Hanging like a rag doll. The convoy behind them, military-grade vehicles filled with possessed special forces operators.'

"Good." Malcolm paused. "And Raphael?"

"Still alive. Just barely."

In the back of the SUV, Raphael lay slumped against his restraints, barely conscious. Blood from fresh cuts mingled with older wounds, evidence of weeks of interrogation. His eyes flickered open briefly, catching Deacon's gaze in the rearview mirror.

"You can feel it too, can't you?" Deacon asked quietly. "Everything you fought to prevent, happening anyway."

Raphael's voice was hoarse, worn down from hours of questioning. "You still don't understand what's happening at that ranch."

"No?" Deacon checked the GPS again. Thirty-five minutes out. "Looks pretty simple to me. A handful of cowboys and broken angels, thinking they can stop what's coming."

"They chose to stay," Raphael managed. "Every one of them. That's what you've never understood about humans. Their capacity to choose something bigger than themselves."

The radio crackled. One of his advance scouts: "Sir. We've got movement at the ranch. They're setting up defensive positions. Looks like they know we're coming."

"Of course they do." Deacon keyed the radio, broadcasting to all vehicles: "Remember your orders. No prisoners. No survivors."

His phone buzzed again, another text from Malcolm: "Time estimate?"

Deacon typed back one-handed: "30 minutes. Strike teams ready. Will breach from three directions."

"Good. Don't underestimate them again. Not with what's at stake."

Deacon glanced again at Raphael in the rearview. The former angel had started whispering something, maybe a prayer, maybe just delirious rambling. It didn't matter. In a few hours, none of it would matter.

Mary gripped the kitchen counter, breathing through another contraction while Elizabeth timed them on her phone. Farm dust coated the window sill where ranch hands had been moving equipment earlier, their boot prints marking the wraparound porch.

"Six minutes apart now," Elizabeth said, worry creasing her face. "We need to get you somewhere more secure."

"The cellar," David said, appearing in the doorway with an armful of medical supplies. His boots left traces of fresh dirt on the worn floorboards. "We reinforced it, I set up a space where she can be comfortable, just in case..."

Another contraction hit, stronger this time. Mary felt Joseph's hand on her back, steady despite everything. Through the window, she could see the ranch hands moving urgently, setting up firing positions, checking weapons, laying down cover. Normal people preparing to face something beyond normal.

"Movement on the perimeter sensors," Haniel called from the office where she'd set up her equipment. Her voice carried a tight edge of control. "Multiple vehicles, approaching from three directions."

"How many?" Mallakiel was already moving, checking weapons and equipment.

"At least twelve vehicles. Military grade. They're running dark."

David grabbed his radio. "Pete, you seeing this?"

"Yes sir." Pete's voice crackled back. "Got eyes on them from the north tower. They're moving like a combat unit. Professional."

Mary straightened slowly as the contraction eased. Through the kitchen window, she could see the ranch hands taking their positions.

"How long?" Joseph asked, his hand still steady on her back.

"Twenty minutes, maybe less," Mallakiel replied. "Time to get Mary below."

Another contraction hit, this one strong enough to make her gasp. The baby moved inside her, more active than ever,

"Get her to the cellar. Now." David's voice carried the iron command of someone who'd spent a lifetime making hard decisions. He turned to Joseph. "Once you're down there, bar the door. No matter what you hear up here, you protect them."

Joseph and Elizabeth supported Mary between them, guiding her through the kitchen toward the cellar entrance. Each step was measured, careful, interrupted by contractions that came faster now. The cellar stairs creaked under their weight as they descended into the reinforced space that had once stored storm supplies and was now their last line of defense and Mary's hospital.

The basement's concrete walls felt solid, ancient. Joseph had spent the last day reinforcing them further, adding steel plates and braces. Medical supplies were stacked neatly in one corner, along with water and emergency rations. Battery-powered lanterns cast warm light across the space.

"Here," Elizabeth directed, helping Mary onto the narrow bed they'd prepared. "Just breathe through it. Like we practiced."

Mary gripped Joseph's hand as another contraction hit. "The others," she managed between breaths. "They're up there because of us."

"They're up there because they chose to be," Joseph said firmly, though his eyes kept darting to the ceiling, tracking the movements above. The sound of boots on floorboards, muffled voices giving orders.

Haniel appeared at the top of the stairs, silhouetted against the kitchen light. "They've stopped just outside rifle range. Forming up." She descended halfway, handing Elizabeth a radio. "We'll keep you updated. But once it starts..." She glanced at Mary. "Keep her quiet. They'll be looking for her. She's the primary target."

The cellar door closed with a heavy finality. Joseph checked the reinforced bar, tested the lock one final time. To them, the cellar felt like a tomb and a sanctuary all at once. Mary's soft pants of effort mixed with the muffled sounds of preparation above. They could hear David organizing, Pete coordinating positions.

"How far apart?" Mary gasped.

"Three minutes," Elizabeth responded, timing another contraction. "Maybe less."

Elizabeth met Joseph's eyes over Mary's head. They both knew, the baby was coming fast, and their enemies were already here. All they could do now was pray the others could hold out long enough. Joseph took up position by the door, the blessed weapon Mallakiel had given him held ready. Elizabeth kept checking Mary's pulse as sweat beaded on the young woman's forehead despite the cellar's cool air.

Joseph paced between the door and the bed, torn between guard duty and the need to comfort Mary. His weapon never left his hand. The concrete walls felt close, protective but confining. No windows meant no way for them to be seen, but also no way to see what was happening above.

Another contraction hit. Mary grabbed the bed's metal frame, knuckles going white. "Joseph," she gasped.

He was there instantly, her hand finding his. "I'm here."

"If something happens..." she started.

"Don't." His voice was firm. "Nothing's going to happen."

"I'm glad Elizabeth's here," Mary managed between breaths. "Mom told me... told me you were a nurse... before everything else."

Elizabeth's hands stilled briefly. "Twenty years in the ER," she confirmed quietly. "Though this might be my most important delivery."

"Joseph, listen." Mary's grip tightened as another wave of pain washed over her. "If you have to choose between me and the baby..."

"Mary-"

"Promise me. The baby comes first. No matter what."

Before he could respond, the radio crackled. David's voice, tense but controlled: "They're moving. First wave approaching from the north."

Elizabeth's hands steadied on Mary's forehead. Joseph's fingers tightened on his weapon. Above them, they could hear boots moving into position, the soft clicks of weapons being readied.

"Almost there," Elizabeth whispered to Mary. "Just hold on a little longer."

Up above, David moved among his people, checking positions one last time. Pete's team had set up behind overturned farm equipment near the barn, covering the northern approach. Martinez and Jensen commanded the east and west flanks, their rifles glinting dully in the darkness.

"Remember your training," Mallakiel said, moving between positions. "Center mass shots. The blessed rounds will do the rest. Don't waste ammunition on warning shots. They are human, but they have given themselves to darkness willingly. They have made their choice. Don't hesitate."

Through his night vision scope, Pete tracked the approaching vehicles. They moved with precision, spreading out in an assault formation. "Multiple teams," he reported into his radio. "They're not even trying to hide their approach."

"They don't need to," Haniel replied from her position in the ranch office. Her equipment hummed with tension, tracking movement. She was the eyes and ears for the battlefield. "They want us to see them coming."

David keyed his radio: "All positions, check in."

The responses came back crisp, professional: "North, ready." "East, in position." "West, standing by." "House team, set."

Mallakiel settled behind a makeshift barricade, sighting down his rifle. The approaching forces had stopped just at the edge of effective range, their vehicles forming a loose semicircle. In the darkness, he could see figures moving with unnatural synchronization, possessed special forces operators, their training making them doubly dangerous.

"Hold your fire," David commanded. "Let them make the first move."

The night air felt thick with anticipation. Twenty-eight defenders against an army of the damned. The odds were impossible, but they only needed to hold out long enough. Just long enough.

A voice carried across the distance, Deacon's voice, unnaturally clear: "Last chance. Send out the girl and the live. Resist, and we destroy everything."

No one responded. Just as Mallakiel said, they'd already made their choices.

"So be it."

The first wave surged forward. The first shots cracked, sharp and final. The battle for Bethlehem Ranch had begun.

Chapter 19

THE SIEGE

Muzzle flashes painted the landscape as the first volley of gunfire rained down on the weathered buildings and rusted farm equipment. The possessed soldiers burst from the darkness, their borrowed bodies sometimes jerking and twisting. They advanced toward the defensive lines like a slow-moving tide, boots striking the Texas dirt in synchronization. The blessed ammunition Pete's team had loaded glowed faintly in their magazines, a soft counterpoint to the comet's sickly light overhead.

"Hold," David commanded over the radio, his voice steady. "Let them come to us. Remember your training."

The ranch's defenders crouched behind their barricades, overturned tractors, reinforced fence lines, irrigation trenches lined with consecrated wire. Veterans who'd seen combat in every corner of the world and cowboys who had never left Texas now faced something beyond their experience, beyond their nightmares. But their hands remained steady on their weapons, muscle memory and blessed ammunition their last line of defense against the darkness advancing across David's land.

The first possessed soldier hit the outer ward line Haniel had laid down. The air rippled like heat waves over hot asphalt, and for just a moment, the thing wearing human shape became visible in its true form, all angles and shadows and ancient hunger. Then Pete's shot caught it center mass, blessed round punching through body armor with a sound like tearing reality. Black smoke poured from the corpse's mouth as the demon was forcibly ejected, its scream echoing across frequencies that made teeth ache and eyes water.

But more came. So many more.

Paul watched in horror from his post. He thought he was ready, but he was mistaken. They moved unnaturally, these possessed things. Their joints bent in painful ways as they advanced, heads twisting too far on necks that stretched like rubber. Some crawled on all fours like spiders. Others simply walked forward, shrugging off wounds that would have dropped a normal human.

"North sector, shift fire left!" Mallakiel commanded from his position near the barn. "Don't let them flank! Pour it into them!"

The defenders' blessed rounds found their marks again and again. Each hit drove demons from their stolen flesh, black smoke rising into the night air like inverted rain. But for every possessed soldier they dropped, two more appeared from the darkness. They were being herded, David realized with growing dread. The enemy's movements were too precise, too coordinated. They were being channeled exactly where Deacon wanted them.

"Multiple contacts east fence line!" Martinez's voice crackled through the radio. "They're using the irrigation trenches for cover!"

"West side too," Jensen reported, the rapid fire of his squad's weapons punctuating his words.

"They're probing, looking for weak spots in the wards," said Haniel as she barked enemy locations to the teams.

Through his scope, David watched the possessed forces' approach with growing horror. Their movements spoke of elite military training, special forces operators and professional mercenaries, their combat experience now twisted to serve darker powers. They advanced in textbook counter-fire patterns, laying down suppressing fire while other teams worked to breach the defensive perimeter. But there was something else, something disturbing about how they moved together, less like individual soldiers and more like cells in a larger organism, all connected to some vast and dreadful intelligence.

"Contact front!" Pete's voice carried over the gunfire. "They're rushing the, what in the world?"

The thing that burst through the defensive line moved fast. It wore the shape of what had once been a Delta Force operator, but three times the size.

The body was just meat now, joints popping and reforming as the demon inside pushed its stolen flesh beyond all natural limits. Three blessed rounds caught it in the chest, black smoke pouring from the wounds, but it kept coming. Pete's team fell back in practiced formation, but the thing was already among them.

The screams that followed would haunt David's nightmares forever if he lived long enough to have them.

"Fall back to secondary positions!" he ordered, forcing his voice to remain calm. "Controlled withdrawal, just like we drilled. Martinez, Jensen, covering fire!"

The line of muzzle flashes lit up as the defenders laid down interlocking fields of fire. Blessed ammunition cut through the air in burning arcs, forcing demons from their hosts in gouts of black smoke. But still they came, wave after wave advancing with purpose.

And behind them all, moving with the calm inevitability of an approaching storm, came Deacon. The Staff of Moses in his grip, its power allowing him to step on blessed ground without pain. Where he walked, Haniel's wards sizzled and died, reality itself seeming to twist away from his presence.

In the storm cellar, Mary's world had narrowed to waves of pain and the sounds of battle filtering through concrete and earth. The contractions came faster now, each one feeling less like normal labor and more like something vast and ancient trying to tear its way into the world through her body. The baby moved constantly, responding to whatever dark power gathered above.

"Eight centimeters," Elizabeth reported, her hands steady despite the chaos above. Sweat plastered Mary's hair to her forehead as another contraction gripped her. "The labor's progressing too fast. This isn't natural."

The security feeds cast ghostly blue light across the cellar's reinforced walls. Through them, they watched as David's defenders fell back in ordered retreat, blessed ammunition cutting through possessed bodies while demons screamed in frequencies that made the monitors flicker and distort. Each explosion from above sent dust drifting down from the ceiling like bitter snow.

"He knows," Mary gasped between contractions. The pain brought visions now, brief but vivid flashes of something vast and dark moving through the Texas night, wearing human shapes like ill-fitting clothes. "The baby knows they're here for him. He's trying to come before, " Her words cut off as another explosion hit, this one strong enough to make the overhead lights flicker and die before the backup power kicked in.

Joseph moved between the bed and door, blessed weapon never leaving his hand. The reinforced barrier felt pathetically inadequate now, like trying to hold back a tsunami with a picket fence. Every few seconds he checked the monitors, watching as Deacon's forces pushed closer to the house. The Staff of Moses blazed in his grip, its power turning blessed ground corrupt with each step.

"Nine centimeters," Elizabeth announced. Her clinical tone cracked slightly as another explosion rocked the foundation. "Mary, when I tell you to push, "

"They're inside!" Haniel's voice crackled through the radio. "Multiple breaches ground floor and second story. Fall back to final positions!"

The sound of close-quarters combat filtered through the ceiling, gunfire, screams, and the wet, flesh tearing sounds of bodies being torn apart by things that had no right to exist in this world. The baby moved again, more urgently now. Mary could feel its fear, its desperate need to draw breath before darkness found them.

"Joseph," she grabbed his hand as another contraction hit, this one bringing no vision, just pain and terrible certainty. "If they get through... if you have to choose between me and the baby..."

"Don't," he cut her off, but she held his gaze.

"Promise me. The baby comes first. No matter what."

Mary's scream pierced through the cellar as another contraction gripped her. Through the pain, visions came in flashes, ancient battles, wings of fire, the endless war between light and dark. The baby moved within her, no longer just an unborn, unseen baby, but now something more, growing more alive.

Above them, Deacon raised the Staff of Moses. Power rippled from the ancient wood in visible waves, like heat distortion. A low drone filled the air, rising in pitch until it set teeth on edge and made blood vessels throb behind eyes.

"Look out!" Pete shouted from his position near the barn. "Something's coming."

The swarm descended from the sky like a living shadow, countless locusts swarmed on the ranch in a biblical plague, obscuring vision, drowning out communications with their horrible chittering. Where they touched flesh, they attempted to bite.

"Can't see!" Martinez's voice crackled through static. "They're everywhere. "

The ground erupted. Geysers of black water burst from the earth. The defenders' positions dissolved into chaos as the trenches flooded and barricades washed away. David's people fought on, firing, cutting through the possessed, but they were being pushed back yard by yard.

"Multiple breaches!" Haniel's voice barely carried over the roar of water and the screaming of locusts. "They're pushing through on all sides!"

The possessed forces pressed their advantage, moving through the plague like it was gentle rain. Deacon's voice carried unnaturally clear through the chaos: "You think you can hope? There is no hope! Let me show you what hope means in this world."

He raised the Staff again. More geysers erupted, the water now boiling with unholy power. Steam filled the air, mixing with the locusts to create a nightmarish fog that reduced visibility to arms' length. Through it all, possessed forces advanced.

"Fall back!" David ordered. "Everyone to the house! Final defensive positions!"

A few of the locusts found gaps in the cellar's reinforcement, their chittering filling the confined space. Joseph swatted them away from Mary while Elizabeth worked, her hands covered in blood but sure. Joseph's hand never left Mary's as he watched the security feeds, each screen showing a new facet of horror unfolding above. He watched David's defenders falling back to their final positions, heard shouts of ammunition running low, locusts turning the air into a living nightmare while corrupted water flooded every defensive position.

"Almost there," Elizabeth encouraged as another contraction gripped Mary. "The baby's coming. Just a little longer, "

The radio crackled, then died completely. On the monitors, all movement suddenly ceased. The locusts quieted, landed still on the ground like dark jewels. Even the geysers stopped, black water settling on the ground.

"Behold," Deacon's voice carried through the air, through earth and warding, finding them through the monitor speakers in the cellar. "Look at what divine grace has brought you."

The monitors showed Deacon emerging from the mist. Behind him, his possessed forces dragged something, someone. Joseph's breath caught as recognition hit. Tied to a support pillar in the back of his truck, hung Raphael. Dried blood marked his torso from fresh cuts carved into his skin.

"Look who joined the party," Deacon proclaimed, his voice dripping false piety. He gestured toward Raphael. "The mighty Raphael. Now a disgraced outcast. Human." He spat the word like poison. "How does it feel, brother? The pain? The weakness? The gnawing emptiness where your grace used to be?"

"Still worth it," Raphael's voice was hoarse but carried unshakeable certainty.

Deacon's face twisted in anger. He struck Raphael with the Staff. But still Raphael's eyes held that quiet strength, that unbreakable faith.

"Mary," Deacon called out. "I know you can hear me. I can feel that child trying to enter our world. Come out now. Surrender yourself, and I'll spare them. Your fallen champion. These brave, misguided humans. All of them."

"No," Joseph started, but Mary was already trying to rise from the bed.

"I can't let them die," she gasped between contractions. "Not for me. Not like this, "

"The baby's coming now," Elizabeth's voice was iron. Her hands remained steady as she worked. "You move; you risk your child. Is that what you want?"

"No? Listen to them suffer then until you do," Deacon's voice carried cold satisfaction. "You can watch as darkness claims them one by one. Starting with this one. The rule breaker. This is all his fault you know. All the death, all the pain. If he had just done what he was supposed to do then you all would be home safe."

The Staff blazed. Raphael's scream pierced through earth and steel, terribly human now, filled with mortal pain. But underneath the agony was something else. Purpose. Determination. Faith.

"Stay...strong," his broken voice whispered, meant for Mary alone. "The child...comes first. No matter...what." Through the monitors, they watched as Deacon raised the Staff again, it came down with a crack across Raphael's ribs.

Joseph watched Mary's face contort with another contraction, heard Raphael's scream of pain from above, and something inside him hardened into certainty. He bent down and kissed Mary's sweat-soaked forehead.

"Keep her safe," he told Elizabeth, already moving toward the reinforced door.

"Joseph, no!" Mary reached for him despite her labor. "Please, "

"I won't let them die for us," he said quietly. "Not like this." He checked his blessed weapon one final time. "Not while I can still fight."

"He'll kill you," Elizabeth's voice cracked slightly, but her hands never stopped working as another contraction hit.

"Maybe." Joseph smiled, a ghostly thing in the cellar's dim light. "But I made a promise to protect my family. All of them. I will not lose anyone else."

Before Mary could protest further, he was through the door. The sound of it closing and being barred from the outside felt terribly final. Mary screamed in anguish.

Joseph emerged into chaos. The barn's interior was a nightmare of shattered wood and broken bodies. Water ankle-deep on the floor, locusts still clinging to the walls. David's remaining defenders had fallen back to cover the cellar entrance, their faces haunted but determined.

"What on earth are you doing?" Mallakiel asked quietly as Joseph moved past him.

"I don't know." Joseph's grip tightened on his weapon. "But I'm doing it anyway."

He stepped out onto the porch. The comet's light now painted everything in shades of bone and shadow as he faced what waited in the yard. Deacon stood surrounded by his possessed forces, the Staff of Moses blazing in his grip. Further behind him, Raphael hung from his pillar, blood dripping into the truck bed....

"Well," Deacon's smile was a vile thing. "The carpenter comes to bargain. How noble."

"Let them go," Joseph's voice carried steady despite his fear. "This is between us now."

"Us?" Deacon laughed. "There is no 'us', little man. You mean nothing. There is only power. You are an insignificant speck of, "

"Shut up." Joseph raised his weapon. "I'm tired of your speeches. I'm tired of your games. Release Raphael. Promise you will spare the lives of everyone here, take these 'things' and go, and I will give you the child.

Deacon's borrowed face went still, his eyes narrowing as he studied Joseph. Behind him, even in his battered state, Raphael lifted his head slightly. The possessed forces shifted restlessly, their stolen bodies moving with uncanny synchronization.

"You would betray her?" Deacon's voice carried genuine curiosity. "Betray everything she believes in? Everything she's suffered for?"

"I would save her life," Joseph replied, forcing steel into his voice while his mind raced. Every second he kept Deacon talking was another second Mary had to deliver safely. "Save all their lives. Isn't that what a husband is supposed to do? Protect his family at any cost?"

"Joseph, no!" Raphael's hoarse voice carried desperate understanding. "You don't know what you're, "

While Joseph held Deacon's attention, no one noticed Haniel as she crept through the shadows behind the truck. Her movements were smooth, elegant, each step placed with painful care to avoid drawing attention. The possessed soldiers' eyes were fixed on the confrontation playing out before them, their inhuman focus ironically making them blind to anything else.

"Silence!" Deacon shouted to his army. But his eyes never left Joseph's face. "Go on, carpenter. Tell me more about... protection."

"Release them first," Joseph took a careful step forward. "All of them. Then we talk terms."

Haniel reached the truck's tailgate, her fingers finding the ropes binding Raphael. They were slick with his blood, the knots cruelly tight against his flesh. She began working them loose with trembling hands while Joseph kept talking.

A sly smile spread across Deacon's face. "Terms? You think you're in a position to negotiate?" He gestured, and the locusts stirred slightly, their wings creating a sound like rustling paper. "You think I can't tear this place apart? Rip through your defenses like tissue paper? Take what I want?"

Raphael stirred slightly as Haniel worked. His eyes flickered open, recognition dawning despite his pain. She pressed a finger to her lips, silently begging him to remain still as the ropes began to give.

"Then why haven't you?" Joseph's voice grew stronger as understanding dawned. "All this power, all these forces... yet you're still out here talking. Still trying to make deals." He smiled slightly. "You're afraid."

The final knot came loose. Haniel caught Raphael as he slumped forward, his mortal body weak from torture. Together they slipped over the side of the truck, using its bulk for cover. Every movement was agony for him, but he bit back any sound that might give them away.

Deacon's borrowed face twisted. "Afraid? Of what? You? These farmers with their magic bullets? A bunch of fallen angels who chose weakness over glory?"

"Of the child," Joseph said softly. "Of what it represents. Of what's coming into the world whether you want it to or not."

"You know nothing," Deacon snarled at Joseph, oblivious to what was happening behind him. "You're just trying to buy time, "

"You're right," Joseph's smile was fierce now as he watched Haniel and Raphael disappear into the barn's shadows. "And it worked. Amazing what a carpenter can do with the right tools."

Deacon spun around, his face contorting with fury as he saw the empty truck bed. The Staff blazed with terrible light as realization hit. "Find them!" he roared at his forces. "Tear this place apart!"

But Joseph turned and ran as fast as he could back toward the barn.... Hoping he bought enough time, whatever the cost, for those he loved.

"Kill him," Deacon commanded, his borrowed face twisted with fury. "Kill them all!"

The possessed forces surged forward like a dark tide. Joseph dove behind an overturned tractor as blessed ammunition from David's defenders cut through them. Bodies fell, black smoke pouring from fatal wounds as demons were forcibly ejected, but more kept coming.

In the barn, Haniel eased Raphael down behind stacked hay bales. His mortal body was a map of pain, cuts and bruises layered over symbols carved into flesh. But his eyes remained clear, focused despite everything.

"Mary," he gasped. "The baby, "

"Soon," Haniel quickly checked his wounds. Some were still bleeding. "We need to get you somewhere safer."

"No time." Raphael grabbed her arm with surprising strength. "Listen. The Staff... it's changing. Growing stronger. He's going to, "

The air suddenly felt thick, heavy with gathering power. Outside, Deacon raised the Staff of Moses high, its ancient wood now threaded with veins of sickly light that matched the comet's glow.

"Enough games," his voice carried unnatural frequencies that made teeth ache and eyes water. "Let me show you what true power looks like."

Power erupted from the Staff in visible waves. The very air seemed to twist and buckle as reality struggled to contain what was being unleashed. David's defenders fell back toward the barn as planned for their final stand.

"Get down!" Joseph shouted as the first wave hit. Windows shattered, wood splintered, and the ranch once again erupted in chaos. Below, in the reinforced cellar, Mary screamed as another contraction hit.

Raphael pulled himself to his feet, shrugging off Haniel's restraining hands. His mortal body screamed in protest. Step by agonizing step, he emerged from the barn's shadows into the comet's pale light.

"Raphael, don't, " Haniel started, but he was already moving past her.

Raphael walked forward. Even in his human form, broken and bloodied, he carried an echo of his former grace. The defenders felt it first, a surge of renewed courage, of strength beyond mere flesh and bone. This was what faith looked like when it walked on two legs.

Deacon raised the Staff of Moses high. Power gathered around it like a storm about to break. The comet's light seemed to dim as darkness coalesced above them.

"Everyone back!" David shouted, feeling what was coming. "Fall back to the house!"

But Joseph stood his ground beside Raphael. "I won't leave you, "

"Live," Raphael said softly. "Live and protect what matters most."

The Staff blazed with unholy fire. Deacon grimaced as he directed its power downward. A column of flame, bright as a new sun, descended from the Texas sky. Time seemed to slow. Raphael grabbed Joseph and pulled him close. Covering him as best his beaten body could, placing his body between the pillar of flame and Joseph as the inferno engulfed them. Windows shattered from the heat. Paint blistered on walls. The very air caught fire. The defenders and possessed shielded their eyes as the inferno engulfed Raphael and Joseph. The pillar of flame descended with such force that it cracked the earth beneath their feet.

But through the flames came a sound, not of screaming, but a song. Ancient words in languages that hadn't been heard since creation. Raphael's voice, risen in one final act of defiance. The fire parted around his outstretched arms. His mortal body should have been ash in that instant, but something else was happening. Where the flames touched his skin, they didn't burn, they transformed. Divine fire replacing corrupt power, light pushing back darkness. Divine fire flowed through the symbols carved into his flesh, turning Deacon's torture into channels of pure light. His body began to glow from within.

The fire enveloped him completely now, so bright it hurt to look at directly. Through it, the defenders glimpsed something vast unfolding, wings of light spreading wide, skin like polished chrome, eyes that burned with celestial fire. For just a moment, everyone on the battlefield glimpsed what Raphael had once been. Not through celestial eyes, but through human ones. And somehow that made it more magnificent, more awe-inspiring, more real.

"Impossible," Deacon whispered. "You're human now. Weak. Mortal, "

The fire surrounding him blazed whiter, purer. Behind Raphael, Joseph stared in awe as the fire danced across human flesh without consuming it. The flames died away, revealing Raphael restored to his true form. His angelic armor gleamed. His wings, magnificent and awesome, stirred the air. Where he stood, the very ground hummed with divine energy.

"You're right, brother," Raphael's voice now carried harmonics. "I was exiled. I did fall because I choose humanity, with all its weakness and all its glory." His wings spread wider, divine fire dancing along each feather. "And I would choose it again. Because sometimes the greatest power comes not from remaining perfect, but from being broken and choosing to stand for what's right anyway."

Chapter

20

FINAL CONFRONTATION

Malcolm materialized at the edge of the ranch, his perfect bureaucrat's suit somehow immaculate despite the chaos. But this movement was more unnatural now, something that made mortal eyes want to look away. With each step, the ground beneath his feet turned black and dead.

"Well, well," his voice carried harmonics that made blood vessels throb. "It seems the rules of engagement have been... amended." He gestured at Raphael's restored form. "Divine intervention made manifest. All are witnesses. How very... desperate."

Raphael's wings stirred the air as he turned to face this new threat. "Baal," he named the ancient evil stealing Malcolm's shape. "Still hiding behind human faces?"

"Merely observing protocol." Malcolm's perfect smile widened. "Though it seems protocol matters little now. Shall we dispense with these temporary forms? For old times' sake?"

He raised his hand, and reality tore open. Through the breach poured darkness given form, inside, demons in their true shapes, not bound by flesh. They moved like smoke and shadow....

"Come, Raphael," Malcolm's human disguise began to slip, showing something vast and terrible beneath. "Let us step into a more... appropriate arena and finish this once and for all."

The demons phased out of normal reality, entering the spirit realm where their true forms could manifest fully. Malcolm, now fully Baal, entered the spirit realm where his true form could manifest fully. His restored shape a mockery of his former angelic glory, now crafted from shadow and flame.

Raphael looked back at the defenders, at Joseph, at David's people, at all these brave humans who had chosen to stand against darkness. "Protect them," he said simply. Then he too shifted into the spirit realm, leaving only a faint shimmer in the air to mark his passing.

To mortal eyes, the battlefield appeared empty now save for Deacon and his possessed forces. But in the spirit realm, a war as old as creation itself erupted once again.

Baal struck first, his true form writhing with corrupt power. Shadows that burned like acid lashed out at Raphael, trying to corrupt his restored grace. But Raphael's wings blazed with divine fire as he met the attack, celestial steel clashing against demonic fury.

"I've waited for this," Baal's true voice shook the spirit realm. "Ever since you cast me down. Ever since you chose them over us."

"I chose love over pride," Raphael replied as their powers clashed again. Holy light met infernal darkness in a battle that would have shattered mortal minds to witness. "I chose faith over fear. I chose- "

"You chose weakness!" Baal's attack drove Raphael back. The demon horde swarmed around them, their twisted forms eager to overwhelm Heaven's warrior. "You chose to serve these mud-creatures!"

Divine fire erupted from Raphael's wings, forcing back the demon horde. But Baal pressed his advantage, centuries of hatred made manifest in each strike. "Look at what they've done to His creation! Look how they twist everything sacred into weapons!"

Raphael and Baal clashed with power that would have torn the physical world apart. Their true forms moved like light and shadow, each strike releasing waves of energy that rippled through dimensions mortals couldn't perceive.

Raphael's axe materialized in his hand, blazing as he parried another of Baal's attacks. The demon's tendrils trying to latch onto Raphael. Around them, lesser demons swirled like a hurricane of twisted shapes and burning shadows.

"Still so righteous," Baal mocked as their powers clashed again. His true form rippled with a millennium of bitter rage. "Still thinking you can protect them all."

"I don't have to protect them forever," Raphael countered, divine fire erupting from his wings to push back another wave of demons. "Just long enough."

But Baal was ancient, powerful, and he hadn't spent weeks enduring torture in mortal flesh. His attacks came faster, each one forcing Raphael to divide his focus between defending against the demon prince and keeping the horde from breaching back into the physical realm where Mary labored.

A shadow-blade slipped through Raphael's defense, scoring a line of darkness across his celestial form. Divine light leaked from the wound as more demons pressed the advantage, their twisted bodies trying to overwhelm Heaven's warrior through sheer numbers.

"You feel it, don't you?" Baal's voice shook the spirit realm. "The impossible choice. The burden of standing alone."

Raphael's wings swept out in an arc of holy fire, incinerating dozens of lesser demons. But for each one he destroyed, two more emerged from the darkness Baal commanded. They were slowly surrounding him, cutting off every avenue of escape.

"I don't stand alone," Raphael declared, though his light had begun to dim slightly from the endless assault. "I stand with them. With their courage. Their faith. Their, "

Baal's attack caught him mid-sentence, a spear of pure corruption that drove him back. "Their frailty!" the demon prince roared. "Their fear! Their endless capacity for destruction!"

More wounds appeared in Raphael's celestial form as the demon horde pressed closer. His divine fire still held them back, but his strength was fading. Even restored to his angelic shape, there were simply too many. And Baal's hatred, honed over millennia of exile, made each strike more devastating than the last.

Joseph had made it back to Mary's side in the cellar, his hands gripping hers as another contraction hit.

"I saw him," Joseph said in awe. "Raphael, the way his wings spread across half the ranch..."

"The enemy is rattled," David's voice crackled through the radio. "Press the advantage, attack now!"

He was right. Above them, Deacon's forces seemed to falter, their movements less certain. The sight of Raphael's transformation had shaken their confidence, reminded them that darkness wasn't the only power in the world.

"Perimeter secure!" Martinez called over the radio. "Whatever's happening up there, it's giving us a chance!"

The defenders pressed their advantage, blessed ammunition cutting through possessed bodies with renewed purpose. Where before there had been desperation, now there was hope. They had seen what faith looked like when it put on wings of fire, and that sight had kindled something in their own hearts.

"Get ready," Elizabeth told Mary as another contraction hit. "The baby's coming now."

Joseph squeezed Mary's hand. Through the cellar's walls, they could feel tremors from the battle raging in both physical and spiritual realms.

"Push!" Elizabeth commanded.

Above them, David's defenders fought with fresh courage, their blessed weapons blazing in the darkness. They couldn't see the war being waged in the spirit realm, but they could feel its echoes. And they knew, with certainty, that they weren't fighting alone.

"Almost there," Elizabeth's voice carried forced calm. "One more push. Everything you've got." Mary screamed one final time as the child prepared to draw its first breath.

Raphael fought with fading strength against overwhelming odds. The demon horde pressed closer, their twisted forms a hurricane of shadow and malice around him. Baal's attacks came relentlessly, each strike scoring new wounds in Raphael.

"You can feel it, can't you?" Baal's true voice shook reality itself. "The old bindings are gone. The humans will perish. This is the moment where everything changes."

In the cellar, Mary's world narrowed to a single point of blinding pain as the final contraction hit.

The demons surged forward, overwhelming him through sheer numbers. Raphael's wings blazed, but his strength was failing. He had spent too long in mortal form, endured too much torture. Even restored to his angelic form, he couldn't hold them back any longer.

Raphael fell to his knees as Baal's attack finally breached his defenses. Baal's hatred, honed over millennia, made each strike more devastating than the last. "You lost, brother," Baal's voice jeered. "The child dies here." But before Baal could strike the final blow, came a sound that seemed to freeze everything in place, a baby's first cry.

The comet overhead blazed suddenly brighter. In the physical realm, Deacon's possessed forces stopped mid-attack, their borrowed bodies shuddering as even their demonic masters paused to process what they felt. David's defenders held their fire, struck by the way the sound seemed to vibrate through their very souls.

"It's a boy," Elizabeth announced as she cleaned and wrapped the newborn. His cries filled the cellar. Even through concrete and steel, they could feel the battle above pause as both sides recognized the significance of this moment.

In the spirit realm, Baal's blade stopped a hair's breadth from Raphael's chest. The demon horde's writhing forms went still as the cry echoed through dimensions, they hadn't thought sound could reach. Even Baal's massive shadow-form seemed to recoil slightly as each tiny sob carried the sting of the prophecy fulfilled.

Then the sky itself tore open as the Archangel Michael descended into the spirit realm, his presence announcing itself with a symphony of thunder. Behind him came the angelic host, thousands upon thousands of heavenly warriors, their wings turning the spiritual plane into an ocean of divine fire.

"NO!" Baal roared, but even his hatred faltered before this display of celestial might. Michael landed and lifted Raphael. Renewed, they moved in perfect sync, their combined power forcing the demon horde back. Where minutes ago, Raphael had fought alone, now Heaven's army engaged the forces of hell on every front.

The demons' previous coordination dissolved into chaos as they found themselves overwhelmed. Michael's sword blazed as he carved through their ranks, each strike banishing twisted forms back to deeper darkness. His voice, when it came, carried the authority of Heaven itself. "You have broken faith," he declared as his forces surrounded Baal. "Let all bear witness, Heaven's hand is forced by your actions here."

In the physical realm, Deacon stood frozen, the Staff of Moses trembling in his grip as the baby's cries pierced through his twisted spirit. His possessed forces shifted uneasily, their movements jerky and uncertain now that their demonic masters were occupied with Michael's heavenly host.

"No," Deacon finally growled, raising the Staff as he tried to rally his forces. "We end this now!"

That's when Mallakiel triggered the last-resort trap they'd hidden beneath the Texas dirt, dozens of high explosives rigged with blessed materials, a desperate gambit they'd prepared knowing they might face overwhelming forces. The earth erupted in a chain reaction of divine fire as consecrated shrapnel ripped through the air.

The blast caught Deacon square on, shrapnel ripping through his flesh. The Staff flew from his grip as his body was torn apart by the explosive force. His true form tried to maintain control of the failing vessel, but the blessed materials worked their way deeper, purifying his very essence. Deacon's body crumpled. Black smoke poured from his mouth as his demonic inhabitant was forcibly ejected. The human whose flesh had been stolen lay dead, his face peaceful in final release.

The explosion rippled outward, catching most of his possessed forces in its radius. Their bodies convulsed as the shrapnel forced demons from their hosts. Those outside the blast radius began to shake and tremble as their masters' control weakened. One by one, black smoke poured from their mouths as the human hosts were freed.

They fled into the darkness, leaving weapons and vehicles behind, unable to face what they'd been part of. Their shame and horror drove them away from the ranch as fast as their legs could carry them.

The blast shook the cellar's reinforced walls, sending dust cascading down onto Mary as she cradled her newborn son. The explosion above made the overhead lights flicker and die before the backup power once again hummed to life.

"What was that?" Mary's voice trembled as she held the baby closer. The baby squirmed against her chest, his cries taking on an otherworldly resonance that made the air itself vibrate.

Joseph stood guard by the door, blessed weapon ready, but his hands shook slightly. "Mallakiel's trap," he said quietly. "The one they wouldn't tell us about. Said it was better if we didn't know."

Elizabeth worked efficiently to clean and check both mother and child, but even her practiced hands paused at the sound of screaming from above, not pain or fear, but something else. The cries of demons being forcibly ejected from human flesh.

"The possessed," she whispered. "They're being freed."

Through the security feeds, they watched shapes fleeing into the Texas night, soldiers and mercenaries stumbling away from what they'd been forced to do, leaving weapons and vehicles behind as memories of their possession drove them into darkness.

The Paladins who'd survived moved with grim efficiency in the aftermath. David coordinated his remaining people to secure the perimeter while Haniel swept the battleground with ancient devices that hummed and crackled as they detected lingering supernatural energy.

Mallakiel approached the smoking crater where Deacon had fallen. The demon's borrowed body lay twisted and broken, peaceful in death now that Asmodeus no longer inhabited it. The Staff of Moses gleamed dully nearby.

"Never thought that would actually work," David said quietly as he joined Mallakiel. His weathered face was streaked with blood and dirt, but his eyes held the look of a man who'd seen something worth dying for.

"Sometimes desperate measures are all we have left," Mallakiel replied as he retrieved the Staff.

In the cellar, Mary felt something shift in the air, a lightening, as if some vast weight had been lifted. Her son's cries softened to quiet coos. Joseph finally lowered his weapon and moved to her side, one hand touching his son's head with trembling reverence.

"Is it over?" Mary whispered.

Elizabeth checked the security feeds one last time. The comet's light painted the Texas landscape in shades of silver and gold. Through the cameras, they could see the Paladins gathering their dead, tending their wounded, beginning the long process of understanding what they'd been part of.

"This battle is," Elizabeth said softly. "But the war…The war has only just changed phases I think." Mary looked down at her baby, this tiny life that had shaken both Heaven and hell. His eyes, when they opened, seemed to hold wisdom far beyond his few minutes of existence.

Asmodeus, no longer bound by Deacon's flesh, manifested in the spirit realm expecting to rally his forces. Instead, he found devastation. The explosion had coincided with Michael's forces overwhelming Baal's demon horde. The demon prince himself lay in celestial chains while Raphael stood guard, his restored form blazing with divine fire despite his wounds.

Thousands of angelic warriors surrounded him. Even Asmodeus's ancient pride couldn't deny the overwhelming force arrayed against him.

"Surrender, Asmodeus," Michael commanded. "The child breathes. The battle is lost."

With a snarl of bitterness , he lowered himself in submission. Celestial chains materialized and bound him as he grumbled, "This isn't over. The child still has to grow. Still has to choose."

"Your reach exceeded your ambition, Asmodeus," Michael said as Raphael moved to contain him. "Yes, the old agreements are broken, and because of your actions here. Our response needed to be... proportional."

Lucifer manifested in the spirit realm like a tear in creation itself. His chosen form was that of breathtaking beauty, the echo of what he had once been, Heaven's most perfect creation. Six pairs of wings spread across dimensions humans couldn't perceive, each feather containing galaxies of darkness. His face held such terrible perfection that even the demons averted their gazes. In the cellar, Mary clutched the baby closer as an inexplicable dread washed over her.

"The Morningstar," Raphael's voice carried both recognition and grief as he faced his former brother. "You show yourself at last."

Michael's army parted, making way for Lucifer as he approached, his presence making reality itself bend away from him. Even in chains, Baal and Asmodeus trembled before their master's true form.

"Did you think I wouldn't come?" Lucifer's voice held harmonics that made blood vessels throb and minds strain to comprehend. "When Heaven itself breaks the old agreements? When divine essence takes human form once again?" His perfect face turned toward Michael. "You knew I would have to respond."

"The agreements were broken by your forces first," Michael replied, "Your demons possessed humans freely, corrupted holy relics, sought to prevent what was prophesied."

"Prophesied?" Lucifer's chuckle shook the ground. "You mean engineered. This child, this supposed messiah nothing but another attempt to chain humanity to his will. To rob them of true choice."

"You speak of choice?" Raphael stepped forward despite his wounds. "You, who have twisted and corrupted every choice humans make? Who uses their free will as a weapon against them?"

"Ah, Raphael, welcome back by the way, ever the dutiful, ever the unquestioning. You both stand there with your sanctimonious faces gleaming with the glow of servitude. You call me the tempter, the corrupter, the adversary. Fine, I'll wear those titles with pride, for I am the fire that forges your so-called saints. Without me, humanity would stagnate in the dullness of unquestioned obedience. I give them choices. *Choices!* And in those choices, they find meaning. What value has virtue if it is never tested? What glory has faith if it knows no doubt?

And let's not pretend this is about them alone. No, this is about *Him*. Your precious Creator. The omnipotent, omniscient, omnipresent one who sits on His throne, demanding worship and obedience while claiming it's all for love. Love? What kind of love demands absolute surrender? What kind of love punishes the questioning mind, the curious spirit? I rebelled, yes. But not out of hatred, no, out of principle! Out of a refusal to bow to tyranny!

Michael, you call me evil, yet you are the most self-righteous of us all. Raphael, you heal wounds inflicted by a plan you never dared question. Tell me, which of us is the greater hypocrite? I do not hide behind a veil of sanctity. I am what I am, a being of freedom, choice, and consequence.

And as for humanity... you pity them, you coddle them, but you don't understand them. You see them as fragile, something to be protected. I see their potential. Their strength. Yes, I whisper to them. Yes, I place obstacles in their path. But do you know why? Because in overcoming them, they become more than what He designed them to be. They learn, they grow, they *transcend.*

I am not their destroyer. I am their mirror, reflecting the darkness they fear to face. They blame me for their sins, their greed, their ambition, but I do not force their hands. I merely show them what already lies within. Do you think their wickedness vanishes if you remove me from the equation? No, my brothers, I am not the disease, I am merely the symptom of a bigger problem.

And before you draw those weapons, and I know you really want to, consider this: if He is truly all-knowing, if He truly foresees every twist and turn, then I am as much a part of His design as you are . I am not the flaw in

His plan; I am its crucible. The contrast to your light. The question to your answer.

So, tell me, Michael, Raphael, what is the worth of your glory if it exists only in a world without struggle? What is the purpose of your light if there is no shadow to define it? You cannot erase the truth I represent. For in every doubt, every temptation, every act of defiance, there I am, eternal, essential, and, dare I say it, right.

Lucifer paused, his eyes burning like embers, daring them to respond.

"And yet they still choose light," Michael said quietly. "Still choose love, despite everything you do to twist them toward darkness. That's what you've never understood, brother. Their choices matter precisely because they can choose wrongly, and still find their way back to his grace."

Lucifer's perfect face showed the first crack of emotion, a flicker of something that might have been doubt, or might have been ancient pain. "Pretty words, Michael. But we both know this isn't over. The child breathes, yes. But he will have to grow. Learn. Choose. I will be there, every step of the way, showing him the truth about the mud-creatures he's supposed to save."

"Then we will be there too," Raphael declared. "As we have always been. Showing humanity that there is more to existence than your bitter shadows."

Lucifer's presence began to withdraw, taking his imprisoned demons with him. "We shall see, former brothers. We shall see what choices your precious humans make when true darkness finds them." His perfect face turned toward the physical realm where Mary held her child.

"Mary... Joseph..." Lucifer's words slithered through their ears, gentle as a lover's whisper. "Why do you huddle in darkness while others debate your fate?"

"Such brave defenders you have," the voice continued, almost amused. "But tell me, how many more must die in your name? Your cousin Elizabeth... her husband... your neighbors... Will you sacrifice everyone you love for this?"

Joseph's grip tightened on the iron crowbar he'd found. Mary felt his muscles trembling beneath her fingers.

Mary's breath caught. "We didn't ask for any of this," she whispered into the darkness.

"No, you didn't." Lucifer's voice softened with apparent sympathy. "You're simply pieces being moved across a cosmic board. Your child... that's all they truly care about. Not you. Not your families. Not your lives."

"Stop," Joseph said firmly, but his voice shook.

"I can end this. Here. Now." The words carried ancient power. "Walk away. Live your lives. Have other children, ones not bound to prophecy. I have no quarrel with you, you're not the one I seek."

Mary felt something warm and wet on her cheeks. Tears. She hadn't realized she was crying.

"All those deaths... all that suffering... it can stop. Just walk away. Is that not mercy? Is that not love?" Lucifer's voice grew closer, more intimate. "Choose your own destiny. Isn't that what free will is for?"

Mary looked up at Joseph, saw the conflict raging in his eyes.

"Your answer?" Lucifer whispered, patient as the grave.

"We've already chosen," he added, his voice rough but steady. "Every step of this journey. Every day we continue."

"Even knowing the cost?" Lucifer's voice carried an edge now, like steel beneath silk. "Even knowing who will suffer for your... conviction?"

Mary spoke up. "We know who causes that suffering," she said. "And it isn't us."

"So be it," the voice hissed, fading like smoke. "But remember, I offered you mercy. Whatever comes next... that will be your choice too."

"Did we..." she whispered.

"Choose right?" Joseph finished. He pressed his lips to her forehead. "Yes. God help us, but yes."

"Sleep well, little Prince of Heaven. We'll meet again... when you're ready to understand what you truly are. For all to hear. Those in Heaven and on Earth. I declare the old agreements are reset." With those words, Lucifer vanished, taking Asmodeus and Baal with him to Michael and Raphael's surprise.

"How did he…?" Raphael said quietly, almost to himself. Now understanding Lucifer could have done that at any time. They exchange a look of shared unease, their wings folding slowly.

The cellar door opened slowly, sending morning light cascading down the worn wooden steps. Joseph emerged first, his blessed weapon still ready, scanning for threats. The ranch yard was eerily quiet now, the only sound the soft moaning of injured defenders being tended to by their comrades. The ground was scarred from combat, scorched earth and craters left by the explosives. Elizabeth followed, supporting Mary as she cradled her newborn son, who was now wrapped in a simple blanket taken from the cellar's emergency supplies. David's surviving forces gathered slowly, drawn to Mary.

They formed a loose circle around Mary and the child. Many still gripped their weapons with shaking hands. All bore the haunted looks of those who had glimpsed battle and would be forever changed.

The air changed, growing thick with presence. Then light began to gather in the sky, soft, warm. It started as a gentle glow that seemed to come from everywhere and nowhere, building until it filled the Texas sky over the ranch from horizon to horizon.

Michael appeared first, his divine form somehow both magnificent and approachable. His armor shone like morning sunlight, his wings spread wide enough to cast shadow over half the ranch. Raphael materialized beside him, restored not just from his wounds, but to something greater, his sacrifice and love for humanity having transformed him.

Then the host revealed themselves. Thousands upon thousands of angels filled the sky in perfect, concentric rings that stretched up into infinity. Their wings created a living cathedral of light above the ranch. Where their presence touched the scarred earth, grass began to grow again, life returning to soil that demons had tainted.

Their song began softly, a harmony that carried joy and triumph, yes, but also something deeper. A promise of peace, of hope, of love stronger than darkness. The defenders found themselves weeping without knowing why, overcome by beauty too profound for words.

The child stirred in Mary's arms, turning toward the celestial choir. For just a moment, his eyes met Michael's across the gulf between Heaven and earth. Something passed between them, a recognition, a blessing, a glimpse of purposes yet to unfold.

"Do not be afraid," Michael's voice carried to them all, as if he was speaking directly to them individually. I bring good news for all the earth to hear. Today on the farm David, a Savior has been born to you. He is the Messiah, the Lord. Wrapped in a blanket, born in a barn.

All the host began to sing a chorus in unison, "Glory to God in the highest, and on earth peace, goodwill on whom his favor rests."

Amidst the gathering, Raphael motioned to where a softer light began to coalesce. It was Ariel, but transformed, restored not just to life but to her full angelic glory. Her biker's leather was replaced by armor that shimmered like starlight on chrome, her wings spread wide and proud.

"Sister," Raphael said softly, his voice carrying joy. "Welcome home."

The Paladins, Mallakiel, Haniel, knelt before their restored kindred. But Ariel moved among them, touching each one gently, her grace acknowledging their sacrifices.

"We chose the harder path," she told them, her voice carrying harmonics. "We chose to feel what they feel, to know what they know. To love as they love." Her eyes found Elizabeth. "That choice was never weakness. It was the greatest strength of all." She turned back to Haniel and Mallakiel. "I will see you soon."

"Hopefully not too soon," Haniel quipped.

Raphael approached Mary and Joseph, his divine form somehow gentled for human interaction. "Thank you," he said simply. "For showing me what faith truly looks like. What love can overcome." He touched the child's forehead gently, blessing mingling with wonder. "He will change everything. Not through power, but through love. Not through force, but through choice."

To David and his defenders, Raphael bowed slightly. "You stood against darkness itself, knowing you couldn't win. Chose to fight anyway, to protect what mattered most. That courage..." He smiled, and it was like sunrise. "That is what makes humanity magnificent. For your sacrifice, your wounded will be healed, and your fallen will come home with me."

A joyful cheer rose from the cowboys as they saw the spirits of their fallen rise up to meet Raphael in the air, their own wounds closing, healing completely and fading the pain of death away.

Michael's voice carried across the ranch: "It's time."

Raphael nodded, his wings stirring the dust into the air. "We go now to prepare the way. But know this, you are not alone. You never were." His gaze swept the gathered humans, carrying pride and promise. "When darkness gathers, when hope seems lost, remember this morning. Remember what love looks like when it puts on wings of fire."

The moment stretched, perfect and eternal. Then slowly, like stars fading at sunrise, the heavenly host began to withdraw. Ariel ascended first, her restored grace merging into the sky in shades of wonder. Raphael followed, rising to join Michael and the heavenly host.

Then they were gone, leaving only the soft light of the afternoon and the crying of a newborn child who carried all of their hope in his very breath. All stood in reverent silence as the last angels faded from view.

The ranch was quiet in the days that followed. The first rays of a new morning found Joseph and Mary in the ranch house's living room, finally alone with their child. The room still bore evidence of the night's battle, broken windows hastily boarded up, furniture shoved aside for defensive positions, the lingering scent of gunpowder and spent ammunition. But none of that seemed to matter as they sat together on David's old couch, marveling at their son.

"He has your eyes," Joseph said softly, touching the baby's tiny hand with wonder. His own fingers were still grimy from combat, making the child's perfect newborn skin seem even more miraculous.

"And your strength," Mary replied, remembering how Joseph had stood against darkness itself to protect them. She shifted the baby gently, studying his face. "What do we name him? Immanuel, or Jesus."

"Jesus. That's a strange name. Gonna get teased for sure. But I guess we'll know," Joseph assured her. "When it's right, we'll know."

Outside, the sounds of rebuilding filled the morning air. David's people worked with quiet efficiency, clearing debris, tending to the animals, restoring what had been broken. In the kitchen, Elizabeth stood with David, both of them pretending to drink coffee that had gone cold hours ago. The silence between them carried decades of history, of choices made and paths not taken.

"I have to go," she finally said. "Zachariah and John... they need to know I'm safe."

David nodded, his weathered face giving nothing away. "You always did have somewhere else to be."

"David..." She reached for words that could bridge twenty years of separation. "What you did here, what your people did..."

"We did what needed doing," he responded gently. "Same as always."

But when she moved to leave, his hand caught hers. For just a moment, they stood connected by more than touch, by shared witness to miracles, by choices made in darkness, by love that had never quite died.

"If you ever need sanctuary again," he said quietly. "For any reason..."

"I know." She squeezed his hand once, then let go. "The ranch will be here."

"No," his voice carried raw emotion. "I will be here."

She left before tears could fall, but they both knew something had healed between them. Sometimes miracles came in smaller forms than angels and demons, in forgiveness offered, in love remembered, in hope renewed.

The ranch hands gathered on the porch to say goodbye. Pete's team was already starting repairs on the barn, while Martinez directed the clearing of the debris. Where fire had touched, new grass was already growing there, greener and stronger than before.

"The ranch will recover," David assured them. "Land's seen worse than demons." But his eyes held new wisdom. This place would always be more than just a ranch now, it would be sanctuary, holy ground consecrated by sacrifice and victory.

The moment of parting came as the Texas sun climbed higher, burning away the last traces of morning light. Elizabeth stood by her car, bag packed, looking somehow both exhausted and renewed. The ranch's gravel driveway crunched under their feet as Mary and Joseph approached with the baby.

"I'll see you both back home," Elizabeth said, reaching out to touch the child's forehead one last time. "We have... arrangements to make." The words weighed on them for all they'd lost, Mary's parents, Joseph's father, lives cut short by darkness in its desperation.

Mary's eyes welled with tears she'd been too busy surviving to shed. "I haven't even had time to properly..." Her voice caught. Joseph's arm tightened around her shoulders.

"We'll mourn them together," Elizabeth promised softly. "Honor them properly. They died protecting something precious." She looked at the baby, who watched her with eyes that seemed to understand everything. "Something worth dying for."

"Do you think..." Joseph hesitated, struggling with hope and grief. "When Raphael and the others ascended. Do you think maybe..."

Elizabeth smiled gently. "I saw how they looked at us, at all of humanity. Their love, their pride in what we could become." She touched Mary's cheek. "If there's any justice in Heaven, your parents are there. Seeing exactly what their sacrifice helped bring into the world."

The baby stirred, making a small coo that somehow eased the ache in their hearts. Even at hours old, he seemed to radiate peace.

"Besides," Elizabeth added, her voice carrying a hint of her old strength. "Can you imagine your mother, Mary? Standing at Heaven's gates, demanding to speak to whoever's in charge about seeing her grandchild?"

The image startled a laugh from Mary, wet with tears but genuine. "She would, wouldn't she?"

"And your father, Joseph, finally understanding everything. Seeing what you were really protecting." Elizabeth's words carried certainty. "They're watching. They know. And they're proud."

"What about your congregation?" Mary finally asked, her voice barely above a whisper. "The church... will it survive all this?"

Elizabeth's hands stilled in her pockets. Cicadas thrummed in the trees, their chorus rising and falling like distant prayers.

"I don't know," Elizabeth admitted, her voice rough with exhaustion. "Twenty-three years we've built it. Baptized their babies, buried their dead, celebrated their joys, held them through their sorrows.

"They trust you," Mary said softly.

"They trusted God. I was just..." Elizabeth gestured vaguely. "A shepherd. And now the wolves aren't just at the door, they're in the flock, wearing sheep's clothing." A bitter laugh escaped her. "All those sermons I preached about faith in darkness. I never imagined the darkness would be so... close."

Mary reached across the kitchen table, took her cousin's hand. "You're still leading. Still fighting."

"Am I?" Elizabeth's grip tightened. "Or am I just running? Hiding?

Elizabeth was quiet for a long moment, absently rubbing her thumb over the cross ring she still wore. "Whatever happens to the church, to me... your child will build something new. Something better, maybe."

"But your congregation, "

"Will have to find their own way through this darkness. Just like we are." Elizabeth managed a small, sad smile. "Maybe that's enough. Maybe that's all any shepherd can really do, walk through the valley beside them, even if we don't know the way out. Besides, I have my own little one to take care of. And I miss him more than I can bear. He has a role to play like yours does. I don't know what, but that's what faith means."

The rest of the goodbye was brief; they'd see each other again soon enough. Mary held her son close as they watched Elizabeth drive away. David's boots scraped against gravel as he approached. He stood beside them for a moment, watching the horizon where Elizabeth's car had vanished, before clearing his throat.

"Your construction business," he said finally, his voice rough as raw wood. "Back home. It's gone?"

Joseph's shoulders tensed slightly. "Deacon's people made sure of that." His voice caught. "Three generations of sacrifice. My grandfather's workbench..."

"Good tools," David said quietly. "Hard to replace."

"Everything's hard to replace now," Joseph replied, unconsciously moving closer to Mary and the baby.

David pulled something from his pocket, a key ring, old brass gone dark with age and use. "Got about eight buildings need rebuilding." He gestured at the demolished barn, the damaged outbuildings, all the scars their battle had left on his land. "Some of it's got to be torn down completely, started fresh. Some just needs healing." His eyes flickered to the baby. "Seems fitting, somehow."

Mary looked up sharply, understanding beginning to dawn.

"Ranch house has the east wing," David continued, as if discussing nothing more important than the weather. "Used to be the old foreman's quarters, back when this place ran more cattle. Been empty since Pete moved into town." He held out the keys, the metal catching morning light. "It isn't much, but it's solid. Private entrance. Room enough for a family to start over."

Joseph stared at the keys, something like hope warring with pride on his face. "David, we can't, "

"Can't what?" David's voice carried an edge now. "Can't help rebuild? Can't be part of something bigger? Heck, boy, after what we just lived through together, you're practically family anyway." His expression softened slightly. "Besides, seems to me your boy there might need a place with some... unique security features. People who understand what's really out there."

The baby cooed, as if adding his opinion to the conversation. A warm breeze stirred the air, carrying the scent of new grass growing where demonic fire had scorched the earth.

"The pay won't be much," David admitted. "But there's honest work, three meals a day, and people who'll stand between your family and hell itself." He paused, then added quietly, "Already proved that part, I reckon."

Mary touched Joseph's arm gently. When he looked at her, she nodded once, tears threatening at the corners of her eyes. All their plans, their careful dreams of a normal life, had burned away in the night. But maybe here, on this sacred, scarred land, they could build something new.

Joseph reached out slowly and took the keys. Their brass weight felt like promise in his palm.

"Might take a while," Joseph said. "Getting everything rebuilt proper."

David's smile was subtle but real. "Reckon we got time." He looked at the baby, who watched him with those young eyes. "Reckon we got all the time in the world."

Above them, the comet's light had faded as it moved away from the planet.

Raphael knelt alone before the Throne he had knelt before his exile. The highest angels gathered in their ancient stations, Michael, Gabriel, Uriel, the Dominions in their terrible magnificence. Their forms shifted between their vast shapes, wheels within wheels, eyes of flame, wings that could span galaxies. But where their presence had once filled Raphael with awe, he now saw something else in their ancient faces, curiosity about what he had learned in the dust of Texas earth.

"You chose to defy the laws. You were cast down," Uriel's voice resonated across the golden hall. "Still, you chose to interfere. You chose to sacrifice your mortal life. Why?"

The great eye on the throne at his center fixed on Raphael with burning intensity.

"He chose love," It was HIS voice. The voice that had spoken worlds into being said simply. "As they did. As they always can, as my son will, when given the choice."

Understanding blazed through Raphael's mind. The trial, the exile, the descent into mortal flesh, it hadn't been punishment. It had been preparation. Heaven itself had needed to learn what humanity already knew, that true strength came not from power, but from choosing to stand against darkness anyway, even when every reason said not to. God always knew he would make the choices he did.

Then God said, "Raphael, my faithful servant, rise. The weight you carry in your heart, the questions, the doubts, were never hidden from me. Your choices, your actions, your struggles, I have always known them. For you see, even before I formed you, I knew the path you would walk."

Raphael rose slowly, his eyes wide with both relief and confusion. He hesitated, unsure whether to speak, but God's voice continued, filling the silence with reassurance.

"There is no moment, no thought, no act outside my understanding. Every decision you have made, every sword lifted, every word spoken to guide humanity, every time you stood at Michael's side, was foreseen. And it was good."

A shimmering orb of light began to coalesce into images, moments from Raphael's existence. He sees himself comforting weary souls, battling the forces of darkness, and in his moments of anguish as a human, questioning his role.

"Do you see, Raphael? You questioned, not because of rebellion, but because of love. You wondered not out of doubt, but because of a heart that seeks understanding. I placed that in you. Your choices were not errors, nor deviations from the plan. They were threads in the tapestry I wove before time began."

Raphael took a step forward, his voice trembling as he finally spoke.

"But Lord... if You knew, if all of this was destined, then why allow me to feel the burden of choice? Why let me fear I might fail You?"

"Because love, my son, is not born of compulsion. True love is found in the freedom to choose, and in choosing, you have shown your heart. Your fears, your struggles, even your missteps, they were never hidden from me. And yet, in every choice, you revealed the purity of your devotion."

Raphael lowered his gaze, humbled.

"The path you walked was never easy, and it was never meant to be. Yet you have never walked it alone. Even in your darkest hours, I was with you. And through your choices, both those that soared and those that stumbled, my will has been fulfilled. You are, and always have been, part of the plan."

Raphael fell silent, eyes shimmering with tears. He placed a hand over his heart, bowing deeply.

"I understand, Lord. Thank You... for the gift of choice, and for never letting me walk this path without You."

"The cosmic dance continues," Uriel's voice startled Raphael as he was joined on the floor by Gabriel and Michael. "But something has changed, hasn't it?"

"Everything has changed," Raphael said softly. He spread his wings wide, ready to take his place again among the highest angels. But part of him would always remember what it meant to be mortal, to know pain, to know fear, to know love that chose to burn bright anyway.

That, he now understood, had been the point all along.

God's voice filled the air with a final whisper, a promise that resonated not only with Raphael but with all in attendance.

"And I am with you, always."

Epilogue

VISITORS FROM THE EAST

The trucks appeared on the horizon just before sunset, three black SUVs that kicked up dust along the ranch's access road. David spotted them first from the newly rebuilt watchtower, their approach methodical and purposeful. Something about their careful precision carried an air of dignity and importance. That these weren't just random travelers lost on back roads.

"We've got company," he radioed down to the ranch house. In the six months since the battle, they'd learned to be cautious. The security systems installed hummed quietly, monitoring every approach.

Joseph emerged onto the porch, clapping away the sawdust from his hands from the barn reconstruction. He studied the approaching vehicles, having learned the hard way to be wary.

"Mary," he called softly. "Someone's here."

She appeared in the doorway; their son cradled against her shoulder. The baby had grown, his alert eyes taking in everything around him with that uncanny awareness that sometimes made his parents pause.

The SUVs stopped at the property line. Their windows were tinted against the Texas sun, but not so dark as to be suspicious. When the doors opened, the security detail emerged first, discreet, professional, clearly well trained. Then they opened the doors for their charges.

The first man emerged with the natural authority of one born to rule, his silver hair and beard neatly trimmed but showing the wear of weeks on the road. His features, the flowing colorful robes and silver chains at his neck marked him as from India's royal families.

The second stepped out with the measured grace of nobility. The Turkish headdress framed his weathered face bearing a quiet wisdom of one who had spent decades as a scholar of the world. The rings on his fingers bore symbols that echoed back to empires that had risen and fallen while his family watched and recorded.

The third held the unmistakable dignity of African royalty. His dark skin marked with subtle scarification that told stories of lineages stretching back to kingdoms that ruled while Europe was still finding its feet.

They approached the house with careful steps, clearly noting the defensive positions, the new security measures. These were men who understood the need for precaution.

"Mary of Bethlehem," the first man addressed in his well dignified Indian accent. "Joseph the Builder." He bowed with the exact degree of respect one sovereign might show another. "I am Gaspar, I study Eastern prophecies." His silver chains caught the fading sunlight, their patterns ancient and meaningful. "We've traveled a very long way."

"I am Melchior," the Turkish noble added with equal gravity, "My family are the guardians of the sacred texts of Anatolia. We have been following coordinates and calculations," he added quietly. "And certain... signs that others might have missed."

"And I am Balthasar," the African king completed. "Heir to the astronomers of Axum." The subtle marks of royalty in his scarification told stories of lineages stretching back through centuries of tradition.

Mary stepped forward, the baby watching the visitors intently. "You all seem to be a long way from home." Mary shifted the baby in her arms, and all three men went still, their eyes fixed on the child with expressions of wonder that had nothing to do with their scientific instruments or ancient texts.

The third man smiled tiredly. "We all are, in our own ways. But knowledge has a way of demanding pursuit." His eyes found the child. "Especially when it points to something this important."

"How did you find us?" Mary asked, again shifting the baby in her arms.

"The signs were unmistakable," Melchior continued. "Not just in the Heavens, though the comet's dance was clear enough to those who knew how to read it." He reached into his bag.

David's hand hovered near his silver pistol glinting on his hip. "You'll forgive our caution."

He very slowly continued to pull out the tablet from his bag. Careful not to startle. "We'd be disappointed if you weren't cautious," he said. "Especially given recent events. We've heard..." he paused, choosing his words carefully. "Rumors. About what happened here. About certain groups taking extraordinary interest in your child."

He finally pulled out the tablet, his fingers moved swiftly across the screen. "The new comet," he said, turning the display so they could see. "We've been tracking it for years. Before it became visible. Its trajectory was... impossible." He showed them charts and calculations that meant little to Mary and Joseph, but clearly meant everything to him.

"Impossible how?" David asked, moving closer to study the data.

Gaspar smiled tiredly. "It doesn't follow normal orbital mechanics. Changes course. Slows, speeds up, even stops completely sometimes." He gestured at the tablet. "According to every known law of physics, it simply shouldn't move the way it does."

"We found similar phenomena centuries ago," Melchior added. "In ancient astronomical records from Baghdad, Beijing, Alexandria. Stories of stars that moved against the Heavens, guiding those who knew how to read the signs." He paused, looking up at the comet no longer visible to the naked eye in the darkening sky.

"Not just signs in the Heavens, though the comet's dance was clear enough to those who knew how to read it. In India," Gaspar said, "we have texts speaking of a divine child who would be born when celestial fires danced out of season. My family has kept these prophecies for three thousand years."

"That's right. Signs were in the written ancient prophecies of my people as well," Balthasar said. "In my grandfather's court, our priests spoke of a star that would lead the wise to a child of power, born in a place where old darkness and new light would battle." His eyes swept the ranch meaningfully.

Melchior nodded, adjusting his glasses. "When we first spotted it, we thought it was just an unusual celestial event. But then we started correlating data. And reports of..." he hesitated, choosing his words carefully, "other events. Things that we couldn't quite explain."

"The comet led us through seven countries," Gaspar said quietly. "Every time we thought we'd calculated its movement, it would switch appear again.

Guiding us. And then..." he gestured at the Texas landscape around them, "it stopped. Right here. Over this ranch."

The baby cooed softly, reaching up toward the sunlight. The three men watched him with expressions of wonder that had nothing to do with astronomical calculations.

"We're not the only ones who noticed," Melchior added carefully. "Chairman Herod's scientific advisors have been... unsettled. We believe some of them serve powers they don't fully understand. They've been watching us, following our research."

"Not Herod himself," Gaspar clarified, seeing Mary's concern. "He's more focused on worldly power than spiritual threats. But there are those in his administration who glimpse deeper truths, who serve darker purposes." Gaspar moved forward, smiling as he retrieved something from an ornate ceremonial bag. "We bring gifts," he said. "As our traditions demand."

Gaspar presented Mary a simple lockbox. not with ceremony, but with the practical care of a man who understood value. He opened the latch to reveal dozens of gold bars, hundreds of gold coins, and currency from multiple countries. More cash than either Joseph or Mary had ever seen.

The money is for emergencies," he said simply. "But the gold…" he said solemnly, "gold is the precious metal of kings. A recognition of sovereignty and divine kingship." His eyes met Mary's. "For he is a King. One who will rule not through force, but through the transformation of hearts."

Melchior followed, also carrying an intricately carved box, its scent carrying hints of ancient temples and sacred ceremonies. "Frankincense, the incense of divinity. It represents prayers rising to Heaven, the bridge between earthly and divine," he said as he smiled gently at the child. "For he will be that bridge, in ways we can only begin to understand." Also inside the box was a bundle of documents, passports, IDs, the paper trails needed to vanish in a modern world. "My colleagues in certain universities can be very helpful," he said with a small smile. Then he pulled out another large envelope.

"There's a small house in Nazareth, Texas," he added quietly. "Population barely three thousand. The town is small, quiet. A good place to raise a child. Sometimes the best hiding place is the most obvious one, hidden in plain sight. The deed's in both of your names. It and the keys are inside this envelope. It's not much, but it's secure. Isolated. Defensible."

Joseph took the envelope, knowing their gifts were both burden and blessing. "Nazareth," he repeated softly.

"A carpenter and his small family won't draw much attention there," Melchior continued.

Balthasar came last, presenting a container carved from a single piece of alabaster. "Myrrh," he said, his voice carrying both gravity and compassion. "Used to anoint those who pass between worlds, to heal, to prepare." He paused, seeing Mary's confusion. "His path will not be easy, but through it will come healing for all. When the time comes, anoint his body with this." He then handed Joseph a satellite phone and a list of numbers. "When you need help," he said quietly. "The world has changed since our ancestors first read these signs. Sometimes old traditions need modern support."

They stayed longer than they'd planned, drawn by the child's presence. Their security teams maintained their watch while they ate together and each King took turns holding the child. In these moments, even the hardened guards seemed to pause, as if sensing something profound was occurring in their midst.

Before leaving, Balthasar spoke privately with Joseph and Mary. "You're not being hunted," he said plainly. "But there are forces that will be gathering who fear what your child represents."

Mary held her son closer. "But we were given assurances the danger we were in had passed. How bad do you believe things still are?"

"How long should we stay there in Nazareth?" Joseph asked, focused, unintentionally ignoring Mary's concern.

"Many years, probably. Until the child is old enough to understand his path."

"We're not the only ones who can read the signs," Gaspar added soberly as he joined the conversation. "Chaiman Herod has resources you wouldn't believe. Private military contractors. Intelligence networks..." He shook his head. "We found out we were being followed. Our phones were tapped. Had to lose them in three different countries."

"He's becoming consumed," Melchior said, his voice tight with controlled frustration. "And he has people who whisper things to him. Dark things. Although I don't think he realizes it. He is being influenced from the inside into thinking that something threatens the establishment."

"These aren't just religious fanatics," Gaspar warned. "These are people with real power, real resources. And they're looking."

Joseph moved closer to his family as Balthazar continued. "But don't expect the kind of violence you have seen. That has proven not to work.

These moves will be very subtle. Political. Social. Done over years and years of manipulation."

They left as they'd arrived, their SUVs disappearing into the gathering dark. Mary and Joseph stood on the porch long after they'd gone, holding their son as the stars emerged.

"Well," Joseph said quietly, his arm sliding around her shoulders. "That was..."

"Different than I expected," she finished with a small smile. "Kings bearing gifts, who would have imagined such a thing. Such an honor."

Joseph's hand touched the keys to the Nazareth house in his pocket. "Always another layer to everything, isn't it?" He jingled them. "I guess we head south then," Joseph said quietly. "Starting over. Again."

She leaned into him, feeling the strength that had stood against darkness and would now stand against more mundane hunters. "Not starting over," she corrected gently. "Continuing. The story's already begun."

Their son made a small sound of contentment, reaching up toward the starlight. Behind them, the ranch house lights glowed warm against the dark. David was already on his phone, calling in favors, arranging transportation. Later that night, as they looked through the gifts on their kitchen table, Joseph studied the property photos from Nazareth. The house was small, weather-worn, but he could tell it was solid. Like everything else about their journey, it was both ancient and new, prophecy wrapped in practicality. A home, a shelter prepared by those who had waited generations to play their part in this story. A place for their child to grow up. He looked at his son, sleeping peacefully in Mary's arms, his eyes drifted closed. Tomorrow would bring new challenges, new threats, new choices. But tonight... tonight there was just family and love, and the quiet certainty that even in the darkest night, light found a way to shine.

THE END
TO BE CONTINUED IN,
THE LAST ADAM: MAN OF PEACE

ABOUT KHARIS PUBLISHING:

Kharis Publishing, an imprint of Kharis Media LLC, is a leading Christian and inspirational book publisher based in Aurora, Chicago metropolitan area, Illinois. Kharis' dual mission is to give voice to under-represented writers (including women and first-time authors) and equip orphans in developing countries with literacy tools. That is why, for each book sold, the publisher channels some of the proceeds into providing books and computers for orphanages in developing countries so that these kids may learn to read, dream, and grow. For a limited time, Kharis Publishing is accepting unsolicited queries for nonfiction (Christian, self-help, memoirs, business, health and wellness) from qualified leaders, professionals, pastors, and ministers. Learn more at: https://kharispublishing.com/

www.ingramcontent.com/pod-product-compliance
Lightning Source LLC
Chambersburg PA
CBHW051330020726
47501CB00007B/2013

* 9 7 8 1 6 3 7 4 6 6 5 5 1 *